Caelus

R.S. O'Neal

The Quest for the Aura series: Book Four

Books in the Quest for the Aura series:

- The Lightworker Trials

- Terra

- Aqua

- Caelus

- Incendium

Note to readers: The Quest for the Aura series is set in beautiful, sunny Australia, and all spelling and grammar is consistent with Australian English.

Caelus print edition ISBN: 978-0-9954473-5-6

To the ones we lost
And what they taught us about living
Ma, Keith, Tony and Kay

And to BFFE, Mapleton Mums, Mamma Mia, Lovely Ladies and Book
club pals:
Viq in a cup

"Sometimes a thing of great beauty and value is created only after much time and much pressure" - The Kikkuli Master

"May your wings always find the space to fly
May your eyes always see through the clouds
And may your feet always find the Path"
– Kyori, traditional Caelite blessing

"Whine is a drink made from sour grapes"—Sergeant Tottingham

"The Force is unleashed" – General Gel Silica Lithium (Jengles)

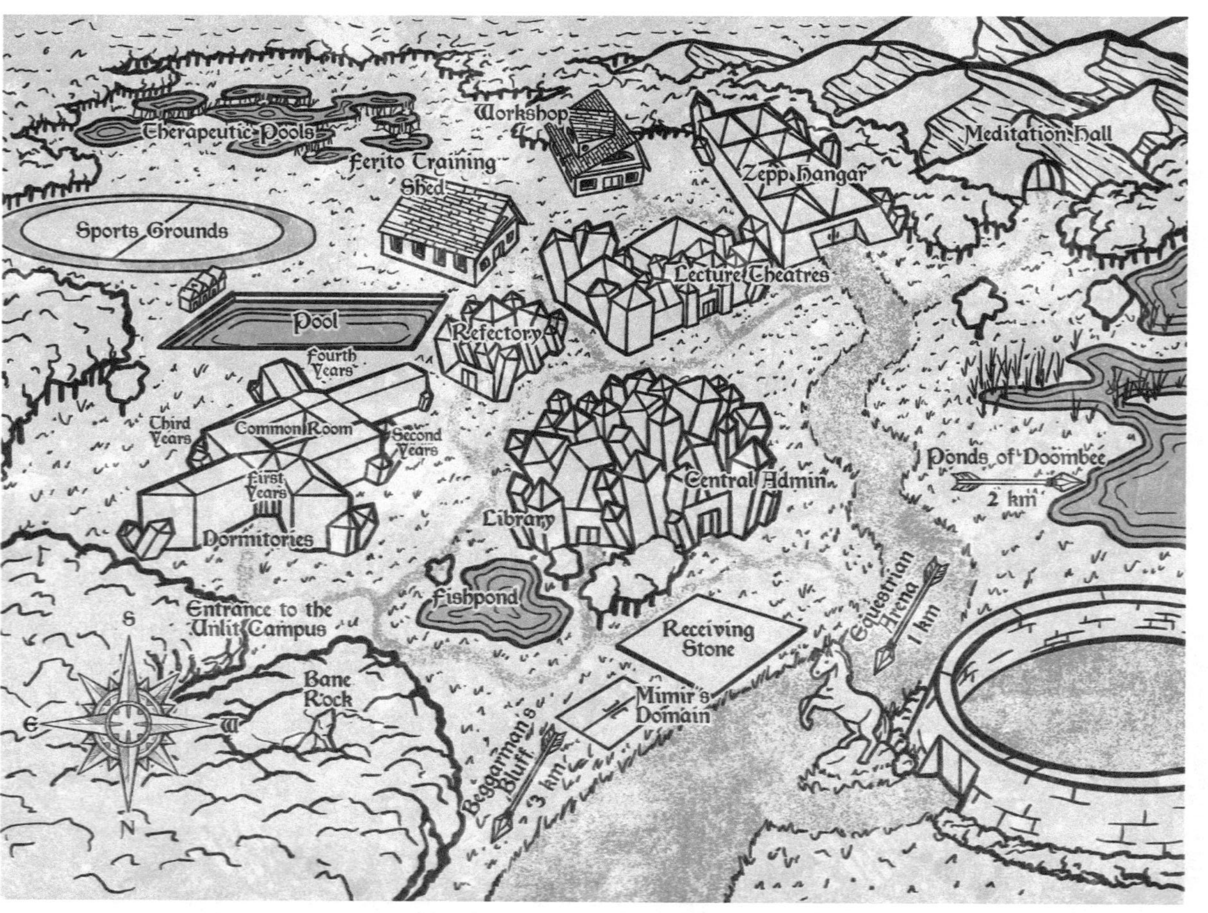

Therapeutic Pools
Workshop
Meditation Hall
Ferito Training Shed
Zepp Hangar
Sports Grounds
Lecture Theatres
Pool
Fourth Years
Refectory
Third Years
Common Room
Second Years
Central Admin.
Ponds of Doombee
2 km
First Years
Library
Dormitories
Fishpond
Entrance to the Unlit Campus
Receiving Stone
Equestrian Arena
1 km
Bane Rock
Mimir's Domain
Beggarman's Bluff
3 km
S
E
W
N

CHAPTER ONE

"TWO DAYS NOW," BEATRICE said, cradling the steaming emerald-green mug in her hands as she sat on Eyre's kitchen bench and leaned against the wall. Her eyes were troubled as she stared out the stained-glass window. "I thought she was getting better these past weeks."

Eyre shrugged. "Maybe the thought of going back to school tomorrow has made it worse for her." She looked down. "This time last year I didn't want to go back either. The thought of facing everyone..."

Beatrice nodded. "I guess. No one's going to blame her though."

Eyre shook her head. "Some will."

"Well, they'll have me to deal with me then," Beatrice said fiercely, putting her cup in the sink with more force than necessary.

Eyre nodded. "Me too," she said softly.

A long silence ensued. Beatrice trailed her fingers over the border of the carved wooden doors that decorated the kitchen cabinets. Her diamond nose-stud glinted as she moved in the light from one side of the cabinetry to the other.

"I wonder why they didn't put two E's on there," she mused, changing the subject as she studied the decoration around the edges of the cupboard doors.

Eyre sighed. "I've wondered that too," she said, and moved closer to examine the ornate border. 'AER' repeated all the way around the cupboards, with bumble bees and vines and horizontal lines in between them. Alia, Eyre, Rufus. Eyre's parents and herself. But her brother Eric, who had died when he was a baby, would have been alive when the cupboards had been carved—so why wasn't his initial on there too? This was a minor mystery amongst many other more important ones, so Eyre had stopped trying to work it out a couple of years ago.

"They did put our initials in the cupboards though." She indicated the centre of the doors. In the middle cupboard, 'A&R' were entwined, and in each of the outer cupboards was an 'E'.

"I can explain it." Nick stuck his head around the door and Eyre jumped. She'd been so engrossed in the doors she hadn't heard him come in. He ran his hands around the border as Beatrice poured him a coffee.

"How's your head?" she asked. Nick just shrugged as he picked up the mug. His face was wan and he looked exhausted. His migraines had become more frequent over the break, and Eyre and Beatrice both looked at him in concern. But Nick waved away their worry, and studied the cupboards.

"The borders were added later," he said. He pointed at the letters in the middle of the door. "If you look at these, you can see they're done in a completely different style, and they're older. The polish over the years has stained them darker than the border. "That border," he continued, "is something else entirely. A master craftsman has done this work, it's exquisite. You know me and whittling," he laughed, his eyes close to the panels. "Wood carvings—the ultimate. I've always admired this work so much. And the inlay of the stones, well that takes a special skill in itself. This was someone with a gift." Beatrice moved closer.

"Well," she said, always competitive. She pointed to the four lines of turquoise inlaid across the abdomen of one of the bees. "I can tell you what those bees are! Flava had Ag with Virens students last year, and we did some beekeeping. They're blue-banded bees. I've seen them in the bush here too. And—native bees can't hurt you," she added, and then grimaced, "unlike many of the creatures out there!" They all looked at each other for a moment as they drank their coffee, and Eyre shook her head. No words were needed after the horror of the past year.

A sudden crash outside made Nick clap his cup down and move carefully towards the window. Eyre understood. Unlike previously, in a world that seemed so distant now to Eyre, nowadays anything out of the ordinary made her instantly react, and her friends were the same. "I'll check it out," he said, as he took a careful look out the window. Then he headed out the front door.

Beatrice's eyes were sad as she looked through the coloured panes of the kitchen windows. "Our cabins used to feel like a refuge, so beautiful and peaceful," she said, "so *close.*" She looked over her shoulder to the door. "And yet, underneath—all this treachery and *Darkness* simmering. So many people affected here—and yet we were supposedly all friends?"

As she stared at the door, her face echoed the sadness and confusion that Eyre felt. It could never be the same here. Ever since Abby's father had betrayed the Lightworkers last year, Eyre felt that she was on dangerous, unstable ground. Nothing was as it seemed, and no one could be trusted, ever. No wonder her parents had kept so many secrets, and had guarded her Wisdom with an unbreachable ward. They knew of the darkness lurking even within their own community. Eyre was filled with an aching melancholy and a nostalgia for the days when Lightworking had seemed such fun, so pure and simple in its purpose. Aeons ago, it felt like, and yet it was only just a couple of years.

Nick thumped up the front stairs and rejoined them. "The Mimir are gathering firewood. One of those huge eucalypts dropped a branch."

Eyre's shoulders relaxed. She realized that she had been waiting for something to happen. Not this time, thank goodness.

Beatrice jumped off the bench. "Come on, we're back at the Academy tomorrow, let's get that hermit out of her cave and go and enjoy the day!"

Following her lead, they headed over to Abby's cabin. As she trailed behind Beatrice, Eyre reflected that Abby was an orphan too, now that her father had died. Lightworker archives were strewn with a history of many family members dying, but the shame of being associated with the Dark side had brought Abby to her knees mentally. It was worse for Abby, because her father had been so highly regarded, and she was suffering desperately as she tried to process his treachery to the Overworld. Nick would understand her feelings very well, as his own father was an Ex, excommunicated by Lightworkers because of his association with the Underworld. But as Gegenees had said, neither of them had to wear their father's coat. Past doings did not define the future. Eyre was determined to help her friend through this; no matter that Abby's father had done the wrong thing, Abby was still grieving him terribly and Eyre desperately wanted to help her with that.

But Abby hadn't interacted with any of them since she got back from Sydney. After her father's funeral, she had gone to stay with her mother's sister and family in Paddington. But she had only stayed there for a week, and arrived unexpectedly one morning saying she couldn't bear the pitying looks and silences from all her relatives. She'd gone straight into her cabin, without saying anything else, and stayed there for most of the weeks that followed. Her grief and shame had turned her virtually into a recluse. Peter and Robyn Edmunsun, and Whittaker Ray, turned up a few times to check on her, but they didn't stay long as she didn't want company. Abby had been whisked away for some counselling sessions, but other than that she stayed most of the time behind closed doors. Time was the only thing that was going to help this problem.

Occasionally Abby would come over and sit in Eyre's attic for hours, and watch the mesmerising stained-glass window change into its never-ending mystical scenes. After the first time that Abby had asked Eyre if she could go upstairs, she hadn't had to ask again. She would appear on the doorstep and Eyre would wave her upstairs without a word. Anything she could offer that might give Abby some measure of healing made Eyre feel that at least she was doing *something*. Abby was starting to come over more often lately, and Eyre hoped she was improving.

But Eyre herself was struggling with a darkness that she found hard to define. This beautiful, peaceful campsite held shadows, a hidden malevolence that had touched all who had lived here. Yet again she understood her parents' need for secrecy—history had shown that even people who seemed irreproachable could not always be trusted. But Eyre knew without a doubt that her own friends could be relied on with her life. The events of the Aqua TACI had bound them together tightly, and their shared experiences had forged a bond that was unbreakable. They hadn't discussed it, but they all knew. They were on a path together now no matter what lay ahead, with a grave responsibility to the world. There were no words that could express that clearly.

Eyre, Beatrice and Nick arrived at Abby's cabin and stood at the bottom of the stairs.

"Hey, Abby!" Beatrice shouted. "Get your butt out here! We're going to make the most of the last day before the grind starts again!"

After a moment the door opened slightly and Abby's pale face appeared in the crack. She studied them for a moment, and then came out onto the porch.

"Eyre, can I talk to you a moment?" she asked. Eyre looked at Beatrice and Nick, then started up the steps.

"Sure," she said. "Won't be a moment, guys."

Abby led Eyre inside her cabin. There was a mustiness inside, and an echoing emptiness, as if something integral had disappeared. The absence of George Wilson cried out from every corner of the cabin. Unwashed dishes piled in the sink, and it looked as if the cabin had not been cleaned or dusted for weeks. Eyre's heart filled, and she felt her old foe—guilt—assuage her yet again. She could have come in and helped Abby with this, at least. *Should have*. But Abby had all but barred the door since she came back to the campsite, wanting no visitors and not inclined to venture out. Looking around, Eyre resolved that when they came back this afternoon the windows would be flung open and all of them would sort this out.

Abby waved Eyre to a soft leather chair. The Wilson's cabin was very like Eyre's in structure, but without the stained-glass and artworks. Everything was comfortable and cosy, designed for relaxing. As Eyre looked around, she wondered yet again what had gone wrong. How could Mr Wilson have been working for the Dark side? He had seemed the very epitome of goodness.

As if following her thoughts, Abby spoke. "Dad was Tyros," she said in a voice heavy with sadness. "The most spiritually evolved of all the Sectors, and supposedly possessing a strength of mind that, combined with their physical prowess, makes them the ultimate psychic defenders." She turned tortured eyes to Eyre. "I was so proud of him." Her voice caught. "I know I apologized to you last year, Eyre, but I've had a long time to think about things over the past weeks. I just wanted to say again how sorry I am."

Eyre jumped up and wrapped her in a hug. "I know," she said softly. "And I don't want you to ever bring it up again. I know how you're suffering. It's not your fault. I don't know why your dad went to the Dark side, but for a long, long time he did amazing things for the Lightworkers and that's what you should remember. That's how I will remember him, anyway." Eyre said the last sentence, although it wasn't completely the truth. She *would* remember that side of Mr Wilson, but she also could not forget the events last year. They would remain with her forever.

Her eyes caught on something on the side table beside the couch.

"Oh!" she exclaimed. "Is that your Lightkeeper?"

Abby nodded and picked it up slowly. "Yes, Mr Ray delivered it over the holidays. Mine doesn't have a tone blow like yours though." Abby was referring to the whistle that hung around Eyre's neck, which opened Eyre's Lightkeeper when she blew it. It was a Lightworking security mechanism, sort of like an audible lock, which Eyre's parents had set up to protect the secrets of Eyre's Wisdom. "I don't have a key for my Wisdom either," Abby said. "My Wisdom just opens." Abby's eyes lingered on the silver whistle and key around Eyre's neck, but then she looked away. She wasn't really interested any more. Eyre could see that around Abby's own neck, she had the gold Argonaut medallion that Gegenees had given her last year, and Abby's left hand played with it constantly.

Eyre took the Lightkeeper from Abby's other hand and exhaled at its beauty. This was only the second Lightkeeper she'd ever seen, apart from her own. It was made with exquisite precision from sapphires of all shades, ranging from a pale cornflower blue to the intense Kashmir brilliant blue, to the dark blue Australian sapphires. The little box glowed in the morning light as if it were alive. Like Eyre's own Lightkeeper, it had an Inguz in the lid. Abby's was made of silver, with Ceylon sapphires inlaid in the centre of the Inguz. Eyre turned it around.

"It's beautiful, Abby."

Abby sat back in her chair, her eyes distant. "I've been studying my Wisdom these past few weeks. I guess I was hoping for clues—" her voice hitched "—as to why things... happened. It's been interesting anyway." Her voice trailed off, and Eyre gathered that Abby hadn't found the answers she was looking for. Eyre looked downwards, feeling so sorry for her friend, and an idea came to her.

"Well, it's a gorgeous day," she said, "and Beatrice and Nick are out there waiting. We have to make the most of it! But you, my friend, are not suitably groomed!"

She sat beside Abby on the couch and lifted her friend's limp, unwashed hair. Abby had always been so aware of how she looked, especially her hair, and to see her so bedraggled made Eyre's heart clench.

"First of all," Eyre said, "we need Bullio!" She waved a hand and a myriad of small bubbles hovered in the air around Abby's head.

"Then..." Eyre clapped her hands and Abby's hair turned into a rainbow of light—all colours of the spectrum danced through her short blonde locks.

"And finally!" Eyre moved a hand again, and a stardust of glitter tumbled into Abby's hair, causing it to sparkle as the sunlight hit it.

"There you go!" Eyre announced. "You are more than ready for a bushwalk!"

Abby looked at herself in the hall mirror and after a moment, broke into giggles. It was a rusty sound, like a gate that had not been opened for a while, but Eyre smiled in relief. This was more like her friend.

"Come on, I've got a great idea," Eyre said, and dragged the girl with her shimmering hair out into the day.

Beatrice and Nick took one look and then applauded. "Hooray!" Beatrice cried. Nick's eyes showed all he felt, and he came up and took Abby's hand.

"So," Eyre said. "I think it's time we took our Lighthorses out for a jaunt!"

Silence reigned. Beatrice's eyebrows rose. "Ah—Ischyros...?"

Eyre snorted. "Well, I would love to give you some comic relief, but he won't come. No, I was hoping one of you might give me a ride. It'll be lovely out in the bush, let's head up to the summit!"

"Awesome idea, Eyre," Nick said softly. "You can ride with me on Prenzel." Prenzel, named after the brilliant wood carver Robert Prenzel who loved to carve Australiana images, was a dark brown gelding, 16-hands-high and could easily cope with another rider.

"Thanks Nick," Eyre said.

Together they stood by the Mantle Basin and shut their eyes. Eyre telepathically called to Ischyros, not because she thought he would come, but for practise, and to at least let him know she was thinking of him.

With a whoosh, horses started appearing in the clearing. Abby's Appaloosa, Cojo, arrived first, which was not unexpected—she had such a communication with animals. Beatrice's Palomino mare came next, Blondie, a spirited 15-hands-high horse who pranced in place when she arrived. Eyre looked at Nick, who seemed to be struggling. He was frowning as if in pain, and eventually put a hand up to his forehead. Eyre started to go over when Prenzel arrived, a gentle giant who nuzzled Nick's shoulder.

"Are you okay, Nick?" Eyre asked. Nick smiled crookedly.

"Yeah, I'm good, no worries," he said, and hauled himself up onto Prenzel, offering Eyre a hand.

But then there was a late arrival. With a clump and a cloud of dust, a shabby brown form appeared in the clearing.

"I hate the Summons," Ischyros complained, stomping his feet.

There was complete silence. Everyone's mouth was agape, Eyre's most of all. So great was her surprise she couldn't formulate words for a moment. But then, a warmth flew up her veins. *He had come!*

"Well," Ischyros grumbled. "Don't just stand there." Eyre raced over to him, trying not to look too eager lest he disappear again.

She knew her friends couldn't hear the grumpy old horse, although they now knew he could communicate with her, and she ran her hands over his tangled forelock.

"Well, thank you for coming," she whispered. "I'm glad you're here."

"Harrumph," Ischyros muttered, tossing his head.

Eyre jumped up on his back, half expecting to be fired onto the roof of the cabins, but Ischyros stood quietly.

"Bea, why don't you lead the way?" Eyre called. "We'll bring up the rear." Beatrice set off with Abby, then Nick following her, and Eyre nudged Ischyros forward and grinned when she found that he would co-operate.

They set off up the track, heading through the eucalypts, and all Eyre could feel was a delighted amazement. She had resigned herself to never getting anywhere with the old horse, but she loved him anyway. Could it be that he was softening towards her, after these past two years? The Kikkuli Master had counselled her that sometimes the things of the highest value were formed only by great pressure, and she felt an updraft of glee at this small step forward. If she achieved nothing more with Ischyros, she felt this would be enough. Just being able to sit on his back was a joy that was worth the long wait.

They moved through the scented bush as the sun rose in the sky, with only the crunch of eucalypt leaves underfoot as time passed. The raucous screech of a white cockatoo cackled through the air from time to time, but other than that there was silence. No one felt the need to talk; they were all tired, and heartsore, and this time outside was a tonic to the soul.

Eventually they reached the summit and watched the birds of prey—the mighty eagles, the sharp-eyed hawks and the swift peregrine falcons—shoot from the heights down into the canyon as their scimitar eyes spotted prey in the outcrops. Eyre would have liked to call Florence for some exercise, but she didn't want to upset Ischyros, who was obviously jealous of the three-eyed raptor. Florence could come another day, she decided as she sat on Ischyros's back, soaking up the sun and the peace.

CHAPTER TWO

IT WAS BEATRICE WHO eventually broached the subject as the high canyon breezes danced through their horses' hair. "We've had a hard year."

Abby's mouth turned down and everyone exchanged pained looks. Beatrice moved Blondie closer to Cojo, waved her hands, and conjured up a heart made of light. She floated it over to Abby, where it hovered above Cojo's ears, and after a moment, Abby gave a grateful smile. Patting Abby on her shoulder, Beatrice continued. "I've been thinking a lot about all of this, these past weeks," she said, "and it seems to me that what happened last year was that we lost faith in each other." There was a silence as everyone looked down. Nick nodded.

"So, I think we need to reaffirm our BANE vows," Beatrice said forcefully. "Let's agree that nothing will distance us from each other again. We need each other, and the Lightworkers need us, and we can't let on about any of this to *anyone*."

Eyre nodded. "I won't keep secrets from any of you, ever again," she said. "We have to trust each other." As she glanced at Nick, she saw a troubled look come over his face, but it was gone so quickly she wondered if she imagined it. Probably his head hurting again, she decided.

"I know Mum and Dad warned me not to speak of the Wisdom's secrets to anyone, but I feel they'd be okay with you all knowing. Especially after the past month. I'm not clever enough, anyway, to work all this out."

"Well," Abby said slowly, painfully, "I want to thank you for being my friends. I am lucky to have you. "And I will always believe you all, no matter what.""

"Back at you!" Beatrice exclaimed. We're not a foursome, we're a force-some!" Abby groaned at that, and a glimmer of sunshine skittered across her face. The old Abby was clawing her way back.

"And what I propose is," Beatrice continued, "is it just me, or is anyone else confused about all the so-called 'helpful' messages that have been given to Eyre? I mean, I can't keep track of them all. How about we start a book where we write everything down? That way, we can go through it and try to make sense of it. Where do we start, Eyre?"

Eyre thought hard. "Well, first of all, there was the message about the Leonids and the Aether. I guess that was worked out, but maybe we'll put it in anyway?" Everyone nodded and she continued. "Then there was the message about the crystals, which was also worked out. The ones that would make the Sea Crone agree to help us."

Abby joined in. "And then, in Aqua, you got two messages—you being illegitimate," everyone laughed and Eyre mock-scowled at Abby, "and the one about the Golden Beryl, hey?"

Eyre nodded. "Yes, but then there is also another one. The Wisdom's code, which gave me the message about the crystals. We should all learn that, so we can communicate with each other if we need to. Telepathy can be intercepted by Lightworkers, so this way we have our own secret system."

Everyone contemplated this, then Beatrice rubbed Blondie's ears thoughtfully. "Well, when we get back, I'll organise the book. Then we can write it all down, and anything we think is important can go in there."

"I'll keep it in the basement," Eyre said. "We don't need anyone to get their hands on it."

A rumble of agreement met this and they smiled at each other. After weeks of feeling like victims, with the loss of the Isar and the horrible death of Mr Wilson, it now felt like they were taking charge again.

Beatrice turned Blondie around. "Well, I guess we'd better..." she began, when the ground began to move beneath her. She looked down in shock as cracks appeared in the path, jagging outwards to the chasm of the canyon. With an agonizing groan, the ground fractured around them, the sandy path suddenly as unstable as a plate of jelly.

"Get out of here!" Nick shouted, pulling on Prenzel's mane and spinning him around. But the ground fell from beneath his horse and he tumbled out into the void. With a shriek, Beatrice, who had been sitting beside him on Blondie, also fell over the edge and disappeared from view.

"Run, Eyre!" Abby screamed as she took off up the cliff line, and as Eyre pulled wildly on his mane, Ischyros stumbled around, heading towards the downwards path. But he wasn't quick enough, and his old legs fell between the cracks opening up underneath him. Desperately Eyre held on to his mane as he fought to stay on stable ground. A screeching thunder filled the air as the earth was wrenched apart, and Eyre's heart stopped as she saw Abby and Cojo thrown up by a seismic jolt and disappear over the edge.

"Come *on*, Ischyros!" Eyre urged, panic filling her like molten fire. Every nerve end fired with dread as she leaned forward desperately, feeling the ground shuddering like a living creature beneath her.

Ischyros pulled with his forelegs and scrabbled with his hind legs, heaving his old body up over the yawning chasm as the earth fell away behind him in slow-motion chunks. Trembling, he balanced on the brink of a raw cliff that had just been formed as the earth cleaved away.

Eyre held tight to Ischyros's mane as hot tears streamed down her face, and she leaned over to stare down into the void, searching frantically for her friends. Where were they? She felt more movement between her feet and pulled Ischyros back from the edge, as she screamed out to her friends. *Are you okay?*

Eyre's mouth fell open as the reason for the cataclysm became apparent. Climbing up the side of the sandstone cliffs was an enormous and hideous creature. Twenty metres long, resembling a ten-legged insect with massive jaws, the creature sunk its clawed feet into the rock and the long, jointed legs moved backwards as it scrabbled up the cliff, impossibly fast. It had burrowed out of the earth from beneath them, undoubtedly one of the Strigis, and its domed eyes were fixed on Eyre as it pierced the air with a strange, high-pitched cry.

She wheeled Ischyros around, but it was too late. The creature was upon them, a huge, chittering predator that crunched and ground its jaws together.

Ischyros heaved and Eyre went flying into the bushes. He stumbled sideways as the pincers of the creature snapped beside him, and then the unstable ground crumbled. But just as Ischyros slipped towards the void, a huge, hairy creature stumbled out from the bushes. With a roar of rage, it grabbed Ischyros's mane, and as easily as a toddler in a tantrum tossing his toys, *threw* the old horse into the bush beside Eyre. She watched in stunned amazement as the ape-like creature roared at the towering creature above him. The Strigis sliced its pincers downwards and, standing his ground, the ape punched it, *smashed* it in the jaws. Shrieking, the insect lunged forward again, but by then reinforcements had arrived.

The Mimir exploded from the bushes, Crescent Blades drawn and baying for blood. As the insect reared above them, they stood in formation in front of Eyre, and the rhythmic stamping of their spears, their terrifying chanting, and the glint on their Crescent Blades was deeply feral, ominous.

When the insect struck down, so did the Mimir, darting in to slice the legs from the horrible creature. It lay snapping on the ground, creating a great swathe in the dirt, screeching in outrage.

And then, the most amazing thing of all. From the depths of the canyon, three flying forms appeared! Abby on Cojo, Beatrice on Blondie, and Nick swooping up high on Prenzel. Like avenging angels, they plunged in and blazed the Strigis with their staffs. Again and again they flew past, cutting hot stripes in the thick carapace as the Mimir attacked from the ground.

Eventually the creature was still. A steaming haze rose from the corpse and the bush was silent. An acrid charred smell rose in the now-silent air. All birds of prey had disappeared, and the cockatoos had fled.

Eyre turned to her old horse. "You saved me!" she sobbed, flinging her arms around his neck. "I nearly lost you!"

Ischyros snorted and stumbled gingerly to his feet. "I did not, and you did not! I slipped, that's all." But he didn't move away as she rubbed his head and scratched his forelock. And his legs still trembled, although Eyre would never comment on it. She looked around for the ape-like creature, but it had disappeared back into the bush.

Beatrice, Abby and Nick landed beside her and dismounted. Eyre could see that their legs were shaking too.

"Snap lesson in flying," Abby said, her voice quivering. "Lucky they're quick learners."

Jengles stepped up and regarded the massive carcass of the Strigis, kicking it with his foot. "A Gryllus Weta," he commented. "They burrow into the rock. We don't normally see them." He peered over the edge of the cliff and shook his head before turning back to Eyre, his eyes desperate. "Are you okay, me Lovey?" Then he seemed to shake himself and was all business again.

Eyre nodded, not looking at the edge. In a way, the thought of the deadly plunge downwards was just as frightening to her as the Gryllus. As shock set in, her legs began to tremble, but she tried to disguise it.

"Wh-what was that creature?" she stammered.

Jengles looked at her, not understanding.

"The one that saved Ischyros," Eyre said, "the gorilla, or something."

"No, the Gryllus Weta is one of the Strigis," Jengles said, uncertain.

There was a blank silence, and then Ischyros spoke. "It was a Yowie," he said. "A mate of mine."

No one of course heard him except Eyre. But again she hugged him tightly. "Any friend of yours is a friend of mine, Ischyros," she whispered.

"Never mind," she said a bit louder. "I was seeing things from the stress, I guess."

Jengles looked fierce, scanning the horizon and the depths of the canyon for more unfriendly fire. But his manner was terse, reminding Eyre of the change in his attitude towards her. At least she understood it now.

"Best be getting back to camp," he said. "Things are changing around here. It's no longer safe to be roaming around. Inguz." He laced his fingers and put thumb to thumb and bowed, and then he headed away.

The four of them walked back down the path in silence. Jengles was right —things were indeed changing. Dangerous events were happening more frequently, and the whole world felt uncertain. Eyre walked beside Ischyros; he'd hurt one of his front legs in the desperate scrabble up the cliffs. He limped along beside her, and all she could feel was a terrible, smouldering rage. Her fear was dissipating as her fury rose, and all she wanted was a chance to get back at the terrible Dark Forces of the Underworld.

CHAPTER THREE

WHEN THEY GOT BACK to the campsite, and within the confines of the Mantle, they all sent their Lighthorses back to the stables. Jengles had told them he would alert the Kikkuli Master, and that Lisa would take good care of the spooked horses. But Eyre noticed there was an edge to the way the horses were behaving; they were hyped up, and nervous. But she realised that this is what they had been bred for, and she could see that there was an element of excitement in their behaviour. Adrenaline and Light—the power of the battle. Except for Ischyros, of course. He just complained the whole way down the trail about his knee, and his back, and the appalling expectations put on a Lighthorse. Eyre was just glad he was still here. And still overjoyed that he had let her ride him. Despite the whole drama of the morning, that was going to linger with her.

Nick left quickly, saying that his head was exploding, and Beatrice, Abby and Eyre exchanged worried looks. Whatever was going on with him seemed to be escalating. Eyre wondered if she should talk to Whittaker Ray about it. But a more pressing thought occurred to her. "Come on you two, we're heading to Abby's place!"

Beatrice's face was questioning, but she followed along. Eyre could see her compassion as she entered Abby's cabin and surveyed the disaster, but she said nothing, her organisational skills taking over.

"I'll put the kettle on," Beatrice said as she looked around, hands on hips, resembling nothing more than a rugby coach making a critical game plan. "Then we'll sort all this out!"

The next afternoon Peter Edmunsun had arrived, punctual as usual, to take them to the Academy. He and Robyn Edmunsun had been with the Echelon for the past two months, as the Lightworking Government tried desperately to formulate a plan of action after the disaster in Aqua. Lachie had been sent to stay with his grandma, who lived at Bondi Beach, and he'd been ecstatic about a summer in the surfing mecca.

But since Eyre and her friends had arrived, a murky desolation had hung over the Highlight campsite. If there was such a thing as group energy, as Mentor Xiphias had proposed last year, Eyre felt that the dark weight of worry and despair was not only affecting Highlight, it was now reaching right around Entis, and indeed, the whole Overworld. Everyone and every *being* must be anxious and stressed; there was an ominous feeling of things about to come crashing down.

When Beatrice's dad walked out of his cabin, Eyre and her friends were waiting by the Mantle Basin with their collection of essential belongings for the year: duffel bags of clothes, musical instruments, Beatrice's usual potted plant, and their staffs, of course. Mr Edmunsun gave a short laugh as he looked at the ungainly assortment of possessions, but then his eyes lighted on Abby, whom he hadn't seen for several weeks.

"How are you, my love?" he asked, his eyes dark with concern. As Abby struggled to reply, he reached in and hugged her hard. "I know," he said. "Don't answer. The burden of a Lightworker." Abby wiped her eyes as Mr Edmunsun patted her back. Then he turned and began to bustle around, trying to lessen the awkwardness as he organised the gear.

Personally, Eyre would have preferred to travel the way they had come back to the camp last year—via Ranger Chrysanthe's bumble bee striped carpet. Not only had it been a raucous and exciting ride, but it was so much better than teleporting, which she disliked intensely, as it always made her head spin. But teleporting was quicker, and once Mr Edmunsun had organised them all to stand with the gear, it was only seconds before they were standing on the metal square, waiting for the distant Zepp to arrive.

Eyre was glad it was the Ranger who picked them up this time, his purple eyes warm as he gave them each a hug.

"The intrepid Gothak-fighters arrive!" he exclaimed, as the beetles twirled madly around his green hair. "I must remind myself never to get on your bad side!"

Today he was wearing an outfit that would do Louis the XIV proud, and he hauled their bags and possessions into the underside of the Zepp, as Eyre and her friends climbed aboard. The last time they had been in a Zepp, they'd been travelling underwater in Aqua. What an awesome ride, Eyre decided, settling back into the comfortable seats. When she had been a 'normal' person, light years ago, the aim of everyone her age was to save up for a car. She decided that she'd rather like one of these instead. Her mind wandered as she stared out the transparent walls while the steadfast vehicle rumbled towards the Academy, past the Ponds of Doombee. As the Zepp's hologram droned on and on about school rules, Eyre wondered who their dorm supervisor would be this year, and what classes they would have. She did know it was going to be busy, and hard, this being the final year for most students.

The Ranger dropped them right at the dorm this year, instead of in front of the Central Admin building. No doubt he had factored in the amount of their luggage, Eyre thought wryly as she hauled everything out from under the Zepp.

Third-years resided in the eastern part of the dormitory complex, or the right-hand section of the Inguz shape, if you looked at it from above. As Eyre walked down the corridor of the dorm, she trailed her hand along the walls of the halls, which were covered in sheets of luminous quartz crystal. Despite everything, it was nice to be back.

Eyre, Beatrice and Abby dumped their gear in their room—a triangle-shaped set-up again—and started to unpack. Staffs were clipped into the special holders in their arms locker and extra possessions shoved under the beds. They had almost finished unpacking when a soft voice called all the students out into the corridor.

Madame Overmantle smiled as doors opened, expelling their new residents, many of whom stared sideways down the hall, regarding Eyre, Beatrice and Abby curiously, even suspiciously. Everyone had heard of the drama last year, and as no one knew about the search for the Isars; the uproar that seemed to accompany Eyre's group on their TACI tests was confusing to most. Pheria in particular shot a sharp look in their direction. "Give me some warning when chaos is about to erupt," she said cynically. Eyre bristled, but didn't reply as Madame Overmantle waved her hands for silence.

"Welcome, dears," she said, her lined face beaming. "Your final year! Unless, of course, you decide to take the Graduate Year to Incendium. There is a lot to look forward to this year, and you will make great inroads into your power and technique. Please feel free anytime to come and see me, my door is always open. Are there any questions?"

No one spoke, so Madame Overmantle motioned for them to go. "The General Meeting is at 4pm in the Common Room and then dinner as usual is in the Refectory. I'll see you all then."

Sorting their gear out was by now a familiar routine after the past years, and the three friends quickly finished unpacking once they returned to their room. But despite the fact Beatrice had set the room lights to a calming aquamarine, Eyre was still seething as she threw the last item in her drawer.

"That Pheria needs a kick," she said furiously. "She's such a pain."

"Agreed," Beatrice said. "But... really, she's jealous." She turned to Eyre with an empathetic look and continued.

"She can't stand that you're getting so much attention. Take it as a compliment, really." She looked sideways at Eyre. "And I doubt you'd worry so much about it if a *certain* person wasn't so frequently seen with Pheria."

Eyre gave a *harrumph* worthy of Ischyros and flung herself on her bed. She lay on her back, looking up at the ceiling, which pulsed with a soft aqua light. "Well, that may be true, but I'm well and truly over *that*. I can't work him out. He's here one minute, gone the next, sneaking around..."

Abby looked surprised. "Sneaking?"

Eyre was sheepish. "Err... one of the things I didn't mention last year." Abby flung a pillow at her, but Beatrice waited.

Eyre shrugged. "Well, he went back to Canada, working with his family last year. His dad was sick apparently. But when he got back..." her voice trailed off as she realised the difficulty of saying what she really saw. No way could she mention Abby's dad.

"Well, anyway, I saw him lurking around in Bathurst, hiding and watching Professor Vela."

Abby huffed. "Probably the only safe way to watch Vela, I'd say."

Eyre thumped the pillow back at her. "Well, anyway, I have no idea what he was doing." Her voice trailed off, and her friends looked away. But Eyre sat up. She was determined that there would never be any more secrets between her friends.

"Oh well, another mystery, I guess. I'm just glad I'm in your classes this year. And that we're all together. Whatever Jax's life is, it's no longer my problem, really."

Beatrice grabbed something out of her suitcase. "Well, speaking of mysteries, here's the Book of Bane! Mum and Dad gave me this journal for Christmas, and I think it's perfect for us to start writing everything down in. Let's get it all done before the meeting!"

Eyre nodded in agreement, but hesitated. "We have to keep it safe. Mum and Dad went to all that effort with tone blows, keys, wards and cryptic messages to ensure the information was safe. We can't just leave it lying around the dorm."

They looked at each other, thinking.

"I know, let's go see the Ranger," Beatrice suggested. "He'll know what to do."

CHAPTER FOUR

THEY FOUND THE RANGER leaving the Zepp hangar, with Lenny under one arm. His face brightened and he waved as he saw them approaching.

"Lenny!" Eyre cried, running over to stroke the little lavender-coloured creature. Beatrice and Abby crowded in too and the Ranger handed Lenny over to Abby, who snuggled the fluffy long-eared pet in her arms. Lenny's little paws stretched out to rest on either side of her neck as everyone leaned against the hangar wall.

"So, what can I do for you today?" the Ranger asked. "Or did you just come over for a Hug?"

Beatrice chuckled. "We want to ask you a question."

"One that is a bit... *sensitive*..." Eyre added.

"And you can't let anyone know we asked," Abby said, looking up with serious cornflower eyes.

"Well then, you came to the right place," the Ranger said. "Sensitive questions are my specialty! Are you after sartorial advice?" They all laughed.

"It's to do with all the information I've received about reinstating the Aura," Eyre said. "There's quite a bit of it, and we want to write it down so we can study it and figure it out."

"And we can't pass it on to the Echelon, because we don't know what's going on there, and who to trust," Beatrice said, looking apologetically at Abby. The Ranger patted Abby on the shoulder.

"But we can't write it down unless we hide it really well so no one can find it," Eyre finished. "And we were wondering if you could suggest anything?"

The Ranger's brilliant purple eyes were serious as he contemplated the question, looking into the distance as he thought. "I understand," he said.

"It's hard to know what's going on, really. And I commend you all for your courage and your conviction in these dangerous times."

After a minute he snapped his fingers. "Yes! I know what you can do. You need to make a cache in the wall of your room, and guard it with a ward. If you bond it to each of your energies, all three of you will be able to reach into the cache and pull it out."

"How do you make a cache?" Eyre asked.

"Well, you disturb the energy of the wall so it forms a pocket, a gap that is unseen from the outside. So, you virtually reach through the wall and put the object in there. No one will see it."

"Brilliant!" Beatrice exclaimed, clapping her hands, and the Ranger bowed, twirling his lemon-yellow cap.

"At your service my lady!" he said, jovially.

Abby looked uncertain. "But can any of us do that?"

"No," the Ranger said. "But *I* can. If you will continue with your excellent babysitting of Lenny, I will nip over and do it for you."

Before they could say anything, he disappeared in a rainbow flash, and a flurry of confetti drifted to the ground. They all looked at each other.

"Well, that was easy," Eyre commented. A few minutes later, the Ranger reappeared in another flash.

"Done!" he exclaimed in a tone that suggested he was well satisfied. "I left you a marker on the wall so you will know where the cache is."

Eyre had to double-check. "So, only we three can get in there?" she asked. As the Ranger nodded, Abby handed Lenny back to the Ranger.

"Thank you, Ranger Chrysanthe," she said. "For doing that, and for the Hug."

The Ranger bowed. "Anything I can do to help the Bane expedition," he said, his eyes twinkling. And then he disappeared.

The girls looked at each other and Beatrice looked perplexed. "How did he know about Bane...?"

Eyre shook her head, equally confused. "How does the Ranger know *anything*, really? Come on, let's go get that book started!"

They started walking across campus when a familiar and unwelcome voice hooted at them from the pathway.

"There they are. Friends of the Gothak. So much for your high and mighty dad, Wilson."

Ben Perrill's malevolent face leered at them, and he grinned with delight at the look on Abby's face. She was stricken, unable to say anything, and a tear rolled down her face. Nothing had been said about Mr Wilson's treachery; people knew that he had been killed in a fight with the Gothak, but the story had been spun so that it seemed that the Gothak had killed George Wilson. The Echelon had decided that no one needed to know the truth.

But apparently, somehow Ben Perrill had found out. He stood smirking at them as Wyatt Rankins and the Curtis twins appeared from around the corner and came to stand by his side.

"You *pig*, Ben!" Beatrice screamed at him, wrapping her arms around Abby, who had slid to the ground weeping. "What is *wrong* with you?"

Eyre felt her head was about to explode with rage, and she stomped across the grass towards him. But someone got to Ben first.

A muscular, tanned arm seized the large boy by the scruff of the neck and lifted him off the ground as if he weighed no more than a bag of flour.

"You need better manners," Gegenees said softly, and with a flick of his wrist, hurled the boy on his butt into a fishpond. Ben stood up, covered in weed and slimy leaves, spluttering furiously. Ben's cronies, who shared very few redeeming traits amongst them, much less loyalty, rolled on the ground in hysterics.

"Going fishing?" hooted Saxon Curtis while his brother Slade and Wyatt Rankins screeched with laughter.

"You stupid oaf, I'll report you for this!" Ben yelled at Gegenees, his face turning purple as water dripped around him. A goldfish fell from his hair, plopped on the ground and wiggled back into the water, causing more screeches of hilarity from his friends.

"I intend to report this to the Echelon myself," Gegenees boomed. "But by all means, you go first." Then he stomped up to Ben, his face so furious that Ben took a step back. The fearsome warrior snapped his white teeth as he bent down, his face close to the dripping boy.

"I could take your nose off in one bite," he said softly. "If I hear you have repeated those words to anyone again, I will hunt you down and do it. Get out of here."

Ben's face changed as he realised that Gegenees meant every word and he stumbled out of the fishpond. "Come on you guys," he said with bravado and tried to walk away with dignity, but Eyre could see he was rattled. She would be too if Gegenees had shouted at her like that. Ben's cronies staggered after him, still laughing raucously, and a violent dislike surged through her. What a waste of space they all were.

Gegenees had come back to Beatrice and Abby, and he knelt before Abby.

"Come on, my warrior girl," he said softly. "You have many battles ahead. Don't let a worm of such inconsequence undo you at the first skirmish.

Stand up, Abby. You only let him win by letting him see."

Abby hiccupped and Beatrice helped her up. Abby's face was swollen and tracks of tears ran down her cheeks.

"I don't know if I'm strong at all," she said softly. "I feel so broken."

"You are stronger than you could ever believe," Gegenees said. "And until you realise that, I am here. Come and find me if you ever need anything."

By now they were walking slowly back to the dorms. Beatrice turned a curious face up to Gegenees. "Are you on campus now, Gegenees?"

The big warrior's eyes clouded a second and then he nodded. "Yes, additional security. I'm hanging around—you'll see more of me. So call me if you need anything." He turned as they reached the door to the hall of the dormitory.

"Thanks Gegenees," Abby whispered as they headed back to their room.

CHAPTER FIVE

ONCE INSIDE THEIR ROOM, Beatrice picked up her journal from her desk. Eyre gave Abby a tissue, and exhaled.

"I'm so sorry, Abby," she said. "I know what it's like to be on the end of Ben's rubbish. He is such a toad. But it seems that someone has a soft spot for you!"

Abby hiccupped. "Maybe he'll follow me around like Jengles does with you?"

Beatrice gave a mock-pout. "No fair, I want a devoted fan!"

"You've got Robeson," Eyre comforted her, teasing, and Beatrice punched her softly on the arm.

The tension dissolved as they all laughed. Beatrice jumped up. "Wait! In the drama, I forgot. Where's the Ranger's cache?"

"He said there was a marker," Eyre said, but they couldn't see anything at all on the wall. After a moment, Abby said, "Maybe turn the lights on?"

Beatrice, who was the undisputed champion of working the lighting system, put her hands on the wall and ran through the spectrum of colours, using her fingertips to change them. Red, blue, green—nothing happened.

"Try the Ranger's signature colour," Eyre suggested.

"I've already tried blue," Beatrice said.

"No, purple," Eyre replied. "He's ditched the blue guys."

Abby blew her nose and chuckled as Beatrice turned the walls purple. "Aha!" she cried. Fully covering the walls was an etching-like image of Beatrice, Abby, Nick and Eyre, outlined in shining silver. They were each standing with mops like staffs, looking fiercely outwards. On the ground in front of them was a bucket and sponges, some rags on the ground, and leaning up at one side of them was a broom, and on the other side, a vacuum cleaner.

"What...?" Beatrice said, puzzled, but Eyre burst out laughing. "It's a joke," she said. "A reference to us hiding in the cleaning cupboard when we spied on the Determinant Dozen and the Echelon. I love it!"

They all laughed and moved closer to examine the image. "So where would the cache be?" Eyre mused, then her eye caught on a detail in the image. The brand of the vacuum cleaner had a small Inguz on it, hidden as part of the logo and almost impossible to see.

Eyre whooped triumphantly and pushed her hand against the image on the side of the vacuum. Instantly her arm went through the wall up to her elbow.

Despite themselves, they all shouted in surprise. "Wow, that's cold!" Eyre said, shaking her hand as she brought her arm out. They all high-fived and looked at each other gleefully. A secret cache! *Awesome!*

"Right!" said Beatrice, "Let's get down to business!" She sat at her desk and opened her journal, then carefully titled the first page: 'The Book of Bane'. She flipped the page over.

"Okay," she said, pen poised. "Where do we start?"

"Well, the first revelation of the Wisdom, maybe," Eyre replied. Beatrice headed the page:

The First Revelation of the Wisdom

Then, as Eyre dictated, she added: "*The Isars can be seen by the Aether during the Leonid*".

Eyre was thinking hard as she tried to remember what came next.

"Okay, let me write the next bit, I guess it should be the Wisdom's code." She looked apologetically at them all. "Christopher and Tina helped me to decipher a message my Wisdom gave me last year. It's a code."

Beatrice smoothed over the awkward silence. They were still adjusting to the new peace between them all, and the secrets that had been kept, and why. "Awesome!" she said. "That's definitely got to go in!"

Beatrice titled the page, then slid the book over so Eyre could draw the details.

THE WISDOM'S CODE

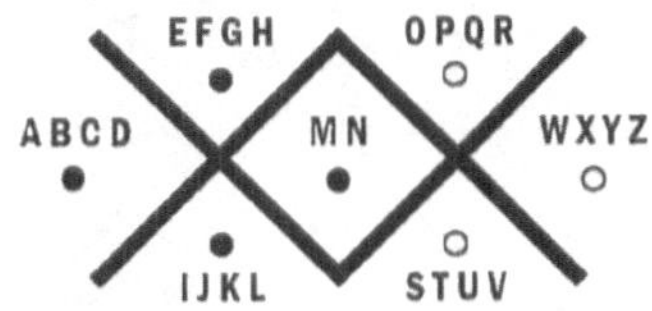

And then she rolled her eyes and grimaced.

"Okay, so I get how it works, but really—it's going to take me so long to work it out. But we need to do it! Bear with me."

She started writing out what she knew, and her eyes turned upwards to concentrate as she tried to figure it out. Her friends watched for a while, but then Beatrice suddenly snatched the pencil out of Eyre's hands in frustration.

"BTL girl! We'll be here for another three years! I get it!"

As she studied the strange shape of the Wisdom's Code, her face had an expression of absolute joy as she wrote the symbols down. Her hands were like lightning as her scrawls appeared across the page in decisive strokes. Eventually she finished and she looked at her friends with a light in her eyes they'd not seen before.

"I *really* want to meet those friends of yours, Eyre. This is *absolutely* brilliant! Wait 'til Robeson gets a look!"

Eventually, after working for quite some time, Beatrice had produced an alphabet. Odd angled symbols, but a code that no one else could read easily:

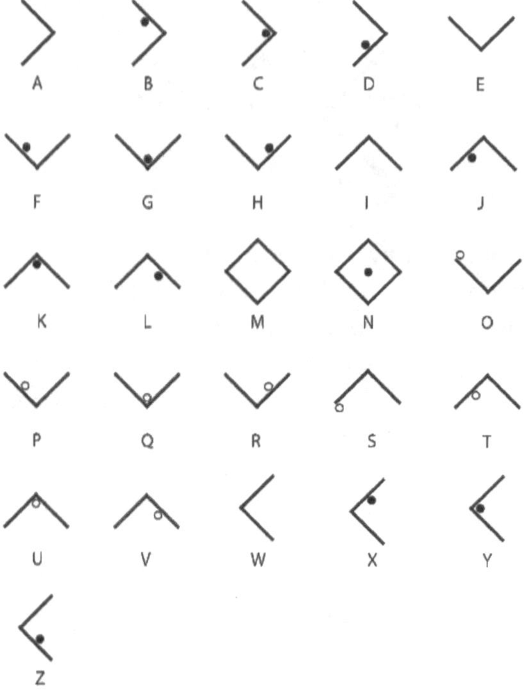

Abby looked horrified. "You expect me to learn that?" she said, looking at the strange angles and dots. It'll take me three years!"

Eyre laughed, shaking her head. "You and me both, my friend!"

Then she slid the book back to Beatrice. "Your writing is better than mine, Bea, here's the second revelation from the Wisdom. Beatrice began writing and Eyre recited:

The Second Revelation of the Wisdom using the code

Search the bottom of the sea
To find the Seer and prophesy
Receive guidance to the light
By bearing a crystal of Angelite
But dry, and also Bloodstone
A gift for the all-seeing Sea Crone
Those who prove their worth
Will receive counsel for the Aura's rebirth
But only the stupid and only the brave
Would dare enter the Oracle's cave

"Ok," Eyre said, "now you need to write in the Sea Crone's prophesy." Beatrice wrote the words she had memorised down carefully.

Sea Crone's Prophesy

"When all seems forsaken
And the Darkness awakens
To dispel chaos and peril
Find the Golden Beryl
And at 7.17
When the colour is green
Free the last gift of Pandora
From the diapaused Aura"

Abby spoke up. "Now my favourite part. Don't forget about the illegitimate girl!" She laughed as Eyre nailed her with a pillow again, but unusually, Beatrice hesitated. "I can't remember it," she said, apologetic.

Eyre laughed. "I can," she said. "I've nearly blown my head up trying to work it out over the holidays. Didn't figure it out, but I know it word for word." She read it out as Beatrice wrote the prophesy in the book.

Nostradamus Century X: 84

The illegitimate girl so high, high, not low,
The late return will make the grieved ones contended:
The Reconciled One will not be without debates,
In employing and losing all his time.

Beatrice sat back with a look of satisfaction on her face. "Well, there we have it. How to reinstate the Aura in five easy pages." They all looked at the incomprehensible jumble of words and broke into giggles. A thought struck Eyre.

"There may be one more piece, but I'm not sure," she said. As her friends looked at her questioningly, she scrunched her face. "Jengles said something strange to me last year. He told me that *"Alexandrite is at the centre of everything,"* but he said he didn't know any more than that. I've tried to figure it out during the year, but I'm none the wiser."

Beatrice shrugged and wrote it in the book under the heading: *'Jengles' Counsel'*. "Well, the more we have in here, the closer we'll get, I guess. And if Jengles said it, it must be important."

She finished writing and then closed the book. "Done! Bags putting it in the wall." She walked over and shoved the book into the silver-lit image of the rag, shuddering as she pulled her empty hand out. "You're right, that *is* cold!" Then she trailed her fingers over the wall and changed the colour to pale yellow, and the light-etching of the four friends disappeared. She looked with satisfaction at the crystal panels. "Safe and sound. If the Ranger has set this up, nothing will get in there!" They all nodded, looking at the wall which guarded their huge secret.

"Come on, just about time for the meeting. Let's head over," Beatrice said, and they trooped out of the room. Eyre was seized by a wave of sudden glee. For the first time in many months, she finally felt that things were getting back to normal with her friends.

CHAPTER SIX

A HUBBUB FILLED THE Common Room as the girls walked in. Students leaning against the walls, drooped over the comfy lounge chairs, sitting at tables, all talking as they caught up with friends they'd not seen since last year. Abby saw Nick chatting to Warrigal and led Beatrice and Eyre over to them. Nick was her personal Buyabarra, a source of peace and solace.

"Hi Warrigal! How were your holidays?" Abby asked. Abby held on to Nick's arm and her voice was hesitant.

The tall boy smiled. "Awesome, thanks. How are you doing?" He said it lightly, but his eyes were concerned. He knew, Eyre thought. Somehow this mysterious boy knew so much.

Abby smiled awkwardly. "I'm okay," she said after a moment.

A voice called from the back of the hall. "Warrigal!" Colton waved at them all, and the spectacular ice-blue eyes in that tanned face met Eyre's for a moment. He had grown even taller over the break and Eyre had to admit, she wasn't immune to Colton's presence. She gave him a small smile as Warrigal left to go and talk with him. No doubt they were planning their practise sessions already. Both boys were driven by a determination that was unusual until you knew their story. Colton's younger brother had been killed by the Gothak, and he pushed himself incessantly, preparing for the day he could avenge his brother. And Warrigal was blessed with a rare and mystical talent—therianthropy—which meant he could shape-shift into other creatures. He was already way ahead of most of the student body, and had an understanding of the environment, and indeed, the Light, that was almost supernatural.

Beatrice was talking to Nick. "So, we finished writing up the Book of Bane and put it in the cache. I bet the Ranger could add you to the ward, so you can access it too."

A shadow crossed Nick's face, and to Eyre's surprise, he hesitated. "You know," he said, "there's not much point really. I'm not supposed to be in your room, so I don't need to access the book."

Beatrice smiled. "BTL Nick, you're *Tyros*—your astral skills must surely help us to solve some of the mysteries! We need you, my friend!" She was joking, not for a second thinking that Nick might be serious about not wanting to be involved.

But after a moment, he shrugged and yawned. "Yeah sure, that sounds great." As if Beatrice had suggested a bbq at a friend's house. Then Nick looked across the room. "Hey, there's Luke, I want to say hi. See you guys soon."

He shrugged Abby's hand off and walked over to Luke as surprise registered on Beatrice's face. Eyre felt the same—had Nick just *dissed* them? Abby's blue eyes were hurt as Nick joined Luke Jordan's group and was soon talking animatedly to them all.

Not wanting to add to Abby's difficult afternoon, Eyre said nothing, and scanned the crowd. Ben Perrill had arrived with his pack of jackals, his hair wet but his clothes clean and dry. Obviously, he'd had a quick change. And then her eyes caught on an unfamiliar, but strangely familiar, face. A new kid, but hadn't she seen him before? As she took in his blonde, styled hair and athletic body, it was the arrogant look on his face that jogged her memory.

It was that boy that had caused all the trouble at the National Ferito trials in first-year! The one that grabbed her arm and called her a freak because of her odd Inguz. *BTL!* What was *he* doing here? As if the boy could hear her roiling thoughts, he looked at her from across the room and sneered, a slight mouth movement that said, *look out.* But it was the chill in his eyes that made Eyre's hair stand on end. Dead, flat eyes like a predator. What was his name? The boy heaved himself off the wall and turned his back on her, heading over to join Ben Perrill's group. That's all I need, Eyre thought furiously. Another black-hearted fiend.

The door opened and Dean Fraser, Whittaker Ray and Sergeant Tottingham entered and walked to the front of the room. As the Dean waved his hands, the voices gradually lessened. As Eyre watched the awful boy saunter over to join Ben Perrill, she had an overwhelming sense that there would always be things she could never understand in this world. Why would they let someone like *that* in to the Academy?

"Welcome to you all," Dean Fraser said. "I trust you have returned—" he hesitated and then everyone except the first-years joined in as he said, "*refreshed and rejoicing!*" Laughter filled the air as the Dean waited again for silence.

"Well, you certainly sound rejuvenated, and I hope the year ahead is going to be successful and productive for you all. Classes will commence tomorrow, so check your Felsics for timetable information. Remember that we have many extracurricular activities on campus if anyone is interested, in particular our renowned rugby team, the Lightning Strike—so see Stratt Galloway to sign up for trials for the team. Or our aerial polo team, the Academy Hawks, which is in the running this year for the Australian titles —please contact our captain Jax Jackson for that one. We also have a solid musical base here at the Academy, and you can contact Abby Wilson for any enquiries about the program."

Eyre and Beatrice nudged Abby and she smiled as the Dean continued. "If anyone has any questions, please see your dorm supervisor, Sergeant Tottingham, Whittaker Ray or me."

The Dean had finished, but before he took his seat he finished as he always did. "Live with courage and Light." Eyre smiled. It wouldn't feel like a normal school year without the Dean's traditional introductory speech.

The Sergeant cleared her throat. "Remembering that you are not to waste our time. Look up the information first, or you will be getting closely acquainted with the ablutions block, a bucket and mop." Everyone laughed again, but taking pity on some of the wide-eyed first-year students, the Sergeant added, "of course, we make some allowances for the newbies in first-year, don't panic."

Whittaker Ray looked at his notes and started to speak as Dean Fraser sat down.

"Professor Vela will be, as he does every year, conducting his weekly tours to the Jenolan Caves for anyone who is interested, remembering of course that for third-year students it is mandatory if you have not yet been there. Please put your name on the sign-up list if and when you would like to join the tour." Eyre groaned silently. The last thing she wanted to do was to join Professor Vela in a dark cave deep under the ground. Unexpectedly, the Sergeant asked Whittaker Ray to pause a moment, and she looked around the room. Her eyes stopped at the new boy, the one who'd caused all the trouble at the National Ferito Trials at Lightning Ridge, and a look of distaste came over her face when she saw he was chortling in Ben Perrill's ear, not even paying attention.

"Since you are third year, Carrison Hamlen, you will be expected to join the Jenolan tour this year. You might do well to listen to announcements too. Generally, we find it helps." Impervious to the Sergeant's sarcasm, the boy returned her gaze with a sneer, as if daring her to do something. Like poking a snake, Eyre thought. He's picked the wrong target.

But before the Sergeant could continue, there was a noise at the door and then it opened unexpectedly. Someone stumbled in, singing at the top of his voice.

"Mr Jackson?" Whittaker Ray said, looking most dismayed.

Jax staggered around the room, dancing a teetering jig as he sang a bawdy Lightworkers song, more suited to a wild mining town than the Academy of Light Common Room.

"If I were a free man, ho, ho, ho
Off through the Seam I would go, go, go
Looking for the lovelies don't you know, know, know
And if I don't come back then I told you so!"

As everyone watched in stunned silence, Jax whirled around the room before finally landing in a stuffed armchair, where he propped his feet up on the armrest. Eyre noticed his hands were bright blue, and his fingernails shone neon yellow.

Sergeant Tottingham's face suffused and her eyebrows turned down. She resembled nothing so much as a bull pawing the ground before a twirling red cape.

"What is wrong with him?" Eyre whispered, aghast, as a low murmuring arose around them. Beatrice's face was just as horrified.

"It looks like he's drunk the juice of the Lorian Tree!" she said, not taking her eyes off Jax, who had now sunk into sudden slumber and was snoring loudly. "It's from Terra, and it's very intoxicating. And it's also illegal in Entis."

The Sergeant's face suffused, and she strode over to the comatose figure.

"Get up!" she shouted, so loudly it echoed around the room. "GET UP!!" The second time she shouted it was so deafening that Eyre covered her ears. Obviously Viq had been used to amplify the order, and it worked, because Jax raised himself groggily and looked around with a bleary eye. He lurched to his feet and took an awkward bow, nearly falling over in the process.

"No applause, you can pay me later," he chortled, waving one blue hand in the air.

The Sergeant shot a massive arm out and clamped him on the shoulder.

"*What* are you doing?" she hissed, and marched him towards the door. Ben Perrill and Carrison Hamlen were looking on with mean-faced delight, snickering as he was propelled past them.

"Top work, Jackson," hooted Ben, and the Curtis twins exploded into laughter, hanging off each other as he stumbled past.

"Silence!" roared Whittaker Ray, finally getting over his speechless shock. All eyes watched the Sergeant heave Jax through the door and disappear after him.

Eyre looked at Beatrice and Abby, and felt strangely like crying. "What on *Entis?*"

Everyone was looking at each other in astonishment. For someone to interrupt the Dean like that, and to be under the influence of an illicit substance, was unheard of at the Academy. With a terrible, sinking feeling, Eyre had a further thought. *And* grounds for expulsion, no doubt.

"Apologies, Dean Fraser, but I think we are finished anyway," Whittaker Ray said, trying to collect himself. "You are all dismissed."

The student body started to disperse, talking loudly to each other, and Eyre heard quite a few snickers amongst the crowd. Obviously many of the students had found Jax's suicidal performance quite entertaining.

"Lorian Tree juice is prohibited in Entis," Beatrice said as they wandered towards the Refectory. "It's so potent and unpredictable, and it's only found in bars on Terra."

"They have bars on Terra?" Abby said, surprised. "I didn't know that."

"Yes, there's an expatriate town there; botanists, geologists and other scientists doing research, and they stay for a year or two gathering data. Dad went there when he was a graduate student to study the physics of the sailing rocks." Eyre remembered back to the strange moving rocks they had encountered on the Pyre of Va, a large desert in Terra. No doubt a good subject for a PhD, she supposed.

"Anyway, it's been easy to control here in Entis, because as you saw, if you drink it, your hands turn blue. No one can sneak around and drink it without everyone knowing. By the Light, why Jax would do that is beyond me. He must have a desire to self-immolate! I've never seen the Sergeant so angry."

Eyre trudged beside her. What a start to the year. Already things had a weird feeling.

CHAPTER SEVEN

THE REFECTORY WAS ABUZZ when they arrived for dinner. Jax's display had set tongues wagging and Ben Perrill's table in particular was snorting with laughter.

"Wonder where I can get some of that stuff," Ben chortled to Carrison as Eyre walked past, determined not to react.

She sat at a golden table as the troll-like Jotnar bustled around the front of the cafeteria. Their imposing horns and scowling faces discouraged much interaction, but they efficiently organised the salad bar and hot food onto servery carts. But Eyre had lost her appetite and sat with only a cup of coffee in front of her.

Abby had joined her melancholy mood, and her eyes wandered occasionally over to Nick, who had sat at a table with Colton and Warrigal. It was the first time he had elected not to sit with them, and Abby was obviously upset but trying not to show it. She picked at her food as Eyre tried to think of something to say.

Robeson and Beatrice, however, ate with gusto, which was the norm. Nothing ever seemed to upset Beatrice's appetite, Eyre thought.

"Robeson's applying for editor of 'The Reflector' this year," Beatrice said, with her mouth full. Eyre smiled and nodded. Robeson would be great at editing the school newspaper. The role was traditionally held by a third-year student, and it was a position that many students vied for.

"Is Zanda doing 'Spotlight' again?" Eyre asked, just as the student in question sat down to join them. He arrived with Scott, who he'd been with since the Sector Fair in first-year, and everyone scooted over to make room for them.

"Of course!" Zanda said, a wicked smile on his face. Zanda's column on gossip and humour had been a new addition to the newspaper last year, and it was very popular. "I'm already off and running—Jax has just supplied me with my first major item. What was he *thinking?* You can't actually sneak around drinking Lorian juice. Headline: *What Third-Year Student Already has the Blues?"* Far from being fazed by Jax's display, he laughed uproariously. "Made my day! Looking forward to this year very much," he said, tucking into his dinner.

Despite the worry about Jax, Zanda's arrival, as usual, had lifted the gloom.

"How was your holiday?" Abby asked, finally taking her eyes away from Nick's table.

"Brilliant!" Zanda said. "We went skiing in Europe—without the Perrills this time! Although I did have to put up with Madam Lash," he grinned, tipping his head towards Pheria, who was sitting with her usual supercilious look at the next table. "The Galloways came too. Pheria's a pain, but Stratt is pretty cool. We did some boarding together." Stratt was Pheria's younger brother, who was in second-year this year. Eyre's eyes travelled to Pheria. She was listening to something Georgia Mahoney was telling her, and Pheria's face looked ready to break into a huge yawn. Obviously, whatever Georgia was saying was not exactly riveting. Pheria looked over and caught Eyre studying her and Eyre felt her face go red as Pheria raised an eyebrow at her. Damn!

But a late arrival in the Refectory caused everyone to look at the doorway. A startled silence descended across the tables as the unexpected visitor stepped hesitantly into the room. Eyre gave a start of recognition as someone she knew from the Unlit shut the door behind her.

It was Tina who moved through the tables, her sharp eyes scanning the students. As the surprised hush continued, Ben Perrill started raucously humming the theme to Mission Impossible and thumping the table in time. Carrison Hamlen stood up as Tina walked by their table and he grabbed the shoulder of her tan-coloured uniform.

"Aren't you in the wrong place, brown bird?" he sneered. "The camp for the Un-*Fit* is out the back somewhere I believe. Don't you have shanties or something down there?" The Curtis twins hooted at this and Wyatt Rankins let out a cackle like a hyena, as they all joined in the thumping of the Mission Impossible theme on the table.

Eyre rose angrily, but she didn't need to move any further. Tina didn't blink an eye at the put-down and calmly lifted Carrison's meaty hand from her shoulder, with no effort at all. Then she picked up some spaghetti from his dinner plate and tossed it on the table in front of him.

"Snake," she said softly. Carrison's face contorted and he let out a squeal of panic. Then he leapt up on to his chair, trembling violently. "No, no!"

he screeched, his face a mask of terror and his hands warding off the strand of spaghetti lying on the table. His friends looked up at him, dumbfounded, as their mouths hung open. Saxon and Slade Curtis looked at each other, then down at the table in confusion. Saxon picked up the spaghetti, causing Carrison to scream in horror. Then he jumped down and ran out of the cafeteria, as all heads swivelled to follow him.

There was a long silence and then all the students erupted with laughter. The sounds of hilarity echoed through the Refectory as the bemused Saxon put the spaghetti in his mouth and ate it.

Zanda had tears of mirth running down his face. "I think Jax has just been knocked off the front page," he chortled. "By the Light, that was beautiful!"

Tina had made her way across to them and Zanda jumped up and pulled out a chair for her. "Oh, join us, join us!" he encouraged. "And let Zanda in on the mystery. How *did* you do that, pray tell?"

Tina's merry brown eyes danced. "Trade secrets, I'm afraid. One of the skills we learnt at the end of last year—'Suggestion'—it's sort of like hypnosis. Apparently, your comrade has a great imagination!"

"He's no comrade of ours," Eyre muttered. "A new guy, and trouble, by the look of it."

Tina rolled her eyes. "Well, it's going to take him a while to regain his reputation after his tangle with the fearsome Bolognese Serpent!"

She sat down as they all laughed. "I can't stay long. I'm looking for Jax."

Eyebrows rose all around the table.

"Ah..." Beatrice started, then stopped.

"He's indisposed," Abby continued. None of them really wanted to pass on the gossip about Jax, except Zanda of course.

"He got busted for drinking Lorian juice!" he chuckled. "He's probably incarcerated for twenty years in a deep, dark cave by now."

Tina nodded sombrely. "I know. UD1 wants to see him."

Eyre was surprised. "Why?"

Tina looked at her calmly. "I didn't ask. I was just sent to get him."

Of course, Eyre thought. Her complete loyalty to UD1 meant it would never cross her mind to ask; she probably thought it irrelevant. Eyre looked around.

"Well, I don't think he's been sent to purgatory just yet," she said. "But he didn't come in here. Perhaps you could ask the staff. How are you doing anyway? Good break?"

Tina nodded as she stood up. "Yeah, it was. Good to be back though." Tina looked fit and tanned, and she had changed in the six months since

Eyre had last seen her. She seemed older, more mature, and very focused. Knowing how much she herself had learned in a very short time with the Unlit, Eyre was sure Tina had advanced immeasurably in the past months. Again, but *better!* The mantra of the Unlit, and she looked like she had indeed gotten better. It was great to see her friend and Eyre felt a surprising stab of wistfulness as Tina left the table. Eyre had loved her time at the Unlit and she realised she would forever miss being part of the campus.

Tina spoke with Whittaker Ray for a moment and then they both left the Refectory. As she watched them go, Eyre felt another familiar emotion come over her. Dejection. The mysteries were already starting again.

CHAPTER EIGHT

"SILENCE!" THE SERGEANT ROARED and all voices stopped. They were in the Training Shed and for many of them it was the first chance to properly catch up since they'd arrived back. Meditation had been the first class that morning, as always, and although some students had no doubt used the time improperly to communicate by telepathy, the walk over to the Shed had been the first opportunity to truly talk to one another after the Christmas break. There had been a lot of laughter and levitation as students re-enacted their summer holiday stories.

Although it was only 9am, it was already hot in the Shed as the late-January sun began to rise in the sky. The summer had been a hot one, with many bushfires across the country, and it looked like the heat was not leaving for some time yet.

Eyre wiped a drop of perspiration from her forehead as the Sergeant strode to the front of the room, her quartz-topped staff keeping time with her footsteps.

"The final year, for many of you," the Sergeant said once she'd reached the front of the Shed. "This is a year when all that you have learned in previous years comes together and you polish your Lightworker skills. Next year you will go out to join the working ranks of Lightworkers, to pursue further education, or some of you may elect to do the Graduate year here on campus. Unless you work hard in third year, you will not be worthy to pursue any of those options. Those who do not pass will have to repeat this year, so I suggest you concentrate and work to your utmost ability."

The Sergeant paused for a moment and frowned before continuing.

"Our experiences in the past couple of years have not been normal here at the Academy. We have had breaches, and interaction with Strigis and the Gothak. Not the usual story by any means in the school's history, and a sign that we need to *focus*. So it therefore behoves you well to hone your skills to the highest ability. Your survival may depend on it—or that of any of your colleagues. We are all linked together and we must work as a united force."

A snide voice whispered loudly. "God help me if I'm ever linked with *her*." Slade Curtis was mocking Carly, nudging Carrison Hamlen as he did so. Carrison's smoothly handsome face was marred by his cold, calculating eyes as he lifted a disparaging lip, his gaze evaluating Carly as if she were a side of beef. Carly flushed in embarrassment and Eyre felt a rage flood through her. The mongrels. How dare they make fun of the kind, good-natured girl! But before she could do anything, the Sergeant spoke. Her head did not move, but her eyes swivelled towards the snickering voice.

"To start the term, I believe a display of Ferito is needed," the Sergeant said in a very low voice. "Saxon, you seem keen to contribute to class this morning, so I feel it would be very good of you if you would step up to the front."

Saxon had the grace to look awkward at least, Eyre thought, as she ground her teeth together. He shuffled up the front, aware that whatever might be following was probably not good. But then he smiled at the Sergeant's next words.

"Carly Henderson, could you make your way to the front also please."

The Sergeant clapped her hands and a pile of short-bladed palum appeared on the ground before her—the palum that were training props for the Antaraks.

"This afternoon you will visit the Depot to receive your arms endowment. But this morning, we will warm up our skills with some Ferito practise. Carly and Saxon, would you oblige please."

Saxon was smirking, looking confident. Although Carly was taller than Saxon, with a strong farm-girl's physique, Saxon was blocky and muscular, with huge biceps. Very much like a gorilla, Eyre thought sourly, but worried for her friend. Eyre wondered why the Sergeant had set this up, as she felt Carly would not be strong enough to take on this brute.

Carly and Saxon each picked up two palum and assumed the stance to begin the Clasis for two-handed fighting. They touched left palms together briefly and shouted "Tollo!" Then, with barely a millisecond from the words leaving their lips, the strong wooden palum smashed together.

Saxon was incredibly strong, and as their weapons clashed Carly stepped back, unbalanced by the force of the blow. Slade Curtis hooted encouragement to his brother and Carly set her mouth. With a flick of her hand she performed movement 12 perfectly, and smacked Saxon's shoulder with her palum. He roared in pain, and responded with movements 6, 8 and

2 in quick succession, the onslaught forcing Carly backwards again. Eyre looked on with worried eyes. Saxon was Rufa, the fighting Sector of the Lightworkers, and he had spent a lot of time practising each of the two levels of the three Clasis, and perfecting the moves. Rufa worked out in the gym to build their muscles, and they were gifted in the fighting skills.

But then Carly surprised everyone. She did a complete 360 degree turn as she levitated over Saxon and whacked him hard in the back as she landed on the mat behind him. He screamed in rage and swung around, flicking his palum wildly. But his concentration was lost in his anger, and his blows missed as he flailed and sliced at her. He drove his 'blade' towards her middle, but Carly sidestepped in position 11 and Saxon's palum went harmlessly by. As it passed, she chopped sharply at his wrist and he shrieked as the wooden weapon hit his bone. The palum fell from his nerveless fingers to the bamboo floor and Carly spun on her toes past Saxon. Then with a blow of such force that the crack of the two weapons meeting echoed through the Shed, she whacked the narrow edge of her palum against the flat side of Saxon's remaining palum, and the 'blade' of his palum split in half. Carly stepped up with crossed blades lightly touching his chest and the bout was over.

"Thank you, Ms Henderson," the Sergeant cried, with more enthusiasm than was probably appropriate. "Well done, you are the winner!" Carly was classy enough to stand at the side of the ring without showing any emotion. But Saxon's face was bright red with rage.

"That's not fair!" he shouted. "She broke my blade, she used levitation..."

The Sergeant swung around to him and the menace in her face silenced him.

"Brute force does not always win with Ferito. Concentration and strategy are the keys to mastering this skill. If *I* were Ms Henderson," she added softly, "I might have been tempted to smack you in your smart mouth. So perhaps you got off lightly."

Then, in a louder voice she said, "*W-h-i-n-e* is a drink made from sour grapes! Levitation, as we all know, is allowable in Ferito in this year. You are not only a loser, Mr Curtis, but a *poor* loser at that. You disgrace your Sector. That is all. We all appreciate, Ms Henderson, your most educational demonstration."

Saxon, still protesting, slunk off to join his friends while Carly, bright spots in her cheeks, left the front stage with her head held high.

"Good for you!" Eyre whispered as Carly made her way past. Carrison Hamlen looked at Eyre and the blackness in his eyes made her shiver. But she couldn't help herself.

"Maybe you can give us a display on spaghetti eating?" she hissed at him. Carrison's face darkened and with a flick of his wrist he sent a pole of Viq into her middle. All her breath left her as she flew backwards and landed on the ground, struggling for air. Completely unfazed that he had used an illegal force, he bent over.

"I'd watch myself if I were you," he said. "You have no idea who you're dealing with."

Eyre wanted to retort, but she was unable to breathe, let alone speak, so she just gazed at him with furious eyes. Another murderous thug like Perrill, she thought. Well, bring it on then, bring it on.

Beatrice stormed towards Carrison, but Eyre finally struggled to her feet and restrained her friend. "No," she whispered. "He's got it coming. Leave it."

But before things could escalate, the Sergeant clapped her hands for attention.

"Right, now it's time for you all to practise. Please find a partner, grab some palum, and we will spend the next half hour practising Basic, Single and Two. Any questions, come and see me. This afternoon you are to meet at the moldavite square so we can go and pick up your arms endowment. And starting tomorrow, you will be learning Level Three Ferito using those weapons. May I suggest you pick up a supply of bandages, band-aids and antiseptic cream before then."

A ripple of laughter ran through the student ranks and they walked up to collect their palum. Cries of "Tollo!" reverberated through the Shed, along with the clatter of palum, heavy breathing and quick footsteps. But no conversation. Evidently the students had taken the Sergeant's speech to heart; they were treating this training very seriously.

CHAPTER NINE

EYRE FOLLOWED BEATRICE AND Abby into their room and flung herself on her back on her bed. She was exhausted from the Ferito training and knew she was going to have to work hard to get back in shape. Beatrice turned the lights to a soft pink and also lay on her bed, breathing hard.

"BTL," she moaned. "I am going to *suffer* this term."

Abby was draped over a large pillow, her head resting against the bed cover as her mouth drooped.

"Nick didn't even come over in training," she said, her cornflower eyes troubled. "Do you think he wants to break up with me?"

Eyre was not sure—it did seem that Nick was avoiding Abby, but she didn't want to say that, so she said nothing. But Beatrice jumped in.

"No way, he adores you!" she protested. "He's probably just trying to settle in."

Abby traced the pattern of her bedspread. "It's not because of—" she took a deep breath—"Dad, do you think?"

Eyre and Beatrice both shook their heads violently. "Of course not," Eyre said. "Nick wouldn't be like that. I think you should talk to him. See what's going on."

Abby gave a deep sigh and rolled over onto her back. "Maybe I'll try to talk to him at lunch then," she said.

But when they arrived at the Refectory, Nick had again elected to sit apart from them. He was already at a table with Luke Jordan and Warrigal, at the opposite side of the Refectory to where they normally sat. Nick waved briefly at them as he saw them enter, then went back to talking to Warrigal without any indication he wanted to join them. Beatrice and Eyre exchanged a look as Abby's face set and they trailed after her to their table.

"Don't worry about it, Abby," Beatrice said. "He'll come around and let you know what the problem is. Give him a bit of time."

But it was a silent lunch; all of them were troubled by Nick's reticence.

Eyre decided to make good use of the time before they were to meet at the moldavite square. She wanted to pay a visit to someone who hadn't been so reticent lately; Ischyros was back in his stable after his recent visit to the Highlight, and Eyre wanted to see how he was doing. And part of her was worried that perhaps he had returned to his normal difficult self now he was back on campus—she wanted to see what sort of a reception he would give her.

So, after lunch she left Beatrice and Abby talking softly in the dorm room and ran down to the stables, her feet flying along the familiar paths that led to the Equestrian Centre. The recording of the Strigis screeches and roars filled the air as she raced past the statue of the rearing horse to enter the slowly-opening bronze doors of the arena. As they closed behind her, she walked hesitantly down the dusty passageway.

Deep in thought, she didn't notice that someone was near until he was almost upon her. Warrigal, as silent as a shadow, apologised for making her jump as he fell in step beside her.

"What are you doing, Warrigal?" Eyre asked. "Going for a ride on Bunu?"

Warrigal smiled and shook his head. "No, maybe later. I'm meeting the Ranger shortly in the far paddocks. We're running through my schedule for the year."

"Ah... *orienteering*," Eyre said wisely and Warrigal chuckled. They both knew the real reason he was studying with the Ranger was to improve his therianthropy skills. None of the students knew he had the extremely rare gift. Eyre had found out about it in first-year, but she had kept Warrigal's secret to herself.

"What does it feel like?" she asked after a moment, unsure if he would want to talk about it. But Warrigal seemed comfortable. His brown eyes regarded her a moment as he thought.

"Well, it might look like I'm hurting when I turn," he finally said, "but I'm not. It's just a feeling of great force, and speed. Sort of like being sucked into a huge plughole."

"How long have you been doing it?" Eyre asked. "It's a spectacular talent."

Warrigal chuckled. "Ever since I can remember. Mum told me once I changed into an emu when I was only two years old and it took the whole family to run me down before I disappeared into the bush forever. Therianthropy is a feeling of being part of all creatures, and just donning the shape that fits the moment the best."

Eyre smiled. "Well, thanks for sharing that with me Warrigal. It's awesome."

Warrigal headed out across the paddock as Eyre approached the rough-hewn stable at the back of the building. A familiar voice filled the air.

"Dratted thing," Ischyros mumbled almost incomprehensibly. "Dimmog! Stay straight!"

Curious, Eyre crept to the door and looked over. The old horse was struggling with something in his mouth, which he was dragging over his hoof. What was it? She leaned a bit closer and gasped. As Ischyros started to turn his head towards her, she ducked down behind the door. There was a clunk as Ischyros dropped the thing on the ground and through a crack in the stall door, Eyre could see him looking out at the other stables suspiciously. Eyre clamped her hand over her mouth so she wouldn't make any noise. The thing he had dropped was a *hoof brush*! He was trying to clean his feet! Could it be that he was trying to smarten up for when she came? Whatever he was doing, Eyre knew he would be mortified if he realised she had seen him, so, concentrating hard, she levitated silently and drifted back halfway along the passage.

Then she landed on her feet and made a few stomping noises.

"Well, see you then, Lisa," she called to the non-existent stable manager, and walked loudly towards Ischyros's stall. She whistled a bright tune and tapped a few doors as she approached.

"Hey, Ischyros!" she called. "Are you there?"

"Well, I wish I wasn't," he answered rudely as she reached his door. "You sound like one of the Strigis. Is it possible for you to make any more noise?"

Eyre looked at the straw on the ground of Ischyros's stable. There was no sign of the brush, and... yes, it did appear that Ischyros's hoofs looked quite buffed. The old horse couldn't help himself and glanced a few times at his feet admiringly, and a strange feeling flowed through Eyre. She almost felt like crying at the joy that rose within her. He *liked* her. *Finally!* She blinked her eyes hard to chase the threatening tears away and leaned over the gate.

"You're looking pretty handsome today, Ischyros," she said softly, and the shabby old creature tried not to show he was pleased.

"How about I give you a brush? It's been a while."

After a second the old horse spoke, almost reluctantly. "I realised I'd rather you were around than not, after the foul Weta," he said, so softly it was almost impossible to hear. "I'm glad you're back."

Eyre was utterly gobsmacked at this comment after the previous years of absolute abuse, but she kept her face straight. "Me too, Ischyros," she whispered. "You saved me. I'd be dead if you hadn't been there."

There was no reply to her comment, so she let herself in and gave Ischyros the best grooming she had ever given him, taking her time, rubbing his old back and massaging his muscles. She finished by glossing his hooves with oil and plaiting his ratty grey mane into braids. Then she pulled some toffee out of her bag.

"We're not meant to give you too much of this," she said, "but hey, it's the new year!"

Ischyros chewed the sticky sweet with his old teeth, his lips smacking blissfully at the rare treat.

"Great!" he said. "Does that mean you'll be leaving next year?"

Eyre chuckled. "Nope, I'm doing the Graduate Year."

Her feet danced down the hall, away from the loud 'harrumph' that echoed from Ischyros's stall.

CHAPTER TEN

EYRE STOOD AT THE edge of the moldavite square and waited for Beatrice and Abby to arrive from the dorms. About half the students were already there, early. It seemed that everyone was keen to receive their Arms.

"How's Ischyros?" Abby asked as they arrived.

"Crabby," Eyre said cheerfully and Beatrice laughed. Beatrice looked around at the growing crowd.

"Well, there's someone I didn't expect to see just yet," she said.

Jax stood on the other side of the square with Warrigal and Pheria, and the three were deep in conversation. Eyre was glad he hadn't been sent home, but she felt her familiar confusion about him. As if he could sense her gaze, he looked up too quickly for her to look away. She rolled her eyes and then grinned. Caught!

To her surprise, Jax grinned back, and her heart thumped. His dazzling white teeth, his black hair and those eyes. She knew he was trouble, and a complete enigma, but she couldn't seem to help her physical reaction whenever he was around. It was like trying to stop the tide being pulled by the moon—impossible. Their eyes stayed locked across the gathering crowd for a moment until a sour voice interrupted the chatter.

"Move away, move away," Professor Vela snapped as he pushed through the crowd. "Gather round please! We don't have long." But most of them couldn't even see him—he was shorter than most of the students' shoulders, and his face reddened as he shoved aside an oblivious Virens student. "*SILENCE!*" he shouted, using Viq, and the sound shredded Eyre's ears. It had the desired effect though; everyone clapped hands over their ears and turned around, their faces twisted in pain.

Professor Vela looked around the mob distastefully and brushed a non-existent piece of muck from his robe, as if he had picked up something unsavoury from brushing against the students.

"Gather in your Sector groups please as we wait for the final students to arrive. Sergeant Tottingham will be leading you down to the Mimir's Domain shortly."

Eyre had lost sight of Jax when Professor Vela arrived, so she jumped when his voice came from over her shoulder.

"Eyre with the red hair," he said softly. "How was your break?"

Eyre turned and looked at him, defensive at first but then she relaxed. She *was* really happy to see him.

"Ah, well, you know—Abby's dad and all," she said in a low voice, careful that Abby didn't hear.

Jax's green eyes clouded. "Tough," he said. "Pretty lousy Christmas, I guess."

Eyre just grimaced. Changing the subject, she raised her eyebrows. "Well, you had a pretty lousy beginning to the semester," she said. "*Lorian Juice?*"

Jax made a face. "Not my finest hour," he agreed. He didn't seem inclined to explain anything, and Eyre had to admit there was no reason he *should* explain anything to her, so she left it alone.

Loud footsteps announced the arrival of Sergeant Tottingham and she repeated Professor Vela's instructions for the students to form into Sector groups. Students began shuffling around and Jax looked down at Eyre, his eyes unfathomable.

"See you soon," he whispered as he moved back across the jade-green square of the Receiving Stone.

"Momentous day!" the Sergeant boomed, her face as close to beaming as Eyre had ever seen. "You have all worked very hard over the past two years, and all of you have earned your Arms Endowment. It's not guaranteed—we have had, in the past, a few students who weren't awarded their Endowment until fourth-year, so you are to be congratulated for your diligence. It is an important day in the life of a Lightworker, so enjoy the moment!

"Right—" She looked over as the doors to the Mimir's Domain swung open and clanged to the ground, lying flat on either side of the dark opening. "It seems our escort is arriving. Please line up with your Sector in this order: Rufa, Arant, Flava, Hese, Virens, Sappir and Tyros. Quickly, and no chatter, please!"

The students gathered into their groups as the Mimir emerged from the opening of the Domain. The short creatures stomped with stern faces up the stairs and out to form long lines at the sides of the brass doors. Shining red hair shone in the sunlight as the fierce platoon assembled. Crescent Blades were hanging in the belts at their waists, and all moustaches and beards were knotted, plaited and tied in a display worthy of the Australian Hair Industry Awards. All stood impassively, unmoving, eyes forward. All but one that is. A movement down the line drew Eyre's eyes towards a distant figure. Corporal Cabochon, risking the wrath of General Gel Lithium Silica—aka Jengles, who was standing fiercely at the front of the troops. Corporal Cabochon was flushed bright red and he waved three fingers at Eyre. She smiled and waved back, causing the young-faced Mimir to almost fall backwards with delight.

"And so it begins..." Beatrice said in mock-despair. "The Glee Club has arrived."

The Sergeant thumped her staff for attention. "Rufa, come with me. Everyone else follow in the lines you have been placed into. We are heading to the Workshop first."

The Sergeant walked towards the opening to the Mimir's Domain and Jengles stepped out before her to lead the way. He waited until all the students were following the Sergeant, and then headed for the brass doors and down the spiralling brass staircase. Eyre was in the middle of the pack and she ran her fingers over the glasslike walls of the passage. The earth of the walls had been hammered to a glossy sheen, and the blue crystals set in the walls cast a mystical glow across the smooth surfaces. The students spoke softly to each other and their voices echoed around the chamber like a whispering gallery. Up ahead Eyre caught glimpses of Beatrice, her lanky frame taller than many of her cohort. And occasionally she saw Jax's dark head as he rounded the staircase several flights below her.

Eventually they emerged in the chamber that Eyre had visited at the beginning of her first year at the Academy. It was a workroom where weapons were being finished, and blades of all styles were lined up around the walls, mounted in holders on the walls and sitting on anvils for more finishing. There were the spiked Flails, Antaraks, Kulbedas and even some Crescent Blades in various stages of manufacture, and exotic-looking tools hanging in a neat line on the walls. Eyre noticed a familiar face in the workshop. Lieutenant Spinel was hammering at a piece of metal, sweat dripping from his craggy face as his muscular arms rose and fell. He looked up as the students crowded into the chamber, and when he saw Eyre he let out an exclamation and kneeled reverently, with his arms crossed in front of him, but fortunately, he didn't throw himself down prostrate as he'd done two years ago when he'd first laid eyes on her. All the same, the other students were looking at her curiously. Eyre sighed inwardly. Evidently, he hadn't received the memo.

After a second, Lieutenant Spinel jumped to his feet and bowed formally. "At your service, madam."

"Thank you, Lieutenant Spinel," Eyre said awkwardly, as low whispers, undoubtedly with *her* as the subject matter, echoed around the walls.

The weather-beaten Mimir stood to attention. "It's Captain, now," he said proudly.

"And well-earned too," Sergeant Tottingham said, acutely aware of the titters, and silencing them with a scowl that would make the Strigis cower.

"Captain Spinel led a team against the Gothak during the breach in first year. He acquitted himself and his team well—they personally dispatched a Menax and a Tuus on the border of the campus. If the Mimir hadn't fought so valiantly it would have been a dark day for the Academy."

Captain Spinel bowed again and then returned to the anvil. As the rhythmic clanking started again, the Sergeant moved the students through the workshop.

"Please keep your eye on Corporal Asscher. He will take you through to the Endowment Chamber." Eyre looked at the slightly flustered Mimir who stepped out from the back of the crowd. He looked familiar and then she remembered. She had met him last year when she had gone to visit Aowx, the fierce dragon who lived way beneath the earth. Corporal Asscher moved to the front of the students, blushing bright red as he passed Eyre.

At one side of the room was the door they had gone through in first-year; it led to the Armament Stores, with its huge piles of raw materials and gold dust. But this year they walked straight past, to the other end of the chamber. There was only a blank wall there, glowing muted blue from the crystals on the walls. As the final students caught up with the forerunners, Corporal Asscher indicated the wall.

"Follow me," he said. "We are about to enter the Endowment Chamber."

Then, he walked straight through the wall. Gasps echoed through the room as the students looked at each other.

"Come on then, mouths closed," the Sergeant said sharply. "Rufa, move along!"

The first Rufa student walked tentatively up the wall and then he too was sucked through. One after another the students walked through like a centipede disappearing into a hole. When it was Eyre's turn, she stepped up and walked through quickly before she had a chance to think about it too much.

Walking through the wall was like walking through a ward. It was cold and unpleasant, and Eyre thought that it must be a security measure to keep unwanted visitors out. And when her eyes adjusted to the light in the room—which was very brightly lit—she realised why the chamber was so well protected.

It was a huge space with towering walls. The rockface had many metal bands attached to the sides of the granite surface, and they ran all the way round the room, spaced about a metre apart. Attached to the metal bands were holders for the weapons they safeguarded. The top row was Kulbedas all the way around the chamber, the next row was Antaraks, then a layer of Flails, and at the lowest level were miscellaneous, strange-looking weapons that she hadn't seen before.

"They're from the Alterworlds," Jax said as he unexpectedly walked up behind Eyre as she studied the bottom row. "Some are gifts, some have been found in battle, some have been bought. The Mimir study them to learn more about the art of weaponry."

Eyre was taken aback. How did he know all that? It hadn't been covered in any of their textbooks. But before she could quiz him the Sergeant followed the last student through the wall. Holding her sturdy staff, she strode to the front of the room and clapped for attention.

"Your Arms Endowment is a priceless gift from the Lightworking community to each of our members," the Sergeant began. "You must respect it, and guard it well. These are special implements, gifted to the Lightworking community by the Mimir. It is an honour and a privilege to own these weapons."

"To receive your Endowment, you will step up to the bronze Endowment Plate here—." She indicated a flat piece of bronze, about a metre square, etched with runes and scrolled designs, that was attached to the ground at her feet.

"Lift your arms," the Sergeant instructed, "like this—." She put her arms in the air, diagonally away from her body, "and recite: If I am worthy, *unisco!*"

"Me first," Ben Perrill said. He hadn't learned any manners over the past three years, Eyre thought sourly. Ben shoved his way through the ranks of Rufa and stood on the brass plate. The Sergeant's face was bright red, but she said nothing as Ben flung his arms in the air.

"If I am worthy, *unisco!*" Ben cried. There was a flash and something appeared in each of Ben's hands as the students gasped in amazement. Ben looked up in anticipation, a triumphant smile on his face. But then the gasps of the students turned to tittering, and then outright laughter as they registered what Ben was holding.

In each of his hands was a fluffy feather duster. The laughter turned to howls of mirth and Ben threw the dusters onto the ground, his face dark with fury.

"It seems you have *not* been deemed worthy," the Sergeant said. "Although I have to say, the feather dusters were my own touch. Perhaps you can wait until the end of the line, and by then you may have been polite enough to have been deemed worthy? Next Rufa student, please!"

Lindi Jamieson stepped up. Eyre had met her in the TEP exams two years ago, and had seen that Lindi had very strong Viq, despite her small frame. She had hurled a sneaker and pulled herself with Viq all the way up a cliff, which had impressed Eyre greatly at the time. Lindi shut her eyes behind her wire-rimmed glasses and raised her arms.

"If I am worthy, *unisco!*" she called. Once again there was a flash, and this time, Lindi held a Kulbeda in her right hand.

"Put it in your belt," the Sergeant instructed, and Lindi tucked the Kulbeda carefully into the special loop on her belt. "Arms up again," the Sergeant said, "and call out '*rursus*'!"

Lindi raised her arms again and shouted, "RURSUS!" and there was another flash. This time she held a pair of Antaraks, their crystal blades gleaming a luminous blue in the cavern. All the students gasped—in admiration this time.

"Well done, Lindi!" the Sergeant said and pointed at the wall on the opposite side to where they had come through from the Endowment Chamber. "You may step back through the wall over that side to the Kit Room where Private Ammonite will fit your baldrics. *Next* please, be ready students or we'll be here 'til next week!"

Lindi disappeared, and the next student stepped up. For the next half hour, Rufa, Arant and Flava students walked onto the bronze square, shouted out the required words and received their Arms Endowment. Beatrice was beaming as she walked past Eyre with her shiny golden Kulbeda tucked into her belt, and the two gleaming Antaraks held tightly in her hands.

"See you on the other side," she whispered as she walked past Eyre and through the wall.

Finally, it was Eyre's turn. Rigmar had just received his weapons and he waved one of his Antaraks as Eyre took her place on the Endowment Plate.

"Good luck," Rigmar grinned. "Hope you catch the right end."

Eyre felt a humming beneath her feet, a force that seemed to travel right through her to the top of her head. And her feet were getting warm, the square was heated, probably from all the energy travelling through it, Eyre thought.

"If I am worthy, *unisco!*" she cried and felt the whack in her right hand as a Kulbeda materialised out of the air and the sheath hit her palm. She quickly slid the Kulbeda into her belt and raised her hands again.

"Rursus!" she shouted. *Wham!* Two heavy Antaraks smacked into her hands. Eyre couldn't help herself, she positively beamed with happiness as she stepped off the bronze plate and walked towards the wall. Kit Room, here I come, she thought, steeling herself for the cold blast of the warded wall as she stepped through.

CHAPTER ELEVEN

EYRE CAUGHT HER BREATH for a moment and then looked around. She was standing in a high-ceilinged wood-panelled room, with bronze sconces containing flaming torches lined around the walls. Nearly half the students were in the room, and they chatted in excitement as they tied on their baldrics and studied their weapons.

The chamber was filled with racks of leather clothing: trousers, shirts, sword belts and scabbards, and several brass trolleys with baldrics hanging from them like black liquorice straps. Shelves across one entire wall held sturdy leather boots of all sizes, and a wooden tree-like structure had armbands and protective leggings made of leather looped over the branches. The whole room smelt of new and old leather that had been oiled to a high polish.

Private Ammonite turned out to be a young-looking Mimir of greater than average stature, with a moustache and beard plaited into two braids and flung over his shoulders. He had dancing brown eyes, and as Eyre entered, he chuckled.

"Aha! She is here!"

Eyre smiled uncertainly, not sure if he was laughing at *her*. She looked over at Beatrice, who seemed delighted at the Private's humour. He bowed low as if in respect, but once again Eyre felt he was not being entirely serious.

"Step this way, step this way," Private Ammonite called to her, waving her over to stand by a rack of leather straps.

Eyre looked at him cautiously and he flung himself on the ground before her, face down. It was so comical that several students tittered, looking at each other. Then Private Ammonite rolled over and started to do a series of powerful sit-ups, and a ribbon of laughter travelled around the room. Encouraged, Private Ammonite then flipped again to do five push-ups with a clap in between, and finished by launching himself up into the air and performing a somersault that would make the Unlit proud. But unfortunately, he didn't land as well as they did, and he ended up flat on his back with a loud "*Oomph!*" At that, the students completely lost it, all except Ben Perrill and his cronies, who remained scowling and unsure in the corner of the room. Peals of laughter echoed around the wood panels as Private Ammonite sat up feebly and looked at Eyre.

"Have I impressed you enough yet?" he asked plaintively.

Eyre's face cleared and she choked with laughter. He *was* making fun of her, and she *loved* it! Private Ammonite leapt to his feet and bowed again.

"Baldrics for my lady!" he roared. "Worthy of the magnificent arms she bears."

Eyre hadn't really looked at the arms that anyone had, including her own. In the flurry of weapons appearing from nowhere and the queue of students moving on and off the bronze square, there hadn't been any time to study them closely.

Private Ammonite rummaged through the racks of leather.

"It's why I'm still a Private," Private Ammonite said sadly as he moved leather straps along the rack, searching for the right size. "My superiors tell me I don't take anything seriously."

Eyre grinned. Somehow, he didn't seem regretful at all, a feeling reinforced by the twinkle she could see in his eye.

She studied her dagger as the Private moved down the rails of the rack. The Kulbeda glowed softly in the light of the flames. It was polished smooth and had sparkling gems embedded in the sheath. To her surprise, Eyre recognised what the gems were—tanzanites, alternating with diamonds. The gems in the Kulbeda matched the ones in her Lightkeeper! Did that mean that every weapon was unique to the student? Tucking the Kulbeda in her belt, she looked closely at one of the Antaraks. The blade was cut from a Zha'kara diamond, which was the gazae that Graduate students sourced from Incendium at the end of each year. The edge was razor sharp, and the shaft of the weapon sparkled and gleamed as Eyre turned it around. The grip was solid and wound tightly with gold thread. On the end of each grip was a tanzanite the size of a pigeon egg, and etched into the crystal blade, at its base, was a series of runes and symbols. The crystal blades were edged with a molybdenum/titanium alloy, and Eyre noticed that the Private kept a careful distance from the blades as he moved along the rack of baldrics.

"Here we go," Private Ammonite announced with satisfaction as he hauled a criss-cross of leather straps from the rack. Eyre had seen the baldrics on third and fourth-year students over the past couple of years, so she knew what they were and how to put them on. Quickly, she slid the black straps over her shoulders, tied them up and then slid the Antaraks into the holders at the back. They slipped in easily and lay across her shoulder blades, the handle just high enough that she could reach across—right hand to left shoulder and vice versa—and pull the blade out quickly. Eyre whipped them out and twirled them around her hands, as she had done many times with the palum. But today she had a special energy, and as the swords twirled, the edges of the crystal blades caught the light, causing prisms of rainbow colours to dance across the walls in joyous speckles. Smoothly Eyre stopped the turn of the blades and slid them over her back, into the holders on the baldrics. Ha! She thought. Ben Perrill had better watch out!

She was so caught up in her personal satisfaction that she had failed to notice that everyone was staring at her, agog. She looked up and caught their astounded faces.

"What?" she said.

Beatrice walked up to her, still fiddling with the laces of her baldrics. "You are confusing people again, Eyre," she said, as she tried to get her own baldrics to sit right. Finally satisfied, she straightened.

"You just gave a display worthy of a samurai and you're asking why we're so perplexed? How did you just do that twirling thing with the blade, and manage to keep your hands on the end of your arms? It's beyond me." Beatrice shook her head.

It was getting quite crowded in the room, so as more students arrived, Eyre and Beatrice moved to the back of the throng, and Abby joined them after she had been fitted with baldrics.

"It's hot in here," Abby said, her face flushed. Eyre realised that the temperature was increasing, no doubt due to all the people packed into such a confined space.

"I'm sure we could wait back in the original room," Eyre said. "Soon there won't be any space in here and it's silly for us all to hang around. I'm going back. Do you want to come too?"

Abby and Beatrice thought for about two seconds. "Yep!" they said in unison, heading for the wall.

CHAPTER TWELVE

EYRE AND BEATRICE LOOKED at each other, baffled, as they waited for Abby to emerge. They'd come through the wall, but realised they'd made a mistake. This was completely new territory—they hadn't been here before. It was a narrow passage-way, very dimly lit by crystals that lined the top of the walls. When Abby came through, shuddering from the cold, the three of them walked down the short tunnel and emerged into a chamber about half the size of a tennis court. It was a plain room, the walls rough-hewn, not at all like the smooth glass-like structures in the chambers they had come through. The walls were chopped at all angles, this area had been not so much carved but *extracted* from the rock with huge blows of powerful blades. The space seemed to serve no function other than as a transit between tunnels, and no effort had gone into finishing it with any precision.

Eyre looked around. As well as the tunnel they had come out of, there were a further seven passages that ran off the room; it was like the hub of a wheel with spokes radiating outwards. What had happened to the Endowment Chamber? It had completely disappeared. Eyre frowned and looked around.

"I don't know where we are," she said. "We'd better go back."

Beatrice and Abby nodded. The darkened openings of the various passageways were hardly inviting; it was spooky in here and they were quite keen to go back to more familiar territory. They hurried back down the passage to the wall they had walked through.

Eyre stepped forward decisively and then marched straight towards the wall. But the wall did not allow her to pass through this time, and she smacked her face hard against the uneven rock.

"Jeesh!" she grumbled as Beatrice and Abby chortled. "I think I just gave myself a nose job!"

One hand rubbing her nose, Eyre explored the walls with her other. She sighed as she pressed her palm ineffectually against the rock. Those walls definitely weren't going to let her through.

"You try," Eyre said in frustration, stepping away from the wall. "Maybe it's something I'm doing."

Beatrice and Abby walked up to the wall, but they were also met with an unyielding façade. They all looked at each other. *Uh oh.*

Eyre looked perplexed. "Hang on," she said, and walked back down the passage to the hub-like space they had been in, with Beatrice and Abby trailing behind. Eyre studied all the passages, then looked at the one they had just come from.

"Huh. I thought perhaps we'd gone down the wrong passage, but nope, that's where we came from. What's that about?"

She thought for a moment, then shrugged. "Well, I guess we could venture down a couple of these passageways and see if they lead to anything we recognise. Although, I don't think we should go too far—we might end up with the Gothak. Some of those tunnels look like they go on forever!"

They all looked unenthusiastically at the dark passages. Eyre had a moment of unrestrained panic as the memory of Ben Perrill attacking her in the tunnels of the Transit two years ago surfaced. The claustrophobic darkness and the terror she had felt during that experience would now always haunt her in confined spaces. But she gritted her teeth, determined that Ben would not have that claim on her mind.

"Let's go down this one," she decided, heading towards the furthest tunnel on the right. "If I'm orientated correctly to how we came out of the Kit Room, I feel like that's the closest to the direction we should head to find the Endowment Chamber."

"Well, I've got no idea," Abby said. "So, it sounds good to me."

Eyre led the way into the darkened aperture. A sudden coolness hit her after the heat of the Kit Room and the previous chambers they had been in. There was a musty smell as she stepped into the murky blackness, as if the tunnel descended into the bowels of the earth, as indeed, it may well do.

"You okay?" she called back as she heard the others following her. At first she could see dim outlines as her friends were backlit by the lights in the hub they had left, but after a few more steps it was nearly impossible to see anything. The crystal lights might be enough for the Mimir to move around, but as she stubbed her foot on yet another unseen rock on the track, she decided crossly that it was not enough for her.

Waving her hands in the darkness, Eyre conjured up her lux and gave it a rub. In a moment there was a gentle glow lighting her way as the lux floated up and bobbed above her head.

"Ah, great idea," Beatrice said in a testy voice. "I've tripped so many times I thought I might end up grovelling at your feet, a la Mimir!"

Abby smiled half-heartedly. "And now at least we'll see whatever the gross creature is, when it comes to get us!"

Eyre laughed. "You prefer to see what it is, when it eats you for dinner?"

Abby chuckled nervously. "Well, if this tunnel starts to go downwards, I'm outta here. Downwards *definitely* means things with lots of teeth and big appetites! And even if the passage is flat, I'm only going to walk for ten minutes before I'm heading back." Her eyes travelled the chamber with a doubtful look on her face. "Not exactly keen on this, I have to admit."

There was no argument about that from the other two, and they started again slowly, all senses alert.

"It would be so much easier if we could teleport," Beatrice grumbled as they continued along the passage. "Definitely looking forward to learning that skill!"

They continued in silence for a short while, until they reached an area that was wider than the tunnel and perfectly circular. They stopped to look around, but realised that only one option for exit was available; the passage continued at the other side of the open space.

"May as well go on then," said Beatrice with a decided lack of enthusiasm. Then Abby, who was at the rear, suddenly whirled around, staring back into the blackness of the passage they had just come from.

"Who's there?" she said, her voice wavering. There was no reply, but Eyre agreed, she could sense there *was* someone there, lurking just outside the lux's reach. *BTL!* She thought. She was so *sick* of hidden threats! Her face grim, she took a step back the way they had come, and, using her best fulminology technique, sent a shard of lightning down the passageway. It blasted into the wall of the passage where the tunnel turned, then ricocheted around the corner out of sight. A second later there was an explosion and a series of oaths. Foul-smelling black smoke curled back towards Eyre from depths of the tunnel as they all waited, fearful of what might emerge.

Before Eyre could send another shot down the dark passage, someone with a soot-covered face emerged, hands in the air.

"I surrender!" Jax said. "Take pity on me!"

Eyre's mouth hung open. "What are you doing here?"

Jax raised a sooty eyebrow. "Well, I was going to ask you all the same thing. I saw you leave the room and I thought I'd come along for the ride." He wiped at the muck on his face, which only resulted in him smearing it comically from one side to the other. His hair stuck up on end, filled with black smut from the firebolt.

"Agh," Beatrice grinned. "You look ridiculous, Jackson!"

Jax rolled his eyes. "Well, it's lucky I deflected that blasted lightning bolt or I'd be *dead* and ridiculous!"

As they all laughed, Eyre tried to explain. "Ah, I'm sorry about that. We thought we'd get out of the Kit Room—it was so *hot*—and head back to the first chamber, but it seems we've gotten ourselves a little lost. I guess I'm a bit jumpy."

Jax shrugged. "Understandable," he said. "Well, I'll come with you, now I'm here. I don't know if I'd be much of a bodyguard, but I might scare them away, looking like this!"

Eyre laughed and turned to start walking again when Jax spoke again.

"You know," he said, "the reason you couldn't get back to the original room is because of the intricate network of passageways down here. The hub where you started is just one of many, and they all have eight passages radiating from them. The tunnels lead to circular 'junctures'—which is the round space we're standing in. At random intervals the hubs spin and the tunnels up to the juncture rotate with the hubs. It's a security measure the Mimir have put in so the layout of their domain is never the same. That way, intruders can't get in and catch them unawares. So, actually I'm here to suggest that you should really go back. If the hubs move, you'll be seriously lost."

Once again, Eyre was bemused at the extent of Jax's knowledge. Where did he get this information? It certainly wasn't taught in class. But she had a question.

"So how do the Mimir know where to go?"

Jax knew the answer to that too. "The Mimir have crystals on their belts that are attuned to the frequency of the ultimate destination. The crystal lights up when you follow the correct passage."

"Wow," Abby said. "Where can we get one of those?"

Jax laughed. "Now *that*, I don't know."

Eyre mused that it seemed there wasn't very much that Jax didn't know, and she felt slightly frustrated at the mysteriousness of this. Perhaps he acquired all his information down at the Lorian Bar, she thought sourly. But she had to admit that he did make sense. It was dumb to keep walking, given that knowledge. And she would also very much like to get back to where they started from.

She nodded as she made up her mind.

"You're right," she said, looking around. "This is a recipe for disaster. I think we should head back and just wait for someone to come and get us. "We'll get completely lost if we keep going."

Beatrice and Abby nodded in agreement. It was eerie in the dark, damp tunnels and the complete silence was unnatural.

Eyre turned to go back up the tunnel, when she was struck by a terrible swirl of vertigo. She staggered and put a hand to her head.

"Are you okay?" Abby asked, putting a hand on Eyre's shoulder. The lux bobbed up and down wildly as Eyre bent over and took a few deep breaths. After a moment she straightened.

"No, I'm alright, I..." and then the dizziness struck her again, even stronger. As she struggled to stay upright, a haunting voice began to call to her, filling her mind with a mesmerising, relentless melody. Over and over the hypnotic vocals repeated their mysterious message, the joyless sounds striking her heart like a melancholic dagger. She felt an overwhelming urge to do something, but she didn't know what, and tears ran down her face as the mournful strains continued on and on...

"Eyre!" Beatrice cried as Eyre began to crumple. Eyre was dimly aware of Abby trying to hold her up, and Beatrice grabbing her other arm, but then the world disappeared in a shimmering golden haze.

CHAPTER THIRTEEN

EYRE OPENED HER EYES and gave a gasp of fright. She was standing only a metre away from the front of a rock wall, and the wall was pulsing and moving like something alive, or like something alive was about to burst through it. To the side of the wall was a statue of a young woman with long hair, reaching up with both hands to the Light.

Eyre stepped back quickly and turned around. Beatrice, Abby and Jax were just behind her, but the expressions on their faces terrified her. They looked like they had just seen one of the Strigis walk in, but they were looking at *her*.

"What?" Eyre cried. "What's happening?"

Beatrice collected herself. "So... you're back?"

"What do you mean," Eyre asked desperately. "And what's happening to the wall?"

Beatrice, Abby and Jax looked briefly at the wall and then back at Eyre. "There's nothing there, Eyre," Abby said softly.

Eyre turned back to the pulsating rock. "It's *moving*," she cried, pointing at it. "And where am I? How did we get here?" She looked fearfully around the room they stood in. Shining gold discs were spaced at intervals mid-way up the rock, in a horizontal line that emerged from the passage at the back of the circular chamber.

"*You* brought us here," Jax said softly. "To this juncture. We've been walking for half an hour through hubs and passages and junctures. The hubs have moved three times, so we have no idea where we are now. But *you* seemed to know somehow. The gold discs appeared as you walked— what they mean I have no idea, but you've been in some kind of trance. We just got here and suddenly, you're back."

Abby's eyes were like saucers as she looked at Eyre. "Are you okay, Eyre? And why did you come here? We didn't know what to do. We couldn't get you to turn around."

Confusion muddled Eyre's brain as she tried to remember. "I, I don't know..." Her thoughts were scrambled. She recalled a heartbreaking melody and an overwhelming urge to do something, but then her mind was blank. She looked around anxiously. Had she really brought them here? And then her scattered mind scuttled back to the wall in front of her. The rock face seemed to move in waves, bulging out and then subsiding again. It was creepy and Eyre shuddered.

"Can't you see the rock moving?" she asked Abby desperately. But Abby just looked bewildered and shook her head. Then she looked more closely at the statue and gasped.

"Eyre! That is *you!*" Abby was pointing at the figure.

Eyre's head was still groggy and she looked at the statue with confusion. She didn't know where she was, or how she got there. But as everyone moved to the statue, she followed.

"St Ria," Beatrice read from the plaque, and then she looked at Eyre with an expression like Edison when the light bulb came on. "No wonder they revere you. They have St Ria *enshrined* down here and you look just like her!"

Eyre looked at the marble carving and thought it *might* look a little like her, but she couldn't concentrate with the moving rock wall in front of her, and her scrambled mind. Then suddenly, the voice in her head was back, but more incessant, more overpowering than before. She couldn't speak, couldn't think and her body turned of its own will and walked her into the bulging rockface. Eyre could hear Abby scream as the wall swallowed her up.

In a second she was out the other side, and her robot-like limbs marched her along another pathway, towards something down the hall that was glowing with a golden light. Unable to stop herself, she could only walk along mechanically as the fervent voice sung on and on in her head.

Eyre heard sounds behind her and assumed it was the others following her through the wall. *Stay back!* she thought desperately, terrified she was dragging them all into danger. She fought against the power that had overtaken her body, but her efforts were inconsequential. Inexorably, the golden light drew her to it.

Racing footsteps echoed behind her and Beatrice, Abby and Jax appeared by her side. Beatrice's anxious face looked at her.

"Stop Eyre, *stop!*" she pleaded. Eyre could only look at her with frantic eyes. Nothing was within her control here.

Her friends ended up walking on either side of her as she moved towards the light, which she could see now was pulsating in waves. The light would brighten almost to the point of blinding them, then it would subside again for a couple of seconds.

They rounded a corner in the passageway and all four of them gasped. Eyre felt the iron control on her body release, but she, like the others, moved forward towards the object in front of them.

The Isar was embedded in the wall in front of them, shining with a dazzling silver light that increased and then faded in an endless cycle. Eyre could hear echoes of the mournful song as she looked with awestruck eyes at the magnificent object.

"It's singing," she said softly. "Singing to the other Isars. It's part of the Aura, and it's trying to find them." She held out a hand to the Isar. "It's so, so sad."

"*This* is what drew you here?" Beatrice said, perplexed. "But why?"

Abby's face was fascinated and she sat on the ground. "Eyre found it, after all this time being lost in Terra. It wants Eyre to find the other Isars. I can hear it now. Isn't it a beautiful thing?"

"Nope," Beatrice said, perplexed, but sat down beside Abby.

Then they all sat beside Abby and watched as the Isar brightened and dimmed in a steady, rhythmic sequence, almost as if it were breathing. Beatrice and Jax couldn't hear the song, but they were just as mesmerised as they regarded the incredible beam of light.

Eyre had to admit that Abby was right. She *did* feel a strange bond with the object, which seemed like a live thing to her. It was calling to her, pleading for her to help. The sheer desolation of the plea would have been enough to drag her into action, even if she hadn't already been on the journey to reunite the four bars of light.

"I'm here, I'll find them," Eyre promised, as her eyes remained transfixed on the glowing bar.

A noise behind them made them turn their heads. Sergeant Tottingham, looking hot and bothered, walked through the wall, followed closely by Jengles. The students jumped to their feet and hung their heads, looking various shades of guilty, and waiting for the inevitable explosion from the red-faced Sergeant.

But Jengles spoke first. He looked at the Isar and then walked up to Eyre. "If I ever had any doubt, I don't have any now, my lady," he said almost inaudibly.

Then, he looked at all four of them and in a louder voice added, "are you alright?"

"They might be alright now," the Sergeant interjected in a tight voice, "but I can't guarantee they will be once I've finished with them. Hold hands."

The four of them grabbed hands so quickly it was like they were playing a party game. None of them wanted to antagonise the already furious instructor any further.

There was a bright flash of light and they all disappeared.

CHAPTER FOURTEEN

EYRE WIPED HER FOREHEAD and groaned as she looked around her. She'd only mopped a third of the Central Administration building lobby, and it had taken her half an hour. The Sergeant had been livid with them all, making reference to their intelligence and potential for living past eighteen years old. She had ranted and raved for ten minutes while the four of them prayed for survival. And then she'd assigned them to various odious duties around campus so that they would realise the error of their ways.

But in truth, Eyre hadn't been sorry about the whole escapade at all. She was really glad she'd seen the incredible Isar, and she now knew a lot more about how the Mimir existed below the ground. It was pretty cool.

She swirled the soapy water around of the floor with the long-stranded mop as she worked her way past the paintings of past Board members on the wall of the foyer. Her thoughts swirled as wildly as the strands of the mop as she thought about yesterday. Receiving her Arms Endowment, travelling through the passages, and then Jax turning up. She thought about Jax. It seemed strange that he had followed them through the wall—I mean, she thought in frustration—what was he doing? Why didn't he make his presence known earlier? Loitering about in the dark behind them, it made her uneasy. She had a feeling he was up to something, and, given his odd behaviour in Bathurst last year and the Lorian Juice this week, she worried that it was not good. If life had taught her anything in these past years, it was that you couldn't trust *anyone*. And now she thought about it, he hadn't batted an eye when they saw the Isar, almost as if he knew what it was. But how could he? Eyre had understood from Whittaker Ray that very few people knew about the Isars, and he'd warned her about talking to anyone about them. But if Jax knew about it, why didn't Whittaker Ray tell her? Jax was certainly an enigma that she just couldn't work out.

The enigma himself was currently cleaning the bathroom facilities at the pool complex, while Abby was assigned to the Common Room and Beatrice had been stuck with the Refectory tables. Once they had finished their tasks they were to go straight to the Ferito Shed with their Arms Endowment for the first training session.

Eyre rubbed her nose and sighed. She'd better get on with it—there was still a lot to do. Pushing the bucket along on its wheels, she worked her way past the Admin Office and back to the end of the corridor. She had just moved behind a column when the lift doors opened and Professor Vela strode out.

He walked straight onto the wet floor, slipped, and fell onto his rear end with a loud *Oof!* Eyre would have laughed, if she wasn't so terrified. Doctor Botolfe followed him out of the elevator and provided him with no sympathy.

"Oh, get up Mandig, you look ridiculous."

Professor Vela scowled and got awkwardly to his feet. Then he looked around.

"What are they doing, mopping at this hour?" he grumbled. "Who's there?"

Eyre stayed behind the column, sweat beading on her brow. Professor Vela and Dr Botolfe! Was Dr Botolfe in on it too? She was such a sour and severe person, there really didn't seem much Lightness in her, despite the fact she had seemed to warm slightly towards Eyre after a Devil Wolf tried to kill her last year and Eyre had saved her. Indeed, if someone gave her a choice between facing Dr Botolfe or one of the Strigis, Eyre would have to think hard about her answer. One thing was for sure, neither of the lecturers were very fond of Eyre, so she was going to stay here until they left.

"No one's here Mandig," Dr Botolfe said impatiently. "You've always been clumsy, ever since high school. You'd think you'd have grown out of it by now."

Eyre started. Since *high school*? So, they had known each other all that time? Eyre already knew in her bones that Professor Vela was up to something, but she was even more suspicious of him *and* Dr Botolfe now. Eyre stood completely silent, scarcely daring to breathe.

Mandig Vela brushed himself off grumpily. "When's the meeting? I don't want to miss it."

"Two o'clock, the Board Room. Make sure you're there, we have to present a united front."

Dr Botolfe stalked off ahead of Professor Vela and out the front doors of the building. After a moment of fussing over his wet clothes, Professor Vela left too.

Once she was sure they were gone, Eyre continued mopping the marble floor, thinking about what they'd said. A meeting. From the tone of Dr Botolfe's voice, it sounded important. Anything those two needed to be united for was something Eyre needed to know about. Perhaps she'd better call a Bane meeting to work it out with her friends.

But then she hesitated, and a sudden sadness sliced through her. It wasn't really Bane anymore, as Nick seemed to have—for whatever inexplicable reason—opted out of their friendship group. He had avoided them for days, and even in the Mimir's stronghold, he had kept away from them, staying in his Tyros sector group rather than coming to talk with them. It was very confusing, and Eyre could see it was breaking Abby's heart. And to add to the pain, Eyre wasn't sure what Jax was up to, and whether he was actually working for good, or just for himself. His family was very successful and wealthy, after all. Perhaps they had a sideline in importing the prohibited Lorian Juice. Whatever the truth was, she wasn't about to consult him on this development.

She finished the last edge of the marble floor and hurried to empty the bucket. Then, consulting her watch she realized she was just about to be late for Ferito, so she skidded out onto the slippery floor and left at a run.

CHAPTER FIFTEEN

EYRE MADE IT IN the door of the Shed and hurried to join Beatrice and Abby. The Sergeant was standing at the front of the room, and behind her was a huge, neatly stacked pile of the weapons the students had received yesterday. When they had arrived back on campus, they had been instructed to leave them in the Shed overnight, where they would be guarded by the Mimir. Two ferocious and large Mimir still remained, one at each door, Crescent Blades drawn and ready across their chests.

"Right," the Sergeant said. "An important day, and a potentially dangerous one."

She waited for the titters to subside before continuing. "Yesterday you received your Arms Endowment, and I am glad that all were *finally*," she eyed Ben Perrill, "deemed worthy.

"Today we will begin learning the techniques to use your weapons without injuring yourself, or others, unintentionally. You will need to learn to summon your weapons so that the right end arrives in your hand. You are no good to anyone if you are injured by your own Antarak." Once again laughter travelled around the room. The Sergeant thumped her staff.

"Yes indeed," she said, "quite funny, unless it happens and you have to spend three months with the Clementis while they reattach a limb. Until now you have had a buffer for training—the wooden palum are designed to give you time to learn the correct techniques. Well, now you are going to have to learn quickly; there is no room for error.

"So, how do we make the transition from fence paling to lethal weapon? You may not realise it, but you have some help in that your body has been programmed as a Lightworker to handle these dangerous weapons, and you will find that your Viq gives you an innate understanding of what to do."

The Sergeant picked up two of the Antaraks on the floor and held them up. "But most important of all is your mind control over your weapons, which have been specifically bestowed to you, when your energy was deemed worthy. It is the connection between your mental power and your body that will cement your skills in Ferito with your arms.

"Aditus—*attack*!" The Sergeant performed an incredible display of speed and force as she moved through the Clasis for Two-Handed Fighting. Some of the moves were unfamiliar, and Eyre guessed that they were getting a preview of the new moves they would learn for Level 3 Ferito this year.

"Tego—*defend*!" the Sergeant continued, and launched into the defensive positions of Tego.

It was fascinating to watch, Eyre thought, and so much more impressive than the practise sessions with the palum. The blades of the Antaraks flashed and sparkled in the morning light that streamed through the windows of the Shed, and as the Sergeant twirled them faster and faster, a hum arose, almost like a low chanting. Finally, the Sergeant stopped, and sweating, she wiped her brow.

"Right then. Please form a line and collect your Arms Endowment from the stage. They are labelled with your name, but from now on you will be responsible for your own weapons, and you must keep them securely locked in your arms cabinet with your staff. Most of the time they will stay there for the next two years, unless you need to take them with you for some reason, or until you summon them."

A queue formed and the students slowly retrieved their arms from the stage. Eyre picked hers up, as well as her baldrics, which were still attached.

"Your Antaraks have been crafted by the Mimir from the Zha'kara Diamonds of Incendium. At the base of the blade, down near the hilt, you will see a series of runes that have been etched into the diamond. This is the name of the student who sourced the diamond for your Antaraks, written in the language of the Mimir. You will have a lifelong bond with that student, who put themselves in danger, and undertook great physical hardship to obtain the gazae.

"Please find a partner and start slowly moving through the positions of Two with your Antaraks. Familiarise yourself with the weight of your weapons. It must become like an extension of your arm. You have been rehearsing for this for two years; you know the movements. Focus, focus, *focus*—your mind will merge with your body and the connection will begin, For the next two weeks you will repeat the Clasis at this speed, again and again until the movements become second nature to you. Begin!"

Abby and Beatrice paired up, and Eyre ended up with Zanda, who also needed a partner. Eyre pulled her unfamiliar weapons out of the baldrics and hefted them in her hands. They were weighted differently to the palum

—heavier, for a start, but also balanced differently. There was greater weight in the blade than the hilt, which caused the blade to constantly tip downwards. Lifting it up caused an ache in Eyre's wrist and she smiled wryly at Zanda as she tried to keep the blade up.

"En garde!" Zanda cried dramatically, posing as if he were one of the Three Musketeers. The Sergeant's roving eyes noticed, and she stomped to the corner of the stage and pointed at Zanda.

"This is not a comedy act, student," she shouted. "The word is 'Tollo' or you may leave the Shed until your attitude improves. Try again."

Zanda blanched. "Tollo!" he cried with alacrity, raising his palm to Eyre's. No one ever wanted to get offside with the huge Sergeant; she had ways of making your life miserable.

For the next hour they fumbled around, trying to recreate the moves in the Clasis that were second nature with a palum. Somehow, the difference in weight and balance of the weapon made it very difficult. And no doubt the threat of being carved open had an influence on their nerve too, Eyre thought.

She was getting very frustrated as she sliced the air with her weapon.

"It's like I've never done it before," she grumbled after tripping over her own feet yet again. A student left on the run for the Infirmary—the third one so far. They'd either cut themselves or their partner had. Eyre sighed and steeled herself to concentrate—she definitely didn't want a three-month sojourn with the Clementis.

Finally, the session ended. Zanda hadn't helped her technique much, with his flippant comments and parody of the Clasis. But he *had* helped her humour—she'd had quite a hilarious workout with all the running in circles. The Sergeant stepped forward as the hour was at the end.

"Head back to your rooms, and put your arms into your locker immediately, students. Your lockers have been warded from today. So if you put your palm on the outside of the door it will lock the cabinet automatically, and only your palm print henceforth will be able to open it. Are there any questions?"

No one raised their hand so the class was dismissed and Eyre eyed Nick, who was hurrying off without a backward glance.

"Well, I have to talk to you guys, but I guess now we're just *Bae*," Eyre said, but immediately felt sorry she'd spoken, as Abby winced. "Let's just talk in our room instead. You never know who might be listening out here," Eyre added.

But Abby just said lightly, "You know you're my Baes. Always!"

They carried their arms to the dormitory room and put them in their arms lockers. When Eyre put her hand on the closed door, as instructed, she felt a warmth shoot up her arm and the metal of the cabinet shimmered with rainbow hues for several seconds. Sure enough, the door was now locked. She put her palm back on the door and with a click the door unlocked and swung open. Better than a locker combination she thought, remembering back to her time at high school where she would often be cursing as the frustrating lock refused to accept the numbers.

She locked the door again and sat on her bed as Beatrice and Abby finished putting their weapons away.

"I have a date for you," Eyre said as they flung themselves on their beds. Beatrice raised an eyebrow.

"This afternoon there's a meeting at the Board Room. I overheard Professor Vela and Dr Botolfe talking about it when I was mopping the floors and it sounded like something is afoot. I think we should go check it out—I really think," Eyre stopped for a moment, unsure. Even despite the experiences last year, Eyre couldn't bring herself to be more specific, for Abby's sake. She took a breath and continued, "Well, we need to keep an eye on Vela. And did you know—he and Dr Botolfe were at high school together!"

"Really?" Beatrice said. "He looks much older than her."

"All the stress of dealing with *disgusting* students," Abby intoned in a good parody of Professor Vela's voice, "has aged me prematurely!"

Then Beatrice jumped, as if she'd had a horrific thought.

"When is the meeting?" she asked. "I hope we have time for lunch."

CHAPTER SIXTEEN

EYRE SIDLED AROUND THE Central Admin building, with Beatrice and Abby close behind, and peered through a hedge of pink camellias as staff members filtered in through the tall front doors. Eyre's eyebrows rose. Chairman Essendon, who was Rigmar's father and head of the Echelon, had just arrived in a flash of light. She looked at Beatrice and Abby. She'd been right—something was definitely going on.

Over the next half hour more distinguished guests arrived, including an unsmiling member of the Thantos Nex; an old man wearing a top hat—Sir Rayburn—who Eyre recognised from two years ago; and a tall black man wearing a golden turban, who she hadn't seen before.

"See anything interesting?" a voice whispered over her shoulder and she nearly levitated over the building.

"Ranger!" she exclaimed as she turned around. "Seriously?" But she was glad to see him—she'd been wondering how they would get into the viewing room.

The Ranger grinned. "Keeping you on your toes, my dear," he said, but Eyre noticed his eyes were lacking their usual cheer.

Before Eyre could say anything else, the Ranger walked around the hedge towards the front door.

"Cheska!" he cried gaily as Madame Overmantle walked down the path. "May I be your escort?"

"Of course, Leo," Eyre heard Madame Overmantle say, and then she patted him on the back. "Are you alright?"

They disappeared inside as Eyre frowned. "What was that about?"

But Beatrice tugged her arm. "Come on, let's go before they close the doors."

There was no need for Eyre to mask to cover them all, as both Beatrice and Abby had mastered the technique in the last year. So, they each generated the protective shield and crept up the first flight of stairs. Sure enough, Mrs Abnett was bent down unlatching the lock that held one of the Boardroom doors open. So they levitated and swept past her just as she began to close the door. Mrs Abnett looked uncertain suddenly and she peered around as the three friends headed up the stairs leading to the higher floors. Something had registered with her—maybe their Viq had changed the energy flow—because she definitely knew something was not right. Eyre held her breath as the old woman listened hard for a moment. Then she shrugged and unlatched the other door before starting down the stairs. She left out the front door and closed it with a heavy clang behind her.

Once Mrs Abnett had left, the three girls lowered themselves to the floor and quickly ran up the stairs to the viewing room. Eyre hauled on the handle. *What?* It was locked! Why hadn't the Ranger opened it for them? And then Eyre thought back to the garden and the Ranger's unusual demeanour. When she thought about it, it seemed that the Ranger had deliberately left before they could discuss what they were up to. And by going in with Madame Overmantle, he had effectively prevented himself from being able to slip upstairs and unlock the door for them. Eyre couldn't understand it. Didn't he want them here? He'd always been so positive about them trying to find out what was going on. It didn't make sense.

But she still wanted to get in the room, so she had to figure out how to open the door. If she were Unlit, she could use one of her many burglary tools to coax the door open. But she didn't have any of the gadgets. Then a thought dawned on her. She did have something that the Unlit didn't— *Viq!* She could use her Light energy like one of the tools the Unlit carried, and follow the techniques for picking locks that she'd learned in 'Breaking and Entering' at the Unlit last year.

Kneeling down, she studied the lock. It was a basic pin cylinder lock with five 'pin stacks', which she'd studied last year in the class with the second-year Unlit students. At the Unlit she'd learnt a technique called Single Pin Picking, which used a lock pick and a tension wrench to work on each pin stack individually. It had been hard enough with the requisite tools; she wasn't sure whether it was even possible to use Viq. The idea of the two tools was to use the pick to align the key and driver pins, then hold the pins in place with the wrench until all five pin stacks were aligned, allowing the 'plug' or cylinder of the lock to turn. Eyre was going to have to use Viq for all these tasks, *simultaneously.* She groaned.

Concentrating hard, she raised a stream of Viq and sent it through the keyhole. Then with her mind she searched and probed until she 'felt' the first pin stack click down. Then, she used a second stream of Viq to hold the pins in place while she worked on the second pin stack. It was fiddly and frustrating, and after the pins clattered down for the third time she almost gave up. But finally, the pin stack gave and she held it steady too with her Viq. Slowly she worked on the remaining three pin stacks until all five were aligned, wobbly, but held in place precariously with her mind. Then, feeling like her head was about to explode, she raised a final burst of energy and sent it through the keyway to turn the plug. *Snick!* The lock was open!

Eyre exhaled loudly and closed her eyes.

"Awesome, Eyre!" Beatrice whispered. "You are now officially a spy! Come on let's go look!"

They raced over to the viewing window and looked down. The meeting was already underway; while Eyre was messing with the lock they had missed the opening comments. Eyre looked down through the glass and saw that the staff were arranged around the boardroom table, with Chairman Essendon in the middle and Whittaker Ray at one end.

Chairman Essendon was rubbing his temples as Professor Vela continued reading from a sheet of paper—obviously a letter—he held in his hands.

"...and we feel he is detrimental to the reputation of the college." Professor Vela sat down.

"Thank you Mandig," David Essendon said, although his face did not echo the words. He actually looked like he would rather be anywhere but here. "Mahogany, I believe you also wanted to contribute?"

Dr Botolfe stood up importantly. "Yes I do," she said. "I've heard from a number of parents about their concerns, and I would like to start with this letter from Melissa Hamlen." Eyre looked at Beatrice and Abby. Carrison Hamlen's mum? This ought to be interesting.

Dr Botolfe raised her voice a little and read out loud. "I had been very much looking forward to my son joining your campus, due to its singular reputation and—" Dr Botolfe couldn't help herself, she preened a little —"the quality of its teaching staff. All but one, however. I strongly disagree with the decision to continue with the Fallen One on the Academy staff and I warn that this may affect your enrolments in coming years. I certainly would have to think again about my son attending this school if you do not deal with the matter. Yours, etc."

Eyre's head was spinning. *The Fallen One?* Who was that? But then she noticed Dr Botolfe was looking at the Ranger, who sat beyond Professor Vela, at the very far end of the table. Surely Carrison's mother hadn't been referring to the Ranger? But her thoughts were confirmed as she looked down through the window. Dr Botolfe shot a triumphant glance at the

Ranger and Professor Vela *smirked.* Smirked! The gall of him, to vilify the amazing being who had saved the world. The calm expression on the Ranger's face made Eyre more furious and she felt her blood begin to boil. What were they doing? How *could* they? Surely Whittaker Ray would intervene? But the travesty continued.

Dr Botolfe indicated the pile of papers sitting on the table in front of her and picked one up. "This one is from Henry and Georgina Rankins." The lecturer proceeded to read out the Rankins' letter, then three more in the same vein as the first. The upshot of it all was that the Ranger was a danger to the student body because of his recklessness and his disregard for authority. Eyre was surprised at the vitriol, even knowing the sourness in the Doctor's soul. What had brought this on?

Chairman Essendon thanked Dr Botolfe in a very insincere voice. "Finally, I believe One One One from the Thantos Nex is here to speak."

The haughty blue being rose, fixing the Ranger with a withering stare. The Ranger, to his credit, did not flinch and kept the same interested expression on his face.

One One One pointed an accusing finger at the Ranger. "We do not intervene in any world, unless it has affected our own. In this instance, our opinion is that *this being*—who would flout the rules of our people, is a dangerous risk-taker who will ultimately cause you terrible trouble, as he did with us. You would do well to heed my warning and send him into exile." Eyre, Beatrice and Abby looked at each other in horror. *Exile!* They couldn't!

The purple-robed man sat down again and the Chairman closed his eyes, as if he had a headache. Then he lifted a hand to the unknown dark-skinned man, who sat next to Whittaker Ray.

"Our final input before we make a decision will be from President Balthazar. Thank you, President." *President Balthazar!* Eyre thought. The President of the Determinant Dozen! He had been missing from the meeting they had spied on in first-year after the Gothak attacked. But he was the most important individual in the Overworld, and wielded great power.

As the tall man rose Eyre had a flash of understanding about why the Ranger had not unlocked the door for them. He was too proud, and hadn't wanted them to see this, she realised. Her rage grew again as she regarded the green-haired, kind-hearted mentor who sat with such dignity throughout the speeches. This was terribly unfair, and so disrespectful, given what the Ranger had sacrificed for—well, the whole Overworld, really.

If President Balthazar said one off thing about the Ranger, Eyre thought she would explode through the window and perform Occido on them all.

But the exotic-looking man did not speak for a moment and regarded the room with calm eyes. His gilded turban shone as he turned from one staff member to another. Then he looked at the Ranger.

"Every couple of years, this issue is raised again," he said. "Generally, around the time of the Echelon elections." Sir Rayburn nodded and Professor Vela looked mortified. Chairman Essendon hid a smile. "And every time, we eventually arrive at the sensible decision."

President Balthazar raised a hand to One One One. "We realise that the Ranger has offended the deepest of your beliefs and we understand your anger. However, we must acknowledge what he has achieved for the future of our own people. The Ranger saved us all, something some of us would do well to remember." His gaze, not so soft now, turned towards Dr Botolfe. A flush crossed her cheeks and she lifted her chin defiantly.

"I understand that the latest complaint has evolved from reports that the Ranger—" President Balthazar consulted some notes in front of him, "—has been teaching—uh, er, so let me quote directly... *"recklessly"*—fourth-year students to fly upside down?" His face looked out at everyone impassively, but Eyre could tell, this man was *seriously* annoyed at the letter.

Chairman Essendon nodded to confirm this, looking slightly embarrassed. He obviously didn't like the Ranger being criticized either. President Balthazar paused and shook his head.

"Whilst my personal views have always been very clear on this, we must consider the desires of the whole Lightworking community. Therefore, while we process all the information to make a decision, I am going to recommend that the Ranger finish out this semester. Depending on the outcome of our discussions, we will decide whether he will be back next semester. Thank you, Andrew."

President Balthazar sat down and Chairman Essendon stood up, looking most unhappy. "Well, that concludes this Special Meeting." He looked at the clock on the wall. "Meeting concluded at 3.04pm. Thank you all for coming."

Professor Vela and Dr Botolfe stood, and the smiles they gave to each other were like a facial high-five. Eyre wanted to send a blast of Viq down that would knock their smug selves onto their rear ends. She wished she'd put more water on the floor that morning. But another thought was intruding. Why would the President of the Determinant Dozen come to a meeting about piloting lessons? It hardly seemed serious enough to warrant all this fuss. And why did Whittaker Ray not speak up? She was disappointed in him. The Ranger deserved better.

But it was time to go. The last of the staff had filed out of the Board Room, and they had to get out the front doors before they closed again. So, the three of them quickly masked and headed out into some much-needed fresh air.

CHAPTER SEVENTEEN

THE NEXT COUPLE OF days were subdued as Eyre and her friends got back into the routine of classes. The meeting about the Ranger had depressed them—they could not understand how such a brave and kind person could be treated so unjustly, and it had broken Eyre's heart to see that no one stood up for him. Where was the Lightness of being in all this?

And Abby was feeling down also—Nick had virtually stopped acknowledging her at all and she was hurt and confused. All had seemed well at the cabins, and now, within only a week, he was completely ignoring her.

"It would be better if he just broke it off," she said to Beatrice and Eyre. "At least I'd know where I stand. But he won't even talk to me long enough *to* break it off!"

Eyre had nothing helpful to contribute. How could she, when Jax seemed to be avoiding her as well? She shook her head despondently. What was with these guys?

The morning was cool as she headed to the Equestrian Centre. Late summer mornings in the Blue Mountains usually started with a light chill before the searing sun drove it away. This was the best time of the day and she ran along the track, breathing the fresh air deeply.

Today was her first riding class with Ischyros and for once she felt optimistic that she might make it around the arena without being shotput face-first into the dirt. Ischyros's new attitude towards her gave her hope. Ever since the Weta had attacked at Highlight, Ischyros had been, well, not exactly *friendly*, but definitely more receptive to Eyre being around.

Students were bustling up and down the passageways when she arrived, leading their Lighthorses to the arena. This year the classes had been organised into groups of approximately twenty students, based on the subjects they had chosen and how it fit into their timetable. That was all very logical, Eyre supposed, but unfortunately it meant that she had Ben Perrill in her class. For the rest of the year. She couldn't believe it.

She also had Colton though, which was great, especially as she was hoping to get some riding tips from him. Carly and Luke were also in her class, as was Zanda. On the downside, the brainless Curtis twins and foul Carrison Hamlen were there too. It was going to be an interesting year, she thought.

The Kikkuli Master waited patiently in the middle of the arena as the students brought their horses out.

"Please wait until everyone is ready," he called.

Eyre felt very self-conscious as she stood in the ring. All eyes were mentally on her, although people were not turning their heads to stare. Most of them anyway. The brief look she had at Ben and his cronies showed they definitely *were* staring at her, anticipating an amusing show when she finally got on Ischyros's back. But even those who were sympathetic to the struggle she'd had over the past two years with her troublesome steed were obviously curious about how she would go. She'd made quite a name for herself in the Equestrian Centre, she thought wryly: possibly the worst rider in the history of the school.

"Okay, please mount your horses and walk around the ring," the Kikkuli Master instructed.

Saying a prayer to the Light under her breath, Eyre grasped Ischyros's mane and swung herself up onto his back. She tensed for a moment, anticipating the moment she might be ejected into the air. But it didn't come. Ischyros stood docilely until she gave him a gentle kick to get him walking. He plodded around the circumference with the other horses and after the first lap, Eyre realised that he was going to co-operate.

"Ask your horse to trot," the Kikkuli Master called, and Eyre nudged Ischyros into a shambling trot, the first time he had ever done it. She felt positively gleeful!

"Thank you, Ischyros," she said softly, and the scruffy creature harrumphed. As they headed around the ring, Ben overtook them on his big bay horse.

"You look like you're on a carousel," he hooted as he passed. "That horse goes higher up than it does forward."

Eyre smarted. Ischyros did have an unusual gait, but he was old and his bones probably hurt. "Well, you look like someone's hung you," she retorted.

Ben's face darkened. He was particularly sensitive about the red scar that circled his neck and always tried to cover it up. Eyre suspected that it wasn't really because of the look of it, because it wasn't really disfiguring, but more because it was a reminder of someone teaching him a well-deserved lesson. Jengles had decided Ben needed educating in first-year after he attacked Eyre in the Transit caves and had nearly killed her. Eyre didn't know what Jengles had done to Ben, but apparently it was frightening enough, and had hurt enough, and it had definitely left a permanent mark. Eyre was just glad that Ben mostly kept away from her now.

So, for the rest of the class, every time Ben passed Eyre, Ischyros would mutter, "Ned Kelly," the infamous Australian bushranger who was hanged, or the old horse would make firing rifle noises, and he was so funny Eyre ended up spluttering with laughter. Ben was furious, but he couldn't hear Ischyros, so he didn't know what was going on. Eyre suspected the Kikkuli Master did, though, because he didn't pull her up for her lack of attention.

The other students progressed on to cantering, and a few of the more advanced riders like Colton and Carly headed out to gallop in the paddock. But Eyre was content just to trot around the ring, ungainly though they were.

At the end of the class Eyre jumped down and threw her arms around the bedraggled horse's neck.

"Thank you Ischyros," she whispered. But the old horse pulled away grumpily and Eyre sighed. It was obviously a step too far for him.

"Where's my dinner," he complained as she led him back to the stall. "My back is hurting."

CHAPTER EIGHTEEN

THAT AFTERNOON EYRE HEADED to her lecture with great anticipation. It was her first lecture about Caelus and she was interested in finding out about the Alterworld and what the gazae would be this year.

Eyre had just left her 'Tenets of Management' class which was taught by a new teacher called Mr Shimizu. Although the good-natured lecturer had a great sense of humour, the subject was starting out just as boring as always. Eyre didn't know how she had ended up in Hese; she seemed so grossly unsuited to the Sector. Beatrice and Abby didn't take the course, so she had organised to meet them for the Alterworlds lecture after her 'Tenets' class.

The lecture theatre was buzzing as she climbed the stairs and took her seat beside Beatrice. Everyone was curious about the Caelus lecturer and what the Alterworld would be like. Eyre was muttering to Beatrice about the agonies of a wages spreadsheet when someone sat beside her. For a moment she hoped it was Nick, and then was disappointed and slightly flustered when she saw it was Jax who had taken the seat. His mesmerising eyes twinkled at her.

"Not who you were expecting?"

Eyre's mouth opened and then she laughed. "Well, I was sort of hoping Nick might come and join us," she admitted, "but he seems to be avoiding us of late."

Jax looked over his shoulder at Nick, who was sitting with Zanda at the back of the room. "I'd noticed that," he said. "It's sort of strange, after all the time you four have spent together. He's a good guy though. There must be some explanation."

"I wish he'd give it to us, then," Eyre said with an edge of irritation. But then she looked at Jax curiously. "What are you doing here?"

"I'm in this class," Jax laughed, deliberately misunderstanding her question.

Eyre rolled her eyes and then tapped his hand, which was still a light shade of blue. "What was that about? You going into bartending?"

Jax hesitated. But then he just said lightly, "A lapse in judgement, for sure."

Eyre nodded. "And timing, definitely! Not exactly the best moment to show off your new blue gloves. But they've obviously let you off—I'm glad you're still here."

Their eyes met for a moment and then Jax spoke.

"Actually, I did come up here for a reason. I have something to tell you."

Eyre looked at him quizzically. "About...?"

Jax's face turned serious. "You need to watch out for Vela," he said. "Things are not as they appear."

Eyre felt almost a sense of relief. *Finally*, someone agreed with her! "You don't need to tell me that," she said with feeling. "I know!"

Jax took her hand and Eyre felt an electricity run all the way to the top of her head. Jax leaned over and whispered, "Promise me you'll be careful."

Eyre faltered at his nearness. A heat rose across her shoulders and travelled up her face. "Okay," she said softly.

Jax's eyes were suddenly intense. "Come for a walk this afternoon," he said softly, "Before dinner. I'll meet you at the moldavite square and we can stroll across the Ponds of Doombee."

Eyre hesitated. She didn't really know much about Jax; she was suspicious of his motives and couldn't figure out what he was up to, with his constant disappearances and reappearances. This was definitely not a good idea, not only because she wasn't sure what was going on, but especially because it was going to make her heart very vulnerable. But despite the logic, it seemed her subconscious had taken over, wherever that might lead her.

"Sure," Eyre replied weakly, her eyes drowning in his for a moment. Then she broke the spell and looked away, fearing she'd be lost forever if she didn't.

As her eyes travelled down, she noticed Jax had a leather thong around his neck, and she couldn't help giving a surprised smile as she recognised it. Jax noticed her gaze and pulled the polished plume agate from beneath his shirt.

"I never take it off," he said. Eyre had spent two days last year cutting and polishing the beautiful stone as a gift for Jax and it made her unexpectedly glad to see that he wore it.

There was a noise down the front as a few more students entered the theatre, Pheria amongst them. She looked around and spotted Jax, then headed across the front of the room to the stairs. As she ascended the steep steps towards them, Jax chuckled at Eyre's expression.

"She's not so bad really, greatly misunderstood," he said.

Eyre shrugged. "That's your business, nothing to do with me," she replied as Pheria sat down on Jax's other side. The tall, tanned girl's short hair was gleaming black and slicked back, like a seal freshly-emerged from the water. Her intense amber eyes surveyed Eyre with dislike. Evidently their feelings were mutual.

But they were distracted as the door swung open and Jemima Periwinkle entered, followed by a small bird-like creature with purple and white wings, edged with gold. Eyre knew it was a Caelite—she had seen one a couple of years ago when she had hidden to watch a meeting of the Determinant Dozen and the Echelon at the Central Admin building. The Caelite had large watchful eyes and a lime-coloured green beak, and it stood quietly at the front of the stage.

"Students!" the annoying, high-pitched tones of Jemima Periwinkle assaulted Eyre's ears. "Quiet please! But before I begin, where is Mr Jackson?"

Jax waved his hand and Jemima Periwinkles face hardened. "Mr Jackson, your presence is required at the Central Admin building."

Jax stood up slowly and picked up his Felsic and bag with his blue hands. His green eyes twinkled at Eyre. "It seems I am the man of the moment," he said softly as he left. "See you a bit later."

Jax headed out the side door of the theatre and Jemima Periwinkle straightened her neon-yellow dress self-importantly.

"I would like to introduce you to Miss Kyori, from Caelus," she said, with the pompous tone of one who was trying to impress her guest with her skills as a toastmaster.

Kyori! Eyre recognised the name. It was the same Caelite who had attended the meeting two years ago! Kyori must be important to have attended that meeting, so why would this particular Caelite be teaching a lowly third-year class on campus? It didn't really make sense.

As if reading her thoughts, the creature turned and looked at her. The bird regarded her calmly, sizing her up, as Jemima Periwinkle gushed on.

"So, please make Miss Kyori welcome," Jemima finished effusively, and the class clapped politely.

Kyori turned her beak to the ceiling and emitted an ear-piercing string of sounds, almost like a high-pitched kookaburra, Eyre thought, as she tried not to cover her ears. The calls rose and fell in waves, and as Kyori let out the last cry, she flapped her wings, rose a metre off the ground and then descended lightly.

A shocked silence fell on the room after the wild cacophony. But as usual, Ben Perrill wasn't lost for words.

"What was that, microphone feedback?" he snickered, just that bit too loudly. Eyre felt embarrassed for the Caelite at his rudeness. If the Sergeant were here, she wouldn't stand for that behaviour, but her froufrou sister just sat vapidly in the corner, oblivious.

Fortunately, the Caelite didn't seem offended, or if she was, she didn't show it.

"That is the Caelite greeting, wishing you luck, happiness and good health," she said in a soft, melodic voice, quite unlike the screeching ruckus earlier. "It equates in our language to: May your wings always find the space to fly." Eyre felt even worse then; the words were so goodhearted.

Kyori touched the crystal on the podium with one wing, so that an image streamed up onscreen.

It was a picture of towering clouds of many colours, drifting above a pebbled landscape, with dark, craggy mountains far off in the distance. Below the pebbles and the ground, Eyre was amazed to see clear air and more clouds wafting around. It was like an island floating in the sky!

"Caelus is mainly constructed of a pumice-like stone that is filled with an energy similar to your Light energy. Over the aeons Mt Crepitus, the highest peak in Caelus, has erupted in a massive explosion that deposits fragments of pumice onto our landscape. The eruptions are extremely dangerous, but necessary so that our world does not erode away. So we try to anticipate the eruptions and prepare for their arrival. The next major event is predicted in 90 years, so you should be safe when you come for your TACI test."

The students laughed and Kyori clicked another image onto the screen. This one was a closer view of the mountains, and showed jagged, pitch-black rock formations jutting up into the air, with deep ravines and narrow paths cut into the sides of the steep façade. It looked foreboding and dangerous. How were they going to navigate *that*?

"These are the Caedes Mountains, which include Mt Crepitus, and they are found at one end of Caelus. They are a treacherous range of precipitous peaks, mostly comprised of obsidian, where unfortunately, but necessarily, the gazae is found. Being so high, the area is subject to wild atmospheric storms that can arise at any moment, so we aim to go in quickly to get the gazae, and out again just as quickly. This year the gazae is a fulgurite comprised of Electrum."

Seeing the blank looks on some of the student's faces, Kyori explained. "In Entis, a fulgurite is formed when lightning hits sand and creates a glass-like tube. Electrum is a metal comprised of a combination of gold and silver. It has been around for thousands of years in Entis, and is also found in Caelus, in the Caedes Mountains. In Caelus, where the lightning is extremely intense, when it strikes Electrum it forms a molten spear that solidifies and must be dug from the ground. An Electrum fulgurite contains an immense amount of energy that is used to power the Zepps. They are rare and difficult to find, and you will have to work very hard to recover this gazae. Electrum is most prevalent on Mt Crepitus, so you will be heading to the highest elevation of Caelus. Needless to say, the lightning at that altitude is extremely dangerous."

"Caelus, in general, is a cold place, so you will have to focus your Viq to stay warm. You will have to train hard to achieve that. In addition, in the coming weeks I will be teaching you the prohemium for Caelus, which you will use to travel with your Lighthorse."

Eyre rolled her eyes upwards and groaned silently. Well, that counted *her* out then; although Ischyros was being more co-operative recently, he was way too old to go gallivanting around an Alterworld, especially one like *that*. Eyre would have to talk to Whittaker Ray to see what she could do.

For the next hour Kyori presented images of Caelus that showed the terrain, the creatures, and how the Caelites lived. She also showed briefly the island where the Clementis dwelled, the strange beings with super-healing powers. But there were no photos of buildings, or indeed the Clementis themselves, and Kyori explained that this was because they were a very private race of beings who hoped that none of the Lightworkers need ever meet them.

By the time the hour was over, Eyre's head was spinning. They certainly had their work cut out for them. There were hidden dangers everywhere: potholes in the beds of pumice-like stone that a person could step into and then disappear into the atmosphere through the bottom of Caelus; horrible creatures (as usual) like the Zeguardagen, a four-winged dragon-like creature that stalked the skies of Caelus; and the Vampire Vultures she'd encountered at the Unlit arena last year. Not to mention the violent weather changes that could happen at any moment—tornadoes and thunderstorms and acid rain. Add the possibility of Gothak and the Strigis to the mix and it sounded like a real fun time, Eyre thought gloomily.

But she did like Kyori, who was quick, and funny and obviously very smart. Eyre looked at Beatrice, who had been writing furiously during the lecture, already planning for her A++ grade.

"Come on, you must have writer's cramp my friend," she laughed, as they left. "Time to go!"

Eyre walked out with her friends and tried to think how to explain that she was about to go on—what was it—a date? with Jax. After their discussions on how strangely Jax was behaving, it might be a little awkward. She decided just to launch into it.

"So, I'm going for a walk this afternoon," she said.

Abby looked happy. "I need some exercise, I'll come with you!"

"I daresay I could clear my schedule too," Beatrice said grandiosely.

Eyre stopped walking. "Well, actually," she said, "I've already arranged company."

Beatrice's eyebrows shot up her head. "*Who?*"

But Abby, the psychic, knew already. "Jax seemed to be deep in conversation with you this afternoon. *He* wouldn't be your hiking companion, would he?"

Eyre shrugged and nodded and Beatrice squealed. "By the Light, he'll be hauling you off to a Lorian dive somewhere!"

"Possibly not the *best* influence," Abby agreed solemnly.

Eyre laughed. "Well, I'll do some sleuth-work then, and find out once and for all! If I don't come back, you'll find me at the Ponds of Doombee."

She strode away, leaving her friends spluttering behind her.

CHAPTER NINETEEN

EYRE WAITED ON THE moldavite square for Jax. Eventually the bronze doors of Central Admin opened and the athletic form of Jax slipped outside. His black hair shone in the afternoon sun as he strode towards her, his lithe frame moving as easily and as gracefully as a panther. When he neared, he smiled at her, and her breath caught. He was so handsome, with perfect white teeth in a tanned face, and eyes glowing like clear green facets of tourmaline. And she had to admit, part of the spell was the mystery that surrounded him, the element of danger.

"Do you have your hiking boots on?" Jax joked and Eyre laughed feebly. "As long as I don't need my scuba gear. I'm not sure if I can make it the whole way across and back without ending up in that algae soup!"

"Come on, I've done it before," Jax said. "I know the best way. I'll look after you."

They walked along the road that led into campus for about half a kilometre until they reached the interlinked Ponds of Doombee. The ponds were an interconnecting series of smaller ponds attached to a larger one, surrounded by eucalypts and marsh plants and inhabited by a wealth of birds and other fauna. A startled wallaby jumped out of the reeds and bounded away, outraged at the intrusion. The throaty croaks of green tree frogs provided a steady background to the general hum of insects. Every ecosystem was an Alterworld in itself, Eyre thought, as she noticed more and more hidden creatures and plant life around the edge of the ponds.

Jax stepped out over the top of the water. Eyre remembered how adept he had been at the skill two years ago at the TEPs, and his ability now had increased so much that he might have been standing on a sidewalk, so steady were his feet. He held out a hand to her and she stepped up uncertainly, her feet wobbling as her Viq adjusted to the surface of the water. Like a toddler learning to walk she turned with Jax and he pulled her with him out further over the water. Then her mind took over and her Viq control kicked in—her feet were suddenly steadier, no longer trembling with the effort. Jax registered that she had found her feet—literally—and let go of her hand.

"You okay?" he asked. Eyre nodded.

"Well then, follow me," Jax instructed and took off *running*! Eyre was caught unawares and then she laughed. She hurried after him with uneven steps that went up and down, sometimes striking the surface of the water, sometimes half a metre above it. Her technique was more like striding through a boggy, muddy swamp, and she spluttered with laughter as she careered along. Jax was way ahead; he had so much control of his Viq he might as well have been on a running track and Eyre exhaled in exasperation. Surely she could do better than *this?* She stopped, took a deep breath and closed her eyes, using the techniques she had learned in meditation to focus her mind. Then, after a moment she started off again.

This time, her path was steadier; not completely smooth like Jax, but better. She was able to run along the top of the water now and finally she caught up to Jax, who had stopped to wait for her.

"Fun, hey!" he said as she arrived, panting. Eyre nodded as she tried to catch her breath, her eyes bright with laughter.

They stood for a moment in the middle of the pond as the water lapped below them. Eyre looked at Jax. "So, what happened at the Admin building? Who wanted to see you?"

Jax grimaced. "It seems my behaviour on the first day rather incensed Mr Ray. I don't think he's going to forgive me. I was there for more interrogation."

"It doesn't seem like you," Eyre admitted as they walked slowly towards the other side, "it's more the type of thing Ben Perrill would do."

"I know," Jax said, after a moment. "Silly of me, really. I've learned my lesson though." He seemed anxious to change the subject, and Eyre supposed he was embarrassed, as well he should be. Drinking Lorian Juice was something that Exes did in the darkened alleyways of cities, not athletic students from a respected college. But she supposed that she herself had made errors in the past, and Jax was obviously not going to be forthcoming, so she decided to drop it.

Jax held both her hands and spun her around in a circle a few times. "Have you ever been ice-skating?"

Eyre shook her head as she turned dizzily.

"Well, try this then," Jax said, letting go of her. He took off, gliding over the water as if he were indeed ice-skating, with long smooth strides that made him skim quickly into the distance. He turned and slid back to her.

"Come on," he said, "follow me!" And he started off again towards the other side of the pond.

Determined not to lose him, Eyre copied Jax's technique and found it wasn't too hard to do. It also used a lot less energy than running, and was much faster. Within a few moments she had accelerated to quite a speed, and the trees on the side of the pond were whizzing past her in a blur. Up ahead she could see that Jax had reached the other side of the pond and was sitting on the edge on the bank on a bed of fibrous reeds. Eyre was sliding along smoothly now, and she sped in to join him. Suddenly, her foot dipped in a pothole of her own mind's making, she tripped and went cartwheeling through the air. With a great splash she landed in the shallow water's edge and floundered out on her knees with duckweed hanging from her hair.

Jax roared with laughter as Eyre stood up, laughing.

"You're so hilarious, Eyre Lightward," Jax chuckled. "I swear, I've never met anyone like you."

"Probably just as well," Eyre said ruefully as she waded out of the shallows, brushing off the sopping duckweed. With a snap of his fingers, Jax conjured up a towel and passed it to Eyre. She sat down beside him and dried her face and towelled her hair, marvelling.

"How did you do that?" she asked. Jax was obviously way ahead in some of his skills—she hadn't seen anyone manage anything like that before.

"It's a variation of the Summons," Jax said. "The key is identifying the target well enough so your Viq can retrieve it. It's taken me a while. I spent a lot of time receiving all sorts of things I didn't want—animals, rocks, my brother. Once I even summoned up a lawn mower but I have no idea why."

Eyre chuckled and draped the towel around her shoulders, very glad that he'd been able to fetch it for her. She sat beside Jax as the late summer sun cast an orange hue over the ripples on the pond. It was still hot at this time of the year, and she started to dry off as they sat in companionable silence, watching the sun sink lower over the water. The waves lapped against the shore with a rhythmic, peaceful sound and a gentle wind stirred the reeds. Back in the distance where they had started out, they could see the magnificent spires of the Academy, the crystal quartz shards catching the final descent of the sun and turning them into golden spears of light.

"Eyre—" Jax began, speaking at the same time as Eyre said, "I wanted to ask you—"

They laughed awkwardly, and then as the moment drew out, and the breeze drifted across her shoulders, Eyre looked into his eyes and couldn't remember at all what she had wanted to ask. All she could think was, *"Jax."*

Jax reached over slowly, and pulled her towards him, not seeming to care that she was still wet. He brushed her damp hair from her face.

"You are the most beautiful thing I've ever seen," he breathed, and then suddenly his mouth was on hers and he pulled her into a strong embrace, tightly against his chest. Her mouth was on fire, and she was drowning, drowning in that searing kiss as she kissed him back passionately. She knew she had been lost since the first time she had laid eyes on the laconic, smouldering boy two years ago at the TEP trials. With a feeling like she was falling, she gave in to the emotion she felt running wildly within her.

Jax lifted his lips from hers and looked down at her with an unfathomable look in his green eyes. "You are amazing Eyre Lightward," he whispered, running his fingers down the side of her face.

Eyre held him close and closed her eyes. She couldn't believe this was happening to her, and she was seized with a pure joy that was like nothing she had ever experienced before.

She sat silently within his embrace as the sun slowly went down, and by the time the last rays petered out, the frog chorus had started in earnest. Jax pulled her to him for another slow, burning kiss and Eyre wrapped her arms around his neck as she succumbed to a tidal wave of emotions. Jax swooped her up into his arms and gently lay her on the edge of the pond in the rushes and she didn't protest. Her sapphire eyes glowed as she looked up at him and reached out her arms.

Jax pulled off his shirt and the plume agate glinted in the approaching darkness. She almost gasped at his perfectly sculpted body, and a strange energy zinged across her nerve endings. If he didn't hurry up and lie down with her, she thought she would burst into flames!

But then, forcing its way into her consciousness, came a spine-chilling sound that Eyre was all too familiar with, and it snapped her instantly out of her dream-like state.

A low snarl came from the side of the pond and she sat up as Jax turned towards the sound. He jumped up between her and the source of the noise, motioning silently for her to get up.

A hulking form emerged from behind the shadowy shape of a nearby eucalyptus, and Eyre backed away, her hand in Jax's.

"The water," he said softly. "We'll go back the way we came."

They quietly backed towards the water as the Saevus stalked them, its red eyes fixed intently on them and its lips drawn back in a snarl to reveal enormous, lethal teeth. Just as it sprang, they turned and levitated over the water, then started to run over the surface towards the other side. But the explosion of water as the Saevus hit the shallows disrupted the smooth surface, unbalancing Eyre's feet and making her stagger. Jax was slightly ahead and he turned just as she disappeared beneath the waves. She struggled desperately, feeling the water churn as the savage creature plunged towards her. The commotion made it impossible for her to pull herself back up and the Saevus was suddenly upon her, its muscular body slamming into her as its sharp claws slashed. Desperately, she dived down beneath the horrible creature, trying to evade its attack.

But despite its size, the Saevus was *fast* and it whirled around like a shark chasing a seal. Just as it was about to grab her with its sharp talons, there was a blast of Viq from above and the water boiled as a spear of lightning seared into the creature. It screamed and stopped, giving Eyre a moment to launch herself from under it. Filling her mind with Viq, she released it in a blast and exploded out of the water in a fountain of spray.

Eyre stayed beside Jax, hovering three metres in the air, and they both sent bolts of lightning and searing flames at the Saevus, which surged and lunged at them with gnashing teeth. As the burning energy hit its dark hide, deep red tracks were scorched into the creature's skin, and the Saevus shrieked in pain and rage.

But it couldn't reach them, and eventually their attack drove it back onto the edge of the pond. It howled in fury and paced up and down the banks, but finally slunk back into the reeds and foliage beside the pond.

Eyre lowered herself down to conserve her Viq and Jax came down beside her. He embraced her as she shuddered, both from the cold and her fear. It was completely dark now, with only the rising moon shedding a vague light across the water.

"Come on, Eyre, I'll get you home," Jax whispered, and he held her hand all the way back across the water.

CHAPTER TWENTY

EYRE STRUGGLED TO OPEN the dorm room door. She was exhausted, wet and cold, and she smelled like the inside of an aquarium. Beatrice's eyes widened as Eyre walked in and she rushed to shut the door behind her.

"By St Illuminado, Eyre, what happened?" she cried.

"I knew that Jax was bad news," Abby said darkly. She raced over and got Eyre a towel.

"No, no, it wasn't Jax," Eyre said softly. "It was a Saevus. We had to levitate over the ponds and..." And then she lost consciousness.

Eyre opened her eyes slowly and tried to focus. Slowly she realised where she was. She was lying in an Infirmary bed, clean and warm now, and Beatrice and Abby sat anxiously in the corner. Eyre tried to sit up but found she couldn't move at all.

A gentle voice came from over her shoulder. "Don't try to sit up, dear," Madame Overmantle said, "your Viq has been exhausted and it will take a while for it to come back. Let your body rest."

Madame Overmantle was sitting in a chair by the door, knitting a strange-looking, four-legged garment out of what appeared to be cotton wool. As the garment grew longer, it floated up into the air. Madame's sparkling knitting needles clinked and clacked as she churned out the stitches as fast as a knitting machine. The old woman noticed Eyre watching her and explained. "It's a coat for Lenny. Winter is coming and I'm knitting her a warm jacket out of clouds. They are very light and make the best insulation!"

"The Ranger will be happy," Eyre replied in a croaky voice. "Did Jax tell you we saw a Saevus?"

There was a silence as Beatrice and Abby looked at each other, and Madame Overmantle suddenly developed an extreme interest in one of her stitches.

"What?" Eyre said. "Did you talk to him?"

"Ah—Mr Jackson seems to have disappeared," Madame Overmantle finally said, and gave Eyre a kind look over the top of her glasses. "I'm sure there's a perfectly good explanation for it, but he was supposed to be doing detention this afternoon and somehow, he absconded."

Eyre's head swam. So Jax was supposed to *stay* at the Central Admin building that afternoon? And yet, he had sneaked out to be with her? Part of her felt an incredible warmth at that idea, but another part of her was confused. It seemed there were many dimensions to the enigmatic Jax. Why didn't he tell her he had ducked out of detention when she asked? And where had he gone? A burst of irritation surged through her. But then she remembered being with Jax on the edge of the pond and a blush ran up her face. *That* had been nice. More than nice.

"You mean, he went for a stroll with Eyre, got chased by a Saevus, dropped her home and then just disappeared?" Beatrice was incredulous. "What on Entis is he up to?"

"He's a *jerk* and he should be expelled," Abby pronounced decisively. "He's up to no good, that's fairly obvious." No doubt Abby's attitude towards the male of the species was being coloured slightly at the moment by her hurt at Nick's behaviour, but Eyre had to admit that Jax's actions were starting to look a bit suspicious. And how *could* he desert her, after what had happened at the ponds? He hadn't even hung around to see if she was okay. A dark gloom settled over her.

"I think Eyre needs to rest now," Sister Murphy said as she bustled through the door and saw Eyre's pale face. "You too, Madame if you don't mind."

Beatrice and Abby filed out the door, waving at Eyre, and Madame Overmantle packed her knitting away and rose to go. But she hesitated before she left.

"Would you give this to the Ranger for me, dear?" she asked. Somehow, in the last ten minutes she had managed to completely finish the little coat. Eyre took it in her hand. It was light and fluffy, and swirled with a medley of whites and greys.

"Just keep it in this box and it will stay put," Madame added, passing over a little carved wooden box. Eyre smiled. The Ranger was going to love it. But then her smile faded, and she sighed. Madame Overmantle's eyes were understanding.

"When I am feeling confused about life, and people," she said softly to Eyre, "I think with my heart, not my brain. I generally find it is the more accurate of the two organs."

And then, as Sister Murphy started to harrumph, she left, leaving Eyre to stare at the ceiling for a long time.

Eyre was fine the next morning, the combination of her natural tendency to heal quickly and a good night's rest returning her almost back to normal. Except her heart, of course. *That* was going to take a bit more work, despite Madame Overmantle's advice.

She left the Infirmary and headed towards the dormitory, the little wooden box under her arm. Students were scurrying in all directions. The year was picking up momentum quickly, and the pressures of third-year were already in play. Subjects were harder, expectations were higher, and the TACI test at the end of the year was going to be the most difficult so far. They were going to have a lot of pressure this year.

Up in the distance she saw a familiar form bobbing up and down along the pathway, striding forward in crimson tails and striped black and white trousers.

"Ranger!" she cried, running down the track after him.

The Ranger stopped and looked around, then smiled as Eyre caught up with him.

"Hello, my dear," he said. "I heard you had a bit of excitement yesterday."

For a moment Eyre flushed bright red as she misread what he was referring to. The first image that had come to her mind was lying on the bank with Jax. Then she understood.

"Er, oh the Saevus, yes, well we were lucky. Fortunately, we got away."

The Ranger contemplated Eyre with his strange purple eyes. "A Saevus should not be able to get through the double Mantle," he said, referring to the security measure that had been installed after the breach on campus in first-year. "It's a mystery how it got in. Whittaker Ray will be running in circles trying to figure that out."

Eyre could only shrug. He was probably right, but she knew what she'd seen. Then she remembered the box under her arm.

"Oh! I have this for you from Madame Overmantle," she said. "It's for Lenny."

"Really? What is it?" the Ranger asked. Not wanting to spoil the surprise, Eyre said nothing and waited for him to open the box, completely forgetting that the garment would float. So when he slid the lid back, sure enough the fluffy jacket wafted out and started to spiral slowly upwards.

"Oh sorry!" Eyre cried, as both she and the Ranger grabbed for the escaping apparel. It drifted just out of the Ranger's hands, bobbing away every time he made a lunge for it.

"Quite irksome," he said in a mild voice as he wiped his brow. "I may have to summon my carpet!"

"I'll get it, Ranger," Eyre said, and levitated next to the coat, which was heading to the stratosphere in an updraft. She snatched it quickly, before the wave of air from her hands could push the coat away again. Then she lowered herself down beside the Ranger and passed the soft garment to him.

"Well, thank you, Eyre," the Ranger said and held it up. "Madame Overmantle surely is gifted with those needles! Isn't this a lovely thing? Lenny will be very warm this winter." He tucked the coat into the wooden box and slid the lid shut. "I see your Viq has returned."

"I just needed a sleep really, I'm okay," Eyre replied. "But what about you? What are they doing to you? We—we, well, we eavesdropped again on the meeting the other day. I hope you don't mind. It seems grossly unfair!"

The Ranger smiled. "People's motives are often hard to interpret, and often driven by some kind of fear. Fear of losing control, fear of looking silly, fear of things that may never happen. In my case, they are afraid because they see me as different, and they see a threat in that."

Ranger Chrysanthe patted Eyre's shoulder and the bangles on his arms jangled. This made the beetles flying around his head more agitated and the whirring increased and the spinning accelerated. Static from the movement of the whizzing beetles caused his green hair to virtually stand on end.

"Although why," the Ranger said contemplatively, "they see me as different I cannot fathom."

Eyre burst out laughing and the beetles circled around more maniacally. The Ranger chuckled too.

"Thank you for delivering this, Eyre. I'll see you at the Zepp piloting lessons."

And then he disappeared as Eyre's mouth dropped open. *Piloting lessons?*

CHAPTER TWENTY-ONE

EYRE WALKED ALONG TO meet her friends, mulling over what the Ranger had said. She didn't know they were going to learn to fly the Zepps, but blimey, that sounded like *fun!* Especially, she thought with an inward smile, if the Ranger taught them to do it upside down. Then she frowned, remembering how she'd found that out. If the Academy was going to sack the Ranger, they may not be taught to fly, unless it happened in the first half of the year. This was definitely something for discussion with her friends.

She was so deep in thought as she walked along that she didn't notice someone in front of her until it was too late and she ran right into him.

"Oh sorr—" she began and then stopped. Nick gave her a crooked smile, his face pale and strained.

"Hi Eyre," he said. "Are you okay?"

Eyre felt awkward. She didn't really know how to talk to *this* Nick, the one who was suddenly a stranger to them all. "I'm alright, you know, the usual drama swirling around me."

Nick chuckled softly. "Yeah, I know. How's Abby?"

Eyre rolled her eyes. "You know, Nick, you could easily find out if you went and asked her yourself."

Nick shook his head slightly and looked down. "Well, tell her I said hi," he said, and before Eyre could respond, he walked off.

Eyre let out an exasperated huff. These guys were so hard to understand. *What* was going on?

Irritated, she knew she didn't need the next encounter either. Carrison Hamlen was walking towards her, with a mean smirk on his face.

"Ah," he said as he neared. "The girl with the weird Inguz. I'm surprised you're still here, actually."

"Well, I'm surprised you're here at *all*," Eyre retorted. "I thought they were pickier about who they let in to the Academy."

Carrison was a big boy, with solid muscles that would probably put him in the school wrestling team. But he was fast too, and he moved in front of her before she could walk by him.

"*Really?*" Eyre said, furious. "I thought *that* play was reserved for your crony Perrill. Get out of my way!"

"Make me," Carrison said softly, and a rage that Eyre hadn't felt for some time began to boil within her, almost as if her body knew something her mind didn't. It had gone from gleeful supposition about upside-down flying into full attack mode within two minutes. From the soles of her feet to the top of her head, molten energy seared through her body and blasted from her fingertips in crackles of lethal static energy.

"I—am—SICK—of—*mysteries*—and—BULLIES—and—you—can—get—STUFFED!" she screamed, and moved faster than she had in her life. She flicked a corona of energy at Carrison that knocked him flying two metres into the gardens at the side of the path. Her eyes glowed golden as she levitated above him, her hands raised, daring him to move.

He'd obviously lost his breath from the fall, but he stood up quickly, with a violent look on his face. As Eyre watched him, his face seemed to crawl and move, *BTL!*—could she see something sliding under his skin? But the sight only seared her nerve endings more, and it was as if some ancient force within her roused; she knew she was dangerously close to performing Occido for the first time in her life. She lifted her hands higher.

"One move, Carrison," she said softly. "One move..."

A grotesque grin twisted Carrison's face and he stepped towards her.

But then there was a whizz and a thump and Carrison was knocked over again, not by Eyre but by a curved piece of wood that had struck him in the stomach. This time he stayed down, gasping for breath and obviously hurting.

Warrigal appeared from behind Eyre and stepped into the garden to pick up his boomerang.

"So sorry, mate, I was practising and it went a bit off-course," he apologised in a very non-apologetic tone. "Looks like I need a bit more practise. Eyre, I think you and I have Equestrian lessons this afternoon. Do you want to walk with me?"

Carrison's eyes were murderous as he staggered to his feet. "You b—" but he didn't finish, because with a *whump!* Eyre knocked him out cold with a blast of Viq.

Warrigal looked concerned. "Calm down, Eyre, breathe. It's not good for you to stay in that state."

Eyre's eyes lost the golden glow and she lowered to the ground, trembling as if she had a terrible fever. Every muscle in her body ached, and she stumbled as she landed.

"I'm sorry, Warrigal, but he is a total *mongrel*," she said in a voice that quavered. "I don't know why he came to the Academy, but there is something terribly off about that guy."

"No argument here," Warrigal said mildly, and took her arm. Eyre was moving very slowly, but Warrigal helped her back down the track until they reached the door to her dormitory.

"Speak nothing of this," he said softly. "Carrison will be okay and he will not mention it, believe me. But you must be careful. There are dangerous things afoot on campus and you, of all people, must be protected."

Then, tucking his boomerang into his belt, he headed off to the Equestrian Centre. Eyre, who didn't really have riding lessons this afternoon, headed slowly into her room, her head aching terribly. The whole campus seemed woven with strands of energy—dark and light—fighting against each other, and the air seemed filled with an oncoming, inescapable menace.

CHAPTER TWENTY-TWO

EYRE LAY ON HER bed, exhausted. Whatever had happened to her body on the track had left her shaken and so fatigued she could hardly move. She thought back over the encounter with Carrison Hamlen, still shocked at how intimidating he had been, almost as if he had another agenda than just bullying—one that involved actual physical injury to her. Fortunately, Warrigal had come along and defused the situation before one of them was dead on the ground, because Eyre knew, somehow, that would have been the outcome if Warrigal hadn't intervened.

Eyre slept for quite a while and was woken when the door opened and Beatrice and Abby swept in, laughing. Beatrice held a copy of 'The Reflector' in her hand, open to the 'Spotlight' gossip section that Zanda wrote.

"Look at this," Beatrice chortled, turning the paper around to face Eyre. Under his weekly heading of 'Sunbeam of the Week', there was a picture of Carrison lying on his back in the garden, looking like he was sleeping soundly, and the caption read: "New student gives feedback on his opinion of life at the Academy."

Abby broke into peals of laughter. "Zanda wrote in the article that the Academy was gaining a reputation for being a place of 'relaxation' and 'repose' and that some students were taking advantage of the beautiful gardens on campus to commune with nature. How *hilarious!*"

Beatrice handed the newspaper to Eyre. "They're all over campus, everyone's reading it. I wonder what on Entis he was up to!"

Eyre took the newspaper and gave a tired grin. Carrison was going to be *livid.* She wondered how Zanda had managed to get this churned out so quickly. It gave new meaning to the words 'hot off the press'. Done at the speed of light, she supposed. Whatever, she was very glad that Carrison

Hamlen would again be at the receiving end of everyone's mirth. It would do his ego some good to be taken down a peg or two.

But despite her laughter, her mind was troubled about the incident. It seemed that Carrison Hamlen was playing tag team with Ben Perrill now, for the honour of taking Eyre out. Both of them seemed driven by a maniacal energy. And what *was* that thing with Carrison's face. Just thinking about it made her shudder.

She was so tired she just wanted to sleep, but they had solemnly promised each other 'no more secrets' so she rolled onto her side and filled her friends in on what had happened, including the strange movement in Carrison's face.

"His face was probably crawling with fear," Abby chuckled. "Seeing you in death-ray mode would make me shudder too, Eyre. It is not a sight for the faint-hearted!"

Beatrice was deep in thought. "You know, it's time for us to do some sleuth-work," she decided. "We are no further along with figuring out all the mysteries around us. In fact, there seem to be more each day! It's Vela's cave tour tomorrow, and I vote that we start investigating him seriously."

Eyre sat up slowly. The idea made sense, and gave her hope in a weird way. Instead of constantly reacting to whatever situation that was thrown at them, they would be being proactive, seizing the initiative, and taking the fight to the ones who were hiding in the shadows. There was already quite a list.

"Good idea," she said, rubbing her head. "Vela's a start."

"Botolfe!" Beatrice exclaimed darkly and Eyre nodded.

"Then we should do Perrill, and Carrison. We can mask, so they won't know we're there."

Abby's eyes were bright. "Yes! And I will try my psychic trick on them, see if I can read what's going on in those murky minds. I have to stand close to them though, I'm no good at a distance, so we'll have to work that out."

Eyre narrowed her eyes. "And let's do two more: Nick and..." her breath caught... Jax!" Then she collected herself and breathed in deeply. "I, for one, am sick of trying to work out what on Entis they are up to. I am definitely not clever enough!"

Beatrice laughed. "Well, good luck with that. Nick's around, but Jax is in the wind. You'd have to find him first."

But the three of them looked at each other, happy to have a plan. Bae it might be at the moment, but they were taking back the power!

Eyre yawned and swung her feet off the bed. "Well, if I don't get up, I think I'll be here all afternoon. I've got Equestrian. Where are you headed?"

Beatrice had 'Minerals and Crystals 301' and Abby had 'Enhancement of Psychic Techniques' with Madame Overmantle, so they headed out towards the lecture theatres.

Eyre sighed and stretched her weary muscles and started the slow trek over to the Equestrian Centre.

CHAPTER TWENTY-THREE

THE HORSES WERE OUT when she got there and Colton was cantering around the ring already, he and his mount moving as if they were one being. He rode effortlessly and with a natural grace that Eyre envied. As they came towards her, his horse stopped suddenly and took some sideways steps towards her. She thought Colton had done it on purpose, but when Eyre saw his surprised face, she realised that Nox, his black thoroughbred, had made that decision himself. Nox nuzzled Eyre's hand and a warmth grew within her. He obviously remembered her from the riding lessons she'd taken with him last year, when Ischyros was being at his most difficult. The shining black horse blew softly out his nose and she rubbed his velvety muzzle. Colton looked down at Eyre with his ice-blue eyes and smiled.

"He's not supposed to do that," he said. "But I have to confess, I felt like heading over too. How are you going, Eyre?"

Eyre took in his blond hair and his tanned skin and she scratched under Nox's forelock, which she knew he loved. She had a bond with Colton that was inescapable, despite the fact she and Jax were supposedly together. But Colton and Eyre had shared some close moments over the past years—the sadness of his brother's death, and the joy of flying into the clouds for the first time. So she was not immune to this tall, Norse-god of a boy. But then, as always, smouldering green eyes haunted her memory. Jax was an enigma, and possibly working for the other side, but she couldn't let go of him. She felt guilty at her confusion, as she looked up at Colton.

"Yeah, good," she said. "I was glad to join the class last lesson."

"Ischyros didn't do too badly," Colton said kindly. Eyre forced herself not to laugh, for Ischyros's sake, but they both knew Ischyros had not done too well at all. Still, Eyre was not complaining. Just being able to get around the track had been enough for her.

"Well, hopefully we'll improve over the weeks to come," she said. "I'm just happy he's not throwing me into the muck heap!"

Colton laughed and pulled his horse back into the ring. "Well, I know Nox would be ecstatic to have you ride him again. Any time, Eyre."

Eyre walked down to Ischyros's stall, struggling with her emotions. What was wrong with her? How could she be attracted to two guys at once? It seemed to indicate some major flaw within her makeup, a weakness that was not very admirable. She sighed and opened Ischyros's stall.

The old horse looked quite sprightly this morning and he tossed his head.

"Ready for a gallop today?" he said and *pranced* in place. Eyre's mouth hung open. Where had the demonic hell-horse gone?

She brushed him lightly and then swung herself up onto his back and walked out down the alley into the ring, where several other students were warming up. Many of them greeted her, some had quizzical looks and others were just plain amused. But everyone seemed happy for her—they all knew the struggle Eyre had had with the unco-operative animal over the past two years. All except Ben Perrill, of course, who stared at her with a mixture of hatred for her, and derision for her ratty old horse.

The Kikkuli Master entered and asked everyone to warm up by walking around the perimeter. "Your most important task in setting up a good ride is not a physical one, though that may surprise you. No, the most critical thing you must do is to connect mentally with your mount. Feel his or her mood, feel their muscles and how they're moving, sense the vibe from their behaviour. Once you understand how they are on this particular day, at this particular moment, you will understand how best to work with them. And they will respond much better for that understanding. Use your Viq, use your psychic skills if you need to, and connect with their inner well-being."

So Eyre concentrated on trying to 'read' Ischyros as they walked around the ring at an uneven gait. Ischyros, however, was impossible to read. Every movement just communicated his utter disdain for the other horses, really, as he seemed to want to stay as far away from them as possible. Still, he did seem to be trying today, and when Eyre kicked him lightly into a trot, he responded well and they went bouncing around the ring several times.

Ben Perrill's mean eyes watched them closely, and as they jounced by for the third time, he couldn't help himself. "You sure that's not a kangaroo you're riding, Lightward?" Despite themselves, a few people couldn't help chortling, because, with his uneven, bouncing gait, Ischyros did indeed seem to be jumping around the ring, rather than trotting. Eyre gritted her teeth, but she wasn't prepared for Ischyros's reaction.

With a loud snort, he kicked into a canter, and bounded around the ring, careering around other horses and in danger of not only throwing Eyre off (involuntarily this time) but crashing into the walls. A few exclamations rose from some of the riders, and Saskia Anderson's small grey horse got such a fright he ran right out the front gate.

"Woo Hoo!" Ischyros shouted as he cantered around, and then, to Eyre's horror, he started to *gallop!* Eyre hung on desperately. She didn't think he'd meant it when he'd asked her if she was ready for a gallop today. But it seemed as if Ischyros was ready for a real *sprint.*

His hooves thudded in the dust, throwing up a cloud behind him, and he whinnied as he charged at top speed around the perimeter. More riders pulled out of the ring, obviously fearing for their safety as the rollicking animal thundered by. Even the Kikkuli Master lowered his whip, nonplussed by this sudden display of energy.

And then, as Eyre held on desperately, trying to haul Ischyros back, he lifted into the air, a metre off the ground as stumpy wings emerged from his sides. Flapping wildly, he careened around the perimeter, stirring up clouds of dust like mini tornados from the downdraft beneath his wings. Eyre slipped sideways and ended up with one leg on and one off as she desperately held on to Ischyros's mane. Despite themselves, many of the students now were chuckling in strangled voices; she was such a ridiculous sight. And then, Ischyros lost control of his aerial skills and shot off-course into a stack of hay. He bounced backwards, throwing Eyre on her back into the ring, and he himself landed upside down with his feet pedalling in the air.

Covered in dust and hurting, Eyre stood up slowly, gritting her teeth as she heard the smothered chortles from around the ring. She dusted her arms off and headed towards Ischyros, who, after a struggle, had managed to turn himself over. But he was exhausted, and his legs were tucked beneath him, unable to stand up. He was breathing in heaving gasps, his eyes closed.

The Kikkuli Master knelt down by Ischyros as Eyre raced over.

"Are you okay, my old friend?" the Kikkuli Master said gently, stroking Ischyros's side, and then Eyre was horrified to see a tear streak down the dusty horse's face.

She skidded down beside him and threw her hands around his neck.

"Don't cry Ischyros," she whispered, but the scruffy old fellow just wept harder, sobs heaving his sides. The students, ashamed of themselves, stood awkwardly as Eyre managed to help Ischyros stagger to his feet. Then she led him limping down the alley as silence reigned behind her. Even Ben Perrill stayed quiet, which was just as well for him, because one sound from him and Eyre was going to blast him out of her life forever.

CHAPTER TWENTY-FOUR

ISCHYROS STOOD SILENTLY AS Eyre brushed the dirt and muck out of his coat. The curry comb was soon full of dust and twigs, and Eyre kept going until he was completely clean. Then she massaged his legs and polished his hooves until they shone. Finally, she finished by braiding his tatty grey mane into cornrows and brushing the knots out of his forelock. He looked much better by the time she was done, but he still hadn't said a word. His head hung low and his eyes were shut, and it was as if she wasn't even there. Eyre would have given anything to hear a rude comment come from him, but he seemed lost in a trance, unaware of her presence.

Her heart sore, she packed up the grooming equipment and put some liquorice and molasses in his feed bin, which he ignored. She hesitated for a moment, and then left the stall after giving him a last hug.

"I'm glad you're my Lighthorse, Ischyros," she whispered. "Thank you for trying so hard."

Despondently she put the grooming equipment away in the storage locker, her thoughts roiling. Just when she was making some progress with Ischyros, *this* had to happen. Her heart was filled with a blackness towards Ben Perrill that scared her. He was mean and cruel, and his derisive comments had decimated the old horse and left his pride in tatters. Eyre felt tears well up in her eyes as she understood the old horse's shame. And a burning rage towards Ben that she thought could spontaneously ignite the building, she felt so violent. But she took some deep breaths to calm down, and after slipping the latch on the storeroom, she left via the back exit, through the paddocks. The last thing she wanted to do was walk through the practise ring, to pass by everyone with their cantering mounts, circling the ring like professional show horses. Eyre moved quickly across the lush grass; in a minute or two the best of them would be moving out to the paddocks to practise their galloping and flying, and she wanted to be well away from them when they did.

She still had a while before her next lesson, so she headed to her dorm room and retrieved her Antaraks and her Kulbeda. The mood she was in, she decided it was probably a good time to practise her Ferito. No doubt Simmons, the wise student she had met during her time at the TEP trials, would have counselled that meditation might be a better choice right now, but she wanted an outlet for her fury and she needed to expel some of her burning energy.

There was no one in the Shed when she got there, which suited her fine. She really needed to be alone right now. Drawing her Antaraks from her baldrics, she crossed them in front of her and closed her eyes. She slowly moved through all the moves of the Clasis for two-handed fighting. They had not learned the Level 3 moves yet—those would be taught during the course of third-year. But Levels 1 and 2 were very familiar, as she had spent hours practising the different positions with palum over the past two years, and the moves came easily.

She kept her muscles taut and controlled as she forced herself to take it slowly, to familiarise herself with the weight of the blades, and to get used to the distance she needed to keep between the blades to stop them clanking together, and so she didn't injure herself. For the whole hour she went over and over the moves, never increasing her speed and keeping her eyes shut so she could concentrate only on the feel of her body and her weapons. A line had been crossed today, and she knew she was preparing herself for a fight of the ultimate kind.

After an hour it was time for afternoon tea, but Eyre had no desire to go. Instead, she took her Kulbeda and practised throwing, connecting her mind to the trajectory of the golden dagger as it spun through the air towards the target. It was a new technique to her, and often the blade hit flat against the target and fell to the floor, or missed it completely. But occasionally the timing was right, and the whirling blade struck the coloured circles on the board nailed to the wall. When the Kulbeda hit the target correctly, it dug in with a satisfying thud. One day that would be Ben Perrill's head, Eyre promised herself. She felt no guilt at the thought; to her mind Ben was no longer a Lightworker. He was one of the most foul Strigis, and the day would come when she would deal with him accordingly.

She was so deep in concentration that when a voice spoke behind her, she nearly jumped out of her skin. She spun around and had her Antaraks drawn before she registered it was Warrigal, his hands raised in a 'peace' gesture.

"Sorry," he said. "I should have made a bit more noise."

"No, it's okay, I was just deep in thought. What are you doing here?"

"The Ranger has called a special event this afternoon, a hash house harrier run," Warrigal said. "Normal classes have been cancelled."

Eyre lowered her blades. "Hash house?" she mused. "That's like a paper trail chase, right?" By the Light, she thought, the last thing I want.

Warrigal nodded. "I'm to lead the pack, I'm the 'hare', I guess, and the rest of you are the hounds for the chase. It's part of my assessment for my special studies with the Ranger on orienteering."

Eyre studied him for a moment, still irritated by the thought of the whole thing, and then understanding dawned. "Ah," she said slowly, checking around for any unwanted ears. "Obviously people are getting curious about what you're doing?"

Warrigal raised his eyebrows and nodded.

"So this is the cover story." Eyre laughed humourlessly. "BTL. The good guys really have to work hard, don't they? Well, it sounds like fun, my friend, count me in. Make it a good one so they all have to run their merry asses off!"

"We meet in half an hour, at the moldavite square," Warrigal said. "The run is set for this afternoon, before dinner. See you there!"

Eyre nodded and watched him go. Then she raised her Antaraks again. Half an hour. Time to run through the Clasis twice more. She shut her eyes and began.

CHAPTER TWENTY-FIVE

BY THE TIME EYRE arrived at the moldavite square about half the student body had assembled, milling around and talking in low voices. Most of them didn't look keen to be there; a run through the bush was the last thing they wanted to do.

Carrison Hamlen and Ben Perrill were talking to their cronies in loud voices, designed for all to hear. "When we catch the twerp," Ben said nastily, "let's heave him into the Ponds!"

The Curtis twins sniggered like hyenas and Carrison's lip curled. "Off a cliff might be fun too."

Saskia Anderson, who was so stupid she didn't realise they were serious, giggled and cast Carrison a flirtatious look. She clearly thought the new student was cute and she was on the prowl. Iris Goff, who was standing with Saskia, flicked her hair back and smirked at the group, tucking her shirt in tightly. Wyatt Rankins looked like his eyes were about to fall out of his head and Eyre shuddered. The combined IQ of this group would be akin to the first amoeba that crawled out of the primordial swamp. Their shallow self-absorption made her want to be ill and she had to turn away.

As she did so, she saw Vicky Johnson watching her with an amused smile on her face, and Vicky moved through the crowd to join Eyre. The athletic girl and Eyre had first met at the TEPs, when Vicky had done really well at the trials. She'd also excelled at the Academy in the past couple of years, and was undoubtedly going to carry on to take a Graduate year. Vicky ran her hand through her short brown hair and indicated Saskia and the group behind Eyre. "Maybe the Gothak will get 'em in Caelus," she commented. The black cloud lifted slightly from Eyre's shoulders and she laughed out loud. "They will if I can help it!" she promised. Vicky grinned.

"So how was your break? You settling back in okay?" Eyre asked.

"Yeah, I'm glad to be back," Vicky answered. "It's good to be in third-year. Hey, not to brag, but I have a bit of news, and it'll be in 'The Reflector' next week anyway, I guess. I found out today that I've made it into the Lightning Strike. I tried out last week and I made it."

"Wow! Congratulations!" Eyre exclaimed. "That's fantastic!" She patted Vicky enthusiastically on the back and Vicky beamed. The Lightning Strike was the Rugby League team for the college, and there was keen competition for places in the team. The Academy had been strong contenders in the Inter-School League for many years, and the try-outs were fierce to make it on the team. The Lightning Strike was quite a force.

"Who else made it?" Eyre asked.

"Luke Jordan's in, Lindi Jamieson, Carly, and a few Cro-Magnons from the Perrill contingent," Vicky said darkly, looking like she'd swallowed something foul. "Colton, Rigmar and Warrigal made it, and several fourth-year students that I don't know. Pheria's brother Stratt was selected too. He's awesome at passing, really accurate. And one other second-year—Amanda Lorraine, she's incredibly fast."

Eyre raised her eyebrows. It was a mixed team this year. Rugby League at the Academy was played using Viq, so the players were not necessarily huge and muscled. The ones that were selected were chosen for their proficiency in using Viq for the specific skills of the game: passing, running, tackling, building and holding the ruck, and not least of all, strategy under pressure. Historically, the team comprised mostly third-year students or older, because their Viq was usually stronger. But occasionally a younger student made it on the team. One of the best tacklers in the school's history was a very slightly-built girl who started playing in first-year and was named, appropriately enough for her stature, Little: Anya Little. For years the chant from the Academy Lightning Strike supporters had been 'Onya, Anya! Onya, Anya!' Anya had gone on to join the Australian National team when she left the Academy, and had become quite famous.

Eyre thought hard, as the name Amanda Lorraine sounded familiar. Then Eyre realised that she had seen the willowy girl before, at the Academy Fair, fronting Arant, in first-year. It was startling to think that someone of her physique might perform well in that melee. Light energy at work indeed! Well, onya Amanda, too, she thought!

"Well, I'll be there cheering for you, Vicky," Eyre said, impressed. "It sounds like a really good line-up."

Just then there was movement from above and a black and orange carpet swept over them, did a sharp left-hand turn and then spiralled down to land gently on the moldavite square. The Ranger stepped off, his green hair sticking up in all directions and the beetles whirring madly around his head.

"Good afternoon students!" he said cheerfully. "Today we are in for an unusual treat as one of our talented students exhibits his skills in a very difficult area—orienteering!" From the expressions on many of the students' faces, Eyre could see that they didn't actually consider it a treat at all, but the Ranger continued on, unfazed.

"Warrigal Gundungurra has been working very hard over the past year to hone his skills, and today we will be assessing his performance to see if he is eligible to pass Level One of the President's Outdoor Achievement Award. This is a very difficult feat, and one Warrigal has worked hard towards. Please give him a round of applause. Good luck Warrigal, and make them run!"

Warrigal stepped forward, grinning his infectious smile as he stretched his legs.

"The original hash house harriers used a paper trail through the bush," he said. "But I'll be scattering light beams for you to follow that will last one hour. If you don't find them by then, you should head back to campus because the trail will disappear. If you can't see which way to get back, use your Viq to connect with the Academy quartz crystals. It will give you a direct line to campus."

He paused and smiled widely. "However, I encourage you to keep up! I have a surprise at the end for those of you who can track me. Any questions?"

No one replied and Warrigal moved off to the outer edge of the square.

"I will be monitoring progress from above," the Ranger said, settling back on his carpet, which rose straight up into the air. "The first horn is for Warrigal to take off. Five minutes later, the second horn is for the rest of you. Play fair, and have fun!"

Then he disappeared.

A loud klaxon like a circus clown's hooter rent the air, so deafening it hurt Eyre's ears, and Warrigal grinned. Then he took off at amazing speed and was soon lost to sight in the bush. As the minutes ticked by, Eyre walked across the polished green square to join Beatrice and Abby, who had arrived quite late. Abby in particular was looking very unimpressed at the thought of a run through the bush. Her cornflower eyes were mournful and she sighed dolefully. "Torture," she complained woefully as her amethyst and feather earrings swept from side to side. "It's just torture."

The second hooter blasted and everyone walked off in the direction Warrigal had taken, studying the ground for the light beam trail that

Warrigal had left.

"Here!" Zanda called, and everyone crowded round to have a look. The light beams were small circles of pulsating light about the size of a twenty-cent piece. They glowed against the earth, but not too brightly. Eyre supposed that if it was too bright, the trail would be easy to follow. Obviously, they were supposed to work at it.

"Off we go!" Zanda shouted gleefully. He started off in an ungainly run as others quickly overtook him, their eyes on the ground as they followed the gleaming trail.

"I'm taking it easy," grumbled Abby. "I have no desire to kill myself."

Beatrice was always competitive, but it was clear she didn't want to move at Eyre's pace. "Well, I want to get there, but I can't keep up with you, Eyre. You go on ahead, and I'll see you at the end," she said. "Robeson and I will run together."

"Well, you all can tell me all about it—I'll see you back at the room," Abby said, rolling her eyes. "Give it ten minutes and I'll be heading back to those gleaming spires!"

Eyre and Beatrice laughed, and Eyre took off, her eyes following the glowing spheres on the ground. It was easy to find them at first, because everyone had seen the route that Warrigal had initially taken, and they all charged into the forest after him. But after a while, the discs of light became farther apart; the idea was to make it difficult so that the chasers had to deduce where the 'hare' had gone. And sometimes it was just pure luck if someone stumbled over the trail.

After half an hour of steady running, many of the students had dropped off. By the third year, the demands of study and other activities had meant that only the most dedicated had kept their running fitness up. The other students could go for a while, but the run through the bush was difficult and hilly, and it was weeding the unfit students out fairly quickly.

Eyre managed without too much difficulty for that first half hour. There were enough students ahead of her following the trail so she didn't have to search for it. But then, as the numbers began to dwindle, she overtook enough of them that she was at the front of the pack. And then the running was slowing down because the discs were getting harder to find. Luke Jordan was with her as she searched the ground, trying to pick up the light beam trail, which had suddenly disappeared. There were about fifteen students still at the front, and they fanned out to search for the elusive glowing discs.

"Got it!" cried Vicky. "It passes under the tree here. Come on!"

They took off again, down a well-worn track that suggested wildlife used it as a regular route. The glowing discs formed a straight line heading downwards, and Eyre felt her energy return at the respite as they ran down the hill.

At the bottom, however, was a wide, open clearing with jutting rocks around the edges. There was no sign of the trail anywhere, and it was obvious it was going to be difficult to find.

"Okay," Luke said. "Let's spread out and see if we can find it. Everyone take a different direction."

Just then Beatrice, red-faced and gasping, and Robeson staggered out of the bush.

"We'll help," Beatrice gasped, leaning over with her hands on her hips to catch her breath. "My lungs might be destroyed, but there's nothing wrong with my eyes!"

Robeson chuckled in a breathless sort of way, and the two of them walked slowly over to the easterly edge of the clearing. All the other students began to search the perimeter carefully, looking for the glowing lights that would direct their way.

Eyre ducked under the branches of a paperbark tree, causing red spiky blossoms to fall in a shower all over her. She brushed through the cascading blooms as she pushed further into the bush, looking around for signs that someone might have run through the foliage: a broken twig, footprints, trampled undergrowth. Then, up ahead, something shining slightly on the ground caught her eye and she raced to see what it was. Sure enough, it was a light beam! And further on was another one, leading the way through the undergrowth. Eyre was just about to call out to the others when someone grabbed her from behind with a hand over her mouth, and dropped her to the ground. Her heart lurched in fear, and she started to fight back, but a voice whispered to her.

"Stop, stop, it's me, Eyre." The hand left her mouth slowly. "Don't shout out, no one can know I'm here."

Finally recognising the voice, Eyre sat up angrily. Her hair was in disarray, with red blossoms stuck through it, and she was covered in the sandy soil that was characteristic of the area.

"What are you doing Jax?" she snapped, brushing the sand off her clothes. She was about to stand up when Jax put a cautionary hand on her shoulder.

"Don't," he asked. "I can't be seen." From the clearing, the other students could be heard searching through the bushes, dry eucalypt leaves crunching under their feet and comments being yelled out to each other.

There was also the sound of more students running down the track into the clearing, finally managing to catch up with the leaders.

Eyre looked at Jax for a charged moment, a million emotions running through her. Why on Entis should she have faith in this strange and baffling person? What had he done to gain her trust? Nothing, actually; in fact, he had only shown that he was yet again doing something that not one of the Academy staff would approve of. His whole life was completely mystifying and unfathomable.

But then, despite all logical thought, an uncontrollable force took over her and she flung herself into his arms. Part of her was so annoyed with herself that she wanted to zap herself with her own staff. But Jax held her tight, his chin resting on her head. And all sensible thought was no longer of consequence.

"Where have you been?" Eyre cried. "Why did you disappear? Everyone's saying such awful things about you."

Jax kissed the top of her head softly and then turned her to look at him. "I can't say, Eyre," he said reluctantly. "But I wanted to say goodbye before I leave."

"You're leaving *again?*" Eyre said disbelievingly, her heart plunging in despair. "But why? Where are you going?"

Jax studied her with his deep green eyes and a look of pain crossed his face. "I can't tell you," he said after a moment. "But I'm coming back. I'm just not sure when."

He pulled something from his pocket and held it out to her. It was a rough, diamond-shaped rock that flashed with brilliant greens, reds, and blues; an incredible, glowing gemstone containing all the colours of the rainbow. When Eyre didn't take it, Jax gently took her hand and put the fiery stone in her palm, wrapping her fingers around it.

"It's a black opal from Lightning Ridge," he said. "I found it on my travels. It's incredibly rare. Ever since you gave me the Plume Agate, I've researched rocks and gemstones and their meanings. The black opal is for luck, and for bringing Light to the Aura. But opals are also a symbol of faith. Please have faith in me Eyre."

Eyre wiped her eyes and pulled away from him, her blue eyes flashing like the stone she held in her hand, and she shook her head. "No, no, *no!* You tell me what's going on *now*, or we are *over*," she said fiercely. "I am sick of trying to work things out, and for all I know, you could be a Lorian trafficker from Terra! Why can't you tell me? I'm not going to tell anyone. You ask me to have faith, but if you want me to trust you, *you* have to trust me *too!*" She was so agitated that the red blossoms cascaded out of her hair like a floral waterfall, and Jax's eyes followed them with a wry smile. He trailed one finger down her cheek, and then kissed her gently on her mouth. But his eyes were sad, as if he knew what was coming.

"I can't tell you Eyre," he said simply. "I'm sworn to silence."

Eyre looked furious, and then suddenly grief stricken, as a clear certainty came to her. She turned away slowly, as if in great pain. "Then I can't be with you," she said softly. "There's obviously something grossly wrong here, and I can't take any more mysteries. When you come back—if you come back—maybe we can talk again. Good luck with whatever you're doing."

Before Jax could say another word, Eyre waved her arms to the searching students. "Over here! I've found it! The trail is here!"

When she turned back, Jax had disappeared. She looked at the brilliant stone in her hand and shoved it in her pocket, tears running down her face as a terrible pain speared through her heart. She felt like she'd lost something forever.

CHAPTER TWENTY-SIX

WARRIGAL, NO DOUBT BECAUSE of his years spent travelling through his country, left no physical signs at all that he had passed through the bush. So, the students acting as hounds in the hash chase had to rely completely on the light beams he left as a trail. As the time went on, the trail became harder and harder to find, as the distances between the discs of light became greater. After another half hour of running along the uneven tracks, most of the students had been left behind and several had opted to head back to the Academy. Abby had made an extremely half-hearted effort at participating in the race, and as she'd said, headed back after a very short while, almost as soon as the track had started to climb uphill. Beatrice and Robeson were much more determined and had made it to the clearing, but they couldn't keep up with the pace of the faster runners, so by the time they got to where the light trail should be, it had disappeared, and they'd also had to give up the chase. Eyre knew Beatrice was going to be very annoyed about that! But even Eyre, who was now a strong runner and had fairly good stamina, was finding this chase hard.

Right now, the few runners left—only eight of them—were scanning the bush for the light source, as they'd temporarily lost the trail. Eyre was using the pause as a chance to catch her breath. Her lungs were on fire and her legs were trembling—this was quite a run. Not only long, but over some fairly difficult terrain. Vicky was still here, and Luke and Rigmar, surprisingly. Rigmar wasn't the fittest person, but he had somehow managed to keep up with them. And Nick was there, pale and taciturn, keeping to himself. Eyre ignored him. If he wasn't willing to communicate, she couldn't do anything about it. Unfortunately, Carrison Hamlen was with them too. He may be a completely vile person, but he was undeniably a great athlete, and he hardly seemed out of breath as he searched around for the tell-tale discs of light.

Time was ticking on, with still no sign of the elusive light trail. The students became more desperate, searching farther afield and aware that time was running out; shortly the light discs would fade and disappear and the chase would be over. Luke Jordan lifted up a heavy rock, groaning with the weight of it, and flipped it over onto its back. A stream of alpine ants, their nest disturbed, came streaming out over his boots and he flicked his feet to dislodge them. But when a large brown snake came shooting out he wasn't quite so calm, levitating two metres into the air as the creature slithered away beneath him.

"*BTL!*" he swore as he lowered himself back down. "This is turning into a potentially lethal undertaking. There'd better be something worthy at the end of this charade!" Huffing and puffing he returned the rock to the position it had been in, and continued the search into the dense undergrowth.

Eyre stood with her hands on her hips, completely stumped. You'd think there'd be some sign of the trail—surely it couldn't be this hard? After all, the discs did glow—softly perhaps, but definitely visible from a fair way. Where had Warrigal gone?

And then an idea dawned on her, based completely on knowledge that she alone knew about the gifted student. She looked up, searching the tree trunks, up into the overhanging canopy. After she'd studied the third eucalypt, she saw a sign. About two thirds of the way up the mottled trunk a circular light glowed softly. About a metre on from that, another glowed. Eyre laughed to herself. Easy for a possum, or a koala perhaps; not so easy for third-year Lightworking students. She suspected Warrigal was having a great laugh at their expense.

"Here it is folks," Eyre smiled. "Get your Viq ready, we're in for some fun."

The other seven students wandered over, curious, still not able to spot the glowing clues. Eyre just pointed up and Rigmar groaned. "Awesome," he said dismally. "Levitation. Not my strongest skill." Eyre laughed. Rigmar hadn't been great at it during the TEPs and he hadn't improved much over the years. His talent lay more in strategy and defence; he had a sharp mind like his father, for management and tactics, and very keen eyes, so he was brilliant at anything involving hand-eye co-ordination. But levitation had always proven a challenge for him. Still, he was always game.

"Well, I guess that's where we need to go then. Up, up and away!" He closed his eyes and wobbled upwards to the shining disc. "Come on," he called down to the others. "If I can get up here, you can, and this is most definitely the way we need to go!"

They all levitated up to the first disc, and then moved upwards to the second. After a couple more vertically placed discs, the next ones travelled through the foliage on the tree branches, threading their way through the canopy of leaves across the top of the forest. Initially the students were awkward, bobbing up and down, trying to gain a constant level as they searched for the shining lights. But then their minds seemed to lock on to the right height and it got a bit easier. For ten minutes they swung though the tree tops, holding on for stability, and using Light energy to propel themselves across the branches.

With a sudden surprise, Eyre realised that she was having *fun!* It was fantastic flying across the green canopy of the forest, and she felt like a Venator herself as she swooped from branch to branch.

And then the discs lowered again, running down the tree trunks to the ground. Eyre and the rest of the students dropped slowly through the leafy branches and onto the crunching layer of eucalyptus leaves on the ground. Brushing the eucalypt blossoms off her, she looked around. So, where now?

Luke spotted the disc first. It was tucked away under an overhang of sandstone shelves, one single shining circle of light to mark the way.

"Here it is!" he called, and the others crowded over.

"Are we supposed to go through that?" Vicky asked dubiously, looking at a small aperture in the rockface, low to the ground and only half a metre wide. It seemed a very dark space to crawl into.

Eyre kneeled down to look and sure enough, inside the hole another glowing disc shone, casting a dim light that revealed a narrow tunnel.

"Looks like it," she called, her voice echoing in the confined space.

Rigmar grimaced, looking at the size of the hole. "Well, I'll go last," he said. "If I get stuck, no one's going to get through!"

Eyre had only one thought; she didn't want Carrison Hamlen right behind her.

"I'll go first," she said. "I'll clear the spiderwebs out."

"And it's probably a good idea to go by size," Lindi added. "Vicky and I'll follow you, Eyre."

Eyre kneeled down and crawled into the tunnel. It was sandy inside and there were tree roots dropping from the roof, but fortunately no spider webs. Just a dank, dark crawl space. She pushed through on hands and knees and was hugely relieved it didn't take long until she could see an uneven circle of light that announced the end was near. She could also hear the roar of rushing water and as she pushed out the other end of the tunnel she could see why. Balancing on a narrow ledge, she saw that a powerful cascade of water tumbled from the side of the canyon, disappearing into a froth of spray as it dashed against the rocks below. BTL! She thought dismally. We don't have to get down *there*, do we?

By the time the other seven students had emerged from the tunnel, it was fairly cramped on the sandstone ledge and they held on to the rocks at the side for stability. None of them looked particularly happy.

"The Ranger didn't say it was going to be a death-defying experience," Rigmar said gloomily, watching the water smash down below.

"Well, is that even the way we have to go?" Lindi asked. "Where are the light beams?"

"Over there," Nick said, the first time he'd spoken all afternoon. They all looked in the direction he was pointing and saw a trail of light on the other side of the canyon, not heading down to the lethal waterfall, but upwards into the bush.

"Well, at least we don't have to go down *there*," Vicky said, looking down at the churning water, "but how on Entis do we get across?"

Carrison looked unconcerned. "Light-beam tightrope," he said. "It's easy." He flicked his wrist and a bright beam of light shot from the sandstone ledge they stood on, straight across to the other side. Despite herself, Eyre was impressed. How did he do *that*? It would require an awful lot of energy to maintain that force.

Carrison swung himself up and stood at the end of the strip of light. "Bond your Viq to the beam," he said and took a few steps forward until he was standing over the yawning chasm below. Then he tipped sideways, causing Lindi to yelp in shock. But Carrison didn't fall off, he swung completely around the beam a few times and ended up standing on top of it again. He took a bow.

"Easy, see?"

Tec Langford applauded, but the others looked dubious.

"It's a long way down," Rigmar said. But Carrison walked effortlessly across the light to the other side.

"Come on," he called. "It's the only way across."

Tec jumped on first, his desire to impress Carrison overcoming any misgivings he might have had. When he made it safely, Nick followed, and then Lindi and Vicky. Luke helped Rigmar up, as the heavily-built boy found it harder to clamber up on to the light beam, and Rigmar tottered across, sweat dripping from his brow. When he reached the other side, he fell to his knees and kissed the ground.

"You next, Eyre," Luke said as he laughed at Rigmar. "I'll go last."

"Thanks Luke," Eyre said, "but I'd rather let you go before me. I'll keep watching so I can learn the technique to get across." Eyre was already quite confident about the technique, but she wanted to get Luke across safely in case Carrison tried anything. Because although the others might be impressed with Carrison Hamlen's Lightworking skills, all Eyre had noticed was that dead, calculating look in his eyes. Carrison never did anything without a reason.

Once Luke was across, Eyre leapt up lightly on to the light beam. It was warm beneath her feet and slightly elastic, but immediately she felt her Viq bond to the energy of the shining shaft of light. She took a tentative step forward and found it was indeed easy, just like walking along a line drawn on the ground; it was all just a mental challenge. She moved quickly to the middle of the stretching band of light and then looked over at the waiting group of students. But then, as she looked at Carrison, some sixth sense alerted her, and she *knew* he was about to do something bad. She tensed her muscles and leapt as hard as she could towards the edge of the canyon, just as the light beam disappeared from under her. She landed just short of the solid ground and her fingers scrabbled at the rocks on the side of the cliff. For a second she thought she was going to go tumbling down into the violent cascade of water, but Luke and Nick grabbed a hand each and hauled her up over the edge. She sat on the edge shivering; that had been awfully close.

Carrison had a contrite look on his face. "I'm so sorry!" he said. "I just couldn't hold it—*BTL*, Eyre are you okay?"

Vicky and Lindi rushed to reassure him. "It's not your fault," Lindi said. "You did really well to get us all across! You must have incredible Viq to manage that."

Rigmar and Luke slapped Carrison on the back to console him, but Eyre saw the look in his eyes as he turned away from her. He might have everyone else fooled, but she knew that had been deliberate. She knew what he'd done. The only question Eyre had was what *was* Carrison Hamlen?

CHAPTER TWENTY-SEVEN

THE DAY WAS GETTING late now and shadows snaked across the sandy tracks as they followed the sparsely-placed discs. Eyre was pretty much over the chase now; she felt it had gone on a little too long and she wasn't keen on being out here as darkness neared, with the malevolent Carrison as part of the posse.

The track led in a meandering route that in any other circumstances would have been beautiful and serene. The dappled light slipping through the eucalyptus leaves; the flitting birds amongst the blossoms; the fresh air that blew from up the canyon; and the crisp, familiar scent of the Australian bush. It was a place Eyre was normally happy to spend hours just wandering, but today she felt isolated and on edge.

Someone fell in step beside her and Eyre was surprised to see it was Nick. He looked at her with an expression that seemed creased with pain. The scars that covered his body were more obvious than usual and he walked as if every step was hurting. Eyre didn't know what to say.

"Watch out for Carrison," Nick said quietly, although Carrison was striding on ahead, leading the pack and probably couldn't hear them.

"Well, I already am, but thanks," Eyre said after a moment. "What makes you say that?"

An expression of such torture and despair twisted Nick's face that Eyre sucked in a breath. She wanted to wrap her friend in a tight embrace, but the distance that had grown between them made it impossible. She put a hand on his shoulder, but he moved away.

"I get a bad vibe," was all that Nick said. "Keep well away from him." And then he strode off to join Luke at the front of the pack.

Lindi called from up the track. "The discs are fading, guys. Unfortunately, I think we've taken too long, they're going to disappear—we'd better hurry now!"

A mass groan filled the air, but they took off running as the sun lowered in the sky. One benefit of the approaching darkness was that the discs were more visible, and they could see them stretching off down the track and around the corner.

And then, after they rounded the corner, they reached a spot where they couldn't find the discs at all. Despite searching the ground, up trees, under rocks, the light beams had disappeared. Eyre was exhausted from the fast pace they'd set, and she sat down for a second on a smooth-faced rock. Then she nearly leapt in the air as something soft nosed at her arm.

"Argh!" she shouted and turned, half expecting it to be Lenny, after all the times the little Hug had surprised her with a nuzzle. But a soft grey face looked at her, beaming. Eyre did a double take. "Thumper?" she asked hesitantly, and the rabbit jumped in her lap. It was! Thumper was Abby's rabbit from the class they'd taken last year, 'Speaking with Rabbits'.

Eyre grinned as she stroked the soft little creature. Then all of a sudden, a whole pack of rabbits loped into the clearing and surrounded Eyre—a 'fluffle', as a group of rabbits was apparently called. The other students turned and looked, completely confounded as the little creatures swarmed all over Eyre. Carrison Hamlen sneered. "Well, at least dinner's sorted. Rabbit tastes pretty good on a spit."

Eyre looked at him and fire seared from her eyes. "Demons are pretty good roasted too, so I hear," she said softly. A darkness turned Carrison's eyes almost black, but then, aware of the students around him, he laughed lightly and put his hands up in mock fear. "Just kidding, Lightward. Of course I wouldn't mess with you."

But his face showed that he really *would* like to mess with her. The swarming rabbits weaved in and out of Eyre's legs, jumped all over her and nuzzled her face with their soft noses. "Love, love, love," she heard them say, telepathically, and was rather pleased. Last year in Dr Botolfe's class she hadn't been able to hear anything at all, so she must be improving. And then Thumper jumped into her arms and nosed her ear. "Big danger demon here," he said. Eyre hugged him tight, and stroked him. She already knew that, but it was good to have her feelings confirmed. Thumper jumped to the ground and his nose twitched. "Warrigal-one-of-us has left the trail in the path of the sun."

Carrison took a step towards them, and like a school of fish when a shark approaches, the whole group of rabbits swarmed like one surging entity, disappearing in a couple of fleeting seconds. To the other students it had just been a rather cute interaction, but Eyre was left feeling unsettled and anxious. She looked where the sun was setting, and sure enough, the beams headed off in that direction, very difficult to see because of the back-lit orange light from the sunset.

"There they are!" she called, rather unenthusiastically. All the students reacted and raced towards the beams. But Eyre was despondent. The last thing she wanted to do was to start following the trail again. They'd been running almost all afternoon and she was exhausted. But the other students had all set off, so she joined in yet again, and for twenty minutes they ran swiftly up and down the sandy trails, chasing the last rays of light and anxious to finish the race. By now, the hounds were all heartily sick of the 'game'.

"How about we let the hare go, and head back for dinner?" Rigmar grumbled, and got a chorus of rueful agreement. But they knew he wasn't serious and they reluctantly kept going up the path. Despite the fact they were all sick of it now, none of them were going to give up. Eyre sighed. Her muscles were protesting and she really was over it. But then they rounded the corner and were greeted by the most amazing sight.

Tables and chairs completely constructed of light were hovering a metre above the ground, laden with the most delicious food imaginable. Seafood, hot breads, multi-coloured salads and mouth-watering roasts piled on platters. Swirling rainbow-coloured flames rose from five-armed candelabras that sat at intervals on the gleaming tables. Warrigal stood beside the incredible feast and applauded as, heaving with exertion, each student staggered into the clearing.

"Well done my friends!" he congratulated them. "That was a difficult task, and you've done so well. Traditionally the Hash House Harriers finish their chase with a nice cold beer, but I hope you'll find this acceptable!"

Then, with a flash, the Ranger appeared. "I hope you've set me a place," he stated as his bumble bee carpet settled on the ground. "I'll send you home once this delicious repast is finished. Thank you, Warrigal! Let's tuck in!"

So they all sat up on the light chairs and gorged themselves on the most delicious meal imaginable. Eyre decided that it had definitely been worth it after all, as the moon rose and lit their meal with a haunting, golden light, while a deliciously cool breeze swept across their shoulders and the eucalyptus leaves stirred and fluttered around them in a joyous dance of their own. And the harriers talked to each other—sharing dreams and thoughts, bonded by a physically exhausting experience; it seemed the walls were down for a moment, and they could talk to each other, all knowing, poignantly, that it was probably a transient thing. All except Eyre, who was trying to contribute, but mostly kept quiet and watchful, loving the honesty of all her friends, but feeling terribly anxious. She did notice, though, that Nick didn't say a word. Or Carrison Hamlen, who sat silently during the whole meal. It was significant, Eyre thought, as her friends laughed and shared around her while Carrison just sat watching with such a cold gaze amongst the general camaraderie. Who was he? She knew her friends had no idea that they sat amid the most incredible danger.

When they had all eaten as much as they possibly could, the Ranger snapped his fingers and one by one they disappeared.

Eyre landed on her bed in the dormitory, causing Beatrice to drop her chalcanthite crystal and thereby lose the crystallography round.

"Oh well done, Eyre," Abby cried, "I win!" and burst into giggles.

Beatrice scowled and cleared the board and pieces away. "Well, come on then, give us the goss, and don't leave anything out!"

And Eyre didn't leave anything out, except for the part about Jax and the opal he had given her, which she had thrown at the back of her drawer without even looking at it.

CHAPTER TWENTY-EIGHT

BEFORE DAYBREAK THE NEXT morning, Eyre and her friends bustled around the dorm room, throwing things into daypacks and checking the list that Madame Overmantle had given them. The trip to the Jenolan Caves was a one-day event and it was expected that the students organised everything they would need for the journey. Madame had warned them that Professor Vela was not tolerant towards any student who left anything behind—something she really hadn't needed to warn them about. Everyone knew that Professor Vela was not tolerant, period.

Despite the fact it was Vela who was taking the tour, Eyre was looking forward to it, as were Abby and Beatrice. The caves were famous for their ancient beauty and intricate limestone formations, and they had a mystical history with the traditional people of the area that stretched back tens of thousands of years. Eyre had not been before and she was keen to see the unique site that was famous throughout Australia.

The rumble of a Zepp could be heard outside as it pulled up beside the third-year dorms, and Eyre shoved her water bottle into her bag, feeling a sudden exhilaration. Apart from her desire to see the caves, a day off school was worth celebrating in itself!

"Enjoy the day, girls," Madame Overmantle cried as they dashed down the corridor.

Outside, more students waited on the path by the dormitory building as kookaburras filled the air with their pre-dawn cackle. The Zepp was parked nearby, a stout, portly vehicle whose appearance belied its power and versatility. Eyre could see the Ranger sitting in the pilot seat, and she was glad that he was coming along. Despite his wacky, madcap image, there was no one in the entire universe that she had greater faith in.

Professor Vela, sour-faced as usual, stalked up to the waiting students, a clipboard under his arm, a briefcase slung over his shoulder and his blacktopped staff in his right hand. Eyre hadn't seen his staff before, and felt it rather fitting that it was made from polished black ebony, with a sharp-edged obsidian crystal embedded at the top. Black from top to bottom, just like the lecturer's soul, she thought darkly.

Professor Vela whacked his staff on the ground for attention as he looked at the scraggly group who faced him. His tours were never well-attended, despite the allure of the wonderful destination; most students were not keen to go anywhere with the bad-tempered, unpleasant lecturer. So, by third-year, when everyone was required to have participated in the tour, he was left with the most reluctant students, and he knew it. He looked at Eyre in particular with a downturned sneer.

"So kind of you to finally make the tour, Lightward," he said. Eyre, galvanised by her distrust and utter dislike of the lecturer, couldn't help herself.

"Building up Viq, Sir, so I could best enjoy this experience," she replied coolly. Professor Vela looked slightly nonplussed, processing this remark, then frowned in annoyance as the possible meanings for her comment registered. He scowled as he consulted his clipboard to disguise his aggravation.

"So, we have fifteen students here today," he said. "Thank you for joining us. Please acknowledge your name as I read it out."

"Saskia Anderson."

"Here," Saskia said from the back of the group.

"Advika Bhaduri?" Professor Vela intoned, looking around. Advika waved a hand. "Here!"

Professor Vela continued through his list, checking off each name as they responded. "Sophie Brown? Carrison Hamlen? Slade Curtis? Beatrice Edmunsun? Rigmar Essendon? Colton Ford? Pheria Galloway? Todd Lewis? Amanda Lorraine? Phillip Outray? Robeson Paul? Abby Wilson?"

Eyre was just recovering as she remembered that of course, Carrison would be coming—Sergeant Tottingham had mentioned that. But those thoughts were chased away by a bigger shock. Eyre gasped and looked at Beatrice and Abby as Nick appeared, walking down the path to join the group. What was *he* doing here? He'd taken the trip last year, so he didn't need to come.

"I thought he'd do anything to avoid my company," Abby muttered bitterly, and Eyre patted her shoulder awkwardly. It did seem quite weird to see him there.

Professor Vela marked the last name off the checklist and slid the clipboard into his briefcase.

"Nick Richards has agreed to come along and assist with the tour. He is familiar with the caves, so if you have any questions you can ask him also." Eyre felt the colour drain from her face. *Nick was working with Vela?* And since when was he familiar with the caves? She was so shocked she could only just stare at Nick, who was deliberately avoiding looking at them.

Professor Vela hesitated a moment and his disagreeable face looked uncharacteristically uncertain. His discomfort was obvious, and his next words took Eyre completely by surprise.

"I know you're all here because you have to be," the lecturer began after a long moment. "However, I entreat you to soak up this amazing experience. You are privileged to be part of this, and I know it will be an experience you will never forget. Please board the Zepp and we will be underway. We will be travelling to Katoomba, and then continuing on by minibus." Several of the students gasped. This would be great fun in itself—they so seldom travelled by automobile! Professor Vela waited a moment and then continued. "The journey from Katoomba to the Jenolan Caves is 1 hour, 11 minutes, a magic number in the realm of the Lightworkers. That alone should tell you that you are about to encounter something rather special."

Eyre shared a look with Abby and Beatrice. They knew it would be special. But, given what they also knew about Professor Vela, the worry was just how special it might be.

Professor Vela waited by the stairs as the students boarded, then climbed onboard himself. Nick sat beside Phillip and Robeson, and Abby made sure she sat a few seats away around the circle, so that she wouldn't have to sit opposite him. Eyre sighed to herself. She missed Nick, and this estrangement was hard on all of them. And as she contemplated his new association with Professor Vela, she realised he was becoming more and more of an enigma to them. She took her seat beside Abby and Advika as the ramp closed and the Ranger revved the engines. The walls vibrated and after a moment they became transparent. Outside, the darkness was slowly lifting as the sun began to rise, and the shadowy shapes of familiar campus structures came into view. The Zepp roared as the Ranger gunned the engines, and the unlikely vehicle took off towards the clouds.

The Zepp swooped and soared through the atmospheric conditions, which were unsettled this morning due to a cold front coming in from the east, and an upcoming warmer stream from the south. The Ranger held his craft steady, but then broadcast a message to the passengers to make sure their seatbelts were done up tightly.

"It seems we have a windblast approaching," he said. "Probably nothing to be concerned about, but please secure your belts to be sure."

They roared through towering clouds tinged with pink from the sun and were buffeted by crosswinds that blew them up and down, but Eyre was enjoying the ride. Through the transparent walls she could see birds and far-off airplanes and she loved diving into a billowing cloud and shooting out the other side. A windblast wasn't so bad at all, she thought.

And then, like the roar of a primordial beast, something slammed into the side of the Zepp with a wailing howl, and the Zepp suddenly rose twenty metres. A force of equal magnitude came crashing into the other side of the Zepp and sent it into a downward, dizzying spiral as the students shrieked and hollered in fear. Eyre held on tightly to her seatbelt and shut her eyes; the clouds were whizzing past the windows so fast it was making her ill. Then there was a last upsurge of wind that flung the Zepp sideways out of a massive cloud and finally into calm air.

Eyre opened her eyes and saw equally terrified faces staring back at her. Poor old Todd had lost the contents of his stomach, but showing great initiative, had used Professor Vela's briefcase to contain the mess.

"Sorry, Sir," Todd apologised, as he handed the briefcase to Professor Vela, looking like a mouse sitting before a particularly vicious cat. Eyre kept a deadpan look on her face, unable to look at Todd or she knew she would lose it. The sight of Professor Vela was worth every minute of the violent ride. His face like thunder, he zipped up the briefcase, carried it with two fingers and shoved it into a storage cabinet. His expression as he looked around the Zepp dared *one student* to make a comment. Wisely, no one did.

A cheery voice came from the front of the Zepp. "Everyone ok back there?" the Ranger asked. "That was a windblast. Quite fun really, when you get used to them."

Todd didn't look like he agreed with that, but Eyre, Beatrice and Abby finally exchanged a sneaky smirk with one another.

"That's one for Zanda's column!" Beatrice whispered.

"Professor Vela's barf-case," Abby added, and they all spluttered as the Professor whipped his head around.

The rest of the journey to Katoomba was smooth and event-free. It took only another half hour before the Ranger began his descent, going down in a gentle arc to land in a flat clearing in bushland on the outskirts of Katoomba. It was near a road, but traffic was erratic and as the Zepp trundled to a halt, not a person or residence could be seen. A white minivan was parked at the side of the clearing and the students were instructed to get onboard and take a seat.

"We generally find that the minibus attracts a lot less attention than the Zepp," the Ranger said, "or for that matter, teleporting. It's rather hard to arrive in the middle of a tourist mecca in a flash of light." The students laughed as they filed out and the Ranger waved. "Have a great trip, I'll see you back here this afternoon!"

The students climbed aboard the minibus and Professor Vela took the driver's seat, with Nick in the passenger seat at the front. Eyre felt an awful unease as she looked at Nick sitting upright and unmoving beside Professor Vela as the 1 hour and 11 minute trip started. It might be a magic number, but to her, this trip had the troubling vibe of *black* magic.

CHAPTER TWENTY-NINE

THE DRIVE TO THE Jenolan Caves, through the small town of Katoomba and up and down the narrow winding highway, was scenic and enjoyable. Many of the students had not spent much time in a traditional vehicle for years, so it was a great way to start the excursion, and they shared snacks and drinks as the minivan journeyed through the mountain range. Once they'd gone through Katoomba, they joined a line of buses and cars all heading the same way; the Jenolan Caves was a popular destination.

Sure enough, exactly 1 hour and 11 minutes later they drove into the Caves parking lot, where large buses and cars with roof-racks crammed with gear and neat rows of motorbikes jammed into every available space. Queues of people were lined up outside the ticket office, waiting their turn to join one of the guided tours through the many caves.

Nick, without being asked, disappeared towards the management building as Professor Vela fussed around the minivan.

"Take all your belongings," he snapped. "We won't be stopping for lunch, so if you haven't brought anything you'll have to go without. The Academy has a special tour arranged every year, separate from the general visitors. Please be respectful to your guide and don't lag behind. It's very easy to get disorientated and lost in the cave system."

Professor Vela led the line of students up to the entrance to the caves where Nick waited with their tickets. The attendant at the gate signalled them through, causing the long queue of people behind them to look rather disgruntled. But the Professor just ignored the muttered complaints, he considered the crowds to be inconsequential Entis beings of no importance. He waved his ebony staff at the students and entered the caves. "Follow me, don't lag behind!" he ordered.

In they went, struggling to keep up with Professor Vela, who strode ahead like a man—or rather, a Lightworker—on a mission. They left the other groups of tourists behind and, as they moved out of sight down the narrow, dark track, the Professor touched his staff to the wall and a fissure opened, revealing a bright light within.

"In you go, quickly," he said. "Can't let people see us." The students ducked into the cleft in the rock wall and it quickly sealed behind them, just as a tour guide was bringing a group of sandshoe-clad tourists through.

"And here we have—" Eyre heard, just as the wall sealed back up behind them. Somehow, she felt they were in for a much more interesting tour than that group of people.

Professor Vela stamped his staff for attention. "I would like to introduce you to our tour guide, Sergeant Spodumene, who is our expert on the underground labyrinth of the Jenolan Caves. The cave system eventually joins up with the massive tunnels and passages of the Blue Mountains, to the domain of the Mimir and, eventually, the famous Transit cavern. It takes years to learn the layout of these intricate pathways, so keep together. Sergeant Spodumene does not need to go searching for a lost student."

Sergeant Spodumene was a massive Mimir, with broad muscles and a double-forked red beard that he had plaited down to his knees. He had a Crescent Blade tucked into his belt and a lux floated above his head as his craggy, unsmiling face surveyed the students.

"Entis offers us miracles and beauty, and we are to respect the opportunity to travel down these passages. "Be very quiet, just listen, and don't talk or you will miss some of the most divine aspects of this tour. I've had a few chatterboxes over the years who have been zapped back to the minivan to wait out the tour." Eyre felt quite happy to hear that; if she had to endure Saskia Anderson's inane babbling for the whole day she thought she would go insane.

The Sergeant waved up to the towering ceiling, where pure white stalactites hung down in uneven formations. "This is the oldest open cave system in the world," he continued. "Eleven caves, yet again the magic number, with their own rich history, and indeed venerated by the traditional owners. We must respect our journey here and leave no trace behind us. First, we will travel down to the River Cave via our own set of tunnels, to avoid the crowds. The Jenolan River has created this geostructure, and the River Styx pools are where we will culminate our tour. Be prepared for some challenging walking; this is not an easy stroll—it is the most difficult of the cave tours."

Eyre chuckled at the look on Abby's face. After yesterday's hash harrier race Abby was obviously horrified that yet more body-shattering exercise was on the cards, and her face was doleful as they took off, following Sergeant Spodumene at a pace that was just a bit too fast to be comfortable.

Through the dank tunnels they walked, past stunning formations of stalagmites that lined the pathways, created by the steady drip of water from the ceiling above, and reaching up to the stalactites that hung irregularly from the ceiling, creating the impression of a huge jaw of some primordial creature gaping open. As they walked silently through the majestic formations, Eyre understood the need for quiet. The peace and calm that resonated through the almost holy structure was an experience in itself. It was so rare to be surrounded by complete silence. Only the occasional footstep resonated in the fusty, dimly-lit passages as they traversed the magnificent formations.

After an hour of hard climbing, including ascending a steep metal ladder embedded in the rock face, they emerged into a wider clearing that overlooked the River Cave. Below, tour groups were passing over the constructed bridge and pointing and gesticulating at the towering structures around them. Flashes of light punctuated the chamber as people took photographs of the amazing formations.

But Eyre was most entranced by the water that flowed through the caves. Mountain-pure, and crystal-clear, it was lit by ethereal blue light as it passed under the bridge. The gentle sound of water flowing had a music of its own that lulled her into an almost hypnotic trance. She shut her eyes and listened for a moment, and when she opened them again, she caught Sergeant Spodumene studying her with a strange expression on his face, almost as if *he* were looking at a spectacular limestone formation.

It was an awkward moment for both of them, but Eyre just smiled and the Sergeant hurried to lead them on to the next passage. As they travelled through the spectacular caves, they saw the huge stalagmite called the Minaret, the famous Grand Column, and the Queen's Canopy, a spectacular formation of limestone structures. Eyre's legs were aching as they trudged through the passages, but she barely noticed. She was so overwhelmed by the enormity and wonder of this incredible geostructure.

The last stop on their tour was the 'Pool of Reflections', part of the River Styx system and famous for its still, beautiful water that created the most amazing reflections of light.

Sergeant Spodumene talked to them as they stood on the side of the crystal pool by the bridge.

"The next official tour will not be here for an hour," he said. "Our route takes us a shorter way to enable us to get here earlier, although it does make it quite hard work."

Red-faced Abby could only huff in annoyed agreement. But Sergeant Spodumene continued as if he hadn't heard. "Today, we have something special organised for you." As he said this, he looked at Eyre again, and she smiled ruefully. She supposed she should be grateful that the Mimir no longer flung themselves at her feet, but she still felt awkward at being singled out, even in a small way. To alleviate her awkwardness, she looked around at the other students and raised her eyebrows. "That's great, hey!" she said. Professor Vela just looked at her like he'd swallowed a lemon. The Mimir might be keen on her, but he was definitely not a fan.

"Nick," Professor Vela said. "Would you organise the students appropriately please?" Nick jumped to attention, apparently having completely forgotten his previous dislike of the teacher who had set him up for a terrible fight with Ben Perrill at the TEPs two years ago. Eyre felt ill as she watched him direct the students to sit evenly around the edge of the Pool of Reflections; almost an automaton, she thought, and when she caught Professor Vela watching her with narrowed eyes, she lifted her chin and stared back, determined not to flinch.

But then she breathed deeply and turned away from him. She didn't want to waste this magical time in the caves with dark thoughts on her mind. Channelling the instructions from her meditation classes years ago, she let the ambience and the power of the incredible place she was visiting fill her soul with peace and stillness.

And then the most amazing thing happened. From the depths of the cavern, an intensely beautiful and haunting melody began. Its mournful, poignant tones danced through the limestone structures and drifted around the students like a seductive curl of smoke. Eyre opened her eyes and caught her breath at what she saw.

Small phosphorescent creatures fluttered on diaphanous wings amongst the forest of stalactites. They drew their tiny hands down the limestone structures to create each tone that contributed to the music, like a chime struck with a magical mallet. Professor Vela stood and addressed the students and his expression and speech were unusually reverent.

"Erik Satie's Gnossienne No. 1", he said. "The Faerie of the caves have emerged for one performance today, because of recent events, to honour the Lightworkers who have fought so hard for our lives and our world. His voice hitched on the last few words and Eyre was beyond confused. *What?* Who was this strange, strangled man? But then the haunting notes took over her mind and she watched as the beautiful, shining creatures flew up and down the stalactites on their glimmering wings, creating the melancholy music. The blue, reflective pool transmitted the images of the magical creatures high into the air like a hologram as the music drifted through the cavern. It was a gift to the students who sat spellbound, and Eyre knew she would never forget this experience. When the last tones of the beautiful melody faded, she felt an awful sorrow that it had finished. It had touched the very core of her being.

Abby sat immobile with a tear streaking down her face. One of the delicate little beings flew down and fluttered before her. The iridescent colours on her wings caught the blue from the reflective pools and cast a rainbow pattern across Abby's face. "You are Nefelibata," the little one said. "One of the chosen. Satie walked a different path, the dreamer who had no faith in himself. You should believe. Our thanks go with you."

And then the petite being fluttered over to Eyre. As if in a trance, she chanted:

Since the black cloud arose
The dark one dwells amongst you
You, who are blinded by a protective light
A great imposter
Masked as a guardian
Hidden in plain sight

And then it was over. The beautiful, fragile creature disappeared in a flash of rainbow light.

Although it had been such a wonderful experience, Eyre was left with a feeling of deep melancholy that she'd never experienced before. And what was the meaning of the strange message? Yet another entry for the journal back at the Academy. Another enigma to work out. She hoped Beatrice had remembered the words, because she certainly couldn't.

But beyond that, the mournful tones seemed to fill her soul. It was obvious that the other students had felt it too, as a reverent silence lingered in the cave.

Then Carrison said, "That was the most boring music I've ever heard. I can't believe I'm awake."

At his derisive comment, Eyre felt an absolute fury ignite within her, and with one heave of Viq she *blasted* him headfirst into the glorious Pools of Reflection. There was a massive splash in the turquoise water, and rings from the percussion as he plunged deep under the water spread outwards to the edge of the pool. With a desperation and rage not entirely befitting a Lightworker, she wished that he might not resurface. But if he did, she hoped that his dousing in the magical waters might help him understand. The Pool of Reflections—*reflect on that!* she thought furiously.

CHAPTER THIRTY

AS CARRISON STRUGGLED TO the surface the other students grinned, greatly entertained by Eyre's action. The Faerie had long departed, but Carrison's comments after such a beautiful musical gift from the timid creatures had struck a chord with all of them, and they were glad to see him floundering in the water after his offensive words.

Carrison spluttered as he reached the surface of the pure blue water, and several people laughed, but then he suddenly levitated out to land on the edge of the reflective pool. There was a horrific energy emanating from him as he raised his hands. Something dark had ignited within him, and he faced Eyre as if there was no one else in the area.

"You think you're so powerful, you insignificant little girl," he whispered. And then he raised his hands. The calm pools of beautiful blue water suddenly churned in a mad whirlpool, and waves chopped on the surface, leaping up to the stalactites above. As Professor Vela turned in horrified shock, the stalactites broke from the ceiling and speared towards the students on the edge of the pool.

But Eyre, her eyes swirling in a sudden golden madness, stopped the flight of the lethal limestone spikes with one flick of her wrist, and reversed their trajectory, forcing them back up to re-attach to the ceiling with a sear of blinding Viq. All the students stepped back warily as Eyre rose into the air, her fiery hair standing on end as she sent bolt after bolt of lightning slamming into the water around Carrison.

"I know what you are, Carrison," she whispered in a deadly voice, and forced the boy under the water with a smash of Viq, forged from a power she had never experienced before. The ancient forces were rising within her, defending that which she held dear, now way beyond her control and driven by some ancient, protective instinct.

"Stay *down*," she spat at Carrison, her eyes holding strong on the water as the boy struggled beneath the water. But then Professor Vela regathered his wits and sent a blast from his staff that knocked Eyre to the ground. She lay there winded as Carrison resurfaced, spluttering and enraged. Abby raced over to Eyre and stood before her as Carrison leapt up onto the railing of the bridge.

"Leave her alone," Abby said in a voice that was fierce and resolute, and Beatrice stepped up beside her, her hands raised. Then one by one, all the students lined up in front of Eyre, blocking her from the view of the furious boy. He was so incensed that red streaks of electricity appeared to flash up and down his body. Professor Vela finally stepped in, raising his ebony staff, as Sergeant Spodumene raced in with his Crescent Blade drawn.

"Get down, Carrison," Professor Vela said in a voice that suddenly filled the caves, bouncing from the stalactites, echoing darkly around the cavernous space. "You will not win this competition, if that is what it is."

The weight of his words resounded like a whirling wind around the motionless students. Finally, Carrison seized control of himself with a force of will that was almost physical, and after a long, fraught moment, he jumped down from the railing, looking at the stand of students with a nonchalant air as water puddled around him.

"Thanks for the dip, Lightward," he said. "I'll repay the favour someday."

The way he said it left Eyre with no doubt that he'd probably prefer the 'dip' to be in the middle of a boiling volcano, but the situation was suddenly diffused, and with relief everyone gathered together again. The violence that had nearly erupted after the beautiful, peaceful performance of the Faerie had been so sudden it felt like they'd been swept by fire.

Professor Vela, surprisingly, seemed the most affected of all. "I think it might be time to head back," he said tightly. "Sergeant Spodumene, could you lead us out now?"

Sergeant Spodumene did not re-sheath his Crescent Blade as he led them back through the fissure in the wall to the paths that headed away from the Pool of Reflections. But he kept glancing back at Carrison Hamlen, who trailed far behind everyone else, and the Sergeant's gaze was fearsome. Eyre doubted even the arrogant Carrison would dare to defy the ferocious Mimir who was so proud of his domain. That Crescent Blade was more than ready to do what it was designed for.

They had almost reached the end of the tunnels when a strange orange glow emanated from the rock wall beside Professor Vela. As the students halted in surprise, the wall appeared to melt, the rock dripping in rivulets as a horrific shape emerged and lumbered towards them with an unnerving, creaking gait.

"So glad to see you, Professor," the Gothak said, "thanks for the heads-up!" Then, he turned to Sergeant Spodumene, and before the Mimir could react, the tall Gothak blasted him with a burning meteor of atra. Sergeant Spodumene disappeared in a cloud of flaming dust and the students cried out in horror. This Gothak had fine, high-cheeked features and reminded Eyre of someone she had seen before, with his black hair tied back and his ghostly skin. As everyone stood immobilised by shock and fear, the sharp-featured Gothak looked around, as if examining an interesting collection of beetles pinned to a board.

"Pray tell me, which one of these amazing specimens might be... Eyre?" he whispered in a voice that was so dangerous it might have cracked the very path they stood on. Beatrice and Abby moved slightly to stand in front of Eyre as Professor Vela raised his staff. The Gothak looked slightly confused but sent a beam of dark light that held the Professor's staff tight, without even seeming to try.

"I wouldn't, Professor," he said softly. "The consequences are definitely not worth it. No, I am looking for one particular Lightworker, and it has taken me quite a while to track her down. I believe she is here today, and can I say, I appreciate your help," he finished.

"So," he stalked towards Amanda Lorraine. "Are you Eyre? You look like a sprightly sort."

Amanda jutted her jaw and raised a hand. "Yep, that's me. Eyre it is. Come on then, you and me, one on one!" She stepped forward and gave a gleeful grin, no fear, and joyous to take on the horrible creature, despite knowing that she was facing certain death.

"Well, Eyre," the Gothak said, moving towards her, his voice like dripping acid. "My name is Mudamir, and you killed my brother Kaar. *Very* pleased to make your acquaintance."

Advika Bhaduri stepped up. "Thank you, Amanda, but I am actually Eyre," she said, her small frame standing side on to the fearsome Gothak, ready for a fight. "And I'm glad I killed your disgusting brother."

The Gothak's eyes turned black and he took a step towards Advika.

"Advika, come on now, we all know that *I'm* Eyre," Vicky Johnson said, her face clenched, but her eyes showing a black joy—she was more than ready to be Eyre should the moment call for it. She faced the horrible Gothak as if she was prepared to die, and probably, she might. She was more than ready for this fight. Eyre was so taken aback at the sudden turn of events. Her face was pale and she was speechless as she looked at her two best friends, who stood like unmoveable stanchions before her, protecting her from view.

Pheria was next, the most surprising of all, as she flexed her strong, athletic muscles and faced the Gothak fearlessly. "What a loser you are, Muddy Meer," she said. "It will be a great delight to pound you into the mud." And she summoned her staff with an effortless toss of her hand. "Oplo will be very happy to make your acquaintance." She stood ready to battle, and Eyre stood speechless. This girl she had *really* disliked was ready to stand up for her, and was even now facing death for her. Suddenly things were so much more confusing, and yet so much clearer.

And then Rigmar stepped up.

"It's very honourable of you all to take my place," he said as he twirled out in a pirouette from the rear. "But you, Sir Mudamir, should know that it is *I* that is Eyre!" He bowed and held out a hand, as students tittered, and then there was a cacophony as everyone stepped up, each claiming to be Eyre. But Eyre was watching closely, and she saw the rising rage in Mudamir, and she knew that someone was about to be blasted like poor Sergeant Spodumene to make an example of them, so she stepped past Beatrice and Abby, to the front of the crowd.

"Thank you, my friends," she said, eyeing the horrible creature. "But *I* am Eyre," she said. "And I am very glad to have dispatched the foul being who killed my parents. Your ridiculous brother Kaar disappeared in a searing roil of smoke, screeching, I'd like to tell you. It wasn't even that difficult," she added, knowing it would enrage the evil creature all the more. So be it. If she was going to go down, she wanted to make it count.

Mudamir stepped up to her and looked her up and down. "So slight of being, how have you such power? Or perhaps, it is a..." He got no further as Eyre, taking advantage of his sermon, flicked a powerful corona of churning lightning at him. But he deflected it with a snap of his wrist, almost effortlessly, and it bounced harmlessly off the ceilings and around the walls until it disappeared out of sight down the tunnel. A low boom somewhere distant indicated it had finally impacted on something solid.

"You might have to try harder than that," he breathed, his dark eyes flaming as he turned to face her. Eyre was more than ready. She hated the foul beings from the Underworld more than she could say, and recently something had ignited within her that seemed like a flaming blade to fight the horrible creatures. But then, there was movement from the hole in the rock and more Gothak flooded into the passageway, far outnumbering the students who had only two years of Ferito and no weapons to fight with. Carrison Hamlen, unsurprisingly, disappeared briskly back down the dark passage and Eyre wished with a heave of rage that she had held him under the water just that bit longer.

Rigmar stood solidly beside Eyre, and the true nature of who he was, not the clown, not the slacker who did as little as possible to pass his classes, or the unfit, puffing student always last in the race, but the essence of his venerated father suddenly shone through; brave, true to the cause, and totally committed.

"Today we may die," he said softly, "but we die with honour." The students formed a circle, facing outwards, each one of them willing to make the ultimate sacrifice as the hideous Gothak neared, laughing, knowing they were about to decimate the outnumbered students. With a snap of their fingers, the resolute students summoned their staffs, and turned them outwards, towards the ghastly beings.

Eyre knew she was about to die. But then, an uncontrollable, burning fire grew within her that she could not understand, and she felt her eyes flame with a boiling energy. Her brain was consumed by a force she could not control as she lifted from the ground, her hair raised on end and her mind was unthinking as she sent a massive shockwave of Viq towards the masses of Gothak, screaming "RUN!!" to her fellow students. The Gothak were blasted into the walls, and the students raced past them, down the tunnels to the exit, past the pale, evil creatures who lay scattered on the ground. Eyre alone stayed to face them as they picked themselves up off the rock floor.

"I am here," she said in a voice she did not recognise. "And I am beyond you." She pointed her staff and stood with the glowing pink diamond aimed at their hearts. She knew now she could hit whatever she aimed at, and she was ready.

The Gothak stood before her, grinning, and Mudamir held his hand to stop them attacking.

"Mine," he said softly. "This will be a pleasure."

"My pleasure too, you abomination," Eyre spat, ready to fight.

But then, there was a flash of bright, blinding light, and everything disappeared. When Eyre opened her eyes, she was standing, ridiculously, in front of the white minibus with all the other disorientated students. She still held her staff in front of her, and was lucky that it hadn't gone off and blown Advika to smithereens.

"Thought it might be time we tootle-ooed," the Ranger said softly.

Professor Vela, beyond speech, piled in the back with the students. Eyre spent the whole 'magical' one hour and eleven minutes until they reached the Zepp directing most unmagical thoughts towards Carrison Hamlen, who had somehow reappeared and seemed the only one pleased with the events of the afternoon.

CHAPTER THIRTY-ONE

THE NEXT MORNING EVERYONE was very subdued as they ate breakfast in the Refectory. The ones who had been to the caves were reluctant to talk about it, and the ones who had not knew better than to ask. The darkness of the experience was beyond discussion.

Eyre was so distraught that she left breakfast early and ran along the track to the Equestrian centre. She wanted to be alone in the quiet of the arena, and she wanted to see Ischyros. Somehow, the old horse seemed so bonded with her, *finally*, and she felt it might help to go and see him.

But she was devastated when Ischyros turned his back on her, as he had done so often over the past two years.

"What are you doing here?" he said. "Go away."

Eyre had become used to his bad temper, but this morning, when she most needed some connection with her Lighthorse, it wounded her more than she thought possible.

She entered the stall slowly, her heart so sore she felt like weeping. "Ischyros? I thought..."

Ischyros tossed his head and kicked his feet at her, and if she hadn't been so fast she would have been knocked out of the stall.

"Go away," he said. "I do not wish to be part of this, ever again. Get lost, you annoying creature." And then he stuck his head in his feed bin, with his rear end and those gnarled old legs presented towards her. She knew that if she took a step forward, he would be only too happy to launch her over the stall door, and probably over the roof of the Equestrian arena if he could manage it. To be honest, given his obvious rage, she thought she might even land in Sydney Harbour. Her heart suddenly broke, and tears ran down her face.

Eyre left quietly. She shut the door, and it felt final. She had tried for so many years, and it seemed that the old horse was never going to work with her. Part of her knew that their recent experience in the arena had influenced his behaviour, but part of her also knew that she was tired of it all. She was fed up. She'd tried hard enough, and she was done. He was not interested, he was difficult, and he obviously preferred to be alone.

"Bye, Ischyros," she said softly, as she tried not to weep, the pain in her chest making her feel like her heart would break. "Sorry it didn't work out."

And then she left, trudging along the passages of the Equestrian Centre, out of the arena and through the huge bronze doors, feeling like it was the last time she would come here. She didn't even have enough energy to run back to the dormitory, such was the weight on her shoulders.

The next few weeks passed quickly, as the routine of the new year became established. Meditation, Ferito training, third-year core classes and the individual specialist classes the students took for their various Sectors dominated their days, and they all tumbled into bed each night exhausted.

Eyre had not been near the Equestrian Centre since the incident with Ischyros. She felt so conflicted, because she now knew she loved the old creature so dearly, and yet he obviously wanted her nowhere near him. Finally, she had accepted that perhaps she should concede to his wishes. She didn't know what else she could have done to make him like her even a little, and it felt like a huge failure and a deeply personal blow. She must have some fundamental defect that no Lighthorse had chosen her, and that the one she ended up with had definitely not only *not* wanted her, he loathed her!

The only bright point in the term was when Ranger Chrysanthe turned up one morning at the Refectory.

"Next year," he said, "those of you who are staying on will be going to Incendium. You will need to learn to fly the Zepps if that is so, in case anything happens to your pilot. So, I need you to put your name on the list for piloting lessons, which will take place once a week this year and also next year, until you head to the Incendium TACI. Madame Overmantle will tell you that it is very difficult to fly a Zepp, but luckily, she is a very experienced aviator after all these years."

He was poking fun at Madame Overmantle, who was possibly the worst pilot to sit in front of the controls of a Zepp, and she knew it. She stood up at the staff table in mock-offence, raised her eyebrows and scowled.

"I fear that the Ranger is being slightly irreverent. However, I have to agree. I am a perfect example of why you should join the lessons with the Ranger," she said. "If you intend to go to Incendium, you might need skills slightly better than mine! Luckily, you have all survived my piloting because my psychic skills help me to predict those dastardly weather patterns." The students all chuckled; they had all had experience with the commotion that was associated with Madame Overmantle steering a Zepp.

After breakfast, Eyre hurried to put her name on the list, along with many other students who were continuing to their fourth year at the Academy. Piloting lessons were to be conducted after Meditation and Ferito on Fridays and Eyre couldn't wait to get in the driver's seat of one of those fabulous vehicles.

However, her first lesson with the Ranger was less than celebratory. Apart from the fact that there were seven gears and two clutches, along with side wings that caused the vehicle to tilt if you got them unbalanced; the Zepp was also so powerful it could tip over and zoom along on its side or even upside down if you got the balance wrong. Then, there were the Alter-aspects of the Zepp to learn: along the track (the easiest of course— Terra), underwater (mildly difficult –Aqua), in the air (high difficulty and not attempted until later in third-year—that would be Caelus), and then, through volcanic mass (arduous, and definitely a fourth-year skill— Incendium, of course). But Eyre didn't care. She felt the same glee she sensed in Madame Overmantle as she swirled the vehicle up through the sky, splashing underwater and racing along the bumpy roads beside the Ponds of Doombee, crashing and bouncing along as best she could. Whatever she was doing, she loved it. Gears crunching, the engine over-revving as the Ranger's face tried to maintain a positive expression, it didn't matter. Piloting a Zepp was *fun!*

Beatrice and Abby had joined her class—there were several groups, as many students were continuing on to the graduate year. Eyre's friends also loved the feeling of controlling the incredible vehicles, and after a few lessons were starting to get a handle on it. Nick had also joined a class, but unsurprisingly, it wasn't with them. He had retreated from them even further after the experience at the caves, and Eyre, Beatrice and Abby no longer expected him to join them when they got together. Understandably, Abby was hurt the most because of his distance, but Eyre and Beatrice were also confused and perplexed at what had gone wrong in such a short time. However, there was so much that Eyre didn't understand, and this was just one more enigma that she had to hope would work itself out.

She was glad that she was learning to fly the Zepps because she wondered if she might use one to travel through Caelus for the TACI later in the year —obviously Ischyros was out of the question. Even if he decided to co-operate, he couldn't fly that well. So, she put her heart and soul into the piloting and she was picking it up quickly. She volunteered for any short-distance trips required by the staff, and took extra time with any fourth-year student who would sit with her while she practised. Her lack of fear made her progress that much quicker over the weeks, although there was the odd occasion when the Ranger clutched at his chest with his jangling bangles and asked her to remember his heart and his age. "I *would* like to live to teach the next year of students," he would say mildly as Eyre laughed uproariously and did a loop-the-loop.

"Rubbish!" she said. "You *love* it! I heard them at that meeting! When are you going to teach me to fly upside down?"

And so the Ranger did, although warning her that it might speed up his exit from the Academy. Eyre told him, quite seriously, that if he left, she would too. But she kept that part of her training a secret.

The flying lessons used up a lot of her free time, and helped with the terrible pain of losing Ischyros once and for all. She hadn't been to the Equestrian Centre for four weeks now, so she was surprised when a second-year student found her in the Refectory one lunchtime and said the Kikkuli Master was looking for her.

"Is Ischyros alright?" Eyre said, a terrible fear creeping over her.

"As far as I know," the student said. "I'm sure the Master would have told me if it was bad news. He just asked if you could go over there sometime to talk to him."

No doubt it would be about trying to get her to the TACI test, Eyre thought. The first time ever someone wasn't able to fly their horse up in Caelus—what a wonderful thing to be known for.

"Well, thanks," Eyre told the student. "I'll head over after lunch."

So, a short time later, she ran down the track to the Equestrian Centre, through the eucalyptus trees as she had done so many times before. It was a bittersweet feeling, as she loved the run, but knew that she wasn't going to see her grumpy old horse this time. The closer she got to the huge bronze gates, the more of a failure she felt. She didn't really want to face the Kikkuli Master, as she was ashamed at how badly she had done.

The arena was deserted when she entered—even Lisa had finished her chores for the day. The Lighthorses were safely stabled in their stalls, and they were all munching on hay and grain. It would have been a very peaceful scene, except for the ruckus that was emanating from the far end of passageway. Neighing and kicking, stomping, the splintering of wood, as if some ferocious beast was smashing its way through the walls of the barn. Needless to say, Eyre knew the beast was Ischyros, and a tear ran down her face.

"He's been like that since you left four weeks ago," a quiet voice said at her shoulder, and Eyre turned to see the Kikkuli Master regarding her with a sympathetic expression.

"Poor Ischyros," Eyre said, and rubbed her eyes. "I just don't know how to help him. He doesn't like me at all. Maybe someone else should take him as their Lighthorse?"

The Kikkuli Master said nothing, just kept looking at her with his gentle, powerful gaze. And then a flash of self-awareness nearly struck her to the ground, and the anger towards Ischyros melted away. Eyre lowered her head in awful pain as she suddenly realised the true reason for the shame she was feeling, and undoubtedly why the Master had summoned her. It wasn't because she hadn't done well enough with Ischyros; no, the truth was that her shame came from knowing that she should *never* have given up on him. She had left because she was tired, and angry with the old horse for being so difficult for *so* long, and because she thought he would never like her, and she was sick of it. But she should have persisted, and *that* was the reason she had been feeling so bad these past weeks. The wise Kikkuli Master had made her understand this without saying one word.

"I'm sorry," Eyre whispered. "I am not worthy of a Lighthorse if I give up. I will try again, and I will never leave him again."

The Kikkuli Master put his hand on her shoulder lightly. "I know Ischyros has been a trial for you and you've tried very hard over the past years. Ischyros's last master deserted him and he he's never got over it," he said. "I'm glad you came back."

Eyre gave a deep sigh and looked down the passage towards the abysmal noise.

"Wish me luck," she said in a tired voice. "On my headstone I'd like it to say: *She tried her best.*"

The Kikkuli Master chuckled and started to head towards his office at the end of the building. But he hesitated, and turned back to her and said: "No one has ever been worthy of Ischyros, you know." And then he continued on.

For a long moment Eyre felt unable to move, not really understanding the Kikkuli Master's comment. She didn't know why *she* might be worthy— blimey, what an ambiguous statement! Was she so hopeless that she was the only one appropriate to get stuck with the ancient, feeble steed? Or was it just not worth her while at all—that no one was ever going to make any progress?

But then she decided that didn't matter; all she wanted to do was make amends to the poor creature, and she took a reluctant step towards

Ischyros's stall.

As she approached, her main feeling was amazement. How could the old horse muster up so much energy? The damage done to his stall and the stable door was immense—parts of the boards were completely missing and straw had been kicked over the gates out into the main passageway. His feed bucket was dented and twisted in a strange figure-of-eight shape from the powerful hammering of his hooves, and his water bucket was lying way down the alley towards the paddocks. And a cloud of dust whipped around in the air like a tornado had centralised above the stall, about a category F5 by the look of it.

Eyre bit her lip desperately. What should she do?

The only thing she could think of was to start singing, so she softly began the strains to a lullaby she'd been taught in primary school, lifting her pure voice above the rhythmic pounding and crashing. There was a temporary lull in the pandemonium in the stall, and then all hell broke loose! The kicking and thudding at the door increased tenfold as an enraged voice shouted "BE QUIET! BE QUIET! *BE QUIET!*" over and over again, until, with a massive crash, Ischyros broke through the door and out into the passageway. Eyre stood stock-still in terror; Ischyros looked like a demon from hell. His eyes were completely red and terribly inflamed from the onslaught of dust in the air, his mane and forelock were a tangled clump of dust and dirt, his hide, never the best at any time, was ragged and covered in grime, and his old legs were injured and bleeding from the attacks he had made against the hard wood of the stables.

Ischyros looked like he was going to charge her and run her down, but Eyre's fear dropped away at the sight of the wounded old horse. She dropped to her knees and sobbed.

"I'm so sorry, Ischyros, I'm SO sorry!" Her heart felt like it was going to break, and she had never felt so awful about herself in her life. If he did trample her into the ground, she felt that she only deserved it.

The enraged horse thundered up to her and skidded to a halt in front of her. Then he raised himself onto his hind legs and Eyre covered her head, knowing he was about to crush her into the ground. But his forelegs landed harmlessly either side of her as she quivered beneath him, and Ischyros heaved great lungfuls of air.

"I HATE YOU!" he screamed, tossing his ragged head up and down wildly, the whites of his eyes, now blood-red, rolling back in his head.

Eyre put out one hand and slowly stood up, ignoring the likelihood of Ischyros running right over her or killing her with one swing of his huge head.

"I know," she said softly. "And I deserve it. I left you when I should have stayed, more than any other time. I'm so ashamed of myself. Can you forgive me?"

Ischyros was so out of control that his whole body was trembling, but he stood still as Eyre approached. She cried as she looked at his bleeding feet and legs, and then she suddenly hugged him around his disgusting, dirty neck, even if it meant the old horse killed her for it.

"Give me another chance," she whispered. "You are my Lighthorse and I will *never* leave you again!" She was distraught with horror that he had been like this for weeks, and she had never once come to check on him. Her own pathetic frustration had caused this, and the shame that engulfed her made her feel like she was on fire.

To her huge surprise, Ischyros let her stay that way, and slowly the trembling in his old frame eased. Eyre let go of his neck and hung her head.

"Let me take care of you, Ischyros. Let's start again." She took a few steps towards the stall.

After a very long moment the old horse finally limped behind her, and she walked back into the chaos of the stall. It was like a bulldozer had driven through the structure: dirt everywhere, holes in the wood, no feed or water bucket brackets left. Just one huge barren, filthy space.

Eyre looked around and then back at Ischyros, who returned her gaze unapologetically.

"It's all your fault," Ischyros said in a cantankerous tone, and Eyre huffed in surprise, then chuckled, then laughed until tears ran down her face. He was back! Her horrible, difficult, awful old Lighthorse.

"It sure is," she agreed. "So I'm going to sort it out."

CHAPTER THIRTY-TWO

EYRE WAS EXTREMELY BUSY for the next two months, rectifying the problem that she had created—for that was the way she looked at it. Ischyros's words had been true. First of all, she raked the churned-up ground in the stall until the furrows and trenches in the earth were smooth again, then she lay fresh, clean straw all around . It took days for her to nail all the boards back in place, and to find new ones to replace the ones that were missing. The walls and the gate were severely damaged and it was very hard work, and frustrating as she tried to figure out how to make it all sit straight again, especially the hinges, but she insisted on doing it herself. Weeks passed as she sorted it out. It was a lesson to her on the pain that one's actions could cause another—horse or not, and she wanted to make amends.

But by far the hardest, and most painful, task was cleaning up the poor old horse himself. It was hard to know where to start, but she first of all bathed his sore, wounded legs with medicinal wash, and the Kikkuli Master gave her special healing herbs to guard against infection, which she mixed with his feed. She trimmed his hooves, and polished and oiled them, and she washed him carefully with a warm soapy bath, loosening the grime that tangled his mane and hide. Then she brushed the knots out, along with the excess hair from his hide, and soon he started to shine again.

After several days of care, Ischyros finally began to look better, and his eyes, to her relief, were clear once more. Eyre was exhausted; she had fitted all this extra work around classes, piloting lessons and training, and she fell gratefully into bed each night, only to get up and do it all again the next day. But it was therapeutic for her, and necessary; each day she visited the Equestrian Centre she told Ischyros how glad she was that he was her horse, and she repeated it every time, despite his rudeness, or what he said back to her. And she knew it was true. She *did* love the old creature, no matter what he did or said. And from now on, that was all that was important. She didn't care if he couldn't fly, or run fast, or do the things the other Lighthorses did. Ischyros was the one she wanted, and she knew that he was finally coming to believe that.

Eyre had returned from another session at the Centre, and had just finished showering when Abby came rushing in. Eyre was brushing her hair, and the door opened with such force that she reacted instantly, raising her hairbrush like a weapon. Ridiculous, she realised, inwardly rolling her eyes; what was she going to do—brush someone to death? Even Beatrice had taken defensive action at the ruckus, but, showing much more sense than Eyre, had summoned her redwood staff, and she strode to stand beside Eyre who stood with her upraised, threatening hairbrush.

Completely embarrassed, but laughing very hard at herself, Eyre took one look at Abby and chortled. "Need a new do, my friend?"

And then Beatrice pointed her staff at the pink-tipped girl and threatened: "I am about to blast the rose highlights out of your hair. How do you answer?"

Eyre tossed the brush on the bed laughing, but then she suddenly realised something was actually amiss. "What's going on?" she asked, her face concerned.

Beatrice lowered her staff and walked over to her friend.

Abby's face crumpled as she saw their caring faces. She was completely beside herself as she collapsed into Beatrice's arms, crying, "Nick's gone. He's disappeared!"

Eyre shook her head, confused. "What? What do you mean? He's become Vela's best friend lately, By the Light—sure, that would mean he's *definitely* disappeared!" She tried to laugh, but found it impossible—they were all horrified by the events at the Jenolan Caves and its implications, and it wasn't actually funny at all.

She breathed in deeply, worried. "But what do you mean? Has he wandered off, or do you mean he's been zapped into the ether? He's been a mystery lately, I know—but what? What are you talking about?" And then her own pain overtook her. "How could Nick just disappear anyway?" she said painfully. "He's one of *us!*"

Beatrice was patting Abby's back, horrified by the wrenching sobs that wracked her small frame.

"He's gone," Abby wailed. "He walked out of the dorm and hasn't been seen since yesterday."

"We'll find him," Beatrice said fiercely, with a resolve that sounded like the clang of the Mimir's bronze doors shutting against the Strigis. "By the

Light, we've waited far too long to figure out what's going on with him. We should have persevered despite him not wanting to speak to us."

Eyre could only agree. As usual, Beatrice had nailed it. Why had they waited all this time to work out what Nick's problem was? Maybe out of respect for his personal space, but really... this was something else. As Eyre regarded the useless hairbrush lying on her bed, she had an overwhelming feeling of guilt that she was just like that stupid hairbrush. Useful to a point, but dumb. Why hadn't she gone and talked to Nick about what was going on? Eyre knew that if the situation was reversed, Nick would never have waited so long to sort it out.

Abby obviously felt the same way. "I was so worried he didn't like me anymore," she sobbed, "so I didn't ask him what was going on. How selfish! And now he's gone. I went to his dormitory this morning to finally have it out with him, and *no one* knows where he is. Ben Perrill said he saw him heading out towards the Ponds yesterday afternoon, but Ben is such a liar, I mean, who knows?

"Master Swiss-Bel—that's Nick's dorm supervisor," Abby's voice hiccupped with tears, "I didn't even know his name until yesterday. Says it all, really, doesn't it? How could I not know that?" Her mouth turned down and her face was agonised.

"Well, he doesn't know where Nick is either, and he's meeting with staff this morning about it. Poor Nick. I knew something was wrong—why didn't I talk to him?"

Beatrice could only hold her close, and Eyre patted her shoulder ineffectually as the dark guilt assuaged her. She knew Beatrice felt it too, and their eyes met above Abby's shoulder. This needed to be dealt with, now.

When the sobs finally subsided, Eyre turned Abby's blotchy, tear-streaked face towards her.

"Abby," she said softly. "You, of all of us, have the skills to find Nick."

Abby blew her nose and stared at Eyre, her stunning blue eyes still wet with tears. "What do you mean?" she said. "I'm useless at everything, pretty much. Unless you want me to play the theremin."

Beatrice and Eyre chortled. "We want him to come back, not go further away," Beatrice quipped. But she understood what Eyre meant.

"Come on, Abby, you're the psychic!" Beatrice said. "And apparently, like the Faerie said, a Nefelibata!"

At this, both Eyre and Abby looked confused and Eyre raised a questioning eyebrow.

"It means cloud-walker," Beatrice confessed, shrugging. "I looked it up the night we got back, when I wrote what they'd said in our book." She looked over to the wall, where the journal lay hidden. "A cloud-walker is one who lives in their dreams, who thinks laterally and moves on another plane from others. Tyros Sector are the astral travellers, and you have some of that skill too, your psychic skills are the best in the year, everyone knows that. *You* can find out where Nick is, just go up there, wherever it is, and search for him!"

Abby rubbed her eyes. "I don't really know how to do it," she said. "I can't control what I do, it just comes to me sometimes. I've never tried to search for anything specific before."

Eyre snorted. "Well, now is the time to try, my friend," she said.

There was a sudden knock at the door and they all jumped.

Eyre opened the door, and saw, incongruously, Madame Overmantle standing there, holding something spherical in her hands, and beaming like a friendly neighbour delivering a casserole. She smiled at them as she entered and sat on one of the desk chairs.

"You'll need this, my dear," she said to Abby, and held up a large globe that radiated with the spectacular aquamarine of an inner ice cave. Pale and magical, a hue that was unlike anything they had ever seen. Eyre gasped, because she recognised it from her joust with Aowx, the fearsome dragon, last year.

Madame Overmantle handed the glowing ball to Abby, who looked completely confused as the heavy sphere settled in her lap. "The beryl orbuculum. Use it well." And then she turned to Beatrice and nodded at the wall, "You must protect it in the same place as the journal," she said. "It is the only secure place. The orbuculum stays with you now." All the girls' mouths were hanging open as Madame Overmantle stood up to leave. For a start, to be given this glorious object, but also—how did she know about the journal? And the wall? Eyre shook her head. No wonder Madame Overmantle was revered for her psychic skills.

Abby held the crystal ball desperately. "Can't you just tell us where Nick is?" she pleaded, lifting it up to the old woman in a great panic.

The ancient seer turned to Abby, her face unreadable. "There are some things that even my eyes can't see," she said. "The ancient beryl has revealed to me that only yours should now gaze into its secrets. The Nefelibata." And then, so quietly that Eyre wasn't even sure she heard it, the old woman added, "my eyes have certainly not proven worthy of late."

As Eyre stood in shock, the greatest seer the Overworld had known turned to her and put a soft hand on her shoulder.

"Your times of trials are just beginning," she said to Eyre. "Be strong."

And then she left, leaving the three friends staring at each other in complete bewilderment.

"Did you hear what she said about her eyes?" Eyre stuttered. The others looked blank. "She said she couldn't see things properly, that's why she's given you the orbuculum, Abby."

Abby shook her head. "How can I see something she can't? That's ridiculous!"

Beatrice was more focused on another statement Madame Overmantle had made. "What about the 'times of trials'? What does that mean?"

"I thought my times of trials began about three years ago," Eyre said in a resigned voice, unable really to think of anything else to say. But her comment held sadness, and fear. "So, what are we in for *now* then?"

Abby echoed her plaintive thoughts as she looked at the priceless object in her lap. "And the only thing I can think of to do with *this* is roll it down a bowling alley and hope I hit a few pins!" She looked desperate, unsure what to do with the magnificent orb.

They gathered around the shining spherical globe, the very palest of green-blue in colour, studying it in awe. Eyre really hadn't had much chance to look at it the previous year, as she'd been charging through piles of golden treasures, trying to outwit a cunning dragon intent on eating her. When she'd eventually won the orb, Whittaker Ray had whisked it away for safekeeping, and it had obviously ended up with Madame Overmantle. Undoubtedly a wise choice, given the old woman's world-renowned skill in the psychic and scrying realms. But why would she give such a rare and beautiful object to them? If she couldn't use it, surely none of them could?

The orb seemed to have a life of its own, almost seeming to float as the light within it curled and swayed, and strange shapes formed and disappeared at intervals. All three of them had had some introductory lessons to scrying, or fortune-telling with a crystal ball, but none of them had made great progress with it, not even Abby, the most psychic of them all.

Beatrice grimaced, confused. "Well, all I can say is that Madame Overmantle must know what she's doing. She thinks you can do it, Abby, so you'd better try."

"Do you want us to leave?" Eyre asked, wondering if it might help Abby to concentrate. But Abby shook her head and sighed. "I'm sure it won't make any difference whether you're here or not," she said, clearly not expecting much success.

Still, she put the spectacular object reverentially on her desk and drew her hands over it for a moment. "It's so exquisite," she breathed. Then she sat down before it and put her hands flat on the desk on each side.

"Come on," she whispered. "Speak to me." The clouds in the pale blue ball seemed to jump and sway as she spoke, and as she focused deeply into the interior of the crystal, they began to move faster. Shapes and forms swirled around, and Abby seemed lost to the world as she concentrated on the mystical silhouettes that formed within the sphere.

Eyre tried *so* hard, but she couldn't see anything in the cloudy outlines, although they did look spectacular floating within the crystal. Beatrice was also staring intently, but Eyre could tell she was equally mystified. It all made as much sense as trying to read hieroglyphics in clouds on a windy day.

But finally, Abby looked up at them, her eyes glowing with an unnatural fire.

"I saw!" she said, her voice wondering and awestruck. "I know where he is!"

"You did?" Beatrice was initially disbelieving, then totally amazed, and finally ecstatic. "Well, where is he?"

"He's at the cabins," Abby said. "Alone, and he's in pain."

They looked at each other for a moment, all of them dismayed.

"It's not so surprising that he's at the cabins, I guess," Eyre said. "But why is he in pain? Our poor friend. *BTL!* We need to go and help him!"

Beatrice and Abby just nodded; no words could articulate what they were all feeling.

Abby carried the beryl orbuculum reverentially, and Beatrice controlled the lights in the wall so that it turned purple, and the etching the Ranger had designed appeared. Abby quickly pushed the orbuculum through the indistinct Inguz on one of the rags in the image, anxious to safeguard the precious sphere. They were all awed that such an ancient, powerful object was now under their protection. Before Beatrice changed the colour back, she reached in and grabbed the journal.

"*This* is coming with us," she said grimly. "It's time to start solving some mysteries!"

CHAPTER THIRTY-THREE

THEY STRODE RATHER DRAMATICALLY out of their room, Beatrice with the journal clutched in her hand as they stalked down the passageway of the third-year dorm. Each of them summoned their staffs in a flash of brilliant light, and they stomped along, their objective clear to them. Down the hall they went with great purpose, looking as if they should be accompanied by a burst of dramatic music. Off to Highlight! Mission in mind, going to save Nick! But their steps began to falter as reality dawned on each of them. Slowing down with every step, they cast awkward glances at each other, and gradually they lowered their staffs.

Eyre tried to look nonchalant. "Hey, yep, we'll go sort out Nick!"

Beatrice was fierce. "Indeed! Maybe we should have talked to him, but well, of course he should have talked to us too!" But her steps were slackening.

Abby said nothing, despite the fact she was the most worried about Nick. But she'd already realised the obvious. She looked at her friends and laughed, despite herself.

How were they going to *get* to Highlight? Teleporting was a fourth-year subject, and only able to be mastered if you were especially talented. So by the time they got to the dorm door they had considered their predicament, and all of them were looking a little disconcerted. Eyre started snickering and opened the door for her friends.

"Onwards!" she announced, and then let Abby through. "My lady—I am hoping you have your chariot waiting!" Eyre said with a bow and a flourish. Beatrice then strode through the door with a dramatic twirl of her staff, and she pirouetted and grinned back at her friends.

They ended up sitting outside the dorm door as it slammed shut behind them, laughing so hard that they collapsed in a heap on the ground beside the building.

"Ooonnnnwarrds…" Beatrice hiccupped.

"To war, and valour—" Eyre declared, her fist clenched at the sky.

"To save the Overworld!" Abby added, and they all laughed uncontrollably, thinking how far from that goal they really were. They had great intentions, but they now knew… they were well and truly stuck! Their staffs lay on the ground, crossed over each other like pick-up sticks, and probably just as useful. They hooted in self-deprecating glee as they leaned on each other, helpless with laughter; the mission aborted before it could even begin!

But then, suddenly, unexpectedly, they were saved. As they chortled and wiped hysterical tears from their eyes, a black and yellow-striped carpet twirled down in a wild circle from above and a manic, green-haired angel grinned at them, seated on the battered old rug as if he were the pilot of Airforce One.

"Do you ladies need a ride?" he asked, as he settled the worn-out old carpet on the ground beside them.

Abby regarded him with serious eyes. "Only if you do it like last time," she said.

And as they roared with laughter, the carpet took to the wind with them all aboard.

⨯⨯

The Ranger obviously had a sense of humour, because rather than delivering them in a gentlemanly way to the door of their cabins, he did a sequence of loop-the-loops, upside-down flying and a wild series of spiralling movements that eventually landed them beside the Mantle Basin at Highlight with their heads spinning.

The girls looked at the Ranger dizzily, but he was completely unapologetic.

"My payback for the Zepp lessons, Eyre," was all he said as he flew off into the distance, the wonderful, undulating carpet looking like a striped stingray as it soared into the clouds.

But Abby, who was looking definitely unwell, shook her head at Eyre.

"You have such an entourage of people who are out to get you," she said in an annoyed tone. "Can you please tell them I'm not your friend?"

Eyre, who had loved every minute of the uproarious ride, exploded with laughter.

"Yes indeed," she said. "I know it's dangerous being my friend!"

But their faces turned sombre as they looked at Nick's cabin. There was no sign that anyone was there; the windows were shut and the curtains drawn. And leaves and dust lined the veranda: he'd obviously made no attempt to tidy up since he'd returned. There was a dark, foreboding air about the whole campsite, as if something malevolent was sitting and watching.

Eyre shivered. "I'm not liking this much," she said.

Abby and Beatrice nodded. "Something's not right, hey," Abby said, not needing any of her psychic skills to pick up on that today.

Beatrice had put in an aquamarine nose stud today, for courage and protection she'd told her friends, as she'd deliberated over her jewellery box this morning. Obviously taking that to heart, she raised her redwood staff and lifted her head. "Onwards!" she said. "To solve the mystery!"

They walked up the stairs of Nick's cabin and Eyre rapped on the door. For a moment there was no sound, and then heavy footsteps slowly moved to the door. When Nick opened the door they all gasped; he was almost unrecognisable. His eyes were bloodshot, he had a ratty stubble over his chin from not shaving, and there were deep circles under his eyes. His skin was pallid and unhealthy-looking, and he was so thin that Eyre thought he couldn't have been eating for days. He leaned against the doorjamb, so weak he couldn't stand properly.

"What do you want?" he said, looking like he just wanted them to leave.

Abby had a hand to her mouth, she was so shocked. And Beatrice just had her mouth hanging open in surprise; she was uncharacteristically speechless. So Eyre, who also couldn't think of anything better to say, chuckled painfully, filling the resounding silence. "Just in the area, thought we'd drop in."

"Well, go away," Nick said, his expression tortured, and slammed the door in their faces.

Eyre looked at her equally gobsmacked friends and said, "I think Ischyros has been giving him lessons on etiquette."

Beatrice puffed air out her mouth in disbelief, for once at a loss. "So now what?"

Abby had a tear running down her face, not just because of Nick's behaviour, Eyre knew, but because he had looked so sick. There was definitely something wrong.

Abby rubbed her head wearily. "Jengles," she said. "We've got to go and talk to him."

Beatrice raised the journal in her hand. "What about this?" she said. "We can't walk around with it. Perhaps we should go and put it in your basement, Eyre."

Eyre nodded. Beatrice was right. The information in the book was far too valuable to carry around.

They turned to go down the stairs and jumped in fright, because a very angry, red-haired curmudgeon stood at the bottom, hands on hips.

"*What* are you all doing here?" Jengles bellowed. "You're supposed to be at school!"

Unexpectedly, Beatrice grinned at Eyre. She was delighted that they were *all* in trouble this time!

They walked slowly down the steps, feeling like they were about to be put on detention.

"We're here to get Nick," Abby said. Unexpectedly, her words diffused Jengles' anger immediately as his brows turned downwards in confusion.

"Nick?" he said. "Nick's not here! I sensed activity here the moment you all arrived. But I had nothing before that."

"Yes he is, Jengles," Eyre said, pointing at the door of Nick's cabin. "We just spoke to him."

Jengles was so nonplussed that Eyre was confused. Beatrice filled the gap for her. "Jengles *always* knows when someone is here. He monitors the energy, and the Mantle keeps it protected. It actually *is* weird if he didn't know Nick was here."

Obviously needing to check for himself, Jengles strode up the stairs and knocked on the door. There was no movement at all this time from within the cabin. Eyre ran up and tried to peek between the gap of the curtains.

"Nick!" she yelled. "Come out!"

When Nick didn't appear, Jengles crossly turned the handle on the door and stomped inside. And then a few seconds later in a huge blast of energy, he was blown back outside, landing in the dirt on his back. If it wasn't so frightening, Eyre would have laughed. Jengles was completely flabbergasted. Slowly he stood up, dusting himself off as Nick appeared at the door, holding on to the sides as if trying to keep himself from flying out at them.

"Keep away from me!" he cried desperately. "*I* am the imposter, the dark one dwelling amongst you! I can't control it any longer—" and then his voice changed and a demonic tone burst forth. "Enter at your peril," it hissed. As if he were struggling with something massive, Nick used every fibre of his being and slammed the door again. The sound of the lock turning within echoed into the silence.

"I was right," Jengles said slowly. "*That* was not Nick. Nick is not here, really. Although, I should still have known that something was amiss. But what was he talking about... 'the imposter'?"

Beatrice raced over to him and flapped the pages of the journal open to the last entry.

"Here," she said. "The Faerie at the Jenolan Caves gave Eyre a prophecy, and Nick was there. He says it's *him* they were talking about."

Abby looked dismal. "He might be right," she said, casting a look at the barricaded door of Nick's cabin.

They crowded around the book to read the words the Faerie had spoken, although not Beatrice, who had memorised the prophesy already. She spoke it out loud slowly, trying to work out the words of warning.

"Since the black cloud arose
The dark one dwells amongst you
You, who are blinded by a protective light
A great imposter
Masked as a guardian
Hidden in plain sight"

"What is the black cloud?" Eyre asked, stuck on the first line, let alone the rest of it.

"It means the Gothak," Beatrice said as she thought through it, suddenly understanding the nuance of the words. "The dark occurrences that have happened over the past couple of years. Ever since that terrible scene on the basketball courts at the Sunshine Coast, the Gothak have been more fierce, more active, and their horrendous deeds could indeed be described as a black cloud that has arisen!"

"So Nick thinks he's the dark one," Abby said. "And he definitely doesn't look normal. *Could* he be an imposter?"

"But he's not really masked as a 'guardian'," Beatrice said, mulling the riddle over. "And he's not hidden in plain sight."

"Well, he *is* hiding, if he's something else, not Nick," Eyre said, still shuddering as she remembered how Nick's voice had sounded just before he slammed the door. But it had seemed like he was battling something within him, *not* 'masked' as a guardian at all, and it seemed that he'd actually been trying to protect them somehow. And in that sense, a most courageous guardian.

"Blinded by a protective light," Abby said in frustration. "*BTL!* Why do they speak in such riddles? Couldn't they just say it so we could understand?"

Finally, Jengles spoke. "That's because they did not wish for certain ears to hear their warning, and to understand it."

They'd certainly done that well, Eyre thought wearily. *No one* could understand that cryptic message, so it was extremely safe. And no doubt the ears they were hiding the information from were Mandig Vela's, who always seemed to be somewhere nearby when anything concerning the Gothak occurred. Dismally, she thought it would be more likely that *he* would decipher the message than they would.

Jengles frowned and looked with a concerned face towards Nick's cabin. "Nick is Tyros, is he not?"

Abby nodded, but it was obvious she was not certain why he was asking. Jengles studied the words again, frowning in concentration. Then his eyes widened in sudden understanding, his face was horrified and he shook his head incredulously. "Yes," he said softly. "Hidden in plain sight indeed. This does explain a few things that have troubled me very much recently. We must act fast."

He snapped the book shut and handed it back to Beatrice. "You are a wise girl to contain all this valuable information in a source of reference. Guard it well. It has proven a great aid today." Beatrice looked like she might faint from surprise at the first words of praise she had heard from the General's lips in seventeen years!

Jengles strode away from Nick's cabin, not towards it as the girls had expected. Following along, trying to keep up, they were amazed when he stopped beside the Mantle Basin and looked at it with something like grief.

"*This* is the imposter," he said, and he could hardly bear to look at it.

Eyre studied the metal dish, with its silvery matrix of glowing branches that stretched high into the air, sending out the brilliant light that protected the whole campsite. She couldn't see anything wrong with it, and it had certainly kept the Strigis out for the years that she'd been there. How could it be an imposter?

And then to the surprise of all the girls, Jengles clapped his hands together with one loud whack, and the light of the matrix snapped out! It was the first time since the Zyx had attacked two years ago that the shining beacon had been extinguished, and they all stood frozen in shock. Jengles took his Crescent Blade and with a few sharp chops, decimated the tower of branches and they scattered to the ground around the Mantle Basin.

Jengles knelt before it, as if he was about to treat a wounded animal. His face was creased with dismay as he emptied the ashes from the bottom of the dish and studied it carefully, wiping his fingers down the inner sides of the bowl. After many minutes he shook his head and turned the dish over. Then he let out an exclamation of rage as he saw a large irregular blotch between the legs of the curved metal container.

"*DIMMOG!*" he exploded, and used his Crescent Blade to scrape off some of the dark purple, mould-like substance. He looked at it carefully with one focused eye, then smelt it and then wiped it off into the dirt. He shook his head again in rage as he regarded the confused girls.

"This foul *atrocity*," he spat, "is Violite, which comes from the veins of the magma in the Underworld. It is an extremely toxic compound that will eventually poison everyone who comes in contact with it. But it specifically affects the nervous system, and the mind in particular. So those of the Tyros Sector have always fallen victim to the fumes before others, because of the hypersensitivity of their brain, and their association with the ethereal, the Astral world. Violite causes strange utterances first, before the onset of irrational behaviour, then psychotic rages, and finally death, always. It's a mineral, but it grows in a fungus-like manner over time. Most importantly, it needs to be seeded by someone." He was so incensed, he could hardly speak. "*Someone* has brought this killer into our midst."

Beatrice was listening hard, and then her eyes teared up as she turned to Abby. "Your dad," she whispered, putting her hand on Abby's shoulder. "He was Tyros."

Jengles nodded and clenched his fists. "I never could believe that George would have betrayed us, he was such a good man, Abby. But the size of this abomination"—he clanked his sword against the pulsating purple mass —"suggests it's been here a year or more. Violite will drive men mad, even strong ones like your father, dear girl. No one has ever withstood the power of the Violite. It turns Lightworkers into the darkest of forces!"

Abby had slid into a heap beside the upturned Mantle Basin, sobbing with pain and a kind of horrible relief. Beatrice and Eyre could only kneel beside her and hold her as she wept in uncontrollable grief. Her father had not been able to avoid what he did; it was not his decision. It was the result of someone planting the virulent, disgusting seeds from the veins of the tainted Gothak Underworld into their camp. How long had Mr Wilson battled in pain and confusion before he finally succumbed? Abby could not speak as they sat with her while she exhausted the storm of her emotion.

"Hidden in plain sight," Eyre stated, her voice tight with rage. "So, who hid it? *That*, my friends, is something we are going to find out."

Finally, Abby was able to speak. "But how are we going to help Nick?" she said, rubbing her eyes and trying to blow her nose at the same time.

"Nick needs to go to the Buyabarra for an extended time," Jengles said. "He's resisted the negative forces for longer than anyone I've ever encountered. I've never heard of someone with such mental strength. Such a small boy, which seems so unlikely when the Gothak are involved. But he is the epitome, the essence of a Lightworker!"

Eyre felt sure that the trials Nick had described from his younger life had contributed to his mental strength; the things he'd endured at his father's hand had shaped the unbending survivor's toughness within him. But apparently even he could not withstand this toxin forever.

Jengles blew loudly through a cone-shaped object from his belt, and a haunting sound resonated through the air. Lids flipped open in the ground immediately and red-haired Mimir jumped out and raced over to Jengles, lining up in a perfect row with their Crescent Blades drawn. Not sure why they were needed, but instantly ready for war.

Jengles turned to the girls. "You all need to get away from here as we thoroughly cleanse the area; it's still toxic and we will need crystals and fire, and the scent of burning herbs to fully purify it again. Nick is very sick, but it is a sign of quite an incredible strength that he has fought so hard. He should make it, but it is going to take time. He is indeed a true warrior, to have protected you all under these circumstances. Any more time and he would undoubtedly have been unable to do anything but become a pawn of the Gothak."

"*We* will take him to the Buyabarra," Eyre said, with no room for argument. "We are not going back to school. The fight has escalated, and this is our first step of resistance. They *cannot* win. They *will* not!"

"I'm not leaving Nick," Abby said with an unmoveable determination.

Beatrice and Abby turned fierce faces towards Eyre and she realised that they were *with* her, bonded forever in a fight against the unknown forces that were trying to bring them all down.

Jengles scowled murderously as he regarded his precious, beloved Mantle Basin. He looked over at the ranks of the silent, mighty Mimir.

"The force is unleashed," he said softly. "And they are not going to like it."

CHAPTER THIRTY-FOUR

EYRE LOOKED WARILY AT Nick's blockaded door. "Okay, we've got to hurry. But how do we get him out of there?"

"How about you go in in first," Beatrice suggested to Abby. "He actually likes you!"

Eyre laughed, despite herself. She thought that the present version of Nick probably didn't like anyone at all, not even Abby!

Abby shrugged, her face lined with worry. "I'll give it a go, of course," she said as she moved towards the steps. But Jengles put up a hand.

"No, lassie," he said gently. "It will require many of us to move that mali. It has already become a great force."

At the memory of the powerful Jengles being blown backwards out of the cabin, Abby stepped back.

"Poor Nick," she breathed. "What a terrible time he's had."

"A Crasher, and a Restrainor!" Jengles snapped at the first two Mimir in the line, who disappeared quickly. In a few moments they were back, carrying a huge log like a battering ram, and a shining, golden coil that resembled a lariat. The girls stood anxiously as Jengles motioned the first column of Mimir up the steps to the door. The soldiers pounded the door open with the Crasher and then ten troops flooded through the doorway, the Restrainor coiled over the shoulder of the final soldier.

Once they were all inside there was a terrible screaming and such a colossal commotion that it sounded like the gates of hell had been opened. Then followed the agonising sound of splintering and smashing wood, ominous crashes and the thud of falling objects. Two soldiers flew out the door and landed in the dust, grimacing as they staggered to their feet and brushed themselves off.

"*Dimmog!*" one of them exclaimed in a wondering voice. "That be one formidable demon!"

Then they both rushed back up the stairs and charged inside again. An eerie, high-pitched wail pierced the air and all the windows in the cabin splintered outwards in a glittering shower. Eyre held her hand to her mouth in horror. What was going on in there?

Finally, the ten massive Mimir came out the door, with Nick trussed up in the Restrainor. He was struggling and cursing, using words that Eyre didn't understand, and he was completely unrecognisable now. The final vestiges of his sanity had disappeared; he was something else entirely now, cursing in a deep, unnatural voice, with flaming sparks flying from his skin.

"To the Buyabarra!" Jengles shouted. "And quickly! The rest of you, get this festering thing to the Cleansing Fire." He pointed at the upturned dish, and five Mimir leapt to attention, picking it up with difficulty and marching towards the sandstone cliffs in the distance.

"We're going too," Beatrice said grimly. And then she added softly, "Let's hope it works. It doesn't always, but By the Light, we've got to save Nick."

Eyre looked at Beatrice and Abby. "Give me the journal, Bea," she said. "I'll put it in the basement, and then catch up with you."

She grabbed the book and left at a run, charged in the door of her cabin and hurtled through the ward and down the steps. She quickly put the journal in the oak chest, then raced back out of the basement. It didn't take long to catch up with the group as they struggled up the track with their screeching captive.

The three girls hurried along behind the Mimir as they strode along the sandy tracks leading to the billabong. The sound of Nick's voice set Eyre's hair on end, but despite her terrible fear for him, she also had a great sense relief. Because now Nick's reticence, his solitude and his strange behaviour all made sense. He had been infected with a terrible virus, and it was only his unusual fortitude that had kept him from doing the terrible deeds the mali had wanted him to. And to have an explanation for George Wilson's behaviour helped too, in a profound way. She had really liked Mr Wilson, and trusted him, and she was glad there was a reason for what he had done. And she knew it was going to help heal Abby's wounded heart to know that it wasn't her father's fault. The Faerie of the caves had helped them to solve the awful mystery.

The journey to the billabong normally took an hour and a half at a leisurely pace. The Mimir were fast, strong walkers, but with their ferociously squirming bundle it was hard work and it took them all of two hours to get there. The girls were sweating as they struggled up the rocky paths that led to the cliff overlooking the billabong.

"It never gets any easier," Beatrice grumbled, wiping her brow.

"At least it's not summer," Eyre said, grateful that the blasting heat hadn't accompanied them this time.

Abby said nothing for a while, just focusing on the Mimir as they laboured with their monstrous bundle up the rocks. As they neared the summit, she said in a quivering voice, "what are they going to do?"

The answer was quickly delivered, because as soon as they got close enough to the edge, the Mimir *hurled* Nick over without a second's hesitation. Off he went, soaring into the air, howling like a demented beast.

"Noooo..." Abby cried, racing up to the edge, with Eyre and Beatrice following close behind, their eyes wide. As the impassive Mimir stood silently in straight rows, the three girls skidded to a halt and peered fearfully over the cliff.

Eyre's jaw dropped. The trussed, violently-struggling bundle was suspended in mid-air by rays of rainbow-coloured light that emanated from the quartz cliffs surrounding the billabong. The rays converged where the cursing, foul-mouthed creature thrashed and writhed, and they held him tightly. For a while he seemed to be quietening down, and Abby cast a hopeful look at Eyre and Beatrice. But then with a gut-wrenching, frightful scream, Nick—or whatever he was now—blasted the rainbow beams that held him, and he plunged deep into the waters of Buyabarra Billabong. The dark water closed over him and there was no sign of where he was, other than wavelets that lapped against the flat sandstone rocks edging the water.

Abby howled in grief, and Eyre, her heart plummeting to her stomach in horror, reacted instantly, without even thinking. She sprang off the edge, and dived in a graceful arc from the towering cliffs. Then she plunged straight down and into the fathomless waters, following the path of the screeching demon.

As she hit the warm water and speared downwards she began circular breathing, the technique she'd learnt for Aqua last year. It came to her naturally, and to her relief she realised she could breathe underwater, and she swam down desperately, trying to follow the small bubbles that indicated where the struggling form had gone. The billabong was deep, and dark, and it was cold at the bottom, and Eyre had to focus to keep herself from panicking and kicking wildly back to the surface.

Where was he? It was so gloomy and murky down there, not at all like Aqua, where even in the deep water, it was a beautiful turquoise colour, and as clear as glass. Here the water was clouded by water plants, dark green filaments that stretched up from the bottom of the pool. Over thousands of years, sediment from the rocks, microscopic creatures and surrounding foliage had floated in the still water until it all eventually sunk down, piling up in the prehistoric sludge at the bottom of the billabong. The deepest layer of mud was unlikely to move at all unless a rare rain event stirred it up. And little light filtered in through the canopy of eucalyptus trees bordering the pool, so it was almost impossible to see anything in the water. Eyre was swimming blindly, with a horrible feeling that something foul was about to grab her from below.

Finally, she spotted the slight glint of the Restrainor, way below, coiled around the dim form that still struggled as it rested on the on the bed of the billabong. Swirls of muck and leaves rose in a murky veil as he fought against the golden lariat, making it even more difficult to see in the billowing brown clouds. Frantically Eyre swam down, the muddied water curling around her in eddies as she finally reached Nick. Mad panic was crowding her head; What to do? *What to do?*

And then, an overwhelming calm came from within her, a force she could neither understand nor deny. With a primal awareness that was beyond her reasoning, she swam down and embraced him, sitting on the bottom as he fought and railed and tried to bite her. A strength far beyond anything she had ever experienced rose from within her; unbidden, pure, powerful. It was as if a light had been ignited within her and the waters around her glowed golden as her Viq expanded. Eyre wasn't thinking at all—her body just knew what to do as she held the demon tight with an unassailable force, keeping it from exploding out of the Restrainor.

And then, after many minutes, Nick fell still within her arms. The Restrainor uncoiled and, like a golden snake, it headed for the surface. Eyre pulled Nick after it, kicking hard as they rose from the murky depths. She propelled them upwards, hurtling through the inky waters until they finally broke the surface, Eyre holding Nick in her arms as she struggled towards the edge. Beatrice and Abby were treading water beside the sandstone rocks; they'd obviously been searching in the billabong without luck. And the Mimir had scrambled down the sides of the cliffs and were standing on the rocks, desperately throwing weighted ropes into the dark water.

"Help me!" she shouted. "*Quickly!*"

The Mimir raced over and picked up the unconscious boy from Eyre's arms. Then they hurried up the sides of the sandstone cliffs, racing back towards Highlight.

Eyre and her friends hauled themselves out of the water, all three of them exhausted after the terror of almost losing Nick. Eyre bent over, breathing deeply after the enormous amount of energy she'd expended. Finally, she managed to stand up, and she turned to her friends.

Before she could say anything, Abby seized her in a wild embrace.

"*Thank you!*" she sobbed. "You've saved him!"

Beatrice's eyes were round as she regarded Eyre. "Astounding. You are indeed a mystery, my friend. Come here, I'll help you back." She put her arm around Eyre, who was sagging in exhaustion.

And they slowly headed up the sandy cliffs, following the Mimir.

CHAPTER THIRTY-FIVE

JENGLES WAS STANDING OUTSIDE the cabins with the upturned Mantle Basin when they returned. It had obviously been brought back from the sandstone cliffs, and was now being given another treatment. Jengles was blazing it with a rainbow fire emanating from what looked like a redwood branch, and he seemed to be doing it with ferocious satisfaction. He looked up as the troops arrived with the comatose Nick, with Beatrice and Abby following behind and helping Eyre into the campsite.

"Why're you back already?" he barked, his red eyebrows turning down ferociously. "He needs another week!"

The first Lieutenant stepped forward and saluted, holding up the Restrainor. "Was not necessary, General. The demon was driven out."

Jengles put the Firebranch down and stood up, looking confused as the Lieutenant passed him the Restrainor. He looked at it. "How can that be?"

"The demon escaped the Buyabarra Healative," the Lieutenant continued his report. "And the young'un saved him." His face grew a little confused, but then he covered it up. "She brought him up from the water."

Beatrice and Abby had helped Eyre to sit on a log around what used to be the edge of the Mantle Basin. Eyre was so bone-weary she thought she might fall on her face in the dirt asleep. But she looked up as Jengles walked over to her, still carrying the golden Restrainor. He lifted it up.

"This has the power of the Aura within it," he said softly. "To drive out the Dark Forces. What happened down there?"

Eyre was so tired she could hardly move. But then she lifted her sapphire eyes and looked at him with a gaze that was so intense Jengles took a step back.

"*I* drove it out!" she whispered fiercely. And then collapsed.

The next few days were quiet and sombre. Eyre had woken after a twelve-hour sleep to discover that Nick was still unconscious and Jengles was still blasting the firepit with his Firebranch. The Mantle was still down, so hundreds of Mimir ringed the campsite, scanning the air and the surrounding bush for signs of danger as the damage the Violite had caused was dealt with.

When Eyre came out to watch Jengles with his Firebranch, she felt very sorry for the ancient Mimir. He looked tired and shamed and ferocious, all at the same time. She knew he blamed himself for this infraction, and she understood it. She'd had years of feeling guilty for everything that had gone wrong in her life, so she walked up to the old General and touched his shoulder.

"Can I have a go?" Eyre said.

Jengles turned ferocious brown eyes at her and after a moment, passed her the Firebranch. "As long as we keep burning, it doesn't matter who does it," he said darkly.

Eyre took the beautifully-grained red branch from him. It was two-metres long and an irregular shape. A crackling charge of light surrounded the entire branch and intense rainbow flames pulsed continuously from the end. The Firebranch was so powerful that it was difficult to control without using her entire strength. Struggling to hold it, she aimed the scorching flames towards the metal dish and the fire seared at the outline of an irregular purple mass that could still be seen on the base of the revered object.

"The Firebranch is different from a staff?" she asked, as Jengles stared at the dish.

"A Firebranch is a sacred object infused by the Aura, as is the Restrainor, and the Crasher," he eventually said. "Imbued with special power to fight the Dark Forces. Your staff might be able to blast the Violite, but it would take a lot longer. As it is, we still have a few more days ahead of us to cleanse the dish."

Jengles' eyes scanned the lowering light and shook his head. "I just hope we get the Mantle up again before they realise."

Eyre hesitated for a moment and then looked sideways at Jengles as she held the flames on the dish. "No one could have prevented this, Jengles," she said softly, and the fierce General's face worked for a moment.

"Someone should have," he said shortly, "and that someone is me. This be my responsibility. And now I have to fix it."

Eyre said nothing more. She knew how he felt. Sometimes there was nothing that anyone could say that would help,

Then Jengles looked at the troops on the edges of the clearing. "Can you hold that for a while?"

"Yes sir!" Eyre said crisply, and was glad to see a slight smile creep up Jengles' face. He was taking this hard, and she was happy she could help to lighten his mood; she knew what guilt was all about.

After half an hour of violently pointing the Firebranch at the dish, Eyre began to feel despondent as the purple outline appeared exactly the same as when she'd started. Her arms were aching from the force of the fire-stream, and it made her realise how potent this awful stuff was.

Beatrice and Abby were watching Nick in his cabin, waiting for him to show some sign he might wake up, so there was no one to relieve her as Jengles marched up and down the ranks of Mimir, organising them in defensive positions should the Gothak appear.

"Sick of it yet?" a deep voice boomed in Eyre's head.

"Eh??" she said in confusion, looking around, and the Firebranch moved as she did, blasting a flaming hole into the side of the Perrill's cabin.

"*Good!*" she thought defensively.

"You could sort this so much quicker," the deep voice said, and Eyre knew it was familiar, but couldn't place it.

Suddenly an image of a musical staff flashed into her mind, but what she heard was the melody in her head of four notes.

"*BTL!*" she thought, as she tried to hold the branch steady. "What is *this*, now?"

In a rush she realised where she knew the voice from. In her TEP exam, more than two years ago, she had met the ancient tree who had later given her one of its rainbow-coloured limbs to make her staff. With a flash of understanding, she knew now that the voice and the image of the musical staff she was seeing in her mind was the Rainbow Eucalyptus communicating with her. But what was he saying? She tried to keep the Firebranch trained on the dish as she thought hard. What was that melody?

Finally, she got it. She realised that the notes she was hearing were F, A, D and E. *Fade!* They'd been trying to fade the Violite for days—what was the Rainbow Eucalyptus trying to tell her?

"I was about to leave you to it, if you hadn't worked it out," said an impatient bass voice in her mind. "Use your staff. *Fade* the insult."

"General Gel Lithium Silica said the Firebranch was more powerful than a staff," she said in her mind, sending it outwards, hoping the Tree would hear.

There was an awful, intense sound like the feedback of a microphone magnified a thousand times and Eyre clapped her hands to her ears, dropping the Firebranch on the ground where it shot a blazing stream of fire across the ground, hitting the Lodge storehouse, which immediately caught fire. Several Mimir rushed over in a panic with buckets as the Firebranch set the building alight like a bonfire.

"*Not. My. Staff?*" the voice thundered.

Eyre was blown back a step from the force in her mind.

"Apologies, Ancient One," she sent outwards, hoping again it would be heard. "I thank you for your guidance. And for my staff. We will deal with this problem."

Her mind suddenly had a way forward, and she was so grateful. Somehow a force she'd never seen, or understood was at her own call, had revealed itself. She had an unearthly instant where she saw the infinite. The Firebranch eventually dimmed once it was no longer held in a hand, and lay dark on the ground.

Then, focusing hard, Eyre summoned her staff. With a whistling noise, it slammed into her hand with a satisfying *whack*.

Eyre hefted the rainbow-coloured wood with the pink crystal at the top and turned towards the dish. After her time vying with Aowx, the sneaky dragon, with such success last year, she had so much more faith in the powerful weapon. And she knew the Rainbow Eucalyptus was an ancient revered being, who had singled her out by sending her one of its branches as a special gift in her first year at the Academy. Why, she didn't know, but she had felt very honoured by it. So any message from the old tree was worth listening to. *FADE!* Yep, she was happy to give it a try. *Fade* the vile poison indeed.

She turned to the dish again, where the purple stain still made an irregular pattern on the base of the magical receptacle, despite hours of blasting with the Firebranch, treating with crystals from the Transit and smoke from magical herbs from Terra. It was going to take a long time to eradicate the awful toxin, and as long as it was there it would continue to emit the malignant fumes that would cause Lightworkers, and particularly the Tyros, to fall desperately ill and eventually go over to the Dark side.

She felt furious as she looked at the growth put there by someone aligned with the Gothak, who had caused Mr Wilson to die and Nick to suffer so much. Energy travelled down her arm and through her staff and the pink diamond glowed a brilliant crimson as she sent a shockwave of Viq towards the metal dish. There was an explosion and a huge flame seared the Mantle Basin, sending drifts of sparks and soot into the sky. When she'd finished, the metal was burnished perfectly silver, no trace of the Violite left.

The Mimir, at the explosion, had all raised their Crescent Blades and rushed towards the clearing. Jengles was at the forefront, his face contorted in rage and ready to kill every Gothak he encountered.

But when they got to the dish, all the Mimir slowed and lowered their blades. Jengles looked amazed.

"*Dimmog*," he said softly as he examined the perfectly polished silver of the dish. "Did you do this?"

And then he gave a slight smile and a soft chuckle. "Of course you did." He turned to the milling troops. "Well, all of you, get some branches in here, *FAST!* Night is falling. The Mantle must be lit!"

Eyre looked out over the canopy of trees and lowered her staff. She wasn't sure how to communicate with the Rainbow Eucalyptus, but if Viq was any use, it must have heard her heartfelt 'thank you!' from wherever it was.

CHAPTER THIRTY-SIX

THE NEXT MORNING WHITTAKER Ray arrived to survey the scene. The Mantle was now re-lit, its silver matrix sending the protective rays arching once again over the compound. Eyre, Beatrice, with the journal under her arm, and Abby waited patiently as Mr Ray conferred with Jengles. There was a lot of discussion and hand movements, and staring over at the silver dish. Eyre could tell that even Whittaker Ray was shaken by this awful revelation.

Eventually he nodded goodbye to Jengles and walked over to join the girls. For a moment he was quiet, and then he shook his head.

"What a terrible situation," he said. "Eventually the Violite would have affected us all. How did it get there I wonder?"

Eyre gritted her teeth. *That* was something she wanted to know too. But she certainly had her suspicions. Professor Vela had been lurking around the Transit last year—no doubt he had easy access to the Mantle Basin. And he'd had Nick tethered to him at the Jenolan Caves—he must have known something about it. But she didn't say a word. Whittaker Ray was adamant that Professor Vela couldn't have been with George Wilson that day and Eyre knew she'd never change his mind on that.

In any case, it was a rhetorical question, really, and Whittaker Ray continued. He put a hand on Abby's shoulder. "I was very distressed by the events at the end of last year. Your father was my very good friend, and I could not make sense of it at all. If it wasn't for Nick's bravery, this would not have been discovered until it was too late. I hope it helps you in some way to know that your dad was not to blame for what happened."

Abby's lip quivered, but she nodded. "It does," she said softly.

"Well, we'd better get you back to the Academy," Whittaker Ray said. His eyes flicked over to Eyre.

"Nick is going straight to the Infirmary for a week and should hopefully make a full recovery.

"I am asking you all to keep this incident to yourselves. The Echelon will be made aware of what took place and they will share my relief that there is an explanation for what happened in Aqua last year. But we will not make the information generally known. We don't want anyone asking why this campsite should be a target for the Gothak."

Eyre, Beatrice and Abby nodded and Whittaker Ray smiled. "Thank you for your courage and your discretion."

Then he motioned for them to hold hands and a second later they were in their dormitory room at the Academy.

For a moment they just looked at each other, then sat on their beds.

"Poor Nick," Beatrice said. "No wonder he's been having those migraines. Thank goodness he's going to be alright."

Abby gave a wistful smile. "And maybe he might like me again."

Eyre flung a pillow at her. "Of course he will! He was protecting you, you dope! I'll just be glad to have him sit with us again."

The past year had seen a lot of division between the group, and their faces all showed relief at the thought that finally it might be over.

"Well, I guess we'd better get to class; no excuse really to linger here," Abby said. Eyre stood up, but shared Abby's reluctance. It was going to be hard to pick up the normal routine after all this drama.

Beatrice switched the lighting so she could put the journal back in the cache and they gathered their school gear together.

"Just another week at the Academy," Beatrice said, and they chortled as they left the room.

Someone was outside in the corridor, and Eyre, who was first out the door, leapt in fright.

Jemima Periwinkle came charging at them and gave Eyre a huge hug. She was a large lady and Eyre nearly disappeared within her arms. Abby and Beatrice looked horrified, knowing their turn was next.

Once she had hugged them all, the dorm supervisor, dressed in a lilac and rose-pink lacy twinset, stepped back.

"My poor dears!" she said breathlessly. "What a horrible situation for you! We are so lucky you found Nick!"

Eyre sidled past. She didn't know how much Jemima Periwinkle knew about recent events, so she wanted to exit fast before any questions were asked.

"He's going to be fine, Ms Periwinkle," she stuttered, then added brightly, "I'm late for Equestrian class, so I'd better get going!"

Beatrice and Abby, following her lead, shrugged ruefully at Jemima Periwinkle.

"Minerals and Crystals," Beatrice said, edging past.

"Psychic Techniques," Abby explained regretfully as she followed Beatrice. Then before Jemima Periwinkle could say anything else they rushed down the corridor after Eyre, looking like the most enthusiastic students on campus.

Eyre arrived just as the class began and the Kikkuli Master waved her down the corridor. He obviously knew what had been going on. She ran lightly down to Ischyros's stall and leaned over the gate. Holding her breath, she called to him.

"Come on Ischyros, let's go to class."

The old warhorse lifted his head from his feed bucket. "Oh, my aching back, not *that* again?"

But he turned around and let Eyre lead him out the door, and her heart sang. She hadn't been sure if he would ever want to go back to class after the last disaster. But she'd decided that they should go and practise walking, trotting and maybe galloping. After the last calamitous attempt she knew that Ischyros wouldn't attempt to fly again, but if they could just practise riding, she would be quite happy with that.

As they entered the arena heads turned with surprise. But Eyre lifted her chin, stroked Ischyros behind his ear and whispered, "I am proud to ride with you Ischyros. Thank you for trying again."

Ischyros grumbled, but stood quietly as Eyre swung herself up. This time she was ready, and she looked steadily at Ben Perrill, daring him to say one word. He knew her powers were now fully back and after a moment he looked away, sneering. But he didn't say anything.

Eyre and Ischyros joined the group and began walking. Eyre felt a wondrous joy. She wanted to hug the bad-tempered old beast, but restrained herself as the Kikkuli Master led the class through their paces for the next hour.

The students had just dismounted and started to lead their horses to their stalls when the Kikkuli Master asked Eyre to come to his office, once Ischyros was settled in his stall. Eyre nodded but her head was full of questions. What did he want to talk to her about? Hopefully he wasn't going to tell her to stay out of the class.

She took her time and brushed the sweat from Ischyros, cleaning him up beautifully after the ride, making sure she did it properly. Finally, she braided his grey mane, a silent thank you for letting her participate in the group lesson. She put some liquorice in his feed bucket and to the old horse's shock and dismay, kissed him on his forehead.

"*By the Light!*" he exclaimed in a horrified tone. "What was that?"

But as he turned towards the feed bucket, she could see that he looked ever so slightly pleased.

The Kikkuli Master was busy at his desk as she approached the door. He waved her in and indicated she should sit opposite him. She sat down with some trepidation. Something in the Master's demeanour indicated that whatever was coming next was not good. After a moment he finished what he was doing and put his pen down.

"Thank you for coming Eyre," he said, and a wrinkle appeared between his brows. For once, the Master seemed unsure of what to say. Eventually he sighed.

"You've heard of The Lightness Cup?" he asked.

"Oh yes, of course. The horse race at Coober Pedy? We've watched it the past couple of years holographically. Why?"

The Kikkuli Master looked down at his desk and twirled his pen around. "Well, you know that nine of the contenders are always drawn from the best Lighthorses in the world, but there are an additional two spots for wild cards?"

Eyre nodded. Anyone who wanted to enter the race could apply, and the two names were pulled from a draw. It wasn't frequent, but very rarely one of the wild card contenders placed in the race, and once in the history of the two-hundred-year-old race, a wild card had won it. The Kikkuli Master's eyes were regretful.

"Well, this year, Eyre, Ischyros is one of the wild cards drawn."

Eyre leapt up in horror. "*Ischyros?* But how could that be? I didn't enter him!"

The Kikkuli Master shook his head. "Well, it appears someone did, and that is enough to be eligible. In fact, if you don't compete, it could put the whole race in jeopardy due to a mis-draw."

"Couldn't they just pull another name out of the hat?" Eyre said dumbfoundedly, as she sat back down.

"It's not in the rules, Eyre. No one has ever declined the wild card spot before, so the rules and regulations have not allowed for that." He shook his head. "What it means is that if you don't enter, the race will be called off."

Eyre looked at him furiously. "Someone has set us up. They want us to look stupid. Ischyros can't even fly, so how can he be in a race like that?" Then she clenched her jaw. "It will decimate him."

The Kikkuli Master's dark brown eyes were understanding. "I have tried very hard to argue your case, Eyre, and I understand completely. I heard about this a week ago, and I travelled to meet with the Board of Directors. I agree that this is a travesty, and very unkind. Also unfair to those wild cards who would genuinely like to be in the race. But unfortunately, the Board is adamant and there is nothing I can do about it. You have to race."

Eyre sat in shock. She'd just started making progress with Ischyros, and this would embarrass him so badly, the poor old fellow.

"It's on June 21st, isn't it?" she whispered.

The Kikkuli Master nodded. "The Winter Solstice."

"Two weeks," Eyre answered bitterly. "What a farce."

"I'm sorry, Eyre," the Kikkuli Master said softly. "I'll tell Ischyros."

Eyre stood up slowly and turned to go. "It's not your fault, sir," she said softly. "But I just feel that the bad guys seem to be winning at all levels lately."

She left the Equestrian Centre and headed to her next class, her thoughts black and churning.

CHAPTER THIRTY-SEVEN

AS EYRE WALKED INTO the History of Light and headed for her usual seat half-way up, she could see Beatrice and Abby were already there. They gave a questioning look at her furious face as she sat down with a thump.

But before she could open her mouth, someone moved into the row in front of them and leant across the back of the chair.

"Heard you're going to be a jockey," Carrison taunted, his eyes flat and mean. "Can't wait for the race."

He kept walking, but then turned back and mock-whispered, "My dad's on the Board of Directors."

Carrison left, guffawing, and Eyre felt like she had been punched in the stomach. Everyone in the auditorium turned to look at them, craning necks to see what was going on. Beatrice looked like she was going to blast Carrison out of the auditorium, even without knowing what was going on.

Abby put an arm around Eyre. "What's up? What's going on, Eyre?"

Eyre just shook her head, feeling all eyes upon her. "I'll tell you after class —meet you at the Bane rock." Her eyes followed Carrison, who had sat next to Ben Perrill, and they high-fived and looked down the aisle at her. Ben Perrill gave a merry little wave and Eyre felt like she was about to explode.

At that moment the door opened and Professor Vela stalked in. It was just as well, Eyre realised, because her Viq rose like magma under pressure and she was about to shoot a torrent of fire towards the smirking group of boys. The Curtis twins, Wyatt Rankins, Tec Langford, Jeremy Tucker, Carrison and Ben were all chortling amongst themselves as if they'd just won the famous race themselves. A horde of snickering faces. Only the presence of a demon like Professor Vela could have stopped her from completely losing it. She forced herself to look down at the desk and breathe in and out slowly, using the techniques from the classes her parents had sent her to so many years ago. Slowly, the inferno running through her veins began to subside and the uncontrollable energy within her eased, and she finally looked up as Professor Vela started the lecture. Despite the concerted efforts of the grinning jackals at the other side of the auditorium to gain her attention during the lecture, she ignored them completely and she left as soon as it finished.

Eyre took off at a run for the Bane sandstone rock, running as if she was in the Lightness Cup herself. Her heart was beating hard, and she almost levitated and shot there like a comet, there was so much angry energy within her.

Finally, she got there and skidded to a stop, her breath coming in heaving gasps. She slid down with her back against the rock and waited for her friends.

It didn't take long, and they arrived looking worried. Beatrice tried to make light of it as they sat down in front of her. "I hope this won't take too long? It's lunchtime, you know."

Eyre gave a small snort and shook her head.

"What's up Eyre?" Abby asked. "You shouldn't let those mongrels get to you."

"Yeah, what did they mean about being a jockey?" Beatrice added.

Eyre sighed and looked at them flatly. "You're not going to believe this."

Beatrice raised her eyebrows. "Try us. Could anything be weirder than what we've been through in the last year?"

There was a long silence as they looked at each other, and then Eyre huffed, shaking her head.

"Ischyros is one of the wild cards in the Lightness Cup this year," she said.

Abby laughed, and then horror dawned on her face as she realised Eyre was serious.

"*What?*" Beatrice exploded.

"So, yes indeed, things *can* get weirder," Eyre said.

There was dead silence as they all watched the eucalyptus leaves wave gently in the breeze above them.

"BTL!" Beatrice finally said. "You'll be famous!"

Eyre looked at her and suddenly giggled. Then the three of them lost it, and they roared with laughter, tears streaming down their faces. Finally, Eyre wiped her face and rubbed her forehead.

"BTL indeed," she said. "We are going to be famous, alright, but as a laughing-stock. The whole world will be rolling on the floor with hilarity."

Abby, the animal whisperer, suddenly put her hand to her mouth. "Oh no," she said, her blue eyes troubled. "Ischyros will be so humiliated."

"Not just Ischyros," Eyre said drily.

Beatrice looked at her. "It's in two weeks, By the Light, what are you going to do?"

Eyre considered the question. "Well, I was a coward, and I've let the Kikkuli Master tell Ischyros. I really couldn't do it myself. I'm going to visit Ischyros this afternoon to see how he is. Poor old fella."

"You can't withdraw?" Abby suggested. "Then maybe someone else can enter."

Eyre's eyes darkened again. "Carrison's dad has rigged this. I never entered Ischyros—obviously—but apparently anyone can enter a horse. Carrison put Ischyros in, and Carrison's dad has organised it. That's what he was talking about."

Despite her anger, her pain showed, and Abby put her arm around her.

Then Beatrice jumped up. "Well, if it's a show they want, let's give them one! We'll work something out. We're with you Eyre, and we'll applaud when you cross the finish line, don't you worry!"

Eyre looked at her gratefully. "Thank you, my friend. Well, enough about me—how about we go and visit Nick?"

Abby stood up so fast she almost levitated. "Hey, good idea Eyre. We can have lunch with him!"

"And I can stop feeling sorry for myself and think about someone else for a change," Eyre added.

Beatrice slapped her on the back as she stood up and the three of them jogged along the track to the Infirmary.

When they got there, it was a bustle of activity. Ferito training had been going on all term and many of the students had come for an unfortunate but necessary visit over the past couple of months, after receiving their arms endowment. Students were filing in and out, sometimes in a frantic rush, with wounds to be dealt with, and there were occupied beds everywhere with various levels of bandaging.

Sister Murphy was very happy to see them and gave them some patient trays to take for their lunch as she ushered them in to visit Nick. He lay in the hospital bed, very pale, making his scars stand out like shining hieroglyphics all over his body. Dark shadows hung beneath his eyes, but Eyre felt joy rise within her as she looked at those eyes. The old Nick, although exhausted and incapacitated, was definitely back.

Abby flung herself at him, weeping, and his arm curved over her, patting her back gently.

"Nick, thank the Light that you're back!" she cried.

Nick rested his head on hers, and Eyre saw how he had managed to hold the demon at bay. His love for her had given him strength beyond the Darkness.

Eventually, Beatrice walked over and hugged him, and Eyre did too, her eyes tearing up. Then they all sat down in the chairs beside the bed.

"You are a legend, Nick," Eyre said. "If you hadn't made it back to the cabin, we would never have found the Violite. No one would ever have known."

There was a silence and then Nick spoke softly, his voice a hoarse rasp, damaged after all the screeching and shouting when the demon was within him.

"I didn't know what was going on," he said. "I was so worried I would hurt one of you. And I might look bad now, but can I tell you, I feel better than I have all year. I'm so glad my head has stopped talking to me. The pain has gone."

They all looked at each other and then Abby chuckled. "Well, you have to get better quickly, because we need you in a couple of weeks!"

As Nick looked from one face to the other, Eyre, Beatrice and Abby all broke into uncontrollable laughter.

"We're going to the Lightness Cup!" Abby spluttered.

CHAPTER THIRTY-EIGHT

THE NEXT MORNING EYRE ran lightly down the track that ran to the Equestrian Centre. She had left early so that she could visit Ischyros before Meditation and see how he felt about the Lightness Cup. Although there was really no answer she expected from him, other than how she herself felt; doomed. She expected it might be coupled with an anger storm, rating about level 5 on the Saffir-Simpson hurricane scale. And ending with him saying he wouldn't go. I don't want to go either, she thought dismally, so maybe that would be fine, despite the fact that it would make her solely responsible for the cancellation of the Lightness Cup.

She approached Ischyros's stall cautiously, and then ducked as something whizzed by her ear. She picked it up carefully and then frowned in puzzlement. Liquorice? Uh oh, she thought, I'm in for it...

An ancient head suddenly appeared over the stall door, the old horse with the black circle around his eye studying her carefully. No matter how much she groomed him, he would never look anything other than decrepit; he was so old his coat was ratty, his mane tatty and his back bowed. She expected him to bite her as she approached cautiously.

"So, we're in the Lightness Cup," he said, brightly. Eyre nearly fell over.

"Uh... er..." She was lost for words.

"Eat that," Ischyros said, tipping his head towards the liquorice. "I saved it for you. You'll need the energy."

Eyre was horrified. Oh no! Did the old horse think they had a chance? That was by far the worst aspect she had encountered regarding this whole embarrassing situation. What should she say?

Her heart aching, she picked up the liquorice, and held it out to Ischyros.

"Thank you Ischyros," she said. "I thought you might not want to go. But you will be doing the hard work, so how about you have this?"

Ischyros didn't need any encouragement and lifted the stub of black deliciousness from her hand with alacrity with his soft mouth.

"Well, you'd better get in training," he mumbled as he chewed.

Eyre had no answer. She entered his stall and gave him a good grooming as he went on and on about being invited to be in the Cup, and what an honour it was.

"Well, Ischyros," she finally said. "You and I will certainly make an impact. This will be a race to remember!"

Ischyros chewed on the liquorice as she brushed him down. "Of course it will," he said.

Eyre ran back fast to her Meditation class—the first one of every morning. She sat there, trying to dump the thoughts of her poor old horse thinking he might make an impact in the Lightness Cup. An impact indeed, but not exactly in the way he was imagining. Her heart was sore, but then suddenly Colton arrived and sat beside her.

"I sense troubled thoughts," he said telepathically.

"So many," was all Eyre could manage. She knew Colton was the purest of souls, but she still had to work things out.

Suddenly Colton turned to her, his ice-blue eyes regarding her kindly.

"I am here for you," he said, no longer using telepathy. "Whenever, however. I have always felt a bond with you and I know that eventually we'll beat the Darkness."

Eyre felt his goodness run through her like a bright light. She suddenly needed to confide; not that it was a secret really, as everyone would eventually know.

"Well, I'm not focused on the Gothak today, actually. But I am feeling the bad guys are winning. Someone entered Ischyros in the Lightness Cup," she said. "It will be so hard on the poor old fella."

To her surprise, Colton smiled. "We'll all cheer, no matter what happens at the Cup. And it will be a race to remember."

"Thanks Colton," Eyre said wryly. "That it will, no doubt about it."

She left for Ferito next, and her anger about the Cup gave her extra focus and an edge to her practise. She managed her Arms Endowment so brilliantly that even Sergeant Tottingham stopped to watch her. Eyre wanted nothing less than perfection in her Clasis, and she was far from it. So she went through the moves of Clasis 3 over and over again, even when the other students had left.

Eventually, half an hour after the training session had finished, Eyre slid her Antaraks back into her baldrics and her Kulbeda into her belt, heading back to the dorm where she would fasten them in the locker. She wiped her brow as she left the Shed, and then someone stepped in front of her. Ready for anything, as always these days, she raised her hands and then registered in shock that it was Jax. Automatically she looked at his hands, but they were now looking normal. At least he wasn't addicted, was all she could think.

Jax looked at her, his green eyes concerned, and gently pulled her hands down from the defensive gesture.

"Hi," he said.

"You're back?" was all Eyre could say. *Idiot! Obviously.*

"Yep." Jax didn't say more, and Eyre slumped.

"Okay, well, I guess I'll see you around, hey," she said.

"I'm coming to the race," Jax said, and Eyre flinched.

"Should be a good show," she said in a subdued tone, and Jax's eyes softened.

"We're all with you, Eyre, no matter what happens," he said, and kissed the top of her head. Then he was striding away, without looking back.

Eyre walked away slowly, feeling conflicted. She didn't know what Jax was up to, any more than any of the other enigmas she'd been dealing with lately. She couldn't trust anyone, and maybe his behaviour had all been for show. She didn't have faith in her skills anymore to work out what anyone's motives were, so she had to keep to herself. Troubled, she watched the athletic, and to be truly honest, *gorgeous,* Jax walk away from her.

And then, someone else stood in front of her.

"Uh, Zanda?" she said, slightly confused. Zanda had a notebook and pen, and his eyes were focused.

"I hear there's a major story here, Eyre," he said. Eyre looked at him and despaired. Was *no one* capable of stopping themselves from delving into the mire?

She walked away without saying anything, heading for the solitude of her room.

CHAPTER THIRTY-NINE

THE NEXT DAY EYRE walked into the Refectory, and there was a buzz as she entered the doorway. Heads looked up, chatter died, and even the Jotnar stopped their routine for a moment to regard her entrance. Obviously, everyone had heard. She headed towards her usual table, ignoring all the looks, but then, with joy, she registered that Nick was back! Defying the predictions, he was obviously well enough now to join classes again. Forgetting the looks directed her way, she rushed up and hugged him.

"So glad you're back," she whispered. And Abby's face said it all. It looked like she'd received an unexpected Christmas present. She sat close to Nick and he held Abby's hand in his.

"Thanks, Eyre," Nick replied. "It's because of you. I remember."

Eyre waved it away. "The Restrainor and the Mimir were the reason you're here, Nick. But mostly your own strength. It was you, really. How you could obstruct the Dark Forces is beyond me. You are so strong. And we are so glad you're back!"

She beamed at him, and so did everyone else at the table. Then Robeson sat down at their table, slapping a stack of papers in front of him. He passed them around.

"The Reflector!" he said. "Have a look at 'Spotlight'."

Eyre opened the school newspaper with some trepidation. Zanda was clever at making fun of whatever was happening on campus, and she felt sure that poor Ischyros was in for a roasting. But as she read the Spotlight article her heart lightened, and she looked for Zanda in the Refectory. He'd obviously been waiting, as he met her gaze across the room and gave her a captain's salute. Incredibly relieved, and feeling guilty for thinking the worst about him, she saluted back.

"*Academy of Light invited to the Lightness Cup!*" read the headline. Then the story went on to outline how, by a stroke of great fortune, one horse from the Academy had been drawn as the wild card for the annual race. 'What an opportunity for the Academy to support each other', the article read. And, 'How wonderful that we have a profile in this national event!' Zanda went on to write a positive article about the amazing luck that Ischyros had been chosen. Then he made it quite clear that Ischyros was very old, and unable to compete at the level of the other competitors, but that the Academy owed it to each other to turn up and cheer him on. Eyre's eyes moistened as she read the article; Zanda was a very talented writer and despite his opportunity for a hilarious and more newsworthy take on the whole situation, he had taken a moral and kind slant on it all. She looked around the Refectory and was taken aback to see many smiling and sympathetic faces looking at her, including Pheria, to her surprise. Ben Perrill and Carrison, of course, were smirking and nudging each other as they chortled loudly.

Eyre stood up. All conversation stopped around the room.

"Ischyros!" she cried, her fist pumping in the air.

"*The pissy hoss!*" Ben Perrill hooted and his whole table howled with glee.

Eyre was about to incinerate their meals when Pheria started clapping. For a moment Eyre was confused, but then the mean laughter was drowned out as others started to clap too, until the whole Refectory rang with applause.

"The famous race will go on," Eyre declared in an iron voice when the applause finally died away, "only because that brave old horse has agreed to participate." She stalked over to Ben Perrill's group, her eyes flaming, and slammed her hands down on their table. The golden surface hummed and became scorching red and the Curtis twins jumped up in fright.

"So, I'd advise certain *brainless* idiots to make no more comments, or I might decide to go to the Cup's Board of Directors and announce our *regretful* withdrawal." Eyre looked directly at Carrison and *dared* him. Carrison clenched his teeth in fury and looked away.

Beatrice and Abby slapped Eyre on the shoulder as she walked back to their table and sat down.

Nick's eyes glowed. "By the Light, it's great to be back!"

The next two weeks passed in a flurry. Everyone was rushing—finishing classes, getting final assignments in and swotting for end of semester exams. Beatrice was deep in the agonies of '"The Physics of the Aura', and Abby's nemesis was 'Psychic Retrocognition and Precognition'. Nick was spending long hours on the intricacies of 'Alchemy and Transformation'. Eyre found all her subjects equally hard, as she'd had so much to catch up on, and she'd spent many late nights trying to learn everything she needed to.

Since Nick had come out of the Infirmary he and Abby had spent a lot of time holding hands, walking together and talking. It seemed the near-death experience he had been through had brought them even closer. Eyre would often see them together as she raced around campus from one class to another, trying to make up for the time they'd missed.

Eyre also visited Ischyros at dawn every day and they'd practised galloping around the ring. Eyre was determined that they would at least finish the race, which was three laps of the course, and she wanted to make sure she didn't fall off. Ischyros had such an unusual gait, he was harder to ride than Nox, who ran so smoothly that even a beginner was safe on his back. But daily she improved as she got used to Ischyros's eccentricities, and on her last ride before the Cup she was fairly confident they'd make it around the track three times together.

Ischyros was trying hard, and although his old legs trembled at the end of each training session, he seemed to be enjoying it. And Eyre was too. She was just happy that they were finally working together.

"Tomorrow's the big day," she said softly to Ischyros as she massaged his old legs and brushed him down. "I'm so proud to be riding with you."

Finally, she put the curry combs and brushes away and filled his bucket with fresh water.

"Sleep well, see you tomorrow, you great warrior," she said as she ran down the walkway. "We'll show 'em all something they've never seen before, that's for sure!"

For once there was no answering harrumph from the stall.

The next day, Eyre lay awake early as her friends still slept. She'd tossed and turned all night and she had dreamed fitfully. Despite her brave words to Ischyros, she was dreading the race. She knew they were going to look ridiculous, and she hated the fact that people might be laughing at the old horse.

Eventually she realised she wasn't going to be able to get back to sleep and she sighed, swinging her feet over the side of the bed. May as well get on with it.

She dressed quickly and headed out the dormitory towards the stables. But a voice stopped her as she jogged along and as she turned towards it, she smiled.

The Ranger stood at the side of the path, holding a bag in his hand.

"I hope you don't mind," he said, "but I took the liberty of organising you some silks for the race."

Eyre walked over and looked in the bag. Her eyes started to water as she pulled out the beautiful racing apparel. The breeches were deep purple, and the shirt was also purple, but with a design of silver Inguz all over it, with gold centres. The silks were truly magnificent, and then she noticed something else in the bag and pulled out a pair of silver racing goggles, edged with amethysts. She raced over to hug the Ranger.

"Thank you, Ranger," she said. "They are beautiful. Ischyros will be happy to have a real jockey on his back!"

The Ranger's purple eyes twinkled. "Amethysts create spiritual light and protect against psychic negativity. Enjoy the race, my dear. I'll be cheering you on!"

Eyre continued on to the stables, feeling a bit better. At least she would have her friends there and other supporters as the dismal event unfolded. Then she heard the sound of running behind her and again she turned.

Beatrice and Abby, red-faced, staggered down the track.

"Wait!" Abby gasped. "We didn't think you'd be up so early!"

"Couldn't sleep," Eyre said wryly, as they finally they caught up to her. Abby's face showed she understood.

Beatrice's eyes were round as she put her hands on her knees, breathing deeply. "You do this every morning? Shame it's not a running race!" Eyre noted that today she had in her lucky diamond nose stud and she felt a gladness run through her for these wonderful friends.

"We want to help you get Ischyros ready," Abby said as they finally continued on towards the Equestrian Centre. "I've been talking to Beatrice about it and we've made a plan."

The arena was silent as they entered the massive bronze gates and walked towards the stables. Then the slight form of the Kikkuli Master appeared from his office across the arena.

"I have something for you, Eyre," he called.

The Kikkuli Master walked across to join them and handed Eyre a silver racing collar, with the number II in large purple numbers on each side. Lightworkers didn't ride with a saddle or bridle, so the silken racing collar was designed to sit around the neck to identify the horse.

"I—er—wanted to give you something," he said awkwardly. "We've never had a Lighthorse in the Cup before. I have to confess though, that the Ranger did liaise with me."

Eyre took the shining collar, and to the Kikkuli Master's great surprise, hugged him.

"I am *so* lucky to be in this," she said fiercely. "Not because of horses, but because of what I've learned about people. Thank you so much."

The Kikkuli Master smiled as she left. "You have made us proud, Eyre, whatever happens."

Ischyros had his head over the stall door as they approached and he was the most energized Eyre had ever seen him. He snorted and tossed his head and stamped in place, and Abby and Beatrice cooed.

"He's so cute," Abby said adoringly, and Eyre's eyebrows raised.

Ischyros beamed. "Someone understands me," he commented.

Beatrice and Abby hadn't heard him of course, so they all hurried in to get started. Dawn was breaking, but they had a lot to do before the race, which always began at 2pm.

First of all, they led Ischyros out into the horse-washing facilities at the end of the stables. A high powered, fine-holed hose fired water at Ischyros as Beatrice and Eyre washed him completely with shampoo and rinsed him off. It took about half an hour and then Eyre rubbed him down to get rid of the excess moisture. Then she snapped her fingers and a gentle warm blast of air flowed over the old animal. He stood contentedly underneath it. Being winter, it was cold outside, and Eyre knew they had to get him completely dry.

Eventually all the moisture was gone, so they led him out into the walkway, where there was more room. Eyre didn't tether him; if he wasn't going to co-operate now, there was no point going ahead with it, really.

"Can you bear with us Ischyros?" Abby asked. "It will take a while, but we have to make you look awesome for the race."

Ischyros obviously had a soft spot for her since she'd called him cute, and he *nuzzled* her. Eyre's eyebrows rose. Nuzzling? Although she'd done so much better recently with the old creature, she hadn't known that nuzzling was in his repertoire. But at least he was co-operating, so she didn't comment as Abby did her magic.

While Eyre and Beatrice brushed Ischyros carefully, and massaged his legs and body, Abby braided his grey mane, forelock and tail in an intricate weave at the top of the hair, with the rest of it falling free. Amongst the braid she laced amethyst crystals, which glinted against his brown coat and looked spectacular. It took quite some time, and then she finally cut the ends of the forelock, mane and tail so they were dead straight. Smiling with satisfaction, she looked up at Beatrice and Eyre's gobsmacked faces.

"I researched it," she said. "I've done the most difficult weave there is—the Millaa Millaa. After the waterfall. Isn't it beautiful?"

Eyre had to agree. What a work of art! The Mimir would be most impressed.

Then Abby got to work with her art box. She sprayed each of Ischyros's hooves silver, and then sprayed a silver Inguz on his shoulder. Then she painted gold paint in the centre of the Inguz. Eyre had showed Abby and Beatrice the racing silks earlier and Abby winked at Eyre as she marvelled at what Abby had done.

"The Ranger consulted with me too," Abby chuckled.

Finally, Ischyros was ready. He pranced in place and looked at his hooves in admiration.

"Wish you were my Lightworker," he said slyly to Abby, looking at Eyre, and Eyre felt a sudden surge of happiness. This cranky, difficult old beast was still teasing her! All her misgivings about the race suddenly disappeared. Whatever happened today, it would be magical to be part of it.

The Kikkuli Master appeared then and walked around Ischyros with an unfathomable look on his face. Then he smiled.

"You have all done well," he said. "I'll see you at Coober Pedy."

CHAPTER FORTY

EVERY YEAR IN THE week before June 21st, an area five kilometres west of Coober Pedy was transformed from an empty red desert into a bustling construction site. A racetrack was laid out with light beams, and stadium seating completely surrounding the track was erected using strong quartz crystal, and layered in tiers by Master Faceters, who moved at great speed to get everything done. Marquees were set up for those who were able to organise the space for private functions, and food suppliers bustled around getting their services organised. In the centre of the racetrack, a powerful Mantle was constructed, its massive silver matrix sending out protective and shielding rays of light five hundred metres high, to hide the whole event.

Eyre, Beatrice and Abby arrived in the middle of the hubbub. Jemima Periwinkle had rushed down their corridor when they got back that morning to see how they were doing.

"Thank you Ms Periwinkle," Eyre said, as Jemima Periwinkle beamed through their door, "it's kind of you to check on us."

Jemima preened. "It's so exciting—I always like being at the track."

Beatrice, never lost for words, finally spoke. "You're going too?"

Jemima Periwinkle looked at her, her pale violet eyes suddenly focused. "Oh yes, my dears, I wouldn't miss it for the world. The Kikkuli Master was taking you, but since I'm going and I'm here, I thought I'd save him the effort."

"Eyre and her friends looked at each other and Eyre felt a falling sensation within her. She'd sort of hoped that the race might be beamed by hologram and the news ultimately reported by Zanda in Spotlight—'Valiant Lighthorse does his best'; 'Brave Academy steed makes his mark',—or some similar headline. Now, to her horror, it seemed there would be more observers at the race to witness the travesty.

But she rallied a smile. "Great, thank you so much. We weren't sure how we'd get there. That's very kind of you."

"So glad to be part of this National event! Anything we can do!" Jemima said coyly. She looked so excited, and Eyre snuck a glance at her friends and raised her eyebrows. Did the woman not realise she and Ischyros were about to make an embarrassing spectacle of themselves?

Abby looked down at the floor, and Beatrice to the ceiling. They were obviously trying not to laugh. Eyre finally found her voice.

"Well, Ms Periwinkle, we know this race will make history," she said, and Ms Periwinkle lifted a twirling hand.

"I was so hoping it would!" she said. "Come, hold my hands and I'll get you there."

They arrived in the middle of the melee and the first thing that struck Eyre was the focus of everyone who rushed around. Spectators weren't allowed in until 11am, so everyone who was there at the moment had a job to do. People with clipboards marched around giving instructions for the last-minute organisation of the tents and pavilions; the announcers were testing their voices over the noise, making sure they could be heard; magnificent Lighthorses were arriving in a flash of light, skittery and prancing with excitement. A couple of the grooms sent their Lighthorses out with their exercise rider for a slow run on the track. But not for very long. Most of them headed to their stalls to rest and calm down before the race. The Lightworker who belonged with each Lighthorse followed closely behind their magnificent animals as they disappeared into the stables.

Jemima Periwinkle strode along ahead of the girls. "The pre-race examination is at 10am," she said importantly. "You can head that way to the stables where you will find Ischyros and the Kikkuli Master, and you will need to get your steed ready for the veterinarian to check." Eyre heard Beatrice and Abby choke at the word 'steed' and Eyre couldn't look at them; she knew she'd lose it. Had Jemima Periwinkle ever *seen* Ischyros? Ms Periwinkle carried on, oblivious. "I have some people to see so I'll leave you now. Good luck with the race, my dear," she finished, beaming at Eyre.

Once she was out of earshot, Eyre exhaled loudly and chuckled. "Well then, let's go find my trusty steed!" They walked into the stables, where twelve stalls were lined up, six each side across a wide walkway. The stalls were spaced quite far apart, with a grooming pen for each horse between each stall. Eleven of the stalls had horses in them and it only took Eyre a moment to know where Ischyros was, because she could hear his grumbling from the end of the corridor.

"What a furore, too much damned noise," he complained loudly. "Stupid jittery creatures are likely to jump out of their stall and into mine! Dratted Lighthorses. Can't stand 'em!"

Eyre arrived at his stall, which was (wisely, she thought) at the end of the row, and she stuck her head over the door.

"Hello, my mighty racehorse!" she said, and got a loud harrumph in return. Eyre had to admit he looked quite magnificent, with his crystals and glitter, and the beautiful braiding Abby had done. Although he was muttering petulantly, she could see him admiring his silver hooves. And she thought she might even have seen a prance at one stage. The Kikkuli Master smiled at her from his seat down the back of the stall.

"How do you feel, Eyre?" he asked.

Eyre rolled her eyes, but didn't tell the truth, since Ischyros could hear. "Oh, it's going to be brilliant!" she replied brightly. The Kikkuli Master understood.

"It's an experience of a lifetime, Eyre," he said. "It will be a special memory, no matter what the outcome."

Eyre nodded. A special memory it would be, indeed! And she had a fair idea of the outcome actually. But she realised the Kikkuli Master was just trying to be kind.

After a while, the veterinarian arrived to examine Ischyros. He bustled in and then did the biggest double-take Eyre had ever seen in her life.

"Oh, I'm sorry," he said, backing out of the stall. He looked at the number on the door of the stall, then his clipboard, and back at Ischyros. His jaw dropped.

"Are you—er—Ay-Ree Lightward?"

Eyre sighed as Beatrice and Abby sniggered. "It's pronounced '*Air* Lightward' actually. And this is Ischyros, Number 11," Eyre said calmly. "I'm his Lightworker."

The vet's eyes were round, but he was obviously a veteran of surprises at the racetrack, so he didn't comment as he went about his examination. Although Ischyros was ancient, he was in good health, so he passed the required tests to participate in the race.

At 11am the noise at the racetrack increased immensely as the spectators were allowed in, and they streamed across the race-grounds. The stadium filled quickly with thousands of people, and the marquees were packed with groups of stylishly dressed racegoers sipping at special drinks. Vendors selling popcorn peas, drinks and hot food were frantically serving queues of people as the day went on.

"Hi," a voice said in an American accent, and Eyre looked up to see a woman in her twenties looking over the stall door. "I'm Payne. I'm the other wild card, I drew lane 6. I just wanted to wish you luck."

Payne's face was quizzical as she looked at Ischyros, but she smiled. "He looks pretty sharp!"

Eyre looked down the corridor and saw the Lighthorse in Stall 6 with his head over the door, turned their way. He was a big bay horse with a black mane braided and tied in knots down his back. He stood quietly, unlike some of the other Lighthorses, who moved incessantly around their stall with suppressed energy.

"I'm Eyre, and this is Ischyros. Where are you from?" Eyre asked.

"Fort Collins, Colorado," the woman said, and shook her hand.

"You've come a long way then. Good luck to you too, Payne. I hope you go well."

Payne headed back to her Lighthorse and Eyre turned to Ischyros. She, Beatrice and Abby heated their hands with Viq and began to massage Ischyros—his legs, his flanks, his back and his neck. Eyre knew it was going to be hard for the old horse to make it around the track three times, so she wanted his muscles to be as warm as possible.

Time passed surprisingly quickly, and the Kikkuli Master eventually stood up. You need to collar Ischyros and get your silks on," he said.

Eyre quickly dressed in the shimmering purple silks, and pulled on the silver boots. She felt a bit like Ischyros as she admired her beautiful racewear. The Ranger had certainly outdone himself this time!

Then she slipped the silver racing collar with the big number 11 on each side over Ischyros's head and around his neck. She could hear stall doors opening and the riders coaxing their Lighthorses out; there was a clatter of hooves as one by one the entrants headed out to the parade ring beside the starting gates.

As each shining Lighthorse came out there was a reaction from the spectators. Each one of the horses was spectacular, and their race collar co-ordinated beautifully with their rider's silks. Manes plaited, immaculately groomed, they were the most elite Lighthorses in the world. Ischyros was one of two Australian contenders (thank goodness, Eyre thought, at least she wasn't the only Australian representative!), there was one from New Zealand, one from France, one from Dubai, one from the UK, two from the USA, including Payne and her horse, two from Ireland and one from Japan.

It was impossible to tell who was going to win; they were all breath-taking creatures.

Eyre looked out the doorway as the ten other Lighthorses were walked around the parade ring, nostrils flaring and dancing in place. They knew what was coming and they were all eager to race.

Eyre wished she could feel the same, but when she looked at Ischyros, decorated in all his splendour, she took a deep breath and led him outside into the parade ring.

The noise of the spectators gradually died away until there was absolute silence in the stadium as every single eye fell upon her. Eyre tilted her chin and stood calmly in the middle of the ring as the other Lightworkers jumped up onto their horses and walked them around the perimeter of the ring. Eyre climbed lightly onto Ischyros's back, but there was no need for her to walk him. They just needed to get the race over and done with.

A buzz started again in the stadium—no doubt with her and Ischyros as the main topic of conversation—but then there was no time to worry about it, as the race stewards ushered them onto the racetrack and towards the starting gates.

Full of adrenaline, some of the horses balked as they were led into their individual blocks and had to be coaxed into place. Eyre plodded with Ischyros into number 11, the outside lane of the track and the lane closest to the stadium, and he stood quietly. Eyre's heart was beating hard though. For all her understanding that this was an amazing experience, she knew it was going to be embarrassing.

"Three laps of the track," Eyre thought grimly. "Three times, and we're done."

CHAPTER FORTY-ONE

WITH A CLANG, THE metal gates raised and the Lighthorses lunged forward.

"And they're off!" the race caller cried excitedly as the powerful horses charged out onto the track. Eyre was left with a cloud of dust in her face as Ischyros trotted along behind them. Choking, she urged him forward, focusing on the track and determined not to look towards the stadium.

"We're with you, Eyre," Abby called telepathically, and Eyre sent a mental flower back to her. But then she had to concentrate all her energy on the ride; Ischyros was so ungainly that if she didn't focus, she would fall off.

Up ahead she could see the Lighthorses thundering away, vying for positions as close to the rail as they could. It was a tight race and from her position she couldn't make out who was in the lead. And the race caller's voice was just a buzz in her ears.

Along jogged Ischyros as people snickered from the sidelines. Eyre gritted her teeth and kept her eyes forward.

"They're smiling! They love me!" Ischyros said in delight, and danced on the spot, nearly tossing Eyre over the rails.

"Come on, let's just get around," Eyre urged him, her heart bleeding for the poor old horse who didn't realise he was a laughingstock.

The rest of the pack was already halfway round when Eyre and Ischyros reached the first bend. Heartsore, she patted Ischyros's side and encouraged him on.

"Doing well, going great!" she whispered.

It was a long, long journey to get halfway round, with catcalls and boos and jeering faces all the way. Eyre understood the reason for the spectators' behaviour; they had come to see a horse race, the most famous one in the world, and she was taking a spot that a more worthy entrant had missed out on. They all thought she should never have entered.

About three quarters of the way around, Eyre and Ischyros were overtaken by the rest of the horses—flying above them. The second and third laps were always raced in the air and it was traditionally a magnificent sight, with horses taking off from the track, then swooping above and below each other, turning on their sides with great flaps of their wings to try and slide forwards into a better position. The wind from the force of their wings as the mighty herd passed over caused a dust storm on the course, and once again Eyre and Ischyros were left choking in the red haze.

"Keep going, Ischyros," Eyre urged, but she realised that he was slowing.

"They don't love me," he said, as realisation dawned. "They're *making fun* of me!" The hurt in his voice nearly caused Eyre's heart to break, as she felt something ignite within her.

"We are finishing the race," she said in a furious tone. "Don't you listen to them!"

But Ischyros was tiring and his old legs were starting to tremble, and if possible, he went even slower until he was virtually only moving forward at a walk. Tears ran down Eyre's face as the old horse tried to pick his feet up, but it was obvious that he was never going to make a second lap, let alone a third.

As they approached the end of the first lap, the laughter and jeering had increased. The rest of the Lighthorses flew past on their third lap, heading for the finish line and fighting for first place. Eyre could see through the swirling sand because she had her goggles on, but Ischyros couldn't and had to stop. As he lowered his head, Eyre put her hand over her mouth and peered into the dust as the horses swept by.

The race caller's voice got higher and higher as the magnificent creatures charged for the finish line, until with shouts and cheers from the spectators, the first three Lighthorses rocketed over the line, with the other seven close behind. Eyre watched as they soared on ahead for a short while, and then wheeled around, gliding down to land in the centre of the racetrack. Eyre's cheeks flamed and she gritted her teeth as she and Ischyros staggered painfully towards the end of their first lap.

The race was won, so everyone in the stadium was now focused on Eyre and Ischyros.

"Get off the track!" someone called.

"A travesty!" another jeered.

Boos and catcalls filled the air, and as Eyre's rage rose, she noticed a tear run down the red dust that now covered Ischyros's face. His beautiful braids were clogged with dust, and his sides were soaked with sweat.

Then, in a flash of searing energy, the brewing, boiling inferno suddenly exploded within her, an uncontrollable eruption like a bomb going off. She looked at the contemptuous, mean faces surrounding the racetrack and her eyes turned from sapphire blue into swirls of burning golden fire. An eerie wailing filled the stadium as a ferocious dust storm rose from the track. The current of wind whirled round and round, funnelling tons of dirt up into a tornado. Then, with a howl, the funnel exploded outwards and pounded its contents down over the entire racegrounds. The spectators were completely covered in red dust, rubbing their eyes and gasping for breath. Hats were blown off and carefully coiffed hair turned into rats' nests. Food was covered in thick, red Coober Pedy dirt, and drinks became muddy swirls.

A red current of fire that Eyre could no longer control travelled through her, and her hair stood on end as she and Ischyros began to ascend slowly, until they were more than ten metres in the air. Electricity sparked outwards from them in crackling streaks, and then she and the old horse zoomed around the course, so fast that the red dust coating them was blown off into the swirling slipstream of air. In a wild maelstrom of sand, they hurtled past the finish line for the second time.

Mouths were ajar as the spectators silently watched the unlikely pair fly around the track for the third time, faster even than the horse that had won. The jockeys on the ground below looked upwards in dumbfounded shock as Eyre brought Ischyros over the finish line with a telepathic shriek that made the whole stadium cover their ears.

Breathing hard, Eyre's rage was so out of control that she had to use every ounce of her conscious thought to curb the maniacal energy that filled her being. Finally, she started to calm down and she turned Ischyros around and brought him gently down to the parade ring by the stables. Every person, creature and surface in the entire race area was covered in a thick layer of red dust, except for Eyre and Ischyros, who shone brilliantly in their silver and purple silks.

Eyre walked her shaking horse slowly around the parade ring and then led him into the stables without a word.

CHAPTER FORTY-TWO

EYRE WAS BRUSHING ISCHYROS down when Beatrice and Abby came rushing down the corridor.

Abby burst into the stall and wrapped her arms around Ischyros's neck, and Beatrice hugged Eyre.

"Well done, both of you," Beatrice said softly.

Eyre wiped her eyes and returned to grooming Ischyros. "Well, the sooner we get away from here, the better. What a pack of mongrels. What's happening outside?"

Abby patted Ischyros's head as her blue eyes turned merry. "By the Light, Eyre. You said it would be a race to remember, and it certainly was!"

Beatrice laughed out loud. "You should see them out there! Blasting away with Viq air blowers, brushing the course, everyone tidying themselves up with Light energy. It's actually hilarious! You sure taught them a lesson!"

Eyre's eyes were troubled. "Do you think I gave myself away though? I couldn't help it."

A voice from beyond the stall answered.

"It will be explained somehow," the Kikkuli Master said. "Perhaps the Gothak, or a mali. Even a natural phenomenon—an extra-terrestrial cyclone from Incendium, escaping the Seam; that could be a possibility. I believe there are some Armatura here. In any case we will take care to cover it up."

He walked through the door and up to Ischyros. "How are you, my old friend?"

Ischyros didn't reply, and Eyre patted him on his neck.

"He was fantastic," she said in a defensive voice. "The bravest horse I've ever seen."

The Kikkuli Master looked at her. "You did well, Eyre. You showed courage too."

Eyre looked down at her feet. She really would have preferred to have missed the whole event, but at least it was over.

Abby's cornflower eyes were troubled. "Come on, let's go home. I don't want to stay any longer. Do you?"

"Certainly not interested," Eyre muttered.

"Well, I'll organise that shortly," the Kikkuli Master said. "I'll just find Whittaker Ray and we'll come up with an explanation for the windstorm—which blew you and Ischyros completely around the course—" he chuckled, "before we leave."

He walked away down the corridor, and then Eyre looked over the door as she heard the sound of running feet coming towards them.

Nick skidded to a halt in front of the stall. "BTL, Eyre, what a show! Well done! Everyone is finally clean again after your sand shower, but how funny was that?"

"Who won?" Beatrice asked him. It had been such a close race that the stewards had to check it out by hologram, and Beatrice and Abby had left the track before the decision was made.

"One of the Irish horses; then the horse from Japan was second, and the wild card came third."

Eyre smiled. She was happy that the American she'd met earlier, Payne, had made a good account of herself.

"Well, we're not sticking around for the festivities," Abby said as she kissed Nick lightly. "Do you want to come back with us? We're going in about half an hour."

"Sure," Nick replied. "I'm not keen on staying either—what a horrible bunch of people. He hesitated a moment, then added, "but I have something to do first. I should be able to make it back in time."

"We'll wait for you, don't worry. But what's going on?" Beatrice asked.

Looking at Abby, Nick answered slowly. "Well, you're not going to like this, but—er—my dad is apparently here. Jemima Periwinkle told me."

Eyre stopped brushing Ischyros and stood up straight. Abby breathed in deeply.

"He told her he has something to give me of my mother's," Nick finished lamely.

Eyre thought hard. Could that be why Nick's dad had been following him around Lightning Ridge, Bathurst and Coober Pedy? He wasn't permitted to come anywhere close on campus or to Highlight, so perhaps he was making use of the mining tunnels to try and make contact?

But then a hardness descended within her. She was getting used to the bad side of people and wasn't inclined to trust anyone nowadays, much less an Ex. Let alone the man who had given Nick so many of his scars.

"Well, if you're going to see him, I'm coming too," she said in a soft voice.

"Me too," Abby said.

"And me." Beatrice summoned her staff with a snap of her fingers. "I think I'll bring my friend, too."

Nick smiled ruefully. "You won't need that, Beatrice," he said. "I'm ready for anything. But if he is telling the truth, I really would like to have something from my mum. I haven't got anything that belonged to her."

Eyre put away the grooming brushes and produced some liquorice from the grooming pack.

"Here you go, my friend," she said and stroked Ischyros's head. "You did a fine job. We'll be back shortly and I'll get you home."

Ischyros again said nothing, but he chewed the liquorice, which lightened Eyre's heart somewhat.

"I'm meeting him down the end here—he's staying in a caravan behind the stadium, apparently," Nick said as they left the stable area and walked away from the arena. In the distance ahead Eyre could see a form that she recognised, despite having only seen him a couple of times before. It was if the aura of menace that surrounded him was a tangible thing. Nick hugged Abby and then led the way towards his father.

He walked confidently, but Eyre could see his anxiety in the way Nick clenched his fists, and the sweat that gathered on his brow.

And she could see the ferocious look on Abby's face. If Abby was ever to perform Occido, this might be the moment.

Nick's dad smiled at them as they neared, an expression his mean mouth seemed unused to. "Nick, I see you've brought your entourage. Hello everyone."

"What do you have for Nick," Beatrice said, holding her staff firmly.

"Why, his Lightkeeper," Nick's dad said. "I've had it since his mum passed and I thought it was time to give it to Nick. It's no use to an Ex." He shrugged apologetically as he said it, but to Eyre's sharp eyes the gesture seemed totally insincere.

"It's in my caravan for safe keeping. Come with me and I'll hand it over." His eyes studied Nick's resolute face with a crafty look. "Then, you don't have to ever see me again."

Eyre looked around her. Something was not right about this, and her senses were on high alert. But the hopeful expression on Nick's face as he followed his father was enough for her to fall in line too. She had to help her friend. Eyre could see that Beatrice and Abby were just as uneasy, and their eyes were roving the area, ready for trouble.

An uproar in the distance grew louder as they approached an unkempt group of men, circled around what looked to be a fence. A deafening shouting and cheering filled the air, along with loud swearing and the ominous roar of ferocious growling and shrieking. As they got closer, Eyre realised that the fence surrounded a deep hole dug into the red dirt. And in the pit a horrible battle was going on.

Two Devil Wolves, the huge red creatures that Eyre had first seen a year ago in Dr Botolfe's lecture, were fighting to the death in the pit as the rabble cheered them on. The snarling and snapping were appalling, and the sight of the wounded creatures dripping with blood sickened Eyre. Money was exchanging hands as the audience chugged back huge jugs of beer and screamed encouragement.

Nick's dad was watching the fight with a light in his eyes. "I've got a bet on the big'un," he said. Nick's face registered disgust and he turned away.

"I don't have long," he said. "Let's just get the Lightkeeper and I'll leave you to it."

Just then, Eyre looked across the pit and saw Ben Perrill and Carrison Hamlen watching her from the other side, sneering. And with a horrible shock, she saw Professor Vela walking away from the two boys. He had an ugly look on his face, and, as if she'd been hit with a lightning bolt, Eyre suddenly realised that she'd been right about him all along. Why else would he be in this repulsive place, surrounded by what she now realised were Lightworker Exes. A repulsive, dirty rat pack, evil inside and filthy outside. Dread rose within her as she realised that she and her friends were in terrible danger.

But Nick had already arrived at the caravan door and Eyre could see him reaching to take something from his father. Her stomach lurched when she saw Professor Vela moving towards the caravan from behind the crowd.

But then there was sudden chaos as two mighty Armatura strode into sight from behind the racing arena. Their faces were as ferocious as anything Eyre had ever seen, and they raised their mighty weapons as they headed towards the sunken hole in the ground. They tossed several of the Exes into the air before jumping down into the fighting pit. The crowd drew back as the Armatura turned around back-to-back in the centre of the arena and silently dared anyone to intervene. Then, kneeling down, they cradled the terribly wounded Devil Wolves in their arms and with a flash, disappeared.

Beatrice and Abby were still standing in shocked relief, after watching the grisly scene in the pit and Eyre grabbed them urgently. "Quickly, quickly! Nick's in danger!"

The tone of her voice seemed to break their trance, and they snapped around to follow her. But Professor Vela got there first. Eyre, Beatrice and Abby reached the caravan just as Ben and Carrison arrived behind Professor Vela.

The two groups stared hard at each other and then Professor Vela summoned his staff. Something was awry there, but Eyre was too focused on his words to think further on what was bothering her.

"So, you're the Aether," Professor Vela sneered. "It's taken us a while to sort it out, but here we are."

Eyre opened her mouth, and then shut it in shock as she realised that Professor Vela was talking to *Nick*, not her.

"Say goodbye, Nick," the Professor whispered and raised his staff. His first blast was deflected by a searing flame from behind him, and he turned angrily. Beatrice stood furiously with her staff aimed at him.

"Get – *away* – from – him!" she said in a low voice.

Before she could move, however, Carrison had sent a beam of Viq and knocked Beatrice's staff out of her hand.

"Easy," he snickered, a derisive look on his face.

Eyre could tell that Nick would die if she waited even one more second, so she raced towards Professor Vela.

"*I* am the Aether, not Nick!" she screamed, and Professor Vela turned, shock running across his face. Eyre stood her ground, ready for anything, when a jag of lightning hit the ground in front of Professor Vela, and a swift form darted past Eyre, a Mnae in hand.

Her jaw dropped as Jax stood in front of Professor Vela, his sword raised. A Mnae? Eyre thought, bewildered. They weren't supposed to have one yet! Her mind was muddled as Professor Vela summoned his own sword and lifted it up.

"I *thought* you were on to me," he whispered, and then charged at Jax. Their swords met with an ear-splitting clang and they began the most serious Ferito fight Eyre had ever seen outside of the Nationals. A fight that could only have one outcome. Her bewildered thoughts were interrupted as the crowd of Exes surrounded them. But rather than attacking the Lightworkers, money started changing hands—this was evidently a much better fight to bet on than the Devil Wolves. Suddenly, Carrison leapt towards Nick, who summoned his Antaraks with a flick of his wrist. A high-pitched ringing filled the air as their crystal blades smashed together.

"Get out of here and call Whittaker Ray," Eyre called desperately to Abby with her mind, and Abby sprinted off. Beatrice raced away too, blasting with her staff at anyone that tried to reach for the girls. They fought their way through the crowd and out the other side, to a safe distance. As Abby dropped her head to concentrate, Beatrice stood guard and scorched the ground when anyone approached.

Suddenly a familiar, menacing form stepped before Eyre.

"Finally, we get our chance, Airhead," Ben Perrill said, and summoned his staff.

"My pleasure, Perrill," Eyre spat, and her own staff smacked into her hand. "Bring it on!"

The crowd around them roared at the violent battles, the noise interspersed with the clash of weapons and thump of feet on the ground as the combatants moved and somersaulted, trying desperately to improve their Aditus positions.

Nick and Carrison were fighting furiously behind Ben Perrill, equally matched despite their difference in size. Money was passed from hand to hand and more beer tossed down throats as the spectators goaded the fighters on.

And then, a strange silence fell. Confused, Ben stopped fighting, so Eyre did too. Nick and Carrison followed suit, not sure what was happening.

Jax had Professor Vela on the ground, his Mnae at the Professor's throat.

"Reveal yourself," Jax whispered. "Or you'll regret it."

The crowd watched with an anticipation that was palpable. No one knew what was going on, but the Exes were relishing the prospect of bloodshed. And then, the form on the ground began to writhe and move. The face bulged and changed and the arms grew longer. When the final metamorphosis was done, Eyre's mouth hung open. Jemima Periwinkle, her face no longer simpering and vacuous, was glaring furiously up at Jax.

"Do it!" she screamed. "You slimy liar. I should have known you weren't interested in my classes. Sneaking around, following me. Go on, finish the job!"

But her words were just a ruse to give her time, because before Jax could move, Jemima Periwinkle, the ridiculous lecturer who had always resembled nothing more than a cream puff, disappeared in a flash of light. Jax disappeared in a burst of light after her. *Jax could teleport?* Eyre looked at Nick in disbelief, and in the distraction Carrison punched Nick in the face and knocked him out. At the same time, Ben bashed Eyre's staff from her hand and it rolled on the ground behind him. Quick as a flash, Eyre summoned her Antaraks and twirled them in the light.

"Come on," she said softly, and Ben's jaw jutted.

"Kill her!" a woman with long, matted grey hair screeched as she pushed to the front of the crowd. "*KILL* her, my son!"

"Mum?" Ben's face was astonished.

"Get rid of the Aether!" the woman spat. As Eyre waited, nerves on edge for him to move, a huge internal battle seemed to be going on inside Ben's mind. Indecision suddenly coloured his face and as Eyre watched his torturous struggle, she dropped the ends of her Antaraks slowly downwards. It was obvious that Ben was not going to fight her anymore. He began to mutter in strange tongues, and held his head as he talked to something that no one else could see. The Exes started to jeer as Abby and Beatrice dashed into the clearing.

"Kill her, kill them," they chanted. "Fight, fight, FIGHT!" Carrison Hamlen picked up Eyre's staff from behind Ben and an awful smile crossed his face.

"Well, I'm happy to dispatch you with your own weapon," he said softly, sneering. He began to raise Eyre's staff.

And then, with the snap of her fingers, Ben's witch-like mother sparked a fire that surrounded Ben and Eyre in a circle of leaping flames.

"You *coward* Ben!" the woman screamed as the flames scorched the earth. "No wonder I left you behind! You never were any good. You can die together!" The heat from the inferno burned like the inside of hell itself, and Eyre could feel her face blistering from the lick of the flames.

At that moment Carrison aimed Eyre's staff and a burst of energy travelled up the rainbow branch. But the lop-sided crystal at the top of the staff sent the ray of light whirling off at an angle, and it blasted into Ben's mother. She disappeared in a violent explosion, screeching.

Carrison looked shocked, and threw the staff down. As Beatrice and Abby raced towards him, Carrison disappeared.

The flames surrounding Eyre and Ben were so strong that Eyre was powerless to control them. She could see her friends struggling to help, but no amount of her Viq, or focusing her concentration could lessen the blaze. Ben was completely unaware of anything, lost in the mad prison of his mind. But as Eyre's head almost exploded from the effort, she managed to make a small gap in the conflagration that surrounded them, and she pushed Ben through it and out to safety. Before she could follow him, the opening closed and she was unable to break through the wall of flame again. As the towering blaze moved closer, she shut her eyes, resigning herself to the inevitable. Her skin was sizzling and peeling and she cried out in agony as the flames reached towards her.

But then, something charged through the burning firestorm. Ischyros, neighing and stomping, skidded up to Eyre's side. She somehow managed to climb on his back, and was only vaguely aware of the flames engulfing her as they stampeded back through the inferno.

CHAPTER FORTY-THREE

EYRE SWIRLED THROUGH AN agony unlike any she'd experienced before. Her whole body was on fire, melting. A cool hand wiped her brow and blackness overcame her again.

Vague memories surfaced. Pain, more pain. Comforting hands. Blackness. A blur of searing torture and nightmares. A haunting, airy melody. Immobility. Complete silence. Confusion. Kind voices from afar. And a disembodied blankness.

Eyre opened her eyes and struggled not to panic. She couldn't see! Was she blind? Apart from the disjointed, surreal images that flickered through her mind, the last real thing she could remember was Ischyros charging through the raging fire. Perhaps her eyes had been burnt? She had to stop herself from screaming, breathing deeply to get herself under control.

She struggled to sit up but found that she couldn't. Her hands moved through a warm, gel-like substance that held her suspended in place. She could only flail her legs around uselessly—with nothing to push off, she was immobile. Then she tried to shout, but only the echo of her own voice blasted her ears.

Slowly, with great effort, she pulled her arm through the sticky goo and touched her face, to find that she was wearing some sort of mask. Where was she? She suddenly felt claustrophobia grab hold of her mind and she thrashed around in the thick substance, shouting for help.

Then a hand touched her shoulder, and an instant peace filled her mind. Fear and confusion were gone with the gentle touch. She felt herself being drawn upwards and lifted out of the gel into the air. Soft hands placed her lightly on a comfortable bed.

"Keep your eyes closed," a melodious voice murmured. "All will be well."

Filled with a sense of well-being, Eyre didn't struggle, and lay there as the hands took something from her face. Another dressing was lifted from across her eyes, and even with her eyes shut she could sense light filtering in. She wasn't blind!

"Rest for a few moments, and then open your eyes slowly to get used to the light," the voice told her, and Eyre did as she was instructed. She felt tranquil, and she registered the soft tones of a mellow wind instrument in the background. It sounded familiar, and then she realised it was a tortilis— the instrument that Abby was learning. The poignant melody echoed through the room and a peace filled Eyre's body. After the violence of her last memories, she was quite happy to lie in this serenity.

A few moments passed before she opened her eyes and gasped. Before her stood a very tall, long-limbed creature with extremely pale skin and very large, slanted black eyes. It had a small nose and small mouth, and moved towards her gracefully.

As the creature looked down at her with shining eyes, Eyre spluttered, "Are, are you, an—alien?"

The creature smiled and took one of Eyre's hands. Once again, she was overcome with a feeling of goodwill and peace.

"No, my dear, I am a Clementis," the being said. "Are you able to sit up?"

Reluctantly, because she would have been very happy to remain lying on the cosy bed, Eyre eased herself up to a sitting position.

She realised that she was lying on what seemed to be a hospital bed, in a room that resembled a hospital ward. Except that the walls were moving; they were soft and billowy, as if made of clouds. And she could see straight through the floor to the atmosphere below. Suspended in the air a metre from the ground was a huge Bullio bubble, filled with what looked like golden syrup. The tortilis continued to fill the room with beautiful melodies, but whoever was playing it was out of sight.

The Clementis noticed Eyre gaping at the floor and the endless space below it. "Sheets of quartz," it explained.

Eyre's eyes widened. "Where am I?" she asked.

"You are in Caelus, on Medela Island," the Clementis replied, and then added, "you've been here for two months."

"*Two months?*" Eyre gasped. "I need to be getting back then! We have to warn Whittaker—" The Clementis motioned for silence.

"Mr Ray is well aware of the situation. Your friends were able to give him very helpful information. What you need to do is rest and recover. You've been through a terrible ordeal."

Eyre looked down at her arms and wiped at the sticky golden substance that covered her body. In a small voice, not really wanting to hear the answer, she said, "Ischyros?"

"He survived," the Clementis said as it walked to a nearby basin and brought it over. "Although he was very badly burnt. He will need to stay two more months to heal."

Tears slid down Eyre's cheeks. He was alive! Her brave, crabby old warhorse. She knew her heart would have broken if he hadn't made it.

"Bless the Light," she whispered.

The Clementis sat down by the bed, then took a sponge from the basin and started to wipe Eyre's arms and legs with warm water to remove the sticky gel that covered her.

"What *is* that?" Eyre asked, rubbing awkwardly at the golden substance. The Clementis rinsed the cloth in the bowl and continued. The warm water felt wonderful and soothing.

"This is Royal Jelly; it has remarkable healing properties for all injuries, but especially for burns. It comes from the Tub-Bee hives, which are found in Terra. The Tub-Bee is a bee-like creature very much like your bumble bees in Entis, but the size of a sheep. A very beautiful creature, and very precious to all the beings of the Overworld."

Eyre's mind was working slowly, but she remembered back to her time in Terra, when she had seen a huge purple and yellow striped bee drinking nectar from a flower. No doubt that was the Tub-Bee the Clementis was referring to. It had looked quite a portly, slightly ridiculous creature, really, rather than something prized by the whole Overworld.

The Clementis continued, interrupting Eyre's thoughts. "Royal Jelly has saved many lives. You have been suspended in Royal Jelly for two months, to heal your deep burns. That was no ordinary fire. A mali generated the firestorm you endured, and you were very close to death."

Eyre felt her hair, which was only marginally shorter than it had been before the horse race. And her skin seemed pretty much the same. The Clementis smiled, understanding her confusion. "Our healing methods have been developed over thousands of years. We are glad we could help you.

"Whittaker Ray, Madame Overmantle, the Ranger and many other staff have been to visit you. You are very much loved, Eyre."

Eyre wiped her eyes. "So, I can go home now?"

"Yes, you can. The Clementis nodded. "You will spend a few days at the Infirmary on campus, and then you should be able to resume your studies. You will have to go carefully, though, as you still need to regain your energy." Then the Clementis looked slightly perplexed.

"Really, we expected you to be staying here as long as Ischyros, but you seem to have healed much quicker than anticipated, even with our techniques. It seems there are many things we do not know about you, Eyre."

Eyre looked anxiously at the serene creature. "Will Ischyros come home too?"

"When he has healed enough to leave the suspension, yes. We will send him back to the Kikkuli Master."

Eyre's eyes brimmed again. "Thank you," she whispered. "Thank you so much."

The kind, dark eyes looked at her. "Mr Ray will be coming to take you back shortly. I was to let him know as soon as you awoke. They are very keen to have you back."

Eyre was very keen to *go* back, although she had no sense of time having passed at all. It was as if she'd been to the Lightness Cup yesterday; she had no awareness of her time here, other than a few disjointed, nightmarish memories.

The Clementis stood and picked up the basin and walked away.

"Sleep, my dear. When you wake you will be back at the Academy."

And as if the voice had hypnotised her, an incredible lassitude overwhelmed Eyre and she fell instantly into a deep sleep.

CHAPTER FORTY-FOUR

"WELCOME BACK," THE CHEERY voice said. Sister Murphy bustled in the door with a tray of food and helped Eyre to sit up.

"What time is it?" Eyre croaked. She felt as if she had been asleep for days.

"It's breakfast, my girl. And *you* need to eat up. We want you back on your feet as soon as possible!" The Sister fluffed Eyre's pillows and made her comfortable, and then left in a hurry. No doubt, other patients to be seen to.

Eyre looked at her breakfast and her stomach rumbled. She was starving and she wondered if she'd had anything to eat during the last two months. Probably only Royal Jelly. She gagged at the thought and started to hoover the food from the tray into her mouth.

A knock at the door interrupted her and she looked over, with cheeks filled like a chipmunk. Beatrice and Abby rushed in and hugged her tight, one on each side of the bed.

"We thought you'd died, Eyre," Abby whispered.

"Your name is now legend," Beatrice said, mock-seriously. "Although I'm not sure about your table manners."

Eyre snorted and tried not to spray food everywhere. She swallowed hard. Her wonderful friends!

Someone else walked in the door. Nick, his face uncertain, joined them. He sat on the end of the bed tentatively.

"I'm so glad you made it," he said. "And I'm so sorry about my father—"

Eyre interrupted him sternly. "Did you get your Lightkeeper?"

Nick looked nonplussed. "Er, yes? But it's back at the cabin now."

"Well then, it was worth the trip! All the more valuable! Don't you dare apologise, Nick. None of that was your fault. And I want to see it as soon as possible!"

A silence fell for a moment and then Eyre took another mouthful. "I am actually happy about all that, because *finally*, the mystery of Professor Vela is explained."

Beatrice's eyes were incredulous. "Apparently he *is* one of the good guys."

Nick shook his head. "*Not* one of the good guys," he said darkly, "but not working with the Gothak."

"Yes, Jemima Periwinkle can do therianthropy!" Beatrice exclaimed. "Even the Sergeant didn't know that."

Eyre hadn't had much time to think things through since she'd woken up, and her thoughts tumbled around.

"So—in the Transit cave at Highlight, that was Jemima Periwinkle I saw with your dad," she looked apologetically at Abby, "in the form of Professor Vela?"

Beatrice nodded. "Yes. And they think it was probably her who put the Violite on the Mantle Basin."

Abby's eyes were huge. "She summoned the Sublabor centipede at the pool last year."

Eyre tossed this around in her mind. So, Jemima Periwinkle hadn't run away because she was a coward, she had left because she wanted students to be killed. And taking the credit for killing the beast was just a smokescreen to hide the truth.

"And Jemima Periwinkle put the Stibnite in the staff meals," Abby said indignantly.

Thinking hard, Eyre thought of something else. Last year she thought she'd heard Mentor Xiphias call Jemima Periwinkle 'two-faced' in his Thalassa language. Eyre hadn't been at the Unlit for long, and had struggled with the translation, but she did realise that he'd obviously picked up something amiss about the lecturer. Now she knew what he had really meant; Jemima Periwinkle was not two-faced at all, she thought furiously, *multi*-faced would be far more accurate.

Eyre's head was swimming with all this information. So much was beginning to make sense now.

"Wow," she said. Everyone nodded. Then Eyre said wryly, "Well, at least the whole Lightness Cup humiliation will be long past when I get back to campus!"

Abby started giggling, "That s-s-sandstorm," Abby choked, "was brilliant! Microdermabrasion for everyone!" That set them all off, and they spluttered with laughter at the memory.

Finally they stopped, and Beatrice and Abby wiped tears of mirth from their faces. They all looked at one another. It had been so strange, and horrible.

After a moment, Beatrice put her hand on Eyre's arm and brought up the one thing Eyre didn't want to discuss.

"Ischyros," Beatrice said, looking apologetically at Abby, who semaphored with her eyebrows to *STOP!* Obviously, they'd already had this discussion. But Beatrice needed to say what they felt. "Many of the Academy students agree with us. They are furious that the crowd was so *vile* to him! And he was so brave. He was burnt black, you know. He looked like a demon horse from hell coming out of the fire with you on his back. We didn't want to ask you; Abby said we shouldn't. But is he going to be okay?" she asked. "Mr Ray said he was being treated with you by the Clementis."

Eyre had been trying to avoid the memory; she was devastated beyond comprehension at the thought of her courageous old Lighthorse and what he had endured. To think too long on it made her feel like she might explode like a nuclear bomb. Beyond control, beyond logic.

"I was told that he'll be there for a couple more months," she said carefully. "But then he's coming back." She was distraught as she said it. She really wanted to see the old fellow and give him a hug, *now*. Two months seemed such a long time and she was desperately worried that he might not come back, ever. It was such a horrific thought. But her face was impassive. Those responsible would experience her wrath; she would make sure of it.

A knock at the door made them all jump. Sergeant Tottingham stood in the doorway.

"May I come in?" she asked.

"We were about to go, Sergeant," Beatrice said. Eyre realised that Beatrice felt it was a diplomatic time to leave.

"Sister Murphy said we couldn't stay long." Beatrice said as an explanation as they walked away from the bed. "See you soon, Eyre."

Abby and Nick waved and followed Beatrice out of the room.

"Hi Sergeant Tottingham," Eyre said. "It's good to see you."

The Sergeant strode into the room and sat in the chair under the window, her large form filling the chair. Her face was troubled as she spoke. "I wanted to apologise for my sister," she said slowly. "I had no idea she could do therianthropy, it's such an extraordinary skill, and growing up, she never revealed it to anyone. Although," she added reluctantly, this private woman obviously finding it hard to reveal anything personal, "there were many times I got in trouble for things I swore I didn't do. It makes sense now—I guess she was practising using me."

Eyre had to chuckle. "What did 'you' do back then, Sergeant?"

"Well, apparently, I burnt down the science lab, I blew up the Refectory and I smashed our family's priceless objects." She gave a humourless laugh.

"I always felt something was wrong. But I never thought she had this amount of darkness within her. I am sorry you were at the receiving end of it."

Eyre was silent for a moment. She understood the confusion—she'd had so much of it herself over the past two years. Unfortunately, people sometimes were not as they seemed.

"These times are troubled," Eyre said softly. "No one can see their way clearly. You are not to blame—no one knew about your sister. She was very careful to hide it, and obviously very clever with her cover up. Do you know where she is?"

The Sergeant shook her head. "She's disappeared. As has Carrison Hamlen."

Eyre waited for a moment and then her jaw dropped. "Ben Perrill's not back, surely?"

The Sergeant rubbed her brow. "I can't stay too long, and I know Whittaker Ray wants to see you when you feel a bit better. He will talk to you about Ben."

Sergeant Tottingham stood and patted Eyre gently on the shoulder. "Your parents would be proud of you, Eyre," she said. "You walk with the utmost Lightness."

She left the room and Eyre lay back on the pillow.

Despite the Sergeant's kind words, her thoughts were furious. Ben Perrill was back on campus? She knew that allowances had been made out of respect for his father, but surely this was way too much of a reprieve? What would *ever* be enough to get him expelled? Or preferably, *terminated?* Her thoughts were roiling as yet another knock came at the door.

Sister Murphy led someone in. "This is the last one," she said. "It's been like a thoroughfare this morning! You have ten minutes," she added sternly to Eyre's visitor.

Jax stepped from behind the Sister and stood before Eyre, a small smile on his face. He held a bouquet of flowers that he'd obviously gathered from the school garden and tied with a bow of light.

"How are you, Eyre with the red hair?" he asked softly, handing her the flowers.

Eyre's eyes brimmed. She was so glad to see him! "Thanks for helping us," she said. "I'm sorry I ever doubted you."

And then Jax strode forward and gathered her in a gentle embrace. "I thought I'd lost you," he whispered, his voice hitching on the last word. He turned her face to him and put his lips softly on hers. "Life would not be worth living without you," he added softly.

And then Eyre kissed him harder, desperately, her arms around him. Whoever this enigmatic boy was, she knew she wanted him in her life forever. She felt like she was twirling in a helix of light until they pulled away from each other.

Jax took her hands, his fathomless green eyes looking into hers. "By the Light, you're breathtaking, my warrior girl. And you're back."

After a long silence, Eyre thought again about the recent events. "You were following Jemima Periwinkle."

Jax nodded. "The Sergeant had told Whittaker Ray and Professor Vela that she was worried about her sister, and Whittaker Ray thought it would be easier for a student to follow Jemima Periwinkle than one of the staff. A bit less obvious."

Eyre thought back and then stifled her laughter. "Oh, how funny—the extra training with Jemima Periwinkle and the—uh—'*solid*' genealogy lessons?"

Jax strode around importantly and repeated the words he'd said last year at the Refectory, "Oh yes, '*I feel the next Strigis I encounter is definitely going to come off second-best!*'"

Eyre and Jax looked at each other and burst into laughter. "We thought you were going mad," Eyre choked, wiping away her tears.

"Yes, well, she was crafty, I have to say," Jax said. "But after Bathurst I suspected she was up to no good. I saw her appear, but then I lost her. I was supposed to keep an eye on her, and she definitely was acting very strange. That's why I told you to look out for Professor Vela."

Eyre looked confused. "You said that 'things weren't as they seemed'. Did you know she was impersonating him?"

Jax looked rueful. "No, I actually meant—" he laughed awkwardly, "—that you should go to Vela if you needed help. He was part of the team I was working with to try and find out where the leak was coming from on campus. And he was also looking out for Nick at the beginning of the year, when it was obvious something was wrong. That's why Vela wanted Nick to join the Jenolan Caves trip, so he could keep an eye on him."

Eyre's eyes were round. One of the *team*? *That* was a stretch. She simply could not view Professor Vela as anything other than a toad. She shook her head as if to clear it. After a moment she rolled her eyes. "Well, have they located Ms Periwinkle yet?"

Jax shook his head. "Nope, I couldn't catch her. She's disappeared. And Carrison."

"But not Perrill," Eyre said in a hard voice. "Why is *he* still here?"

Jax looked as confused as she did, but he shrugged. "I guess they have reasons. Maybe they want him where they can watch him. I *can* tell you that you don't need to worry about him. My new 'detail' is keeping you safe. Which means I need to keep you near." His eyes darkened, and Eyre shivered. Jax Jackson was a force of his own.

"You had a Mnae at the Lightness Cup," she said, a question rather than a statement. "And you can *teleport.*"

Jax looked rueful. "I've had extra training in the past year with the Mimir, to help me with my intelligence work. I needed to be able to teleport to follow Jemima Periwinkle. They gave me a Mnae then, and I've trained in Mimir's Domain for months. That's how I knew about the tunnel system down there. And when I saw you lot heading off into it, I knew you wouldn't get out again unless I came with you."

"And UDı? He was looking for you at the beginning of the year. What was that about?"

Jax's eyes were serious. He hesitated, but them said, "He's helping me with my intelligence and espionage training. The Unlit are the masters of those skills."

Eyre's sapphire eyes registered understanding, finally. "So, your disappearances were because you were *spying?*"

Jax shrugged. "Guilty as charged. But I couldn't tell you. I had my instructions, and they were to not speak of it with anyone."

Eyre settled back against the pillows, her thoughts swirling. So much information all at once, but she suddenly realised that it was making her feel better. So many mysteries had been explained, and she felt relieved. But she also felt exhausted, and Jax realised.

"I'll leave you to rest," he whispered, and leant over to kiss her on the lips. "See you soon."

CHAPTER FORTY-FIVE

EYRE WAS ALLOWED OUT of the Infirmary after a couple of days. Her friends had been to see her each day, and some of the other students had also popped in to visit.

"By the Light, Eyre," Zanda said in a mock-exasperated tone, "if you keep up all this drama the Spotlight is going to have to be a newspaper of its own, rather than a segment! I've got writer's cramp trying to keep up with your exploits!"

Colton visited and praised her riding skills at the Cup, and Christopher and Tina also appeared in front of her one day. They brought Florence for a visit and until the Venator shrieked loudly, bringing Sister Murphy running and evicting the three of them forthwith, it had been wonderful for Eyre to stroke her beautiful raptor's three-eyed head.

Day by day Eyre felt better, her healing powers as strong as ever, it seemed. So, by the third day she was able to get out of bed. It felt strange to stand upright, and her head swirled for a moment. But then it cleared and she dressed quickly. She wanted nothing more than to get back to classes and start training again. The burning desire to fight that always simmered within her had ignited with a strange, intense force. Her mind was focused on one thing: bringing the Gothak down.

Sister Murphy arrived just as she finished getting dressed. "Now you take it easy this week, Eyre. Don't go overdoing things. You've been through a huge ordeal and we don't want you to relapse."

Eyre nodded obediently, thinking, I'll do nothing of the sort, when Sister Murphy added, "Oh, and Whittaker Ray would like to see you in his office this morning."

Eyre walked outside, blinking in the wan sunlight. Her eyes were sensitive, and she noticed that her arms were browner than they'd been before. Toasted, she supposed wryly. But it was wonderful to be outside again, with the sharp bite in the air and the trees swaying in the frosty winds. In the distance the mountains had a dusting of snow on them, which gave her a sense of how much time had passed. Winter was almost over. A currawong gave a mournful cry as it winged over her head, and the crystal shards of the Central Admin building caught the pale sunlight and sent it glinting in all directions. Eyre felt her heart swell. She was so glad to be back!

She started to jog towards the Admin building, but had to stop after only a few paces. Her lungs were on fire from the cold air and her legs felt very weak. She was going to have to build her fitness up again after so long lying down. And then an unpleasant voice came from behind her.

"Out of breath, Lightward?"

Eyre turned to see Ben Perrill, surrounded by the Curtis twins, Wyatt and Tec all smirking at her.

"Heard you took a rocking horse to the Cup," Slade sneered, and Ben guffawed while the rest sniggered. But before she could reply, with a loud 'plop', they were covered from head to foot in slimy duckweed from the Ponds of Doombee.

Jax strolled into view. "You keep going, Eyre," he called, "I'll clean up this mess."

Judging by the sounds she heard as she kept going, he was handling the problem quite well. And it looked like he'd taken his mission to heart; she now had a bodyguard.

But by the time she got to Whittaker Ray's office on the 7th floor of the Admin building, she was seething. Would she *never* be rid of the loathsome Ben Perrill? She should have left him in the fire.

She knocked on Whittaker Ray's door and was told to come in. He was sitting behind his desk concentrating on something before him, but when he saw her enter, he indicated she should sit on the comfortable lounge chair by the wall. After a moment, he joined her, sitting in the chair facing hers. There was a knock on the door and a Jotnar entered, carrying a tray with tea and biscuits on it. The crabby-faced creature put the tray on the marble coffee table between them, bowed and left.

Whittaker Ray poured the tea as Eyre traced the pattern on the fabric of the chair she sat on. It was decorated with gold thread in the shape of an Inguz, with a deep blue satin background.

"That fabric is woven on looms in Terra," Whittaker Ray said. The best yarn is spun in Terra, and they have quite a textile industry going on. It's beautiful, isn't it?"

Eyre nodded, but her thoughts weren't really on the fabric.

"Why is Ben Perrill still here?" she asked bluntly. "He and Carrison Hamlen were trying to kill us. But even *they* were way behind *Jemima Periwinkle!*"

Whittaker Ray looked regretful and took a sip of his tea. "That is why I wanted to talk to you, Eyre," he said. "You've been through a trial by fire—literally—and you deserve an explanation. The events of the past two months have been a shock to everyone.

"It was extremely brave of you to save Ben that day. Ben is still here because he told us that he didn't realise what was happening at the Exes camp. He had gone with Carrison, but didn't understand the true nature of the situation. He has apologised profusely, and indeed, he didn't run off when he could have. He could have gone with Carrison."

Eyre remembered her fierce battle with Ben, and an angry flush appeared in her cheeks. But then she also remembered Ben's hesitation when his mother had urged him to kill her. He hadn't even tried, so perhaps the events *had* been a surprise to him. A revolting toad he might be, but maybe he wasn't working with the Gothak. She had to swallow hard to contemplate that possibility. But despite that strange situation, the most pressing memories she had involved her violent history with the troubled, and malicious student. She could never forget what he'd done to her. "Well, what about the mali in him?" she asked, shaking her head.

"I have Jax watching you," Whittaker Ray continued, "and he will keep you safe."

A blush of another kind rose to Eyre's cheeks, and she was suddenly unable to find her voice, so she took a sip of tea and waited.

"I wanted to apologise to you—" (more apologies, thought Eyre. She'd never had so many!) "—for not taking more notice when you said you'd seen Professor Vela at the Transit. Although I knew it was impossible, I should have given your words more credence. There have been very few people in the history of the world with the ability to use therianthropy to impersonate another Lightworker, so it never crossed my mind. But I should have known you were certain of what you'd seen." He shook his head regretfully. "It would have avoided so much chaos if I had listened to you."

Eyre shrugged. "I couldn't figure it out either, sir. Professor Vela doesn't seem to like students very much, so it wasn't a big leap to imagine he was working for the Dark side."

Whittaker Ray laughed lightly. "He is not the most affable person, I agree. And as a lecturer, perhaps not as well liked as others." Eyre's eyebrows rose at the understatement, but then a memory struck her from the day of the Cup. When she'd seen Professor Vela, something had seemed wrong, and she suddenly realised what it was. His staff! Professor Vela had an ebony staff with an obsidian crystal at the top. When he had summoned his staff by the Devil Wolves' pit, the staff was made from a light-coloured wood, with a crystal of blue apatite, the stone of deception. The only staff with an apatite crystal that Eyre had ever seen belonged to Jemima Periwinkle. But at the time she was too confused by what was going on to register that. She thought wryly that the Crystal Grotto had understood Jemima Periwinkle well when it allocated the apatite crystal to her.

Another thought came to her. "But what about in the caves when Mudamir thanked Professor Vela for the heads-up? Did you hear about that?"

Whittaker Ray sighed. "Yes, I did—actually, from Professor Vela, who was completely confused himself, and feeling terrible about it in case he had inadvertently let something slip. But we know now—once again working against the Lightworkers, Jemima Periwinkle had alerted the Gothak to the trip to the caves before you left. But she was always careful to stay in disguise as Professor Vela; it was too important that her true identity remained completely unknown, and his was the guise she constantly used. As you said yourself, he is not popular, and it was an easy camouflage for her."

Whittaker Ray continued. "It may not be obvious to you, and indeed, to any of the students, but Professor Vela really is completely devoted to the Lightworking cause. So when we knew something was going awry with Nick, Professor Vela was asked to watch over him."

Eyre shook her head slowly. Jax had mentioned this, but the confirmation made her head reel. She realised she hadn't really believed it.

Whittaker Ray continued. "I know how you feel about Professor Vela," he said. "But I can assure you that he was actually looking out for Nick. We all knew that Nick was gravely—potentially *mortally*—impacted by whatever was going on with him. But we didn't know what, or why, and we just couldn't work it out. Our mistake, and poor Nick had to bear the brunt of our ignorance. We felt he had the signs of a mali, but there was no evidence for us to be certain."

Eyre still couldn't believe what she was hearing, and had to clarify. "*What?* You left Nick potentially in the clutches of a mali? Surely *someone* could have figured it out, or at least tried to help him? And last year, when I heard you and Professor Vela talking about someone being a problem, you weren't referring to me *or* another student, were you? You were talking about Jemima Periwinkle! Why didn't you *do* something about her then?"

Whittaker Ray looked regretful. "The Sergeant had told us of her concerns about her sister's agenda, but there was nothing concrete she could find out. She didn't know about her sister's therianthropic ability. So, we asked Jax to take extra tuition from her, and to watch what she was up to. With good reason, as it turns out.

"It was Jemima, actually, who entered Ischyros in the Lightness Cup—an enquiry was held after the race. Carrison just put pressure on his father to take Ischyros as the wild card, although Oliver Hamlen was led to believe that Ischyros was a worthy contender. Mr Hamlen wanted to help the Academy out after the recent blows to our reputation."

Eyre gave a puzzled frown, and then looked down at the table with a guilty expression. Whittaker Ray gave a wry smile, understanding. "Ah yes, the concerns about the Ranger—who is still with us by the way, but in a different capacity.

"Well, the Ranger told me you watched the meeting about him, so you must have heard Melissa Hamlen's less than supportive letter about the Ranger's piloting skills, but Oliver Hamlen was not part of that. He and Melissa are divorced, and Oliver was an Academy student himself, years ago. So he was quite ready to believe that we had a world-class Lighthorse in our stable. In fact, I've since found out that Carrison secretly brought his father here to watch Colton train in the paddock last term, telling him that Nox was Ischyros. And indeed, Nox could well be in the Cup one day. He is a spectacular Lighthorse."

"So," Eyre was catching up, "Mr Hamlen is not working for the Gothak?"

"No," Whittaker Ray said. "I feel for him. He is very ashamed of his son, who he realises is very much like his own father, and his grandfather, who were not good men. And," Whittaker Ray looked at Eyre regretfully, "Oliver is also ashamed at how the race evolved. He felt very sorry for you and Ischyros, and for his part in how it happened."

"And Jemima Periwinkle just wanted to get us there so she could kill us all?"

Whittaker Ray nodded. "The Gothak thought that Nick was the Aether, but they also knew that something about your entire group was different, that you all had something to do with the Isars. However, they didn't know it's because the Aether can *see* the Isars. That might have affected how they behaved. But after Madame Overmantle's prophesy, they decided to take you all out, and orchestrated your entry to the Cup to get you and your friends there—in a vulnerable situation. Carrison made that happen."

Eyre sighed. Everything was *so* complicated. Even families were divided on either side of good and evil. But at least the facts were becoming less confused. Like a blurry telescope being brought into focus, she was beginning to see things more clearly. Although there was still so much more to decipher.

But Whittaker Ray wasn't quite finished. "We have also determined that it was Jemima Periwinkle, shape-shifted into a cockatoo, who pushed you under the water in the lake and stuck your feet to the ground when the Armatura were chasing you. She also knocked you off the Iridis. Even back then she was hanging around campus, working for the Dark side. The Gothak wanted all the Lightwards—your family—dead, and if it wasn't for the Ranger, you might be. After she targeted you, she turned her sights to the Determinant Dozen, and eavesdropped on many of our meetings." He sighed heavily and said softly, "That woman has caused so much upheaval and death over the years. We are well rid of her."

Eyre was silent for a moment as she finished her cup of tea. Then she put the crystal teacup on the table and stood up. "Thank you, sir," she said to Whittaker Ray. "I appreciate you explaining all this to me. It helps to understand. Unless there is anything else, I need to head to class—it's only two months until Caelus, and I have a lot to catch up on."

With that she determinedly strode out the door, heading for the Ferito Shed.

CHAPTER FORTY-SIX

THE NEXT FEW WEEKS passed quickly, but painfully. Eyre was so out of shape after her two-month recuperation that she found it extremely difficult to find her form in Ferito. She ran out of breath quickly and had to stop frequently.

"Your lungs have been damaged by the heat and smoke," the Sergeant said to her one morning. "You will improve, but you have to take it more slowly. You look like you singlehandedly want to take down the Underworld."

Eyre grimaced as she leaned over, her hands on her knees. She would if she could, but at the moment she would find it hard to take down a grasshopper.

But she persevered and gradually showed some improvement as the days went by. The Clasis came back to her, and she concentrated on learning the positions for Level 3, which the rest of the class had been learning for so many more months. The positions were more complex than last year's, and involved a longer sequence of movements. She practised over and over, slowly at first and then faster, until the sequences became more fluid.

Adding to the difficulty was training with actual weapons instead of the palum. The bravado that one had with a palum did not translate well when learning with real weapons, where a slight mistake could cause major injury. So, she went carefully, getting used to the weight and the movement of the Antaraks and Kulbeda, determined that she would master them by the time the TACI came around. As the Sergeant said, an inbuilt 'knowledge' came with being a Lightworker—the movements were instinctive to a certain degree. But most of the skill came only from hours of practise.

This morning Eyre was starting back at piloting lessons, her first since returning to campus, and she was really looking forward to it. But when she wandered over to the hangar, she was slightly taken aback to see Madame

Overmantle standing there, resplendent in emerald green silk, quite inappropriately dressed for rocketing around in a Zepp.

"Hello dear," the old woman said brightly. "I will be your flight instructor this semester."

Eyre's stomach dropped. Where was the Ranger? Apart from the fact that she thoroughly enjoyed his company, she was worried that something had happened to him while she'd been with the Clementis.

"The Ranger is well," Madame Overmantle reassured her, reading her thoughts. "But this semester he has been given a sabbatical to do some extra study."

"Will he be back?" Eyre asked. Her throat seemed constricted.

"Well, it's open-ended at this point, but at some stage, yes," Madame Overmantle replied.

Eyre was initially surprised, trying to make sense of this sudden news. But then a violent rage shot through her as a thunderbolt of suspicion sliced through her. *A leave of absence*? She knew better, after spying on the meeting of the school Board earlier this year. So, the Ranger had been suspended after all? How *could* they! And then she was struck by another thought—what if her upside-down piloting lessons had contributed to the situation? Her expression must have shown on her face, because Madame Overmantle patted her on the arm. "Don't worry Eyre, all is as it should be. Sometimes you need to throw a whale in the water if you want to catch a megalodon."

Eyre realised that Madame Overmantle must know she had seen the meeting, and her anger was mollified a little by the trust the old woman was putting in her. Eyre really shouldn't be privy to such things, and Madame Overmantle was letting her know that the Ranger wasn't being punished and it was just a political move on the school's part; essentially a tactical move on the chessboard. And Eyre had no doubt that whatever he was doing, it was important.

All the same, she seethed as she climbed in the Zepp. She hated that the Ranger would be seen to have behaved improperly, and that he was being reprimanded for it. How Ben Perrill would love it!

But she gritted her teeth and waited while Madame Overmantle settled in the co-pilot's seat. She wondered why Madame Overmantle had been assigned as her tutor—she was hardly known as the best pilot on campus.

"I suppose you are wondering why I've been assigned as your tutor," Madame Overmantle said mildly, and Eyre's cheeks flamed. The old woman had read her mind, word for word! She really needed to remember about Madame's psychic skills!

But Eyre presumed that this was how she would move around during her Caelus TACI, so she wanted to put in as many hours as she could. And as the lesson progressed, she realised that although Madame Overmantle wasn't great at actually piloting the vehicle, she was an excellent teacher and could explain very well how to shift smoothly from Terra mode, to Aqua mode, and to Caelus mode.

But like Madame Overmantle, Eyre found the understanding of a thing quite different from putting it into practise. So, as she crunched the gears and stalled the Zepp along the dusty tracks, twirled dizzyingly like a torpedo —unplanned, of course—through the dark waters of Lake Altum, and sped along in the air unintentionally upside-down, Madame Overmantle gasped with laughter.

"Oh, my dear," she chuckled, holding her heart. "I feel you are making a great start. But I do hope your prowess exceeds mine fairly soon! You pilot like a windblast has struck us!"

Eyre just grinned and tipped the Zepp back upright awkwardly as they ploughed into a cumulus cloud. She gave a small salute to the old woman as they bumped up and down in the erratic air currents. "I'll keep practising, Ma'am!"

But as she racked up the hours with Madame Overmantle, she realised that the old woman had something to teach Eyre that perhaps no one else could. Madame Overmantle had joked earlier in the year that she was a great pilot because her psychic skills enabled her to predict weather patterns. Well, Eyre gradually realised that this was actually the truth, not a joke at all; the old woman could see a change in air current, predict a change of temperature, or even sense a weather change long before it happened. Over the bi-weekly lessons, with Madame's tutelage Eyre was getting quite adept at reading the clouds and skies to choose the line that would be the smoothest, or catching the currents under the lake that would cause the least turbulence. She came to understand that piloting was not just about technical skill, it was also very important to interpret the conditions around you and pilot to those conditions. Eyre was very grateful to the busy lecturer for taking the time to help her learn these skills, which often only came with years of experience. And as a side benefit, Eyre was also improving at telepathy; after the first few lessons Madame Overmantle refused to speak out loud and conducted all the tuition psychically.

In between piloting lessons, meditation and Ferito training, Eyre trudged back and forth to her classes, trying to catch up with the work she was behind on. Fortunately, part of the time she'd been with the Clementis had been the semester break, so she wasn't as far as behind as she might have been if she'd left during the semester. But there was still a lot to do.

Eyre also spent some time at the Unlit Compound, practising her archery and working with Florence. She did this early in the morning before breakfast, the time she used to go and visit Ischyros, so that she could fit it into her schedule. The Unlit students were happy to see her return, and many complimented her on the Lightness Cup.

"You made 'em all sit up and take notice," Julia said with satisfaction.

"You should have shimmered the whole stadium," commented Thomas. "They'd have thought you'd won!"

The days were going by so quickly, and were so busy, that Eyre was surprised one morning when a second-year student came up to her table at the Refectory and told her that the Kikkuli Master wanted to see her.

"Well, you know it's not about Ischyros this time," Beatrice commented. Ischyros was still with the Clementis, so Eyre was curious too as she ran down the pathway towards the stables.

The Kikkuli Master stood in the middle of the arena and was signalling a dark brown thoroughbred mare through her paces around the perimeter, first walking, then trotting, then cantering. The mare was in beautiful condition, her coat shining and her long black mane flaring behind her. Eyre stopped to watch, waiting for the Kikkuli Master to finish his training session. She loved the way he interacted with the horses; it was like he spoke their language.

After a few minutes the Kikkuli Master asked the mare to stand, and he walked over to Eyre. "This is Eclipse," he said, looking at the mare.

"She is gorgeous," Eyre commented. "And very smart."

"That she is," the Kikkuli Master agreed. "She's also very sad."

Eyre looked at him enquiringly and he continued. "Her Lightworker was an Aether, and she was killed at Terra."

The bottom dropped out of Eyre's stomach and she looked over at the stunning horse. "Oh no," was all she could manage.

"Eclipse hasn't chosen another Lightworker yet, but she has agreed to go with you to Caelus. So you will need to practise working with her in the next month. You will need to ride and fly with her in Caelus to find the Isar, and you have to be ready for it."

Eyre's eyes opened wide. She was going to ride *this* amazing animal?

"Go and say hi to her," the Kikkuli Master said, a warmth in his eyes.

Feeling slightly disloyal to Ischyros, but elated that she was actually going to *ride* in Caelus, Eyre walked slowly over to the dark brown mare.

"Hello, you beautiful girl," she said softly. The Lighthorse looked at her, and with a shock Eyre realised that she could, indeed, see deep grief in those soft brown eyes.

"I am so sorry about your partner," Eyre whispered as she stroked the velvety nose. "That is a very terrible thing to happen to you. But thank you for helping me to get to Caelus."

Eclipse hesitated a moment and then nuzzled Eyre gently. She whickered softly.

The Kikkuli Master smiled. "She likes you. That is good. Why don't you take her out to the paddock and practise riding together? You are proficient enough to train on your own, so I'll leave you to it."

Eyre walked down the corridor with Eclipse and out to the paddock. Her heart clenched as she passed Ischyros's empty stall, but it helped that she knew he was coming back.

They went out into the crisp air and across the cool grass to the paddock, and Eyre unlatched the gate and led Eclipse in. Their breath was coming in frosty puffs; it was a cold day and Eyre was happy they would be moving soon.

She stroked the gentle mare on her neck and then swung up onto her back.

"Come on then, my beauty," she said. "Let's see what we can do together."

For an hour they walked, then trotted and finally cantered around the paddock. Eclipse had a smooth, even gait and Eyre had no difficulty riding her. It was like flying along the ground and Eyre was filled with a wondrous joy. Even riding on Nox had not felt this way. The cool air turned the tips of her ears into ice, but she was working so hard, the rest of her felt warm.

Eyre was just about to call the session to a close when another horse cantered up and, with an expert leap, jumped *over* the fence into the paddock! The fence was high, so it was quite a feat. Amazed, Eyre swung Eclipse around to see who it was, and her face grew warm.

Of course! Her bodyguard was on the job, sitting on Firestorm, his fiery chestnut Lighthorse.

"Hi Eyre," Jax said. "You're doing well on her."

"This is Eclipse," Eyre replied, patting the mare on her neck. "She has agreed to go with me to Caelus, so we're practising."

"I was watching you," Jax said, his green eyes fixed on her. "You're doing really well. So, I wondered, do you want to fly with me?"

Fly? Did she! Eyre could think of nothing more blissful. But she looked at Eclipse uncertainly.

"I'm not sure if we're ready for that yet," she said. "We've only just started."

But as if the mare could understand, she leapt from a standing position into a full gallop, as if she'd been bitten by a horse-fly. Eyre was so startled she nearly fell off, but she held on determinedly as Eclipse galloped wildly around the paddock and then charged for the fence. It was as if something had been unleashed in the Lighthorse, and as they neared the fence, Eyre felt the strong hind muscles of the spectacular creature tense to jump.

They sailed over the fence and then... *upwards!* Two magnificent black wings unfolded and with leisurely flaps, pulled them up towards the sky.

"Oh, wow! Wow! Wow! WOW!" Eyre screeched with delight.

She saw a flash of red as the mighty Firestorm headed up towards them. In a moment he had caught up with them and Jax's eyes glinted as they swept up towards the clouds.

Eyre couldn't help herself and summoned Florence, who she knew would love to be part of this. In a second, the sleek Venator had arrived and was flying by their side as they reached the cloud cover.

They shot into the clouds and Eyre gasped at the cold and the blank grey fog in front of her. But as if Eclipse had an inner compass, she kept her line, and in a moment they had passed through the cloud and into clear space again.

"Charge!" Jax bellowed gleefully as he zoomed into a towering cumulus cloud and disappeared. Eyre shot along the outside of the cloud and met him as he blew out the other side of it. They both shouted with laughter and swept up and down the sky, around and through clouds, flying at top speed straight up, and then plummeting back down.

Even the Lighthorses seemed to be having fun as they spun around each other in a complex dance sequence. Sideways and side-by-side, they charged across the sky, racing each other. Florence was loving it too, and she matched their speed, executing moves that a fighter pilot would be proud of. Rolls and banks and sudden stalls, after which she would shoot like an arrow into a billowing cloud and out the other side.

Eventually, Eyre indicated that she wanted to go down. She was getting tired, and no doubt Eclipse was too. She was also very cold, and despite the joy of the flying she thought it was time to call it. Jax obviously agreed, and he followed her as she glided down from the heights to eventually land in the paddock. Florence landed gently on the fence, her three golden eyes flashing.

Eyre's hair was a tangled, fiery mess and her cheeks were wind-whipped, but her eyes were bright with joy.

"Thank you Eclipse," she said and hugged the panting horse as Jax landed beside her.

Eyre turned towards him with an exhilarated laugh, and Jax swept her into his arms.

"This is why I love you, Eyre," he whispered, and his mouth was suddenly hot on hers, his arms embracing her as if he would never let her go.

After a long moment they finally pulled apart. Eyre's breath was coming in gasps that had nothing to do with the riding.

Without saying anything, they led the Lighthorses back to the stables, walking in perfect synchronicity.

CHAPTER FORTY-SEVEN

WITH ONLY A FEW weeks to go before the TACI test, Eyre intensified her training until every night she was ready to drop from exhaustion. Archery, falconry, Ferito, riding, practising with her staff, the Caelus prohemium and the Summons; she trained for hours until her movements were fluid and her muscles were once again toned and strong.

After the initial hassle with Ben Perrill when she'd returned from the Clementis, Eyre had seen little of him. Whenever she did, however, he glowered and hurled insults at her, but physically left her alone. Whatever lesson Jax had taught him, he'd remembered it.

She'd managed to catch up on all her classwork by 'doing a Beatrice', as she called it—translated as sitting up for hours at night, studying maniacally. Eyre was driven by a compulsion to be as prepared as she could be for the next TACI journey. In her mind, there was no way she was not going to bring this Isar back.

Jax had taken to joining Eyre and her friends in the Refectory occasionally, and after the initial teasing looks and elbow nudging, they all accepted that this was going to be a regular thing. Eyre had to admit that she was completely smitten with her dark-haired, green-eyed guy. And for reasons she could not comprehend, he seemed to feel the same way about her. Just sitting next to him made her feel like a swarm of Zhuzhu Flutters were divebombing in her stomach.

One morning, before Jax arrived, Abby fixed Eyre with her cornflower eyes. She indicated by a slight nod, a table behind Eyre. "She's been very sad, you know. No, *don't look!*" Abby gasped as Eyre began to turn.

Beatrice, who was sitting beside Abby raised her eyebrows. "Pheria," she said, with her mouth full, looking over Eyre's shoulder.

"Oh." Eyre was nonplussed. "Well, who's she sitting with?"

"She doesn't really have many other friends," Abby said, her soft heart obviously sympathetic. "Iris, Ambrosia and Saskia joined Perrill's group quite a while ago and Pheria showed great sense in not going with them. I feel sorry for her really, Jax was her whole world."

"Well, surely you don't think she should come over here?" Eyre said, aghast. Pheria had been a thorn in her side ever since they'd first met, and she certainly didn't want her as a bestie.

"I reckon we could fit another person at the table," Nick said matter-of-factly as he buttered his toast. Nick usually didn't say much, so for him to make a comment was significant.

Beatrice nodded silently, and Eyre was gobsmacked. Were they *serious?*

Jax walked in the Refectory door and Eyre took advantage of the distraction to look over her shoulder. Indeed, Pheria was sitting at a table with students she barely knew, none of whom were talking to her. It seemed that Pheria had been so focused on following Jax around that she hadn't developed any other friendships. She was certainly a prickly person, and blunt, and she hadn't endeared herself to many students, who saw her as aloof and even stuck-up. But then Eyre remembered back to the Jenolan Caves, when Pheria had defended her against Mudamir, and she felt torn. And when Jax walked by and waved hello to Pheria, even Eyre had to feel sorry for her, her expression was so bereft.

Jax brought his tray of food and sat with Eyre and her friends, and the table became a hubbub of laughter and conversation. But Eyre couldn't enjoy it. Reaching a decision, she stood up suddenly and walked over to Pheria's table.

The other girl couldn't have been more surprised if an octopus had fallen from the sky, *splat!* onto the table. She sat with an expression like a blowfish.

"Come and join us, Pheria," Eyre said. "We've got a spare seat."

Pheria blinked and looked over at their table. "But—"

"We'd love to have you sit with us. Here, I'll take your tray."

Before the girl could react or refuse, Eyre had grabbed the tray and taken it over to the table where her group sat. After a moment, Pheria trailed over, looking very uncomfortable. But Abby, always kind-hearted, made it easy.

"We've been waiting for days for you to come over! Here, sit next to me. How's your TACI preparation going?"

And just like that, Pheria became one of the group. As Abby chatted away to the athletic, black-haired girl, Eyre realised that she actually felt good about it. Pheria had shown great courage at the Jenolan Caves, and despite their differences, she had defended Eyre at risk of her own life.

Pheria was a complex person, but she had great Lightworking skills and no one could doubt her motives—she was as committed to decimating the Gothak as the rest of them. It might take a while, but perhaps they might even be friends one day.

Jax looked at Eyre gratefully, and Eyre realised that he had also been feeling bad about the situation. He'd been sitting with Pheria quite regularly, but he'd obviously been finding the situation difficult. Eyre was suddenly thankful for Abby's perceptiveness. She remembered well how she herself had been welcomed unconditionally into this friendship group, and she felt that Abby, the psychic, somehow always knew the right thing to do.

After breakfast, Eyre strolled to meditation with Jax. They walked close together, their arms occasionally touching, and Eyre felt a warmth within her that she had never experienced before. Just before they reached the meditation hall, Jax drew her off the path and kissed her deeply. Eyre shivered with delight. This guy!

"I wanted to confess one last secret to you," Jax said, as he pulled away slowly. Eyre raised her eyebrows and waited. She thought she'd heard them all by now.

"Next week we head to Caelus," Jax said. "And it's uncertain if we'll all come back this time. The Gothak know you are the Aether, and they will be trying to get the Isar too, with all the force they have. Whittaker Ray and the Governments of the Alterworlds are putting together a Defence Battalion, to keep the Gothak away. But there's likely to be fighting," he added in a worried voice. "I wanted you to know, in case—" at this, Eyre flung herself at him and wrapped her arms around him.

"Don't you say another word!" she said fiercely. "I don't want to hear that!"

Jax chuckled humourlessly. "Your wish is my command, fair maiden—I am not strong enough to battle you! But I need to explain about the Lorian Juice, lest I go to my grave with terrible aspersions on my character!"

Eyre rested her head against his chest. It was unbearable to think he might not come back from Caelus—that *any* of them might not come back! There had been too much death already.

"Whittaker Ray has cleared me to tell you about the quest I've been on for the past couple of years."

Eyre looked up at him with troubled sapphire eyes. "You mean, apart from your spying?"

Jax nodded. "I've had another mission, which, unfortunately I've been unsuccessful completing so far."

As students walked past, looking at them questioningly, Eyre made a decision.

"This is far too important for a five-minute conversation," she said. "Let's go to the therapeutic pools. It's meditation of a sort, and that way we can talk in private."

Jax needed no more encouragement—his face lit up. "Winter spa? Sounds fine to me! Meet you there in ten minutes?"

Eyre nodded, and jogged back along the track to the dormitory, her breath puffing out before her in the cold air. In actual fact, it would do her muscles good to soak in the warm water of the pools; she had been working out physically so hard in the past two months. And it sounded as if what Jax had to tell her was important.

She put her swimsuit on quickly and shrugged on the Academy bathrobe, then she grabbed a towel and headed towards the therapeutic pools.

Jax was already there—sitting up to his neck in a turquoise-coloured pool. Around him, at different levels, were other coloured pools of steaming water: yellow, violet, rose, blue—so many different colours that a rainbow hue hovered in the air above them from the reflected water.

Eyre slipped into the warm water beside Jax and closed her eyes blissfully. Not only did the heated water do her tired muscles good, the vibrations from the crystals that formed the pools worked on restoring her energy. For a few minutes they both sat in silence, soaking up the healing qualities of the water.

Then Jax turned to Eyre and took her hand. "The Lightworkers need to go to the Underworld to retrieve the lost Isar," he began. "But how to go there without being detected has proven impossible. Many warriors have been sent over this past year, but none have returned."

Eyre's eyes were round. This had obviously been done in the utmost secrecy; she had heard no whisper of these missions.

Jax sighed. "It has been a futile endeavour, and one that would have been abandoned much earlier, except that Madame Overmantle saw a vision in the beryl orbuculum. Its message was clear; the fruit of the Lorian tree would be the solution to entering the Overworld without the Gothak realising."

"The *Lorian Tree?* So is *that* why your hands were blue at the beginning of the year? Not some secret addiction?" Eyre giggled.

Jax snorted. "I'd spent all summer in Terra, and was still there when school started. Lorian trees are hard to find, and very sought after, so even if you find one, often the fruit has already been taken. I'd been all over the

Alterworld trying to find the trees, and finally had a hot tip on who might be able to, uh, '*help*' me."

Jax and Eyre both laughed, and then Jax continued. "Exes are often the owners of Lorian plantations—they're called Jus Dealers, and they get to Terra through the Seam, helped by Dark Lightworkers. Jus Dealers are very secretive about where their Lorian plantations are located. So anyway, I got in touch with this Dealer I'd heard about to acquire some of the fruit—he took me blindfolded to his plantation and I had to drink the juice to prove that I was a genuine buyer. I didn't drink much. But I can tell you, it's like rocket fuel! I came straight from the plantation to school."

Eyre couldn't help herself. She laughed until tears ran down her face. "Oh no, Whittaker Ray was so annoyed! You made quite an entrance!"

Jax laughed too. "He understood when I explained the situation later, but at the time, he wasn't happy with the disruption. He imagined I might have fallen into the dastardly snares of the dreaded Lorian! And I can tell you, he had a few letters from concerned parents after that episode!"

They both cried with laughter at the thought of the very straight Whittaker Ray trying to deal with that scandal, until eventually Jax wiped his eyes. "Well, it was worth it, anyway. I left a rainbow clip there so we can go straight back to that plantation—he has thousands of trees. We can get as much of the fruit as we need."

Eyre laughed. The rainbow clip was used by students so that lecturers could locate them if they went astray when they were learning the prohemium. "Such a good idea! But what do you do with the fruit? How can you use it to avoid the Gothak? Get them inebriated?"

They both chortled again at the ridiculous thought, but Jax shook his head, puzzled. "That's the essence of the problem. We're not sure. The Lightworkers who have gone to the Underworld have tried drinking it, rubbing it on their skin and clothes, even throwing it in *bucketfuls* over the Gothak. But it hasn't worked, and many have died from these—well, feeble really, as it has turned out—experiments. It's been a disaster, and for now, the Echelon has suspended its attempts. So many grieving families; it's just not worth it. And I feel like a real failure," he said softly.

Eyre held his hand tightly. "I'm sure no one sees it that way," she said softly. "It sounds like you've worked so hard. You found the fruit, and it seems like *no one* has solved the problem of how to use it yet. It's *really* not your responsibility." Eyre raised her hands from the glowing aquamarine water until she held his face gently. She turned it towards her, and kissed his lips, warm from the steam of the pools.

Jax smiled, but Eyre could see that he still felt a deep pain at the failure of the attempts to get into the Underworld.

"What was the vision Madame Overmantle saw? Was it a picture? Or a place?" Eyre asked.

Jax shook his head. "No, it was a rhyme."

Eyre groaned out loud. Not *another* riddle! *BTL!* "Well," she said eventually, "Beatrice is good with that sort of thing, what did it say?"

Jax thought hard. "It's confusing, like all those things are, but in the mists of the crystal ball, Madame Overmantle saw something like this—I mean I'll have to check it because I might not have all the words right, and really, I was just given the task to seek out as much fruit as I could, but it went, sort of:

Find the heavy fruit
Er... uh... something about *the juices blue*—um,
How to escape the black pursuit
No other drupe will do

—or something like that."

Eyre grimaced. "Well, I'm *so* not good at this, I can't even get started. What's a drupe?"

Jax laughed. "You and me both—I struggle with puzzles. But I know now that a drupe is a fruit with a stone or pit in the middle of it, like a mango."

"Well, I guess that definitely means the Lorian fruit then, with the blue juice," Eyre mused.

"And UD1 is sure that the 'black pursuit' refers to the Gothak," Jax said. "The meaning of the rhyme is quite straightforward really, but we haven't worked out how to use the fruit correctly yet. Too many Lightworkers have died trying, so the missions have been stopped. Our alchemists and physicists have been working on it in great secrecy. Apparently, Madame Overmantle has been very distressed by her inability to solve the message. I heard she's spent many hours staring into the orbuculum trying to work it out, but without success."

Eyre thought of Madame Overmantle bringing Abby the beryl orbuculum earlier this year. She had said that the crystal ball should be passed on to the Nefelibata, which the Faeries at the Jenolan Caves had called Abby during the students' tour with Professor Vela. Eyre thought Madame Overmantle had seemed downcast as she passed the priceless object to Abby. And now she knew why. Madame Overmantle was despondent because she felt that she had failed at reading the swirling mists within, not because she was relinquishing a precious and irreplaceable object. As the world-renown expert in her field, Madame Overmantle had expected that she should have been able to read the messages within the ancient crystal ball. And it was obviously a terrible blow to her pride to realise that she couldn't. But it was also a measure of her altruism that she would sacrifice her perceived image for the good of the Lightworkers, by passing the crystal ball on to someone who might be able to read it—the Nefelibata. Abby.

"Abby has the orbuculum now," Eyre said slowly, and Jax's jaw dropped.

"*Abby?*"

Eyre shrugged. "I don't know why. If Madame Overmantle can't interpret the message, then I wouldn't think anyone in the whole world could. But she understood that the orbuculum had to be held by the Nefelibata— Abby, apparently. Abby did find Nick when he was missing, by using the crystal ball, but she hasn't seen anything since, and I know she's been trying."

Jax sighed deeply. "If only we weren't perpetually surrounded by this feeling of dread, of something coming. The Gothak are rising, and we are really at a disadvantage. Give me a Mnae and a solid adversary any day over these mists of confusion!"

Eyre nodded. She was tired too. It would be nice to live a normal life for a while. Or at least to know what they were up against.

But then she pulled Jax to her until they looked into each other's eyes.

Her voice was fierce. "We will get the Isar. And then we'll solve the Lorian puzzle and get the other Isar back!"

Jax stared deeply into her eyes. "Yes we will," he said softly, and drew her towards him.

CHAPTER FORTY-EIGHT

EYRE MANAGED TO GET to Ferito on time, ignoring the winks Beatrice and Abby were giving her, and found she did the best she'd ever done with her Aditus and Tego in the Clasis Levels 1-3. She was working with Rigmar, who was extremely proficient in the Clasis, but she had no problem deflecting his blows and attacking well enough that Rigmar had to retreat and work hard to avoid her tactics. She moved smoothly through all of the positions, and by the end of the bout, Rigmar wiped his brow and grinned. "BTL, Eyre, you've improved! I'm exhausted!"

Eyre slid her Antaraks back into the baldrics on her back and she saw Sergeant Tottingham watching her with approval. The hard work Eyre had put in over the past two months had obviously paid off. Perhaps the power of the Therapeutic Pools had something to do with it this morning? Or maybe it was happiness, she thought to herself, hugging herself mentally. She looked across and saw Jax watching her with a glint in his eye and she smiled back at him. He seemed pretty happy too.

After lunch, she ushered Beatrice and Abby back to their room. "Nick, you come too, we'll sneak you in," she said, pulling him by the arm. "I've got something for the journal."

Once in the dorm room, Beatrice retrieved the journal and Eyre repeated the words that Jax had told her as Beatrice wrote them down. "He's not sure if he's got it exactly right, but that's the gist of it."

"What does the message mean?" Beatrice asked. "What's a drupe?"

Eyre explained, and that the message was the secret to moving through the Underworld undetected. But then she told them about the unsuccessful missions so far, and Nick sat back and rubbed his head.

"Everything is always so shrouded in mystery! So confusing. Why don't they just *tell* us the secret?"

"It's so the Gothak don't know," Abby said, her eyes serious. "It's like a secret weapon for us, and we have to keep the knowledge hidden."

"Hidden is right," Nick grumbled, echoing Eyre's own sentiments. "But it's only useful if we can un-hide it!"

Abby giggled. "Un-hide? Well, that's a perfect way to put it! We need to un-hide the meaning!"

Everyone laughed until they cried, and then Abby continued, "How about I go and check with Madame Overmantle exactly what the message was, so we can get it right in the journal?"

There was a general sound of agreement, so after Beatrice had put the journal back in the wall, Abby left to find Madame Overmantle. Eyre headed over to practise with Eclipse again; Beatrice wanted to research possible meanings of the orbuculum's message, so she left for the library; and Nick headed off to look for Warrigal. "He's been working really hard with the Ranger," Nick said. "I'm going to suggest he takes a break and comes for a walk in the bush with me."

"See you in the Alterworlds class," Beatrice called. "Only three more days 'til we leave!"

Kyori stood calmly before the auditorium of students, waiting patiently until everyone had taken a seat. Her purple and white plumage shone under the auditorium lights, and the edge of her wings gleamed golden. She watched with bright eyes until the last student sat down.

"Today is our last lecture," she said. "I feel that you are all adept at the prohemium now, so I wanted to take this opportunity to wish you well in your quest for the gazae. I do not feel we need any more practise or lectures, but if anyone has any questions, now is the time. You leave Monday, and I wish you the best of luck."

Students looked at each other and shrugged. Really, they just needed to get to Caelus and get started.

After a moment, Whittaker Ray appeared from the side of the auditorium. "I would like you to thank Kyori for her time and wisdom. It's been an interesting year, and I feel you are all very well-prepared, thanks to her careful guidance."

The students applauded and stamped their feet. The small bird had become very popular this year with her wit and her kindness. And as each subsequent year passed, and they actually visited the Alterworlds, the students were more aware of the expertise these guest lecturers were sharing with them, and were more appreciative. Kyori looked pleased and seemed about to reply, but she was interrupted by the sound of feet tramping loudly outside the building, and Whittaker Ray moved quickly.

"Thank you, students, that will be all for today, and good luck," he said, as he and Kyori hurried out of the auditorium.

The students looked at each other. It had been a rather abrupt departure, and the stomping sounds were, if anything, getting louder. Curiosity got the better of them all, and they headed outside in a chattering flurry.

As Eyre, Beatrice, Abby and Nick walked out the door, they stopped dead at the sight in front of them. Across campus marched an impressive array of formidable creatures.

First there were Lightworkers from all Sectors, Terrigal Furnace among them, aligned and moving with purpose, their staffs in hand as they left the Central Admin building. Then the Mimir, forming straight lines with rhythmic steps, Crescent Blades drawn and ferocious looks on their faces, flooded out the doors of the Mimir's Domain. At least a thousand stomping feet. And finally, an array of creatures from all the Alterworlds—the Nemoris from Terra, the Pinnae from Aqua, wearing air suits, Caelites from Caelus, and most strikingly, a huge battalion of Armatura from Incendium. They moved as one unit, stepping in time as they headed towards what Eyre now realised was the Receiving Stone. And already at the Receiving Stone waited many of the staff—Sir Philius Clarembout, Gegenees, Dr Botolfe and Professor Vela. Professor Vela looked directly at Eyre, and raised his staff slightly.

Whittaker Ray and Kyori appeared beside Eyre and her friends.

"I trust you are ready," Whittaker Ray said softly. "You are leaving ahead of schedule. We are hoping to get ahead of our 'friends' from the murk below. Ben Perrill will no doubt have informed them of the official TACI start date on Monday. But the Leonids have already begun, so you are going early, today, *now*. With luck you'll be back before they realise. Summon your Lighthorses and head for the Receiving Stone."

He and Kyori left at a fast pace, as Eyre, Beatrice, Abby and Nick looked at each other, trying to make sense of what was going on. Eyre suddenly realised the wisdom of keeping Ben around—what a great way to feed false information to the bad guys.

"Here we go, then," Eyre said after a moment, and felt a fire ignite within her. Looking at her friends, she knew that they felt it too. She summoned her staff and felt the rainbow shaft whack into her hand.

"Bring it on," Beatrice said with steel in her voice, as her staff suddenly appeared.

A second later, Blondie, the pretty palomino horse, appeared beside Beatrice; there was another flash and Cojo, Abby's spectacular Appaloosa gelding, arrived. Prenzel appeared in a bright light beside Nick, and Eyre felt a bit bereft as she looked at the stunning dark brown horse. But then, in a silver flare, Eclipse arrived without being summoned, putting her soft muzzle on Eyre's shoulder. Eyre felt so relieved and grateful, all she could do was stroke the beautiful horse's nose. She noticed that each Lighthorse had a saddle bag attached around their neck, and a heavy coat was looped through its straps. There had been no discussion about this—evidently the Kikkuli Master had prepared the horses for the journey.

The army was forming, lining up behind the moldavite square. There was a grimness to their movements, and Eyre suddenly realised how serious this was. Life or death. Light or Darkness. She swung herself up onto Eclipse, and her friends followed. Abby and Nick summoned their staffs and they all started walking towards the Receiving Stone.

But they stopped at the sound of someone running up behind them. Jax was moving fast, his sapphire-topped staff in hand, and with a flash, Firestorm appeared beside him, prancing in place with excitement. Jax leapt up onto his back.

"You're not going without me," he said, his green eyes flashing with fire.

And more surprisingly, as they continued over to the Receiving Stone, two more arrived, galloping over to join them. Colton on Nox, and Warrigal on Bunu.

"We're here to help," Colton said simply. "Anything we can do." Both of them had grave looks on their faces; they understood the risk, but they wanted to be here.

The seven of them approached the Receiving Stone, surprised by the sudden turn of events—they had expected to leave next week for Caelus. But it was evident that they were all more than ready right now. As they headed towards the middle of the melee, Eyre saw Kyori waiting for them at the centre of the glowing moldavite square.

Each of the students began to perform the prohemium as the massive lines of troops waited patiently around them.

Eyre turned towards her friends. "Thank you," she said softly. "The Light be with you." She looked further out to the massed warriors from all the Alterworlds and called loudly, raising her rainbow staff, "And with you. May the Light prevail!" The troops roared, raising swords, and weapons and fists. A tribute to the Light.

Then Eyre and her group disappeared into the blinding flash of the Seam.

CHAPTER FORTY-NINE

THE FIRST THING EYRE noticed as she emerged in Caelus was how cold it was. Swirling clouds moved quickly above them, some of them almost touching the ground. They stood and waited on the volcanic pumice, the horses' hooves crunching as they shifted their weight on the uneven ground. The seven of them waited for the rest of the party to arrive as they looked around at this new Alterworld.

In the distance, towering black mountains formed a ragged backbone against the horizon, and a stiff wind moaned through the canyon where they stood. Far away, they could see dark clouds swirling, and jagged streaks of lightning hitting the ground. Stands of crooked grey trees clumped across the landscape, gnarled and beaten down by the weather. It was not a welcoming place.

Leaning forward, Eyre dragged the coat from the saddle bag straps and shrugged it on as fast as she could. She zipped it up and felt immediate relief—the coat had some sort of mica-like lining that was heated, and gloves were attached to the end of the sleeves so that Eyre's hands slipped straight in. Like all Academy gear, it was tailored to fit snugly, to enable ease of movement.

"Ah," she said as she pulled the hood over her head. "That's better! Now I think I can face the Gothak!"

Her friends moved fast and did the same—the sharp wind was icy. Eyre knew she needed one more companion on this journey, and she gave a high-pitched whistle as she summoned her Venator. Florence arrived in a second, swooping down with a sharp cry to land on Eyre's shoulder.

Just then, a Seam appeared and Kyori, Lord Clarembout, Gegenees, Professor Vela and Dr Botolfe walked through. The Seam snapped shut behind them.

"Just giving the troops their marching orders," Lord Clarembout boomed. "They will be arriving shortly, and will be spreading across Caelus in defence formations, to notify us and defend should any Gothak appear."

Kyori stepped forward. "We have decided that we will be heading towards Mt Crepitus," she said softly, looking at Eyre. "It is of course, the destination for the gazae, but it is also the best vantage point for you to look for the sign of the Isar. Being in a group is definitely good strategy in these conditions. Ours is a dangerous world, and one must always be alert." As if she knew what Kyori was saying, Florence emitted another wild, piercing cry. She understood this environment.

A number of Seams began to form in silvery vertical stripes along the landscape, and through them stepped all the beings that had been at the Academy. They marched with purpose in all directions, except for one troop who headed towards Eyre's group.

Jengles was at the forefront of the disciplined battalion, which comprised about twenty Mimir, including Corporal Cabochon, ten adult Lightworkers that Eyre had not met before, three Pinnae and five Nemoris. Eyre wasn't quite sure what a Pinnae could do in this Alterworld, but she was grateful for the support. It would be nice not to be floundering around on their own for once.

"Can you see anything Eyre?" Lord Clarembout asked, and she searched the area in a 360-degree circle, turning Eclipse around as she scrutinised every bit of the landscape from the earth to the sky. But she couldn't see the tell-tale vertical light from the Isar in any direction and she shook her head.

"Then let's get going," the huge warrior said. "We need to get this done quickly. We will walk to the base of the mountains."

They set off along the crunching ground, the Lightworkers on their Lighthorses and the others moving swiftly behind. Every eye was scanning the terrain, watchful and on edge, looking for any sign that the Gothak were here.

It was going to take some time to get to the foothills, but Dr Botolfe explained to the students that they had to conserve their Lighthorses' energy, and that flying used a lot of that energy. Especially up to the top of Mt Crepitus. So they walked along briskly, past the strange grove of stunted grey trees.

Florence gave a shriek and took off towards the trees, and Gegenees chuckled. "Ru-Ru trees," he said. As Florence neared, from seemingly nowhere a flock of Venators shot from the forest and into the air, their high-pitched cries deafening in the still air. Then they flew around Florence in a sort of dance; up high, down low, circling her in what was an elaborate show of welcome. She raced between them, and twirled with them for a few minutes, then shot back over to land on Eyre's shoulder. The Venators settled back into the trees, once again concealed in the branches. Eyre realised then the reason for the raptors' colouring; their grey plumage made them virtually invisible amongst the twisted trees. Only when they opened their three golden eyes could you see where they were.

Half an hour in, the wind, if it was possible, was getting colder, and Eyre shivered despite her warm coat. A terrified cry behind her made her turn sharply, just in time to see one of the Mimir and then a Pinnae disappear into the ground. She watched in horror as the outstretched hand of the Pinnae submerged and the pumice closed above them as if they had never been there.

"A pumice vortex!" shouted Jengles, pushing the troops away from the area where the two had disappeared. And then like an arrow, Nick took off on Prenzel, flying high into the air. Wheeling around, he shot straight down towards the vortex, blasting the pumice away with his staff at the last moment, before shooting straight down the hole. It had all happened so quickly that everyone was shocked and unable to react. But Sir Philius soon collected his wits.

"By St Illuminado, that's one smart boy," he shouted, and turned his Lighthorse to follow. "Stay here!" he ordered as he too flew straight down the hole. Pumice tumbled around the edges until the hole was filled in again, a lethal and invisible trap for the unwitting.

It seemed an aeon, although it was probably only a few minutes, until finally there was a blast and flaming Light energy blew the pumice up into the air like a geyser. Nick exploded out of the hole on Prenzel, with the Pinnae on the back of his Lighthorse. A second later, Lord Clarembout charged out carrying the Mimir on his horse. They flew in an arc and then settled on the ground beside the troops.

The Pinnae and the Mimir slid off the back of the Lighthorses. Despite the fact they had almost died, their stoic faces gave nothing away as they bowed to Nick and Lord Clarembout. They knew the dangers when they joined the journey, and to them, this was obviously just part of the commitment. Moving swiftly, they rejoined their comrades and fell in line.

"Onwards!" Jengles shouted. "Eyes alert!"

Despite herself, Eyre was rattled by the experience. Imagine tumbling over and over to your death through an unending atmosphere? It made her hair stand on end, and she found herself watching the ground carefully until she realised that she would never find the Isar if she kept watching Eclipse's feet. Instead, she focused on the approaching foothills, feeling like it would be sensible to get away from the open plains.

She thought she heard Kyori mutter. And what she said sounded like "oh no."

"Oh no," Eyre echoed. "Oh no, what?"

A dark shadow fell across the landscape, moving across them slowly and all eyes turned upwards.

"What is that?" Abby said, aghast. "Strigis?"

"No," Kyori said softly. "That is a Zeguardagen." She looked at Lord Clarembout urgently. "Your troops must take cover. They are ferocious beasts and will not stop until everyone and everything is dead."

Eyre looked at the four-winged dragon-like creature that sailed above them, its eyes locked with deadly intent on the group below. It was dark blue, covered in rough scales and it had a tail that ended with a ball and long barbs. Its head had a circlet of spikes half a metre long behind its ears. It opened its mouth and let out a spine-chilling screech that echoed across the empty plains.

"I think we've just been invited to dinner," Beatrice said, as she wheeled around on Blondie "and we're it!"

Jengles leapt into action. "To the trees!" he ordered the troops, and those on foot scrambled towards the Ru-Ru stands to try and take cover. Not that they would provide much protection, Eyre thought in desperation—there was nothing to them. They stood like dead sticks on the plains. The Zeguardagen turned and swept towards the running troops, fire scorching the earth before it, as it approached the diminutive forms.

But then Warrigal jumped off Bunu, and as everyone watched the horrible creature stalking the running forms, he started to morph, hiding behind Eyre. "Cover me," he whispered, and she turned Eclipse so Warrigal was out of sight. In a minute, he had transformed into a Vampire Vulture, one of the awful creatures that Eyre had encountered last year at the Unlit Campus. Vampire Vultures hunted Venators, and Florence gave a disconcerted squawk, but she seemed to know there was something different here.

Then Warrigal took to the skies and shot towards the Zeguardagen, screeching loudly. The huge creature was distracted by the large black bird and turned, evidently deciding to go for the easy prey. As Warrigal flew upwards, the dragon followed, shooting fire from its nostrils, but Warrigal was too quick.

A second later, Colton had taken off after Warrigal, and Jax too.

"*Run!*" Colton shouted as the two boys flew high in the air, and then Lord Clarembout pointed his staff at the foothills. "Go for cover!" he ordered the Lightworkers, before charging after Colton and Warrigal. "We will handle this." The army on the ground divided in two and headed for the closer sanctuary—either the Ru-Ru or the foothills of the Caedes Mountains.

Eyre and her group urged their Lighthorses into flight and they soared along, close to the ground, as fast as they could fly, needing no encouragement as the shadow of the massive dragon passed over them. Kyori flew with them, her purple and white wings beating slowly as she easily kept up with the Lighthorses. Bred for this environment, she was having no trouble.

But it was Gegenees who gave Eyre the biggest surprise, because she saw that he was riding in a huge winged *chariot!* He had a sword in his hand and looked like an avenging god as he charged along at the rear. When he'd escorted them to the shelter of the huge boulders at the foot of the Caedes Mountains, he wheeled around, and shouting at the top of his voice, headed back towards the Zeguardagen.

Eyre and her group anxiously watched the spectacle in the skies. The Zeguardagen was immense and ferocious, and it seemed to have incredible manoeuvrability, with those four stretching wings. She held her breath as she saw the terrible creature spin around after Warrigal, getting frighteningly close to him. But then, Colton and Jax flew in behind and blasted the Zeguardagen with their staffs, the powerful Light energy burning searing stripes in its hide. Lord Clarembout and Gegenees arrived and attacked from the flanks, causing the ferocious creature to screech in pain and snap its huge jaws in fury. It lunged for Colton and Jax, but the two boys, whose flying skills were peerless, ducked and weaved as the enormous dragon chased them across the sky. Then Lord Clarembout flew in close and pulled his Antaraks out. With a cross-bladed swipe, he cut part of the foot off the Zeguardagen and it shrieked in agony. When Gegenees smashed the side of its head with his Flail, the Zeguardagen decided it had had enough. Screeching in pain and rage, it fled towards the mountains, eventually disappearing from view.

Lord Clarembout, Colton and Jax soared down from the sky and landed with the Lightworkers and Gegenees brought his chariot down onto the ground gently beside them. Then Abby noticed Bunu standing there riderless and her eyes became frantic.

"Where's Warrigal?" she cried.

A shame-faced form appeared from behind one of the boulders, rubbing his head.

"I—uh—well, By the Light! I fell off and bumped my head," Warrigal said in embarrassment. "Missed the whole show really. Is it gone?"

"Oh yes," Eyre said in a wondering voice. "Lucky for us, those brave guys saved the day." She looked at Warrigal meaningfully and he gave a slight smile. Evidently, he wasn't ready yet to let it be known that he could perform therianthropy, and she was happy to keep his secret. Although she was fairly sure Lord Clarembout knew, as he was looking at Warrigal with an extremely impressed expression on his face.

Everyone congratulated Colton and Jax, and Eyre had to admit, they had been quite spectacular up there. Their aerial and fighting skills were as good as any she'd ever seen, and as a team they had been unbeatable. No matter what this inhospitable place threw at them, she was starting to feel like they all might be okay.

"Nice wheels," Nick commented to Gegenees, and everyone laughed.

"We all have our secrets," Gegenees commented. "This was a gift to me from an ancestor."

They had some time before the foot troops made it across the plains, so as they waited in the lee of the mountain, hiding from the whistling winds, all the students jumped down to admire the shining golden chariot.

"Maybe I don't want a Zepp after all..." Eyre mused, as she stroked the elaborate carvings on the carriage covetously, and grinned as the rest of them laughed.

"From what I've heard of your piloting skills," Dr Botolfe said dryly, "perhaps you'd better stick with the Zepp. I'm not sure what you'd do with a chariot!"

After a second of surprise that Dr Botolfe actually had a sense of humour, the rest of them roared.

"Noted," Eyre chuckled as the troops arrived.

CHAPTER FIFTY

AND THEN THE ARDUOUS climb began. The first five kilometres were to be done on foot, scrambling over rocks and traversing narrow, dangerous tracks to get further up the mountain. It would leave another ten more kilometres to fly when the terrain got steeper, as well as the return journey, which was a long flight for new riders.

Abby was red-faced and gasping, as she trudged up the sheer rocky pathway, with Cojo following. "Why, why, *why* do I do this?" she complained as Beatrice chortled. "There should be a Sector for the inert, I reckon. Ones who want to sit on the couch and relax. Surely that's where I belong?"

Beatrice slapped her on the back. "You're here to make the rest of us feel good, as always, my friend. And you're doing a great job of it!"

Abby harrumphed, but didn't have enough breath for a repartee, so she stuck her head down and plodded on.

The way up was extremely steep, and everyone was finding it difficult. There was a lot of heavy breathing and not much conversation as they slowly moved upwards. The wind was now close to howling, and despite their warm clothing they were all intensely cold. Eyre looked at the brightly-coloured Kyori, who walked uncomplainingly beside them. How could she survive in this inhospitable environment? I think I'd migrate, Eyre thought dourly as yet another icy blast whipped her face.

"Five-minute break!" Sir Philius called, and everyone stopped gratefully. They'd gone about three-quarters of the walking distance, and Eyre felt exhausted already. Walking straight uphill was a lot different than walking —or even running—on the flat. And the altitude made it that much harder to breathe. This was going to be a test of endurance.

In the saddle bags were bottles of water, sandwiches and energy bars, and the foot troops also produced provisions from a bag around their waists.

They all sat on the ground and Eyre ate the food appreciatively. At this point she would have eaten the Zeguardagen's foot, she thought drily, she was so hungry.

Abby sighed happily as she plunked herself down on the pumice and obsidian pathway. "Sitting! My favourite exercise of all!" Then she looked up and her cornflower eyes danced in delight. "Oh wow! How pretty! Look at those clouds! They look like waves breaking at Mooloolaba beach!"

Everyone turned and Eyre agreed—the clouds had formed a perfect wave-like pattern that stretched right across the sky. She'd been so concentrated on the path ahead of her, she hadn't bothered to look up at all.

Nick smiled and took another bite but Beatrice's eyes grew round. Lord Clarembout and Jengles exchanged a look, and Eyre sighed. What now? Beatrice leapt in to explain.

"By the Light," she exclaimed. "They *are* very beautiful, but that's a Kelvin-Helmholtz formation! It's extremely rare."

Abby looked sideways at Beatrice. "I swear, do you ever sleep my friend? How do you know what that is, let alone how to *say* it?"

Beatrice shrugged, as if it was normal. "I knew that Caelus is subject to atmospheric fluctuations, so I did extra reading on weather patterns in general."

"And...?" Abby asked.

Beatrice sighed. "Not good timing, really. It means we're in for some wild weather—turbulence, to put it simply."

"Oh great," Nick commented. "It's been really boring so far; we need a bit of excitement."

Colton and Jax laughed and stuffed the rest of their sandwiches in. "Well, let's get going before it gets us, then," Jax said with his mouth full.

Lord Clarembout seemed to concur and ordered the troops up.

"Best to move along," he said. "Three kilometres more and the Lightworkers will fly. We will see the rest of you at the summit."

The threat in those seemingly innocuous clouds galvanised everyone into action. They already felt exposed on the unfriendly, rocky mountain, and the sooner they got to the top, the better. So, despite their tiredness, they moved faster than they had for the first part of the journey up the mountain. Even the Lighthorses sensed the urgency, and they quickened their pace as the track led interminably upwards.

It was slow going, but an hour later they reached a plateau and Lord Clarembout called a halt again.

"This is where we leave you, my friend," he said to Jengles, and Jengles nodded. "The Light be with you; we'll see you at the top," Lord Clarembout finished.

"May the Light endure, Philius. We will see you soon," Jengles said softly.

CHAPTER FIFTY-ONE

LORD CLAREMBOUT LED THE way, soaring off on his huge black Andalusian Lighthorse, with Dr Botolfe close behind him. Then Warrigal, Colton and Jax took flight, followed by Eyre, Beatrice, Abby and Nick. Professor Vela and Gegenees, in his chariot, took the rear. In a dramatic swirl of dust and Light energy, the group of eleven flew up the mountain. As Eyre saw the rocky track spiralling up the inhospitable mountain beneath them, she felt immensely grateful that she didn't have to walk it.

The horses also seemed happy to leave the uneven ground, and they flew in formation through the freezing air. Eyre caught Jax looking back at her from time to time and her heart somersaulted. No more wondering and second-guessing. Now they were *together*, whatever might come, and wherever it may lead.

As Beatrice had predicted, the turbulence in the air was increasing, making it hard for the Lighthorses to keep on track. The danger for a Lighthorse in rough weather was breaking a wing if a gust caught them unawares, so it was important to keep riding the air currents on an even course. Both the rider and horse had to concentrate, and this was a skill of a very difficult nature.

"Move it!" Sir Philius shouted back to them. "The weather is intensifying! We must be at the summit in half an hour!"

Just then a huge blast of wind blew the horses sideways, and then shot them straight upwards as the unpredictable air currents battled each other. Buffeted from side to side, the Lighthorses struggled to move forwards, and Eyre held on grimly. Surely, they would be through this soon?

But then it seemed as if hell itself exploded. The wind keened louder as a violent twister, growing quickly into a tornado-like funnel, swept towards them from the top of the mountain. Forks of lightning shot out from the funnel, striking the ground in a billow of black smoke as it rocketed closer.

"*Sideways!*" Lord Clarembout bellowed, pulling his Lighthorse to the side of the impending onslaught. Horses peeled off frantically to the right and left of the storming wind tunnel as it barrelled past them down the mountain. Dust flew into the air and chips of obsidian cut their skin as it was tossed up by the violence of the gale. The raging backdraft of the tornado hurled the Lightworkers in all directions as it whirled past.

"Hang in there, Eclipse," Eyre muttered as she struggled to stay on the horse's back. They were flung upside down and rolled dizzyingly in the ferocious airstream. It was like being caught in a violent dumper in the shallows of a surf beach. Finally, they were hurled out into calmer air, where the shattered Lighthorse glided for a few moments, too exhausted to even flap her wings.

Desperate, Eyre scanned the air, doing a headcount. With a weary relief, she realised that they'd all made it. At various levels in the air, all the Lighthorses were swinging slowly around to head back up the mountain. Eclipse eventually raised her tired wings and flapped, bringing them upwards, and they were again on their way.

Half an hour later, they landed at the summit. It was tight up there, not much room for ten horses and a chariot. But Gegenees quickly sent his chariot away, and they all stood closely together. The Lighthorses rested their heads on each other, and the Lightworkers rested their heads on the horses. Everyone was exhausted.

But then Nick spotted something; he knelt down and started digging frantically in the ground. Everyone watched him, too tired to move. Finally, he gave a yell of victory as he pulled an irregular golden spear from the ground.

"I thought I saw it," he cried, holding his prize aloft. "Gazae!" Suddenly everyone was galvanised. The passing lightning storm had struck the ground hundreds of times, so it seemed that everyone might find some gazae. After some frantic digging, it wasn't long before they all held a precious golden fulgurite of Electrum in their hand. Abby danced with glee as she put the gazae into her saddle bag. Eyre could tell that all the students were jubilant at their success. They had come on this mission to find something other than gazae, but to actually take the treasure back with them was a wonderful feeling.

A tramping of feet announced that the foot troops had arrived, and they trailed in a line back down the track, unable to fit on the summit.

"Well done," Sir Philius Clarembout said to Jengles. "You weathered the storm." Jengles lifted his eyebrows at his friend and gave a small smile. "We are masters of rock and earth," he said simply. "T'wasn't too difficult."

Then he motioned for the troops to sit, and they perched on rocks, and on the dust of the trail while they finished off their provisions.

As her breath returned to normal, Eyre lifted her head from Eclipse's neck and looked out over the vista from this massive mountain. And her heart bloomed. It wasn't as if she was at the top of the world, it was like she was at the top of the *universe!* She could see for hundreds of kilometres around—this vast, unwelcoming world had a severe beauty of its own. The air was freezing, but clear now that the storm had passed, and the stretching plains cast auras of light from the sparkling of the ice crystals that had settled upon them. Eyre caught her breath at the beauty of it, and Kyori moved over to join her.

"Even when it's harsh, there is splendour, much as with life itself," the wise bird said, looking out at the world she was so proud of.

"Over there is Medela Island, where the Clementis reside," Kyori continued. Eyre saw a hovering island in the sky, almost like a mirage. It was strange to think that she'd been there just a few months ago. Focusing hard, she sent a telepathic 'get well' message to Ischyros, and hoped he received it. Her heart felt heavy as she studied the shimmering island.

Kyori continued, as if she understood Eyre's pain. "And that is where I live," she said, indicating the base of the mountain at the opposite side to where they'd climbed up.

Eyre was intrigued as she looked down. It seemed almost as if there was greenery growing there. She strained to look—she hadn't realised Caelus had anything like that, but then her jaw dropped.

Because shooting straight up into the sky from the middle of that foliage was the silver beam from the Isar! She jumped with excitement and pointed.

"The Isar," she shouted. "It's there!"

Everyone came running, their exhaustion forgotten as they searched the area Eyre was indicating. Of course, none of them could see it, but they now knew where they had to go. And it wasn't far!

Lord Clarembout acted swiftly. "We will fly down," he said to Jengles. "If you would follow us on foot in case of trouble, I would be grateful. But we must acquire the Isar with the utmost speed."

Jengles nodded. "Indeed, you must make haste."

And in a second, everyone had left the summit of the mountain.

CHAPTER FIFTY-TWO

THE FLIGHT DOWN THE side of the mountain was much more enjoyable than the wild, frightening ride up to the summit. The Lighthorses seemed to revel in stretching their wings and catching the currents of frigid air, and they plunged quickly through the cloud cover that ringed the mountain.

"Wahoooo!" Abby cried in delight as she plummeted downwards. Cojo's mighty wings flapped hard and she shot out from the underside of the clouds just as Beatrice emerged on Blondie. Hurtling beside each other, they raced down the rockface. Eyre followed on Eclipse, loving the feel of the wind whipping her hair and the speed of the mighty Lighthorse. Florence shot downwards like a bullet, demonstrating perfectly the raptor's skill at executing a rapid descent.

It took only a few minutes to reach the base of the mountain and they landed in an area that reminded Eyre of Terra. It was densely forested, with strange plants and trees jumbled together. Flowers of all colours sprang up from the undergrowth, and a tumbling river—coloured orange—led away into the wilderness. Florence landed on Eyre's shoulder as she took in the spectacular view.

"Wow!" Beatrice said, craning to look around. "This is slightly different from the other side!"

Eventually all the Lightworkers had landed, and Kyori sailed down from the sky to stand beside them.

"Home," she said, as if she'd found a priceless treasure.

Eyre was intently focused on the pillar of light, not wanting to take her eyes off it in case she lost sight of it. So, she quickly led the way, with Eclipse following her.

"I will walk beside you," Kyori said. "In case we meet something you need to avoid."

Eyre understood immediately. This was her third Alterworld, and she didn't need any explanation about things that might jump out and kill her.

The vertical light seemed to be about half a kilometre away, although it was hard to judge.

"Should we fly there?" Eyre asked, as she brushed an annoying vine from her face.

But Kyori shook her head. "Here, you are better to remain in the jungle. Predators lurk overhead—like the Zeguardagen, and Vampire Vultures— they know there are a number of food sources in this area. We should keep under cover and push through—it won't take long once we get to the path by the river."

And sure enough, after ten minutes of trekking through almost impenetrable bush, they emerged to find a well-worn track that followed the riverbank. More surprising was a group of Caelites who stood to welcome them. The purple and white birds did the same welcoming dance, screeching as Kyori had at her first lecture.

When they finished, Eyre bowed. "Thank you. May your wings always find the space to fly."

The Caelites chattered delightedly and stood aside as the Lightworkers moved down the path past them.

Kyori smiled at Eyre. "They said, 'And may your feet always find the Path.' You have honoured them."

The orange water tumbled and sang as they walked along. It was crystal clear and Eyre could see strange water creatures swimming through the currents. One looked like a miniature green dolphin, following alongside and watching them, fixing its large blue eyes on Abby, in particular. Occasionally it leapt out of the water and splashed back in. Eyre suspected the lovely creature was trying to impress Abby, who was very taken with it.

"So clever!" she exclaimed, and trailed her hand in the water. Within a minute, the little dolphin had swum up to her, leaped out of the water and performed a figure of eight in the air before it plunged back in.

"Looks like you've got competition," Beatrice laughed at Nick. "Watch out!"

The bright light was now very near, but it was inland through the bush, and Eyre turned to Lord Clarembout. "It's just behind that tall tree, sir," she said. "If you wait here, I'll leave Eclipse and Florence and go with Kyori to get it. It will save you all having to wrestle with the undergrowth. If there's any sign of trouble, I will let you know."

Lord Clarembout knew she meant telepathically, but he looked unsure. He saw the sense in everyone avoiding the unnecessary fight through the tangled bush, but he looked at Kyori for advice. The small bird nodded.

"It is safe here," she said. "A few minutes and we will be back."

So, Eyre and Kyori left the group and headed into the jungle. But before she left, Eyre searched for Jax. Just the sight of the athletic, black-haired boy was reassuring and seemed to give her renewed courage. He saluted her slightly, his green eyes glowing, and Eyre shivered. If there was power to be gained from another person, she'd just received it.

"You need a beak," Kyori said, as Eyre struggled yet again to break through a thicket of unforgiving foliage. "It makes a wedge and helps you get through. We usually keep our head down and run along the ground, under all of it."

Eyre huffed ruefully as she pulled some leaves out of her hair. Right now, she really *could* use a lime-green beak, or any beak, or maybe an *axe*, to get through the snarled jungle. Her staff was helpful, but tended to get caught in the vines rather than clear them. She was sweating and hot as she paused for a moment. Suddenly, something crunched loudly near her ear, and she jumped and swung around, raising her staff in defence. Clinging to the side of a tree trunk, and chomping away mightily with its strong jaws, was a fat purple caterpillar, about a metre long.

Kyori chuckled. "It's a Gossamer Moth worm," she said. "It's eating the leaves to build its cocoon." Eyre took a moment to catch her breath as she studied the portly worm, and lowered her staff. The caterpillar ignored her as it reared up to reach a nearby branch and munched its way steadily through the leaves. Eyre knew from her Caelus class that the Gossamer Moth worm produced the thread that had been used to make the beautiful gown she had worn to the ball in first-year. She wondered how this ungainly and rather ridiculous-looking creature could produce something so glorious.

But she couldn't linger long—she felt the rush of adrenaline spurring her on, as she knew they were very close. So she continued to shove her way through the bushes, ignoring the scratches and scrapes, until she arrived at the tall tree that the Isar lay behind.

She charged around the trunk, expecting that the Isar would be there, but all she could see was a huge pile of newly-dug earth. Her heart sank as she looked up to see the vertical beam a further five metres away. *What?* Kyori followed her, but since she couldn't see the Isar or the beam, she was obviously expecting Eyre to pick it up.

"Have you got it?" she asked.

"It's not here, now," Eyre said, anxious. "It's moved! I think someone dug it up!"

She indicated the heap of dirt and Kyori looked concerned. But then she said pragmatically, "Well, we'll go get it! Where is it now?"

Eyre looked for the beam of light—she still couldn't see the Isar—and then moaned.

"By the Light! It's *moving*!" she said in a desperate voice. "How could that happen?"

Kyori hesitated and looked back to where the Lightworkers, now out of sight, waited.

"How fast is it going?" she asked, suddenly concerned.

"Well, it's like someone is carrying it," Eyre said, a dark stone in her stomach. "But they're not rushing. They're obviously not worried about it." Her thoughts roiled. How could anyone else see the Isar? And who were they?

Making a decision, Kyori looked at Eyre with her bright eyes. "Let us follow for a short while. If we bring everyone, it will alert whoever has the Isar, and we must keep quiet. If it takes too long, we will call Lord Clarembout."

Eyre nodded. Her heart froze at the thought that someone else might have the Isar, and all she wanted to do was blast her way through the forest to get it back.

CHAPTER FIFTY-THREE

THEY CREPT THROUGH THE bush after the moving beam of light. The light bobbed along unhurriedly before them, so they were soon able to catch up. Eyre was ready to summon Florence and any other weapon she could think of to fight off the thief. A Flail, perhaps?

But then Kyori chuckled softly. "Stand down, soldier! No need for Occido here."

Eyre was confused and searched for what Kyori was looking at. She could see the vertical beam of light shooting up to the sky and followed it down to see that it centred above a creature that looked like a bright-yellow turtle, except it was the size of a sheep, with a shell made of a substance that looked like glowing stained glass. Trundling along, the turtle seemed well-satisfied, because it had some sort of mushroom or toadstool clasped in its mouth. And stuck in the mushroom was the Isar.

"Is that where the Isar is?" Kyori asked, watching the ambling creature.

Eyre was nonplussed. "Yep. Er—it's sticking out of that mushroom thing in that—uh—turtle's mouth."

Kyori laughed. "That creature's a Zertle. They eat the fungi that grow around the roots of the Randian tree, which is that tall tree you were heading for. The fungi are a bit like truffles in Entis, but they take decades to grow, sometimes hundreds of years. Obviously the Isar has become encased by the fungus over the years, and our Zertle has discovered it. They are placid creatures. If you reveal the Isar to me, I will get it out of the Zertle's mouth."

Eyre felt a huge flood of relief as she realised she wasn't about to battle for her life again, and she raced over to the plodding creature. It lifted its head to look at her as she approached, and clamped its mouth down harder on the fungus. No way was anyone taking its hard-won delicacy! Eyre touched the Isar lightly and suddenly it shone brilliantly silver and the vertical light disappeared. The Zertle was so startled, it dropped the treat, and Kyori darted in with her sharp beak to snatch it away.

The Zertle looked blindly from side to side, not sure what had happened, and then sniffed the ground, searching for its treasure—not the Isar; but the delicious, truffle-like fungi. Kyori laughed, and with a few pecks of her sharp beak, had freed the Isar from the grasp of the stalk. Eyre tossed the pieces of fungus back to the Zertle, who picked them up in its large mouth, and happily meandered on down the path.

Kyori looked in astonishment at the shining Isar. "So beautiful," she breathed. "So powerful."

Eyre nodded, and picked it up swiftly, suddenly feeling the need to *hurry*.

"Come on, we need to get back. Thank you so much, Kyori."

Then they set off through the wild bush, heading back to the waiting Lightworkers.

"We've got it!" Eyre sent telepathically to Lord Clarembout, and received a message in return, no words, just a feeling. *Relief.*

It didn't take long before they emerged from the jungle. Kyori looked her usual, sleek self, but Eyre was like a wild woman and everyone laughed, despite themselves.

Her hair was a tangled mess, filled with leaves. She had scratches and mud plastered all over, and her clothing was torn. But when she held the Isar aloft, everyone cheered.

Racing over to Eclipse, Eyre stuffed the Isar in the saddle bag, and its brightness was obscured; no one would know it was there. Florence alighted on Eyre's shoulder as she stood close to Eclipse, stroking her neck.

But then Lord Clarembout concentrated, as if hearing a faraway message. When he turned to them, his eyes were frantic. "By the Light," he cried, "mount your steeds! Whittaker Ray has sent a message that it is not safe to return to the Academy. The rest of the troops have arrived at the base of the mountain on the other side and we need to return to them now to await further instruction! We have no time to waste; we are flying out of here! General Gel Lithium Silica is taking his contingent around the perimeter and will meet us there shortly."

Eyre looked at Kyori and put her hands together. "Thank you, Kyori," she said softly, and the Caelite's eyes were soft. "Find the Path, Eyre," she answered. "We are all counting on you."

Then, with a surge of power and wind and wings, the Lighthorses took to the air, forming an aerial battalion as they soared up to the summit of Mt Crepitus. Swooping over the apex, they caught the air currents, and streaked down the other side of the mountain, where the masses of Overworld troops waited. The Lighthorses landed on the unforgiving terrain and the troops looked to Lord Clarembout for instructions.

"It seems we need to wait a bit longer," Sir Philius said. "With any luck, we will be out of here soon." Then they heard the tramp of many feet as Jengles rounded the base of the mountain with his battalion.

But suddenly, from beneath the ground in all directions, surged a horde of Gothak. Exploding from the earth, they caught the warriors unprepared, and Eyre was tossed off Eclipse, landing hard on her stomach. She was unable to breathe for a second, and she saw Eclipse galloping off across the rocky landscape in complete panic. Characs, the hideous symbiotic creatures that existed with the Gothak, swarmed in behind them, their large circular, sharp-toothed mouths gaping open.

Then the Strigis emerged. It seemed that the Gothak had pulled out all stops for this event: Menax Lizards broke free from the earth; packs of Sublabor Pedes emerged from behind the ranks of the Gothak; hundreds of black, sharp-fanged Saevus charged towards the Overworld defence force; and a Tuus Scorpion chittered as it scrabbled across the rocky terrain. Yet more Gothak swooped from above, flying on the deadly Interfector Hornets, and countless hairless Zyx wheeled above the Overworld troops, their blood-red eyes focused malevolently on their prey. Interspersed with these flying abominations were hordes of monstrous Nahtaivel, swooping low as they stalked and hunted.

Eyre looked in despair at the enormous might of the Underworld. Someone had betrayed them! There was no other way this many of the Dark Forces could be here right now. They were trapped, overwhelmed by the dark, gargantuan army. And it wasn't safe to return to the Academy—not when the school was under attack too.

But calmly, Eyre raised her staff. So be it! She would go down fighting! Florence gave a high shriek and took to the air. As Eyre watched her brave bird, she saw a streak of grey spread out behind Florence, as hundreds more Venators arrived to join her. Leading the apex, Florence and the flock of Venators charged into the blackness of the Zyx.

"For the Light!" Lord Clarembout shouted, and his call was echoed by the masses behind him.

"For the Light!" Then, as one, the army charged towards their enemy.

As she raced into combat, Eyre could see a Pinnae moving his hands and raising a wave of water that blasted the first ranks of Gothak onto their backs. Characs floundered in the water too, unable to withstand the raging flood. Choking, they thrashed about as wave after wave smashed down onto them. Recalling her earlier thoughts about the Pinnae, Eyre felt ashamed.

Such powerful beings; she had disrespected their talents. The thought spurred her onwards, and she turned her staff towards the horde of Gothak, determined to join the Pinnae in doing the best she could.

An ear-splitting screech from above made Eyre pause. What new Strigis was attacking? But as she watched, a group of blue Zeguardagen rocketed in from over the mountain, their four wings flapping in excitement. All they wanted was a meal and today they were surely going to get it. They charged down the rockface of the steep cliff and snapped the head off a Sublabor before it could even react. Then, gnashing their huge teeth, they attacked anything within reach—Gothak or Strigis or Overworld troops.

"Eclipse! Eclipse!" Eyre called desperately as she pulled her Antaraks out to face the advancing horde, but the Lighthorse stayed hidden. And then, as the Gothak advanced towards the Lightworkers, Eyre realised why. Because it suddenly became apparent that the Gothak were fixated on *her*. They knew she was the Aether, and they must suspect that she had the Isar. So her brilliant Lighthorse was keeping the Isar out of sight, and out of reach. *Clever girl!*

She battled frantically with her Antaraks, the lethal blades cutting Gothak to shreds and forming a bloody pile in front of her. She picked up her staff, and with all the rage she could muster, blasted her fury through the pink diamond crystal to create a firestorm that burned swathes around her, clearing a space.

But the Overworld Defence Force was grossly outnumbered. It was evident that all the resources of the Underworld had been called for this battle, and the Lightworkers were unprepared for a fight of such magnitude.

Eyre looked desperately for her friends. She could see Beatrice fighting a Gryllus Weta with Warrigal, their joint staffs blasting holes through its sides until it tumbled to the ground. Abby was using her Antaraks to chop the Gothak into stir-fry. Despite her dislike of physical exercise, Abby's incredible mental focus was more than a match for the gross creatures, and she had a wildness about her that seemed to radiate Light energy. Jax and Colton were attacking a Menax Lizard on their Lighthorses, flying in to blast it from all sides, while the foot soldiers battled blade-to-blade with the swarming swathes of Gothak. Lord Clarembout was sending various forms of fulminology to blast the Gothak ranks into the stratosphere, and Professor Vela and Dr Botolfe were fighting back-to-back as the Gothak surged around them. Gegenees was in his flying chariot, his massive blade cutting down any creature that drew near, as he bellowed out an ancient war cry. "Alala! *ALALA!*" and the hated beings cowered before his fearsome attack.

Jengles, in total control of his battle plan, was leading his ferocious troops with Crescent Blades raised, and their deep-throated, hair-raising chants rent the air as they attacked their hated foes. Lightning shot from their feet as they stomped the rocky ground of Caelus. Nick had risen on Prenzel to face a Tuus Scorpion, which towered above him. As Eyre watched, he sent a blaze of Light energy into the creature's mouth. It screamed in agony and fell backwards, landing with a loud crash on the rocky ground. The Armatura rattled their spears with a spine-chilling sound and bellowed in fury as they charged against the Gothak, some of the Armatura elevating from the ground in a choreographed, multi-level attack. And the Pinnae and Nemoris battled bravely against the waves of Gothak that surged towards them.

But despite the valiant effort the defence forces were putting into the battle, Eyre could see it was hopeless. The swarms of Gothak stretched kilometres over the endless plains and more Strigis were emerging; she knew that their sheer numbers would overwhelm them. If only she could get the Isar back to the Academy! But Whittaker Ray had told them not to come.

She resigned herself to dying with honour, and she raised her staff once more. The more enemy she took down with her, the better. And perhaps the Isar might remain undiscovered by the Gothak, thanks to the courageous Eclipse.

And then Eyre saw a horribly familiar form emerging from the midst of the massed Gothak. Mudamir stepped forward, his black eyes triumphant.

"Nice to see you again, Eyre. Sadly, under less than cordial circumstances. But I suggest that you tell me where the Isar is," he whispered. "And I might just let the rest of your colleagues live."

Eyre's jaw jutted. But an indecision was rising within her. Was one Isar worth the lives of all these beings? Perhaps she should just hand it over...

But then Beatrice rose before her on Blondie. Her glowing emerald-topped staff was held high and she blasted the ground before Mudamir into a flaming, molten moat. She flew around Eyre, her black hair streaming behind her like Athena, the Goddess of War.

"Don't listen to that mongrel, Eyre," Beatrice cried, her eyes blazing. "He will kill us all anyway. Fight to the death! He will never get the Isar!" And then she swung her staff around, blasting away the Gothak that surrounded Mudamir. Finally, she aimed her emerald staff directly at Mudamir.

"Look out, gorgeous," she whispered, "you're about to meet your brother!"

But Mudamir just sneered, and with a flick of his wrist, sent a flaming ball of atra at Beatrice.

"Noooooo!" Eyre cried in anguish as she saw the blazing meteor shoot towards her friend. But Blondie turned and put herself in the way of the lethal ball of fire, and it struck her full-on, burning her forelegs and chest completely away. She fell like a rock towards the earth, and Beatrice went hurtling off into the air.

And then the fury in Eyre ignited. Her hair stood on end, her eyes blazed and turned golden, and this time, lightning shot from her fingertips. But despite her ferocious rage, an icy coldness descended upon her as she raised her hands. "I enjoyed sending your brother into nothingness, and now it's your turn," she intoned in a flat, dead voice as she turned her eyes to the sneering Gothak. And she knew without any doubt that Mudamir was about to die.

"Well, then, show me your parlour tricks—" Mudamir began, but was interrupted by an earth-shattering explosion. For a second, all battle ceased as faces turned towards the cause of the blast.

"By-the-*Light*..." Professor Vela breathed as Mt Crepitus suddenly blew its top. The earth rose and buckled beneath the battlefield, and broad cracks jagged across the earth, sucking anyone nearby into them. Sheaves of rock rose and fell, creating great chasms in the terrain, and then molten rock from the explosion began to rain down upon them all. Orange-red magma spilled out of the crater on top of Mt Crepitus, running down the sides of the mountain in lethal torrents. Sulphurous yellow gas filled the air, and those in its vicinity died a horrible death, choking on the poisonous fumes.

"Run!" Lord Clarembout bellowed as the mountain exploded again. "Get to the Academy!"

Eyre was still facing Mudamir as Beatrice slowly lifted herself from the ground where she had landed. She scrambled over to her fallen Lighthorse and hugged her around the neck oblivious, to what was happening around her. "Blondie!" Beatrice wept as she hugged the body of the brave Lighthorse who had sacrificed her life for her Lightworker.

Meteors of molten rock pounded around them but still Mudamir advanced on Eyre with deadly intent. "Where is the Isar?" he said softly.

"Last I heard, it was in your rear end," Eyre whispered, and flung a bolt of lightning so quickly that Mudamir scarcely had time to duck. His eyes darkened.

"Ah, so that is how we will do it then—" he began, then was knocked over as a charging creature attacked him from behind.

Eclipse, barrelling in from the Ru-Ru trees, had seized her moment. Eyre leapt onto her back, dragging Beatrice up with her before Mudamir could get to his feet. Florence descended like a bullet from the Venator flock and landed on Eyre's shoulder, grasping tightly with her talons.

Eyre performed the prohemium and they zapped out of the hellfire.

CHAPTER FIFTY-FOUR

ECLIPSE EMERGED FROM THE Seam on the Receiving Stone and her feet scrabbled on the slippery polished moldavite. Eyre leant over and patted her neck. "You brave girl," she said. "Thank you for saving us." The Lighthorse was skittish from the adrenaline coursing through her veins and she breathed deeply, her eyes wild. Eventually, despite the pandemonium, she started to calm down at Eyre's soothing words.

Lightworkers and the Mimir were arriving in flashes of light, some of them terribly wounded, and Jengles was marching around giving orders.

"To the Infirmary!" he shouted at a group of Mimir who carried the injured on stretchers. Eyre helped the distraught Beatrice off Eclipse's back and sat her at the edge of the stone. Then she grabbed her saddlebag and raced up to Jengles.

"The Isar," she whispered and Jengles seized it in an instant.

"Well done, my Lovey," he said softly, and then charged off, down into the open bronze doors of the Mimir's Domain and out of sight. The doors slammed shut loudly behind him.

Eclipse moved over and nosed Beatrice, who had her head on her arms, bereft. A second later Abby arrived on Cojo and she jumped off and skidded over to sit by Beatrice.

"My poor friend!" she cried, wrapping her arms around Beatrice. Beatrice only wept harder as more and more of the battle-weary troops arrived back. Cries of anguish and pain rent the air; the troops had been decimated by the onslaught of the Gothak and the deluge of molten rock from the volcano.

Sergeant Tottingham and Whittaker Ray were at the side of the Receiving Stone, firing off instructions to anyone who approached. Eyre had the feeling they had probably been standing there ever since the battalion left for Caelus.

"Send your Lighthorses to the Equestrian Centre," Sergeant Tottingham bellowed. "Anyone needing first aid who can walk, head to the Infirmary. The rest of you get home and get some rest. We will have a debriefing tomorrow. Thank you for your courage!"

Eyre noticed that there were no Pinnae or Nemoris there, nor Armatura; nor for that matter, Caelites. The Caelites had probably stayed behind, but she imagined the Pinnae, Nemoris and Armatura had travelled directly to their respective Alterworlds. She hoped they had all made it.

Eyre sent Eclipse back to the stables and Florence took off like an arrow, heading for the Unlit Campus and the forest of Ru-Ru trees. She would need to rest and recover after her arduous experience.

Jax moved up beside Eyre and sent Firestorm to the Equestrian Centre. Then he gathered Eyre in his arms and she sobbed into his chest as he held her tightly. The release of panic and fear, and the thought of all those who had lost their lives, finally caught up with her. Despite retrieving the Isar, it had come at such a huge cost, and she cried for the loss of all those brave souls.

Colton, Nick and Warrigal arrived on the moldavite square and immediately sent their Lighthorses away. Eyre lifted her head and saw that Nick had an enormous burn on his arm and Colton had a deep cut on his leg. Warrigal helped both of them to limp towards the Infirmary.

Eyre kissed Jax softly, her dirty, tear-streaked face turned up to his. "See you soon," she whispered, then slowly turned towards Abby and Beatrice, suddenly incredibly fatigued. It was difficult even to take a step.

She and Abby helped Beatrice up and walked on either side of the weeping girl towards the dormitory. Jax gave a farewell wave then he headed painfully to his own room.

Whittaker Ray intercepted the girls as they passed, concern showing in his bright blue eyes.

"You have done well," he said, "and brought great honour on yourselves. I will talk to you tomorrow, once you have rested."

Eyre could only nod as they walked across campus. Once they reached their room, all three of them threw themselves on their beds, unable even to find the energy to wash. They fell into an exhausted sleep, even Beatrice, whose wearied body finally gave her some respite from her grief.

Eyre woke the next morning lying in exactly the same position she had been in the night before. She didn't think she had moved all night. Her mouth was hanging open and it felt like a guinea pig had been nesting in there—she was so dry and thirsty.

She sat up slowly and grabbed her water bottle, taking a long chug. Then she breathed deeply, leaning up against the wall. Even that small movement had exhausted her.

Abby began to stir and she rolled over and sat up, holding her head. "By the Light, I feel like a Zepp has run over me." Her hair stuck out in all directions and was filled with dirt. Despite herself, Eyre had to laugh. "I suppose I look about the same as you," she said, rubbing her face. "Drink some water, you're probably dehydrated."

Abby and Eyre sat in silence, taking the occasional sip as they waited for Beatrice to wake up. Neither of them wanted to rouse her because they knew she was going to have to deal with the pain of losing Blondie. And they knew it would take a long time to adjust to that.

But eventually Beatrice moved and sat up. Her face was wan and puffy from all the tears she'd cried, and bruises were starting to form after her hard fall from Blondie. But worst of all was the desolation in her normally bright face. She rubbed her eyes and shook her head, unable to say anything. Eyre and Abby were struggling to find the words when a tentative knock at the door roused them from their stupor.

Eyre opened the door and saw Robeson standing there, his eyes solemn. "Do you think, I mean," he stammered, out of depth in this shattering quagmire of emotion. "I thought the Therapeutic Pools? Could I meet you there?"

Eyre felt a great relief. Such a smart boy. "We'll meet you there," she said and closed the door as he headed away.

In a few moments, she'd organised Abby and a very indifferent Beatrice into getting their swimsuits on and grabbing their towels.

"Come on, Bea," Eyre said softly, as she looked into her friend's dull eyes. "Come with us."

Beatrice sighed, and a tear dripped down her face. But she had finally grabbed her towel and followed Eyre and Abby out the door.

They arrived before Robeson and slipped into the first of the heated pools, a deep blue colour; sapphires helped to re-balance the mind and body, Eyre thought, but she knew they'd have to sit there an awfully long time to help Beatrice. No one spoke; they were all too traumatised at the moment for conversation.

"Well, we did it," Abby finally broke the silence, but in a voice that didn't sound like she felt it was a success.

"The hard way," Eyre said. "Thanks to Ben Perrill."

"I'm going to kill him," Beatrice said, the first words she had spoken since they returned from Caelus.

"Stand in line," Eyre whispered. "There's a few of us wanting a turn."

Abby nodded, her cornflower eyes unusually hard. She trailed her hand through the humming water. "How did he find out about us leaving early?"

Eyre shrugged. "There was a lot of activity going on. It wasn't too hard to figure out, I imagine. But the fact that he passed it on entitles him to a meeting with my Antaraks, I think."

"Well, let's go and see Whittaker Ray," Abby said, "and find out what the latest news is. But my Antaraks are ready as well. It's time for us to make the call, since the school seems unable to. If we get the usual 'guff' I'm all for just taking him out."

Eyre and Beatrice both looked at Abby in surprise. Did she just say what they thought she had? Peace-loving, people-loving Abby? Who always did the kind thing? Abby met their gaze without flinching.

"New world, new rules, hey, my friends. Ben's Rufa. I hope my Sappir skills will give me an edge so I can chop his head off. Perhaps my psychic skills will help me to anticipate the blow before it comes. And then I can get him first."

The pragmatic way Abby said it suddenly sounded hilarious, and even Beatrice gave a short laugh. But Eyre noticed Abby wasn't laughing. She meant it.

Before they could continue the conversation, they heard someone coming up the pathway and Beatrice's eyes brimmed as Robeson arrived. He slipped into the pool without saying anything. Beatrice slid into his arms and after a long moment, began to weep silently. Robeson was patting Beatrice's back and his eyes were desolate; he understood Beatrice's pain but was unable to do anything to help her. Eyre and Abby hopped discreetly out of the water and grabbed their towels as Robeson held their beloved friend tight.

The two girls walked dismally down the track back to the dormitory, unable to think of anything to say to each other. But then someone came up the path towards them, and they realised Warrigal must have been looking for them.

"Colton and Nick spent the night at the Infirmary," he said. Eyre and Abby knew that already, because Abby had been checking up on Nick regularly. But the next thing Warrigal said they didn't know. "Whittaker Ray wants to see us all after breakfast. See you at Central Admin?"

Eyre and Abby thanked him, and headed to their dorm room. They both decided not to go to breakfast—all those eyes upon them; neither of them could stand the idea. So when Beatrice finally came back, the three of them showered and dressed and went straight over to meet Whittaker Ray.

They were silent as they walked into the Central Administration lobby. Eyre felt so tired, and so sad for her friend. What words could help? This dark fight had left all of them in tatters.

Colton and Warrigal were standing at the elevator and they all stepped in. Jax scrambled across the lobby to jump in, and just as the doors were about to close a hand stopped them as Nick made a late entrance.

They crammed in together and grimaced. All of them were scraped and bruised, with wounds and cuts and burns from the battle with the Gothak and the explosion from Mt Crepitus. A reminder of how close they had all come to dying.

"I'm so sorry Beatrice," Colton said kindly, and tears sprang into Beatrice's eyes again. But she just nodded as they exited the elevator and headed for Whittaker Ray's office.

The Dean stood up as they entered but was taken aback when Beatrice spoke first, in a very low voice.

"*Where* the hell is Ben Perrill?" It was such an unusual tone for her that everyone swung their heads to look at her. Whittaker Ray looked surprised too; this was not the normal Beatrice.

But then he sighed. "He has gone home for his own safety. Like you, there are many who are very unhappy with him at the moment. But I have to be honest, there is no certainty that it was Ben who let the Gothak know that you'd left early to go to Caelus. Or, in fact, that he'd revealed the date of the TACI in the first place."

Abby's eyes flashed. "Well, who then? Santa Claus?"

"Some people believe it may have been Jemima Periwinkle," Whittaker Ray said.

"But she's disappeared," Eyre said slowly. "Surely she's not still around here?"

Whittaker Ray's eyes were clouded. "A message was sent to Lord Clarembout, instructing you that it was not safe to return here, and for the troops to meet at the base of the mountain."

"But that was *you*, wasn't it, sir?" Nick asked, as they all looked at each other.

Whittaker Ray shook his head. "No, it wasn't. It was someone *pretending* to be me. I wanted you to return as soon as you'd recovered the Isar. And if you *had* all returned then, all the troops would have been safely travelling back by prohemium. We would have lost no one. But the delay enabled the

Gothak to find you. So whoever sent that message was definitely not working in the interests of the Lightworkers."

Warrigal was thinking. "So, do you think it might have been Jemima Periwinkle who sent the message to Lord Clarembout?"

"Yes," Whittaker Ray said regretfully. "That woman has caused inestimable damage to the Lightworking community—and indeed to the whole Overworld. But she is like a malevolent ghost, a shapeshifter—we cannot locate her."

A silence fell. Eyre still found it hard to imagine that the ridiculous cream-cake of a lecturer who'd taught the mind-numbing subject of Lightworker genealogy was capable of such monstrous betrayal, treachery and inhuman brutality. But the thought that she might still be around, in a strange way, actually made Eyre feel better; she didn't want that evil creature to get off easily. One day she wanted to meet that floral monster and make her pay for what she'd done.

Whittaker Ray looked down at his desk. "We were lucky that Mt Crepitus put in an unscheduled performance. It shouldn't have blown for another 90 years, but it is fortunate for the Lightworking defence forces that it did. The confusion allowed many of them to escape, although we have had severe losses and injury."

A sombre silence fell around the room. The memory of that hellish scene would never leave any of them.

Whittaker Ray opened his drawer and pulled out a small wooden box and smiled ironically. "In any case, the reason I have asked you here is on behalf of the Echelon. They believe you have demonstrated valour of the highest order, and have directed me to bestow upon each of you an Inguz Talisman."

From the box he brought out an Inguz, about 2 centimetres long and made out of silver. The Inguz Talisman was a medal given to very few people, so it was a great honour. Whittaker Ray passed each student one of the shining runes.

"I realise this will not help you process what you've been through. But indeed, each of you has behaved with exceptional courage beyond any expectations, especially for a student, and you deserve this. This amulet is to remind you of your bravery, and to help you with your focus as we move further into the fight against the Darkness. Thank you for what you did. You should have been receiving these at a formal ceremony," he stopped and his eyes became distant, "but in light of the circumstances, nothing at the moment is predictable..." He looked at them sadly. "Perhaps in the future sometime."

Eyre held the Inguz in her hand and felt proud, but terribly sad for Beatrice as she saw her stricken friend's face. She knew Beatrice would give a thousand Inguzes to have Blondie back.

"You may head back to your dormitory now. This evening, you are all heading home. It has been decided that you need not finish out the last few days of school. Eyre, could I have a final word with you before you leave?"

The others filed out and Eyre stayed behind, holding her Inguz Talisman tightly.

"The Kikkuli Master would like to see you before you go," Whittaker Ray said, once they were alone. "Eclipse is being sent back to her barracks in New South Wales and the Master thought you might like to say goodbye before she goes. I—uh—well, I didn't want to bring up the stables while Beatrice was here. She is obviously finding her loss very difficult to deal with."

Eyre nodded, impassive. She was getting tired of trying to explain things to Whittaker Ray. "It's tough, sir. Beatrice and Blondie loved each other. They were brilliant partners."

She turned to go. "Thank you for the Inguz Talisman. I will try to live up to it."

Whittaker Ray's eyes were compassionate. "I know you will, Eyre. You have been through so much already and I have the utmost faith in you. May the Light be with you."

Eyre headed out of his office, fury rising within her. She didn't feel much light within her at the moment. Because, despite all they'd talked about, she could only focus on one thing; how could there be yet *another* reprieve for Ben Perrill? And her heart burned with rage. She clenched the Inguz in her hand, sure of one thing only; Ben Perrill was going to pay when she saw him next, of *that* she was certain.

CHAPTER FIFTY-FIVE

THE KIKKULI MASTER WAS in the centre of the arena with Eclipse as Eyre entered through the massive bronze doors. He smiled as she approached and stroked Eclipse's ears.

"Whittaker Ray sent you over," he said and Eyre nodded. Eclipse whickered and rubbed her soft nose against Eyre's face. Eyre wrapped her arms gently around Eclipse's neck and rested her cheek against the thoroughbred's face.

"Thank you for taking me to Caelus. Thank you for your courage. And thank you for saving my life, Eclipse. I hope I see you again sometime," she whispered.

Eclipse's ears twitched as if she understood what Eyre was saying, and she rubbed her head gently against Eyre's cheek.

Then Eyre stepped away, clenching her jaw so she wouldn't cry. "Farewell, beautiful creature!"

The Kikkuli Master waved his hand and in a flash of light, Eclipse had disappeared. Eyre felt a forlorn emptiness fill her heart. In the time she had been with the stunning Lighthorse she had come to love her, and she would miss her so much.

But then she became aware of a ruckus down the alleyway.

"Dimmog!" a cranky voice cursed. "Dratted thing's all tangled up."

Eyre turned towards the Kikkuli Master, a hopeful joy and a question filling her eyes.

The Kikkuli Master nodded. "He's back."

Eyre started running across the arena and flew down the alleyway. Sure enough, Ischyros was in his stall, his rear to her as he chewed at the blanket which covered his old back. The straps had become tangled and he was trying to sort it out with his mouth.

"Ischyros!" Eyre called softly, and he turned around. Eyre got such a shock, she nearly started bawling. The ancient horse had always looked a bit decrepit, but now he was covered in bald patches where his hair had been permanently burnt away. He had scars and burns all over his head, and one eye—the left one, without the patch around it—had a cloudy look, as if he was blind. Only three strands of his grey mane remained, at irregular intervals down his neck.

The Kikkuli Master moved up beside her. "He needs the blanket now to keep warm. He has been terribly damaged by his ordeal."

"I might be a bit blind but I'm not deaf, you know," Ischyros grumbled, turning dimly towards Eyre. "I *can* hear you talking about me!" Eyre unlatched the gate and raced in to hug her cranky, dilapidated old Lighthorse.

Tears coursed down her face as she wrapped her arms around his neck. "Oh Ischyros, I've missed you!" she wept. "You poor old boy, how you've suffered!"

Ischyros harrumphed, but he stayed close to Eyre as she stroked and talked to him quietly. "Thank you Ischyros. You are the bravest creature I've ever met."

Ischyros didn't reply for a moment. Then he said softly. "I got your telepathic message. It helped."

Eyre hugged him gently again, tears dripping from her cheeks. Then she got a soft brush and took off the horse blanket, untangling the 'dratted' clips. It took all her self-control not to gasp at the sight—Ischyros was terribly scarred from the fire and there wasn't much hair left to brush. And he moved slowly, as if it hurt to walk. So she put the brush down and heated her hands with Viq. Then she spent an hour massaging Ischyros's old legs and his wounded body, taking her time and touching him as gently as she could. He seemed to like it, and didn't complain, so she kept going, finishing with his neck and head. Then she found some liquorice and molasses and put it in the feed bin. Nothing seemed to be wrong with his sense of smell or his appetite, because in a moment he was chewing on the black treat, an expression of bliss on his face.

"They didn't give me any of *this* inside that orange blob I was stuck in," he complained.

"Well, you're going to get plenty of it, for the rest of your life," Eyre said as she carefully covered the old horse with the blanket again.

"I'll see you tomorrow," she said. "You're coming to Highlight with me."

The Kikkuli Master nodded. "I can arrange that," he said.

✕✕

Eyre spent the rest of the day packing up her things in the room with her friends. There was a dark despondency about all of them. Beatrice was mourning Blondie terribly, and Abby had been deeply affected by the violence of the battle in Caelus. And Eyre was so sad about Ischyros. He had suffered so much, and was now permanently injured and scarred from the fire at the Cup. What pain he must have endured over the past four months! She hadn't said much to her friends about him when she returned from the stables, just that he was back, and that he needed a bit of care, so he'd be coming to Highlight for the break. She hadn't wanted to make it worse for Beatrice, so Eyre hadn't dwelled on it, and quickly changed the subject after she'd mentioned where she'd been.

"Don't forget to bring the Book of Bane," she said to Beatrice. "We need to do some serious sleuthing this Christmas break! Mysteries are to be solved, and you are the one to do it!"

Beatrice smiled in a lacklustre way and retrieved the journal from the wall. "I'm so very sick of mysteries," she said as she put the journal in the bottom of her bag. "I wish for once they would end well." Eyre silently agreed, but she now knew there was no other way to go forward, it really was up to them.

A knock at the door made them all jump. It seemed to take very little to startle them at the moment.

Eyre opened the door cautiously, then wider as Madame Overmantle stepped in.

"I came to say goodbye," the old woman said. "You have all been very brave this year, under very difficult circumstances. Not only the physical trials, but also the mental ones. I have enjoyed being your supervisor. You are dedicated students, but you have also proven to be astonishing Lightworkers, despite your young age. But it has been proven over the centuries, again and again; age does not define greatness."

She looked at Eyre, but her eyes seemed to be somewhere else. "At the TEPs I read your cards and predicted a long and arduous journey ahead for you, but one with an awakening. It has indeed been arduous for you—and your friends—and I can tell you that this is not the end of your struggles. But the awakening is now beginning. Do not give up hope."

Then her eyes regained focus as she looked at the students in their room. "Well, come on then, put everything in a pile, it will make it easier for me!" And Eyre, Beatrice and Abby all rushed to shove bags, musical instruments, plants and sporting gear into a heap by the door.

"Don't forget the beryl orbuculum," Madame said to Abby as she surveyed the collection of miscellaneous objects that tumbled in the stack. "You will need to study it. There is a secret of great value hidden in its depths and only you will be able to see it."

Abby looked unsure. "Not much pressure then," she said as she headed reluctantly to the wall, and they all laughed. Abby obviously didn't have much belief in her ability, but she carefully packed the glowing crystal ball into her bag.

"I thank you for your faith, Madame, it is very complimentary," Abby said awkwardly, as she wrapped the orbuculum in a soft scarf. "But I feel very inadequate. I will try very hard. However, I have to say—I feel if *you* haven't been able to do it, it would be somewhat egotistical for me to think that *I* could." She shook her head and looked apologetically at Madame Overmantle, then continued, with a hesitant honesty. "I respect and admire you so much, Madame; in fact, I would actually *hate* to see something in there that you hadn't."

Madame Overmantle grasped Abby's hand gently. "That is why you *will* see it," she said. "You are worthy."

Then Madame Overmantle handed something to Beatrice. It was blonde hair, twisted with golden-silver thread into a complex, beautiful braid about 40 centimetres long. At the top of the braid was a large neon blue stone that held the strands together; the middle section was braided and secured with more of the shining thread, and the bottom section flowed free.

"It's from her mane," Madame said softly as Beatrice studied the intricate object, her eyes darkening with a sudden, excruciating understanding. The old woman's face was troubled; she obviously shared Beatrice's pain. "The Mimir brought it to me and I have woven it with strands of Electrum. It will have great protective power for you."

Madame Overmantle passed the beautiful creation to Beatrice, who accepted it with tears streaming down her face.

"Thank you," she whispered, holding it to her heart.

"The year has ended," Madame Overmantle said gently to the three exhausted, distressed girls. "Go and rest. And come back next year with the fire back in your hearts. You three Lightworkers—plus the 'N' in your secret society!—are the secret to the survival of the Overworld, I know that now. You four—*Bane!*—the scourge, the plague, the ruination, and the destruction! The ones who will make the Gothak *quake.* And the quartet who will save the world. Recharge and come back to fight again. The four of you have made more of a difference than anyone in many past decades. And

I should know, because I've been here during those decades! Be safe, be well, and come back ready to *fight!*"

Then she clicked her fingers, and before they could say anything, the three girls and their possessions disappeared in a flash of light.

The entire human race under threat. Evil with one hand on the prize. Can one young girl rise up to save them all?

A secret location, Australia. Eyre Lightward isn't sure she can stomach any more death and destruction. Though with one final powerful shard still missing, the planet's protective shield in tatters and the population defenseless, the brave Lightworker's work is not yet done. But to retrieve the last critical piece of the puzzle, Eyre must embark on a hazardous and potentially lethal infiltration of the dark Underworld.

As the forces for good sustain heavy losses trying to overthrow their enemy deep below the surface, Eyre uncovers a vital clue to breaching the treacherous foe's defenses. And now Earth's future lies in the hands of just eleven determined students...

Will Eyre's daring plan to reclaim power over the darkness require a devastating sacrifice?

Follow the link or the QR code below to grab your copy.

https://thequestfortheaura.com/incendium

About the Quest for the Aura

Discover more exciting facts about the Quest for the Aura and download a free glossary from R.S. O'Neal's website here:

https://thequestfortheaura.com/